SA
FOREVER
Kim Jones
Published by Kim Jones

This book is the final book in a three part series.
Other titles by Kim Jones:

SAVING DALLAS
SAVING DALLAS MAKING THE CUT

www.kimjonesbooks.com
www.facebook.com/kimjonesbooks

Editing provided by:
Mandy Smith
www.rawbooksonline.com
rawbooksbabe@gmail.com

DEDICATION
Punkin, this one is for you.

SAVING DALLAS FOREVER

PROLOGUE

DALLAS

PRESENT DAY

"Picture it, Sicily 1979, a beautiful young woman, trying to find her way in the world, meets an aspiring, handsome, business man for the first time."

"You're talking about you and dad?"

"No, I'm talking about Giorgio Armani. Your father was a schmuck."

Despite the circumstances, I laughed as I listened to Sophia and Dorothy's conversation from the T.V. sitcom, "Golden Girls". Due to the blindfold I wore over my eyes, I couldn't see them, but someone had been nice enough to leave the T.V. tuned to a decent show, and the volume loud enough for me to hear. I knew I was in a hotel somewhere in Atlanta, Georgia. I knew it was three men who had captured me, and I knew that at any minute now, my saving grace was going to burst through the door and rescue me. So far, I had not been harmed, other than my hair being pulled, and losing feeling in my arms and legs, due to the duct tape that bound them. Once again, I had been kidnapped and secured with thick tape that was sure to remove part of my skin when it was finally cut off. I mean, what the fuck was the deal with the duct tape? If this kidnapping shit was going to continue to happen in my life, then at least they could be professional about it, and use rope, zip ties, cables, or something other than damned duct tape. I was in a chair, between two full size beds, in a shitty room that could be rented by the hour. The sound of the door being opened had me smiling. He was here.

"What the fuck is so funny?" the voice asked. My smile disappeared, because it wasn't the voice I'd been expecting. "Oh, I'm sorry. Were you expecting LLC?" he asked, his voice laced with fake regret. I remained quiet and still, my mind racing as I prepared my next move, which wasn't possible, because of the motherfucking shitty ass duct tape. "I don't know what is so fucking special about you. I mean, a million bucks to take you out seems a little extreme. But, I guess if that's what the buyer wants, then that's what he will get. Since I have you here, all to myself, I'm going to have a little fun with you." Don't panic. Don't panic. I kept my mind in a trance, thankful for the yoga classes I had been attending. Well, there wasn't a whole lot of yoga, but laughter was therapeutic too, and there had definitely been a lot of that. I focused my mind, letting the happy memories of the past few weeks block out the rise of the terror growing within me. His footsteps moved closer, and I could feel his hot breath on my face. "Oh, what fun we are going to have." I tried to tune him out. I tried to focus on the sound of the door opening. I took Sophia from the "Golden Girls" advice and tried to picture the moment, the look of shock on the face I had yet to see, the sudden intake of breath, as he realized his life was about to end, and the gunshots that would ring out to announce his death. I tried, and I failed miserably. He moved from in front of me, heading off in the direction

7

of what I knew was the bathroom, giving me time to breathe a little more easily, regain control of my mind, and gather my thoughts. "Dallas, have you ever heard of waterboarding?" my deranged captor called from the bathroom.

"Like behind a boat?" I asked, incredulously. What the hell was he getting at? I guess he wanted to pull a Charlie and take me to Mexico to live out the rest of my days with him. Not gonna happen, shithead. I felt his presence again, and held my breath when he leaned over me. The blindfold was removed, and as my eyes adjusted to the lighting in the room, I saw that the man was wearing a ski mask. Well, shit. I really needed to see his face. He was of a large build, but that's all I could tell. He wore a long-sleeved black t-shirt, black denim jeans, black boots, and black gloves. This man could be anybody. He walked to the door, opening it, and telling whoever was on the other side to put their masks on. Two men entered, one tall and lanky, and the other shorter, with a stockier build. They were both dressed in identical black attire to the first man.

"No, Dallas. Waterboarding is not to be mistaken for wakeboarding. Waterboarding is a form of torture. A towel is placed over the face, covering all airways," he said, walking back to the bathroom, as the two men flanked me. "Then, water is poured over the breathing passages, and it gives the captive the sensation of drowning." My breath quickened, along with my heart, as he talked. He emerged from the bathroom with the room's ice bucket, which I was sure was filled with water. He sat the bucket on the cheap dresser, and went back to the bathroom, returning with two more buckets.

"Please," I begged, my voice shaky and unsteady. All thoughts of staying calm vanished from my mind. I feared death by drowning more than any other, and the mere thought of it had me breaking out in a sweat. I was beyond panicked, as I felt my feet leave the floor. The two men had my chair tilted back, so that my knees were in plain sight. I was so focused on the man with the bucket and towel that I had not noticed the other two had flanked me. The rush of blood to my head made me slightly dizzy as I struggled to try and free my hands. I attempted to move my legs, but they too were securely attached to the chair. Even my waist had been restrained, leaving me with no room to move. "Please. Please, don't do this. I haven't done anything wrong. Just leave me alone," I said, panting, desperately trying to persuade him to stop. He stood beside me, bringing his face close to mine.

"Give me one good reason why I shouldn't." The scent of his breath was minty and cool. This didn't seem right. Even though I had not seen his face, his voice was friendly. He had not done anything to severely harm me, and I figured he had some sort of conscience. He didn't seem like the kind of man who could torture a human being, yet here I sat, immobilized, and at his mercy.

"I'll pay you more than what you were offered. I'll pay you ten times more," I said, my brain keeping up with my hurriedly spoken words, as I thought how this offer could also buy me a little more time.

"Unlike you, I don't have a price on my life. If I take money from you and let you go, then I will die." He started to move, and I stopped him with another rush of words.

"You can still kill me. Just not this way. I'll pay you the money and then you can do what you like with me. Just not like this. Please," I begged, fighting hard to prevent my eyes from turning to the door in the hope that it would open. Where the fuck was he? The man surprised me by laughing.

"Oh, Dallas. This won't kill you. It will just make you wish you were dead. You'd better take a deep breath." He placed the towel over my face, as I screamed and tried to kick, thrashing my head from side to side. It was no use. Somehow, the towel was being held securely over my face. I was gasping for air, struggling fiercely against the restraints. My hands had gone numb, and the pain in my wrist was no longer important, as the fight to survive kicked in. I tried to scream. I had to convince him to stop, but there was no time. My efforts to plead and beg for mercy went unheard, as my head was held in position. I managed to gulp in a breath of air before I was blasted with cold water, which seeped through the towel, and into my nose and mouth. I tried to tell my brain to hold my breath, but as soon as the air left my lungs, I unconsciously sucked in more. I felt the burn as the water hit my lungs, scorching them like fire. I fought hard to free my body from the restraints, but my vigorous attempts had no effect. I was no match for the three men in the room. I tried to cough, but the constant flow of water, and the towel pressed tightly to my face, only allowed the liquid to sink further into my lungs. I felt my eyes bulging from their sockets, and the piercing pain in my chest was so intense that I wished that death would take me instantly. My neck felt strained, as I struggled to move my head to no avail. I was going to die. My heart beat so hard in my chest that I could hear the heavy, thumping rhythm in my ears. My tongue lashed out of my mouth, trying to stop the water that flowed freely, but it was met with the towel that was stretched tautly over my face. Just as the welcome darkness started to close in, I was pushed upright, and the towel was removed, prompting me to see stars, as I vomited profusely down the front of my shirt. I sucked in big gulps of air, each breath burning more than the last, as my teary eyes blinked furiously to regain focus. Each breath I managed to pull into my greedy, burning lungs was forced back out of my body in a stream of watery vomit that I couldn't control. When my stomach was empty of the water I had swallowed, I sat gagging and dry heaving, frantically fighting to will my body under control. After what seemed like an eternity, my vision refocused slightly, and I found myself alone as I sat heaving air into my burning lungs, shaking with the pain in my chest at each breath I took. I was going to live. I wasn't sure how much longer I had, but at this point, I was glad for just another minute. As I sat covered in my own vomit, trembling from the bitter cold water, I closed my eyes, and allowed my mind to drift to happier times. A time when I was with Luke and my family. I wanted to reflect on the past month of my life, and dwell in the peace I had once known. As the gun I wore hidden under my shirt pressed painfully into the small of my back, it encouraged me to think of what once was, and what could have been; not on a plan that had gone horribly wrong.

Chapter 1

Red

Six Weeks Earlier

"Will someone please hold the fucking ladder before I bust my ass?" I yelled to the room, flailing my arms around, and almost losing my balance.

"Damn, Red. When did you become such a bitch?" Big Al asked, smiling up at me from under his flat bibbed hat. I wanted to strangle him with the chain he wore around his neck, which featured the number 13 embossed in a diamond shape dangling from its center.

"They will be here any minute and I don't want these cheap ass streamers I bought to be hanging uneven. Since you have been here, you have been on that damned phone the whole time. Couldn't you take time out of your busy life to just hold the ladder while I adjust them? Please?" I added sweetly, giving him that smile I know he can't say no to. Big Al and Mary had come from Lake Charles to be here with us to celebrate the arrival of the club, and mostly Dallas. Somehow, I had been in charge of the homecoming party, while Brooklyn sat at the table sipping Canadian Mist, informing me that she had had her time in, and it was time for some of us other bitches to step up and take over. She looked up from her whiskey on the rocks to find me staring at her, and pursed her dark red lips, blowing me a kiss from across the room. Bitch. Damn, I love that woman.

"You gonna stand there all day staring at Brooklyn, or hang the fucking streamers?" Big Al snapped me back to the present with his playful scolding, while shaking the ladder causing my arms to reach up and grasp the top of it. Asshole. Damn, I love that man.

"Babe, you want me to hold it?" I looked down to see Mary, standing four-foot nine at her tallest, and laughed. I would crush her if, for some reason, I lost my balance and fell. Mary was the ol' lady that we all dreamed of becoming one day. When her man was ready to ride, she had everything packed and loaded an hour before they left. When they stopped to get gas, she immediately began wiping the bike down, cleaning it of any dust, while the rest of us scurried off to smoke cigarettes and gossip. Yep, Mary made us all look bad and here she was, ever the good ol' lady, doing it again. Skank. Damn, I love that woman.

"I got it, babe, I'm enjoying the view." I heard everyone laugh and turned to see that a crowd had gathered behind me.

"What?" I asked, looking into the faces of the ones I loved. The ones I would give my life for, yet at this moment, I wouldn't think twice about taking any of theirs. It suddenly occurred to me what I must look like. My torso was leaning over the top of the ladder, with my ass stuck out in the air for all to see. Someone, my guess is Brooklyn, so conveniently placed the ladder a little too far out, so that I had to reach to hang the streamers that were looking better by the minute, if I said so myself. "Bunch of perverts," I muttered, causing the room to erupt into laughter once again.

"Come on, Red. Do us a little dance. You know, for old time's sake." I shook my head in disgust, as I recognized Bryce's voice behind me. The six-foot five Sergeant At Arms for the Devil's Renegades, Lake Charles Chapter, was not someone to mess with, but at this point I thought I could take him.

"I am going to pretend I didn't hear that, and y'all better be glad Regg ain't here to hear it either," I said in a chastising tone, but just the mention of Regg's name had me realizing how much I missed him. If anyone was glad all this shit was over, it was me. I needed Regg home where he belonged. I was pretty needy.

"We're just teasing, babe." Big Al attempted to soothe me in his strong Louisiana accent, as he gave the ladder a little shake, and I couldn't help but wonder if he had done this in the hope of seeing a little jiggle from my ass. I looked down at him, and saw him smiling up at me once more, and I knew his statement was sincere. No one in the room would ever use my past against me, unless it was in the form of a joke. Bastards. Damn, how I loved them all.

My head shot up at the sound of pipes in the distance, and the entire house erupted into frenzy. I clambered down from the ladder, which was swiftly pulled away from me, and pushed into a closet. I heard Maddie hollering from somewhere in the house that they were here, and watched as she appeared, her arms loaded down with Devil's kids, and a camera dangling from her mouth. I scrambled to find a mirror to fix my hair, my heart beating excitedly as I started shouting orders at everyone, instructing them to hide. I caught a glimpse of all the women, as I ran through the living room and crouched down behind the couch, while the men stood around shaking their heads at them. I rushed into the bathroom to find it empty, and fluffed up my red hair, which cascaded halfway down my back. The orange top I was wearing was quite a sight, with a scoop neck line that barely grazed the tops of my breasts, and had long sleeves that were slit from the shoulder to the wrists, exposing my tanned skin. The bottom was tight and gathered at my waist, revealing the slightest hint of my stomach. My black skinny jeans sat low on my hips, and showed off my "Property of Regg" tattoo that graces my lower back; my 25th birthday present from him. My killer heels were open-toed, and laced up to my ankles, showing off my perfectly painted, neon-orange toes; another favorite of Regg's.

"Red, come on!" Brooklyn yelled from the kitchen. The bikes were close now, the pipes rumbling loudly as I danced in place for a moment at the thought of seeing my man. I ran from the bathroom to find the house dark, and nearly broke my neck stepping on someone.

"Fuck, Red!" Maddie snapped, as my stiletto collided with her toe.

"Dammit," I heard Mary mutter, as I slapped her in the head, feeling my way around the room.

"Sorry," I said through my laughter. I found a spot next to Logan and hunkered down, listening as the sound of cheerful voices got closer and closer to the door. They were home. My family was home and no matter what happened in the future, nothing could take the happiness out of this moment.

Dallas

On the ride home, I had never felt freer in my life, yet I wore a leather vest covered in orange patches that read "PROPERTY OF DEVIL'S RENEGADES PRESIDENT LLC" that let everyone know that free was something I was not. Adrenaline coursed through my veins, pushing all thoughts of the previous forty-eight hours of my life out of my mind, as we rode home at a leisurely pace of ninety miles per hour. I had to be the luckiest woman in the world. I had found the man of my dreams, a blood sister, a beautiful blue-eyed nephew, and a host of brothers and sisters that I never knew existed. If my life was taken from me tomorrow, I could say that I had lived the dream. Nothing could take this happiness from me.

By the time we arrived at Luke's, the sky was dark and the cool October air had turned frigid with the sun's descent. No one seemed to notice the cold, as we pulled up and dismounted from the bikes. Every face was plastered with a smile as cigarettes were lit, and talk of the ride began in earnest. I learned that every stop we had made between Lake Charles and Hattiesburg served as a memory, permanently imprinted on each of our minds. At a gas station in Hammond, Louisiana, I learned that Ronnie, the president of the Devil's Renegades, Lake Charles Chapter, loved beer infused with tomato juice. He loved it so much that he downed three sixteen-ounce cans, then led us into oncoming traffic. I should have been mortified, but I could only laugh as each bike made a U-turn in the middle of the highway, each full-face helmet shaking visibly with laughter once we made it safely to the median. In Kentwood, Mississippi, we spent twenty minutes trying to figure out how Regg was going to strap a four-foot, stuffed red rose to his bike. He said Red would kill him if he came back with nothing to give her. He managed to bend it enough to sit on his back seat, and secured it with a bungee cord; cursing himself the entire time for not bringing along a PROSPECT, someone who dedicated a minimum of one year to the club in hopes of one day becoming a member. These were just a couple of the memories that were created on our short 5-hour journey back to the new life that awaited me. I removed my gloves, and flexed my fingers, which were now numb from squeezing Luke's leather cut so tight, not in fear of falling off the bike, but in fear of not being able to hold onto him. I turned to him, as he graced me with a beaming smile that made his eyes crinkle at the corners.

"Ready to go inside and thaw out, babe?" he asked, rubbing his hands up and down my leather clad arms. I nodded to him, anxious to see everyone, but my smile died when I noticed no cars and no lights on inside the house. I might have been wrong, or had anticipated too much. I was expecting to see the front yard illuminated with lights from the house, hear music blaring out, and find a slew of cars in the driveway. I mentally kicked myself for being so ungrateful and selfish, a move that was still new to me. Luke reassured me with one of his winks, and the fire inside me ignited once again, as I took in all that was Luke. He was dressed head-to-toe in leather. His thick jacket was zipped up to his neck, and the cut he wore so proudly was displayed on top of it, for all to see. Four chain extenders linked the cut together, each one hanging loosely over his abdomen. His black chaps covered his denim-clad legs, but left that perfectly toned ass of his fully visible, even through his baggy jeans. He grabbed my hand, interrupting my eye-raping, and pulled me toward the door in the carport that led to his kitchen.

"Welcome home, baby," he said, opening the door and gesturing for me to walk inside. I looked behind him at all of his brothers, who stood patiently waiting for me to enter. All that was, except for Regg, who tapped his foot in what seemed to be anticipation. I shook my head and entered the house, my hand feeling its way down the wall for the light switch. When the lights came on, and the kitchen came into view, I gasped at the scene. Streamers lined the large doorway that led into the living room, along with balloons and a welcome home banner. Enough food to feed an army littered the bar in the kitchen, and a large, two-tiered cake, decorated with the words "PROPERTY OF LLC", sat on the table. Had there not been a still-lit cigarette, with red lipstick covering the butt, smoking in the ashtray, I would have thought no one was here. The house was completely quiet, as I walked through the kitchen and to the entryway of the living room. Then suddenly a chorus of "SURPRISE!" rang out, leading me to jump back into Luke's arms, and the lights in the living room were turned on to reveal a host of smiling faces all looking at me. I covered my mouth with my hands, as my eyes filled with tears at the sight of all the familiar, and not-so-familiar, faces. I watched as my nephew Logan's little body made its way through the crowd and into my arms. At the sight of him, my tears fell freely down my cheeks. He smelled delicious as I squeezed him to me; a mixture of soap and little boy.

"Oh, I missed you so much," I whispered into his ear, as I relished the feel of his arms around my neck.

"I missed you too." He pulled his face back, so that he was looking into my eyes, and placed his hands on each of my cheeks. "I'm really glad you're here 'cause I'm hungry." Laughter erupted from deep within my chest at his honesty.

"Well, let's eat." I kissed his forehead, and placed him on his feet, which were propelling him toward the kitchen as soon as they were on solid ground.

"Glad to have you home, baby." I looked up to see Brooklyn standing before me, her arms snaking around my shoulders and pulling me to her. She was typical Brooklyn, dressed in black leggings, thigh-high boots, and a button-up shirt covered in skulls, wearing bright red lipstick, and holding a cigarette between her fingers.

"Thank you, Brooklyn," I said, through a sob.

"Oh, no. We can't be having you crying, now you're home and safe. We have a lot of drinking to do, so dry them tears and start having a good time," she said, giving me a squeeze that was just a little too tight.

"Okay, okay. You have had her long enough, now move on." I recognized Red's voice immediately, and couldn't help a sob escaping from my throat once more.

"Naw, now you are gonna get her all worked up again," Brooklyn chastised, but released me from her grip, and into Red's waiting arms. I felt Red's lips on my hair as she kissed me, then pulled me back so she could get a proper view.

"I did good on the clothes, huh?" she asked, through a smile and tears of her own. I nodded my head and looked down at the leather outfit that she had provided for me.

"Yeah," I said, with a laugh. "You did."

"Okay, I'm not gonna hog you. There is a long line behind me, and I have a man to see." She pulled me to her once more then almost pushed me down to get past me. When I heard her squeal, I knew Regg had presented her with the four-foot stuffed rose. I laughed when I turned to see her jump into his arms, nearly knocking him over in the process.

"Hey, sis." I closed my eyes and smiled, replaying the endearment over and over in my head. I had once longed to hear those words my entire life, and now I could hear them every day. My Maddie was here, and she was safe. Guilt consumed me when my eyes landed on those blue ones of hers that I loved so much. She had my father's eyes. Her smile was almost shy as she stood in front of me. Neither of us was sure what to say at first, but when a single tear fell from her eye and rolled down her cheek, words were not necessary. The reunion was beautiful as we found comfort in each other's arms. It was Maddie who stayed strong this time, caressing my hair and holding me, as I cried into her shoulder. I felt tears of her own stain my shirt as she cried into my neck. Her body, which stood slightly taller than mine, wracked with silent sobs as I tightened my grip around her waist. We stood there in the living room, ignoring the people around us as we tried to squeeze every year we had lost into one single hug. When my tears had dried, and her body stilled, I pulled back to see her face and we both laughed, as our thumbs went to each other's eyes to wipe away the mascara that had smudged against our cheeks. In that instant I wanted to tell her everything. I wanted to tell her that it was me who had taken the life of the only father she had ever known; she deserved to know that it was me who had pulled the trigger. I had had a choice, and I had taken the path I had thought was the best for everyone, but as I looked into her eyes, I realized that maybe I had made the decision on the basis of what was best for me. Sensing my tension, she clasped my shoulders and plastered a smile on her face. "Let's stop all this crying. I think you deserve a drink."

Chapter 2

Dallas

My stomach hurt from laughing so hard at my new-found friend and sister, Punkin. The kids had been put to bed, only after I had read three stories to Logan, not such an easy task when your mind is fogged by an abundance of alcohol; the food was put away, and everyone was ushered into the clubhouse for an adult party that I was in dire need of. I was on my fifth drink, a Red special, and had to take precautions when I took a sip, in fear of Punkin saying something funny that would lead me to spray liquid onto everyone around me. I had recently learned that Punkin was Possum's ol' lady and I was quickly reassured that they had an open relationship, although I nearly died when I remembered a very happy Possum getting a blow job only weeks before. Punkin was in her early fifties, and had spent the last twelve years of her life serving out a manslaughter sentence in the Central Mississippi Correctional Facility for Women. I was alarmed at first, but found myself a cheerleader for the defense team when I learned that she had killed her abusive husband. I didn't really agree with the way she had gone about it, stabbing him forty-seven times in his sleep, but who the hell was I to judge? After twelve years of good behavior, and numerous therapy sessions, we now had a fully reformed Punkin, who loved peppermints, Sprite, and a biker named Possum.

"I'm telling you, I jumped in that twenty-three degree water without a second thought. I was high as a kite while I'll was runnin' from the police, but I was sober as a judge after I hit the bottom of that river. I lost my fuckin' shoe and everything. Them motherfuckers didn't get me though." I laughed through my drink and my attempts at not spraying it failed, as I laughed harder at, a now covered-in-Red-Bull-and Vodka, Red. "You just can't make this shit up," Punkin informed us, oblivious to our laughing, as she sat wringing her hands. Her cigarette, which I noted had never been pulled from the corner of her mouth, dangled loosely with each word she spoke. Red leaned over, wiping the drink from the front of her shirt, and offered Punkin an ashtray. When she refused with a wave of her hand, I laughed louder. I stood, clutching my aching ribs, and left the conversation in search of the bathroom. I thought of how strangely amazing my life had become, and considered how crazy it had been for me to encounter a group of bikers, never knowing that one day I would be a part of that group. I, along with so many others, had assumed that all bikers were trashy, dope-dealing, unemployed felons, whose main mission in life was to break the law and intimidate people. If someone had told me that I would one day be sharing drinks and conversation with a woman named Punkin, who was the ol' lady of a biker named Possum, I would have laughed in their face. It's funny how shit works out. I looked up to find a red-faced Marty exiting the hall that leads to the bathroom. His crimson face deepened when he saw me.

"Oh, hey, Dallas. Having fun?" I had said all of my hellos, and had received all my welcome home hugs, hours ago, yet Marty still looked surprised to see me.

"Hey, Marty. You okay?" I asked, eyeing him warily.

"Yeah, yeah. I'm good. Just checking the bathrooms. It's hard to get over that PROSPECT phase once you have been in it so long."

"I bet. How long did you PROSPECT?"

"Three hundred and eighty-six days," he said without blinking. Damn, did he have a reminder or something?

"I have an app on my phone. It tells me. That's not something you wanna forget if one of the patch-holders asks you. Ya know?" I smiled at his uneasiness, and attempts to distract me with conversation.

"I do now. So, are the bathrooms safe?" I asked, gesturing down the hall with my hand.

"Oh, yes. Of course. They're all yours," he said with a tight smile. I noticed a thin line of sweat break out on his forehead, and was about to again ask him if he was okay, but he got in ahead of me as I opened my mouth to do so.

"Gotta go. I'll see ya around, Dallas. Good to have you back." He all but ran away from me, leaving me to wonder what in the hell his problem was. I walked to the ladies' room, pushing the heavy wooden door open to find a radiant Maddie on the other side.

"Hey!" She said with a surprise. What the fuck was up with everyone being so surprised to see me? I had started to ask, when realization suddenly slapped me in the face.

"You're fucking Marty!" I accused, poking her with my finger.

"What? You're fucking crazy, Dallas," she said, rolling her eyes and avoiding my accusing stare.

"Yes, you are! You just fucked him in the bathroom! He looks just as guilty as you do!" My mouth was agape in an all-out smile.

"Did you see him? Did he say something?" she asked, confirming my suspicions.

"I knew it!" I said laughing. I pushed my way past her to find the toilet, leaving her to panic.

"Dallas, please don't say anything. I mean, it's nothing. I swear." I looked up from my seated position into her blue eyes, which were blazing with fear.

"Of course I won't say anything! What's it matter anyway? Hell, y'all are grown." I froze, and stopped midstream as I gaped at her. "He isn't married, is he?" Marty had told me his story, and he had never mentioned a wife, but I knew that men were fully capable of lying.

"Hell no! It's not that," Maddie said, defeated. I watched as she jumped up to sit on the sink, picking at imaginary lint on her shirt. I resumed my duties as I let out a relieved breath, and watched as my sister struggled to find the right words to tell me about it.

My sister.

I liked that.

"Maddie, you can tell me anything. I won't tell Luke, if that's what you're worried about." Her head snapped up at my confession, and relief flooded her pretty face. I felt like I had been punched in the gut. Did she think I would share her secrets with Luke? Out of fear of my own thoughts, I elaborated, trying to convince my only sister that the things we shared were strictly between us. I had always told Luke everything, because I had had no one else to trust and rely on, but now that I had a sister, things were different. "I promise anything you tell me is for my ears only. I would never sell you out to Luke. But I don't see why it matters anyway. You are both single adults who want to have a non-committal, sexual relationship. There is nothing wrong with that." I had joined her at the sink and stood before her, drying my freshly washed hands on my jeans, as there were no paper towels. Marty had checked the bathrooms alright.

"But it does matter. Luke would never let me date Marty. A long time ago, he told me to never fall in love with one of his brothers. He said it should never happen." I rolled my eyes at Luke's pathetic demands.

"Believe it or not, babe, Luke can't tell you what to do with your own life. If he loves you, which I know he does, he would want you to be happy, and if Marty makes you happy, then that's who you need to be with."

"It's not that easy, Dallas. Luke may woo you in the bedroom, and he may be your knight in shining armor, but he's a force to be reckoned with. Nobody crosses Luke. Nobody."

"Leather." I mouthed at her. Her brow wrinkled in confusion, and it was all I could do not to laugh. "He's my knight in shining leather."

"Well, whatever the hell he is, I tell you one thing he is not, and that is a man who goes back on his word. He gave his word that any man that puts his hands on me will have to face him." I smiled at Maddie's worried expression, and squeezed her hands in reassurance.

"Then it's a good thing you have a man that isn't a pussy. He knows what he wants and he won't let anything stop him. Not even the big bad LLC."

"That's what I'm afraid of." Her defeated tone cut me deep, and I suddenly made it my life's mission to ensure that if a relationship with Marty is what she wants, then that's what she's going to get.

"Do you want me to talk to Luke?" I offered, hoping she would trust me enough to let me help her out.

"What!? Fuck no, Dallas!" She shouted in disbelief. I took a step back at her show of hostility. "Let the man keep his fucking balls, will ya? How's it gonna make Marty feel if you go barging off to Luke demanding he let us be together? I can handle this on my own." I felt pride swell in my chest, as I watched my little sister take a life-altering event into her own hands. Although it didn't quite eclipse the pang of hurt I felt at knowing that there really are things in life she doesn't need my assistance with.

"You're right," I said, surrendering and deciding to let her work out her love-life problems on her own. "I'll stay out of it, but let me ask you a question."

"What?" She snapped in exasperation.

"Is it just sex, or is there more?" I watched as she struggled to answer my question. She jumped down from the sink and started fidgeting with her make-up and hair, giving me the answer I needed before she even spoke.

"I don't know. Maybe more. It's just started. When I got back from Texas, he was here. I needed somebody." She turned to me, and I watched as her eyes turned dreamy when she started to explain, "I was messed up, ya know? I had so much shit going on in my head, and he just came up to me one day with a plate of green apples and peanut butter. It's my favorite, and when I asked how he knew, he just said 'I pay attention.' When Luke left, I found myself in the clubhouse drowning in liquor. He carried me inside after I passed out and I begged him to stay. And he did. The next day we spent all day together. He told me about his ex-girlfriend, and I told him about Logan's dad, and we just hit it off. We haven't even had sex." I raised my eyebrows at her in disbelief.

"Really?" I asked, incredulously. This was so evident in my tone of voice that Maddie actually frowned. Great, Dallas. Make her feel like a slut, why don't you?

"I thought it would be easier for you to believe that it was just sex, but it's so much more. We understand each other. This is my life. This club means everything to me, and he gets that. Imagine being me and trying to bring in

28

someone from outside the club." I stared at a very confused and heartbroken Maddie, as I tried to find the right words to comfort her. Did I understand? Could I be her and choose to love someone outside the club? Luke had taken that chance on me. He had brought me in not knowing how I would react, and it had worked in his favor. Would Maddie have the same luck?

"How do you explain to a man that being around a bunch of guys the majority of your time is normal? How do I keep him from getting jealous, or prevent the accusations that are sure to come? What man would not get pissed at one time or another and throw the words, 'I know you are fucking one of them' at me. Not to mention the turmoil he would have to go through each time I bring him around. It's not possible, Dallas." She was right. The only reason I was able to handle it was because I was here all the time, and had gotten used to the women being around. For a man, it would be different, unless he saw a patch in his future.

"Well, if you feel that strongly about it and think this thing with Marty may go somewhere, then you need to tell Luke," I said, using my best motherly tone.

"And what happens if Luke says no? Then what?" It was apparent that Maddie had zero faith in Luke. She had already convinced herself of the outcome, but I had yet to hear her say she was willing to give Marty up. I tried a different tactic, hoping to persuade her that maybe Marty wasn't the one for her.

"Who knows, this may not even work out. I mean, you barely know him." I shot her a reassuring smile that was wiped from my face immediately, as if she had slapped it from me.

"What the fuck, Dallas? I told you I liked him. It doesn't matter if it works out or not. This is the part where you are supposed to tell me it will work out, whether it eventually does or not. You are a shit advice-giver. And I do know Marty. He has been hanging around the club for years. He has prospected longer than you have been around. I have seen him almost every day of my life since he has been here. You know what, forget I ever said anything." I watched in shock as Maddie stomped out of the bathroom, leaving me staring at myself in the mirror. This sister shit was harder than I thought. I rubbed my hands over my hair, pulling at the ends of it in a frustrated gesture, and let out a long breath. I needed a drink.

The party was still in full swing when I walked back to the bar and took a seat next to a very drunk, very loud, Brooklyn. I greedily accepted another drink from the girl behind the bar and offered her a small smile of thanks.

"What the fuck is wrong with you?" Brooklyn barked, nearly causing me to jump out of my seat.

"Nothing, I'm just a little tired. What did I miss?" I asked, forcing on a fake smile that didn't go unnoticed by the crowd of women that were gathered around.

"Uh-huh. You and Maddie had it out." A very observant Red confirmed. These bitches paid way too much attention.

"And what makes you say that, Red?" I put my drink up to my mouth, looking at her over the rim of my glass, and watched as she smiled coolly at me.

"Oh, just that she stomped out of the bathroom, and only seconds later, you emerged looking like you had lost your best friend." Yep. Too observant.

"It's nothing. Just a minor disagreement." I dismissed the subject with a wave of my hand, and was rescued from the accusing stares when Punkin came up and announced that the new PROSPECT from Lake Charles was catching hell outside. Red, who I had learned had a very soft spot for the PROSPECTS, almost broke her leg trying to get away from the bar to go and see what was going on. I couldn't help but laugh at Brooklyn's attempts to stop her, but soon we were all following Red out the door.

We entered the circle of men that were crowded around, and my heart's steady rhythm intensified. I don't know what I had been expecting, but something told me that whoever was in the middle of that circle was being subjected to great harm. My stomach dropped at the thought of Luke using physical force against one of his brothers, or even his potential brothers. I had never seen the side of Luke that Maddie had spoken of earlier. Sure, I had been subject to his wrath, but I couldn't imagine him ever being mean to one of the guys. I heard Luke's loud voice carry across the yard, as I stepped between Brooklyn and Red to find a guy cleaning Ronnie's bike.

"Don't you ever fucking say you are gonna do something and not follow through. Consider this a lesson. Never offer more than you are willing to give." Luke wasn't shouting, but his voice was louder than normal, and did not contain even a hint of playfulness. I watched as the man paid special attention to ensuring that he did not miss a spot in cleaning the bike, as he worked feverishly, shining it and returning it to its original glory. He kept his head down and his mouth shut, as Luke continued to speak, "You want to clean bikes? Well, now you've got your chance. There are twenty-three bikes in this yard that are the property of the Devil's Renegades and every one of them had better be shining like new. Ronnie, what time do y'all plan to leave in the morning?" Luke turned his eyes from the working PROSPECT toward Ronnie, who stood tall, and bow-legged as ever, next to Luke.

"Oh, I figure we will pull out about ten. I want to get home before it gets dark. PROSPECT, if you can't add, that gives you about eight and a half hours to have our shit looking good." I watched as the guys around them laughed. I looked over at Red, who didn't think this was very funny. I could see her mentally calculating the hours in her head. There was no way he would be able to detail twenty-three bikes in eight hours. Even if he could, he would get no sleep, and he was one of those who would be making the four-hour ride home tomorrow.

"If it's not done, I'll cut that PROSPECT rocker off and give it to someone who deserves it." I snapped my head up at Luke, as he stood with his arms crossed, looking down at the poor guy, who seemed to be breaking into a sweat, and he picked up the pace. Luke must have felt my eyes on him. He looked over at me and his menacing stare melted, to be replaced with a wide smile and a wink that had me breathing a sigh of relief. He was only kidding. I felt someone move beside me, and watched as Red walked back into the clubhouse. The unspoken demand for us to follow was heard, and we all trailed in behind her.

"This is fucking stupid," Red snapped, as soon as the door was closed and we were all inside. "I mean, the poor guy ain't even gonna get to take a fucking break. Come on, Dallas. Get over here and help me." I immediately went to her, fearing if I didn't it would be me she snapped at next.

"Calm down, Red. It's part of it. I don't know why you get all bent out of shape about this shit," Brooklyn snapped, her voice holding a hint of disapproval.

"Well, it just ain't right," Red said, busying herself behind the bar, while I just stood there waiting for orders.

"They all went through it. He needs to watch what he says." It was clear that Red and Brooklyn had had this conversation before. Red had issues with the way the club disciplined the PROSPECTS, while an exasperated Brooklyn seemed to consider it reasonable, and tried to convince Red that it was a normal part of the PROSPECT period.

"If y'all don't mind me asking, what did he say?" We all turned to the softly spoken voice behind us. I was shocked to find a very sweet-looking girl in her early twenties standing there, and staring at us, wide-eyed. Judging by the ring on her finger, and the worried look in her eye, this had to be the PROSPECT's wife. I immediately felt pity for her.

"He got cocky and said he would wash his brothers' bikes. He was talking about Ronnie's, but he didn't elaborate. He said 'brothers'' and that meant all of them. First of all, they ain't his brothers. Second, he shouldn't have offered if he couldn't perform, and third he needs to learn to keep his mouth shut. The less he says the better."

I almost died at Brooklyn's harsh comment. She wasn't cutting this poor girl any slack.

"Oh," she replied simply. She seemed to accept her husband's fate, but Red wasn't going to let it go.

"I thought it was very generous of him to offer. Just because he got a few words mixed up doesn't mean he should have to stay up all fucking night after being up all day, on top of having to make that long trip tomorrow." My mind was screaming at me to stay out of it and keep my mouth shut too, but of course I didn't.

"I really think Luke was just kidding. He winked at me. I think they are just making the guy think he is going to have to do that." The reaction I got was not one I was expecting. The room erupted in laughter at my words.

"You really do have a lot to learn. Honey, if Luke says it; Luke means it. That poor boy will be washing bikes all night. Now, I can't say anything because it's not my place, and I don't want to be screamed at in front of everyone, but what I can do is help him out. Discreetly," Red announced more to the wife than to any of us. Brooklyn's eye-rolling did not go unnoticed, as Red continued with her plan of action. "Katelan? Is that your name?" The girl nodded her head, and Red went on, "You need to stay out of it. Don't talk to him. Don't check on him. Just stay inside and away from him. The last thing you want to do is make him look like a pussy. These guys will use anything as leverage to see if they can break him. I am going to give him an Adderall, make him some sandwiches, and be sure he has all the supplies he needs within reach. Dallas, you are going to help." I nodded quickly, letting Red know that I was on her side, and would do anything to keep the tears that were welling up in Katelan's eyes at bay, as well as make the impossible job for the PROSPECT as easy as I could. "I can't believe he threatened him with his patch," Red mumbled, grabbing Red Bulls from the cooler, and shoving them in a bag.

"It got his attention. If he wants to keep it, when we get ready to leave in the morning there had better be twenty-three Harleys sparkling to their full potential," Brooklyn stated. Red didn't respond, as she grabbed the bag, shot Brooklyn a look, and walked out of the clubhouse with me in tow.

"Will Luke really take his patch?" I asked Red, as we shoved the last few sandwiches in a Ziploc bag. We were standing in Luke's kitchen, preparing a late-night snack for the PROSPECT.

"If he said he would, he will," she replied, deadpan. "Luke is a man of his word." Apparently. I thought about Maddie's issue, and wondered if I should say something to Red. It seemed they all knew Luke much better than I did.

"Are we having operation 'Save the PROSPECT?'" Maddie asked, coming into the kitchen, dispelling any thoughts I had of telling Red about her business.

"You know it," Red said, smiling. "You gonna help?"

"Nah, I'll let y'all handle this one," she said, propping her elbows up on the bar.

"Why? Cause it ain't Marty?" Red asked, and my eyes widened in shock, as I looked at Maddie, who mirrored my reaction. "How many times did you wake me up in the middle of the night for a 'Save PROSPECT Marty' operation? Remember that time he had to go get the letter?" I watched in confusion, as Maddie's features softened, and she relaxed with a laugh.

"Yeah, I remember. It was so funny, Dallas," she said turning to me, her eyes sparkling, as she retold the story, our dispute from earlier seemingly forgotten for now. "He told Luke he was going to go home. Luke told him he had to do something first. He made Marty ride all the way to Lake Charles to get a letter from Ronnie, and then return it to him. When he got back, Luke told him to open the letter. Know what it said? 'Now you can go home.'" I stared in horror at Maddie. That would have been an eight-hour round trip. Shit.

"Rule number one. Never tell the President you are leaving as long as you are prospecting. You ask to leave," Red said, lighting a cigarette, and fanning the smoke away from my face.

"Yeah, I made Red ride with me to Hammond, so we could boost his spirits," Maddie said beaming. I arched my eyebrow at her.

"And just exactly how did you do that?" I asked. Maddie had said they had never had sex.

"Everyone has secrets, Dallas," she said, with a wink. Red laughed and I had a feeling I was on the outside of an in-joke. Apparently, Red knew about Marty and Maddie. It was me that Maddie was so worried would spoil the big surprise. I scoffed, feigning shock, but in reality I was fighting some pangs of hurt and jealousy. Of course

Red was closer to Maddie. She had always been here. It was me that was the newcomer. It didn't matter that Maddie and I shared the same father. Maddie and Red had been sisters a lot longer.

"Okay, so this is how this is going to work. Maddie, are you in?" Red asked looking at Maddie, her eyes turning to resemble those of a puppy.

"Yeah. What the hell," Maddie said, gesturing for Red to continue with the plan of action.

"Good. Dallas, I need you to distract the guys. Mainly Luke, but try to get all their attention. Preferably, get them all in the clubhouse. Maddie, you watch the door and make sure no one comes in or out, and I'll slip the bag to the PROSPECT." Oh, for fuck's sake.

"Red, why don't we just give him the damn bag?"

"Because, Dallas, how would you feel if your man was offered help from another woman and took it, and then had to be subjected to all the shit the guys threw at him for accepting help from a bitch. We want the guys to think that he did this on his own. The chances of that are slim to none, so we are going to help him out, and the guys will be none the wiser." I still didn't quite get it, but if Red thought it was for the best, then I would help. She seemed genuinely concerned about this guy, and if she needed me to help her feel better by helping him, then who was I to say no?

"Okay. How do I get the guys' attention?" I had thought of a few ways, but none would make Luke very happy.

"Give 'em a speech about how much you appreciate all their help and all that shit," Maddie suggested. The thought turned my gut.

"That just feels wrong."

"No, it's perfect. Think of it like this, not only are you thanking them, you are also helping out someone in need. Do you really want to go to sleep tonight knowing that you were responsible for a potential brother losing his patch?" Red asked, looking at me with fake pity.

"And what about that sweet girl he has with him? Do you know how devastated she would be?" Maddie chimed in. They were playing me.

"Fine. But my speech will be sincere. And that PROSPECT better get those fucking bikes finished." Red jumped up, and squealed like a little kid. They ushered me outside and, just like that, the first of what would be many 'Save the PROSPECT' operations was launched.

Chapter 3

Dallas

I was standing on the bar, my glass held high in the air, as I concluded my speech that, true to my word, was sincere. I had forgotten all about the PROSPECT, and the reason I was making the speech in the first place. I was sure that Red had delivered the package and all was good, but at this point I couldn't care less. What mattered to me were the faces that looked at me, most of which I knew, as I laid my feelings bare for all of them. They were an easy crowd. I felt like I could tell them anything, so I did. I told them everything, well, almost everything. I told them how Charlie had taken me and I thought I would never see their faces again. I told them how had I felt when I saw them all standing there, ready to give their lives to save me. I told them about the emotions that had passed through me when their bikes surrounded Luke's truck and led us off the highway. I thanked them for always being there, not just for me, but for Luke too. I let them all know that if the role was reversed, I would do the same for any of them. As I held my glass, I concluded my speech with the words that I would live by for the rest of my life. "This is to all of you and the sacrifices you have made on my behalf. You have all taught me what family is and for that, I will be forever in your debt. To all of you, and to the motto of the Devil's Renegades: Love, loyalty and respect." I closed my eyes and smiled, nodding my head as the chorus rang out from those before me. The brothers, ol' ladies, PROSPECTS, hang-arounds, barmaids, girlfriends, and wives met my toast, and we shared something more than a shot of alcohol. We shared a moment of truth. A moment in which each and every person in that room knew why they were there. This was a moment when we all understood what it meant to be a Devil's Renegade. I was lifted from the bar and into Luke's arms. My hands grasped his muscular shoulders as my legs wrapped around his waist. I felt his hardness through his jeans, as he pulled me to him.

"That was a beautiful speech, babe," he said smirking at me.

"So beautiful that it made your cock rock hard?" I asked, smiling at him, as he grinded his hips into me.

"Fuck, I love it when you talk dirty like that. I want to take you inside right now, and fuck you until you pass out." His eyes were heavy and full of lust, as he ran his tongue along my bottom lip, and delivered another delicious thrust that had me wet and wanting.

"Please," I whispered, taking his tongue into my mouth, and sucking it gently. I felt his grip tighten on my hips, as he let out a groan into my mouth. I knew that groan. It was one that said, 'I can't.'

"I will, baby. Soon," he said, pulling his mouth from mine, and setting me on my feet. I frowned at him, as he adjusted himself, and lifted his head to the girl behind the bar. She placed a beer in front of him, and he shot her a wink, causing my frown to deepen.

"That's my wink," I grumbled, wondering what in the hell it would take to get men behind the bar.

"It's all yours, baby," Luke responded to my grumbling. He kissed me chastely on the lips, then grabbed my hand, and led me over to a group of loveseats that had been arranged to form a semi-circle. The table in the middle was littered with empty drinking glasses and the sofas were filled with ol' ladies practically sitting on top of each other. "We are gonna hold a short church, then you can have me all to yourself." He slapped my ass, and turned to leave before I could say a word.

"Awe, shit. Luke just gave you that 'I'll fuck you later promise' didn't he?" Fucking Red. Why was she always putting my business out on Front Street?

"You know, you pay just a little too close attention," I said, squeezing my ass into the non-existent space between Baby and Jen. I looked around at the group of women, who all nodded in agreement, causing Red to shrug her shoulders in response. I could tell that she didn't give two shits what we all thought of her. Talk between the ladies resumed as more drinks came, including a tray of shots that the lovely Linda presented us with. I felt my cheeks redden, as she winked at me, and I was thankful Red was too busy running her big mouth to notice.

I was introduced to a new group of women from Lake Charles, and was surprised to find that, even though they didn't see each other often, they seemed to have a good relationship with all the ol' ladies in our chapter. There were so many that I was afraid I would never remember them all, but Brooklyn reassured me that I would be seeing a lot more of them. She didn't elaborate, but I could tell there was hidden meaning in her words. I felt, more than heard, the conversation die, as everyone seemed to sense the same thing I did. Brooklyn knew something, and it was a gamble to see if she was going to share. Red must have known what was going on too, and when she took the direction of the conversation in another turn, I knew it for a fact. She was covering something up.

"So, Dallas," Red said, leaning in close, and lowering her voice. I leaned across Jen to bring my head closer to hers, which prompted everyone to lean in; not an easy task, considering there were so many of us. "I'll have you know that the PROSPECT is now hydrated, has a large amount of Adderall pumping through his system, and should have those bikes finished in no time." We all laughed, as we sat back and drank a shot to congratulate Red on her completed mission. I expected Brooklyn to say something smart, but she surprised me.

"There ya go, baby. Your good heart should be enough to keep us out of hell."

"Well, only half of it, because the other half belongs to you," Red said, with a wink. They were so alike, yet so different. It was actually a little scary. If you looked hard enough, you could even find resemblances between their faces. "I'm calling it a night. Maybe I can get a few minutes of sleep in before the insatiable Regg comes to bed, and tries to rape me in my sleep."

"Can't rape the willing," Jen chimed in.

"Ain't that the damned truth! Goodnight all! I will see y'all first thing in the morning." The laughter before seemed muted, compared to that which erupted at Red's announcement.

"You don't even know what morning looks like unless you've stayed up all night to see it," Mary said, through her laughter. I guess Red is not a morning person.

"Ha. Ha. Ha. I'll be up in the morning, and it will be to see your ass off," Red said, pointing at Mary. "Dallas, can I have a minute?" I stood to follow Red to the corner

42

of the room, hearing the ladies placing bets on whether or not she would indeed be up on time.

"What's up?" I asked, noticing the troubled look on her face. I didn't get too worked up, though. Red could be pretty dramatic over the least little things. You just never knew what was going to come out of that mouth.

"So, I talked to Lindsey yesterday and told her we were throwing you a welcome home party." Fuck. I felt my face go ashen and my heart stop. "Don't freak out. I didn't tell her anything; I just said you had been away, which she clearly knows, since she's been taking care of everything while you've been gone. Anywho, I told her and she told me she would be over here. Well, instead of coming, she just sent some stuff, and told me she was feeling under the weather. I know you have a lot on your mind, but I'm pretty sure she is stressed out, so you may want to head over to your office sometime tomorrow, just to make sure everything is okay." Fuck. I had completely forgotten about Knox Companies and Lindsey. I had been so busy with the fight to survive that I had forgotten about the place that had made me who I am. I guess that's how you realize what's really important in life. For me, it was hanging out with a bunch of bikers and their ol' ladies, not running a multi-million dollar company that would probably be in ruins by the time I returned. What was even more foreign to me was the feeling of dread I got at the thought of having to leave the comfort of Luke's arms and this clubhouse to be there. I shook my head, trying to shake the annoying thoughts from my mind. I was too tired and had consumed too much alcohol to think about it tonight.

"Thanks, Red. I'll handle it first thing in the morning. Hey, what was Brooklyn talking about earlier?" I asked, thoughts of Lindsey and Knox Companies going out the door once again.

"I'm really not at liberty to say. If Luke wants you to know, he will tell you." The way she said it made the hair on the back of my neck stand up. It was almost like she was finding pleasure in my discomfort. "Some of the guys let their ol' ladies know what's going on and others just... don't. Maybe after you have been around a little longer he will trust you with more information. Anyhow, I'm off," she said, turning her attention back to the women. I had to cross my arms to keep from punching her in the back of the head. What a fucking bitch! I watched as she disappeared down the hall, leading to the bedrooms located in the back of the clubhouse.

The crowd of women had scattered. I noticed the guys were now done with their meeting, and everyone was departing to their rooms for the night. I spotted Luke across the room, engaging in serious conversation with Possum. I saw Punkin lurking nearby, and decided to join her.

"I wish they would hurry up. Hell, I'm tired," she said, pulling another cigarette from its pack, and sticking it to her painted lips.

"May I have one of those?" I asked, remembering my promise to myself to try it once I had got home. Maybe the nicotine would help with my nerves, which Red had so conveniently got on.

"You smoke?" Punkin asked me, surprised, her black painted lashes reaching her eyebrows as her eyes widened.

"No, but when I was with Charlie, I thought of what I would give to have a cigarette. I just thought I would try."

"Who's Charlie?" she asked, not taking her eyes off me, or making a move to give me the cigarette my mouth was suddenly watering for.

"He was the man who kidnapped me." Did she not know that?

"Oh, no shit? What, did he hold you for ransom or somethin'?" I looked into her bright eyes, trying to figure out if she was fucking with me or not.

"No, he took me and Maddie, then gave Maddie back to Luke, kept me for a couple days, then exchanged me for Frankie." My eyes flitted back to the cigarette pack, hoping Punkin would get the message. She didn't.

"I'll be damned," she said, taking a long pull from her cigarette.

"Punkin, can I please have a cigarette?" I asked impatiently.

"Yeah, honey. Sorry, I get sidetracked." I should have asked what memory my kidnapping had triggered, but I was too busy snatching the smoke from Punkin's fingers. "Don't go to choking on that shit now, or I'll have to give you mouth-to-mouth, and Possum will get jealous." I smiled as I held the cigarette between my lips and allowed her to light it. I pulled a drag into my mouth and blew it out, without inhaling. "You like it?" she asked, smiling at me. Did I like it? It tasted different, but it wasn't bad.

"I think so," I said, putting the cigarette to my lips and taking another drag. This time, I inhaled and coughed as the smoke filled my lungs. "Damn, that burns," I muttered through the smoke that poured from my nostrils and mouth.

"You'll get used to it. But remember, you didn't get it from me." Punkin scurried off in the opposite direction, as I felt the presence of someone behind me.

"You know, those things are pretty addictive." I turned to see Luke smirking behind me. "Do you mind?" he asked, taking the cigarette from my fingers. I followed his movement, as he brought the cigarette to his own lips and took a deep drag, inhaled, then blew the smoke over the top of my head.

"You smoke?" I asked, obviously knowing the answer.

"I did," he said shortly, throwing the cigarette on the floor, and putting it out with the heel of his boot. "I have a promise to keep." Thoughts of cigarettes fled my mind as I felt butterflies form in my stomach. I looked up into Luke's face, still bruised from the beating he had taken to protect his cut.

"Come to bed with me?" I turned on my heel, grabbing his hand and pulling him behind me. I heard his low chuckle, as he allowed me to lead him out of the double doors of the clubhouse. As soon as the cold air blasted us, I was jerked back and pushed up against the outside wall of the building. I could feel the steady bass of the music reverberating through the walls, and vibrating against my back as Luke grabbed my face in his hands and closed his mouth over mine. I opened to him and he began kissing me deep, his tongue working mine over and over, as his hands found the hem of my shirt and pushed it up over my breasts, taking my bra with it. He released my mouth, only to dip his head down to my nipple, which had already hardened from the cool air. I threw my head back against the building as my hands found his head, pushing his face deeper into my chest. The feel of his mouth on my nipple, his teeth nibbling, then his tongue sweeping over it to soothe the pain, had me forgetting everything but him.

"I want you to fuck me. I want you to fuck me right here, Luke," I demanded, gasping as he sucked my nipple deeper into his mouth. He released my breast, reaching his hand down to massage it, as he moved his attention to the other one.

"Oh, baby. I'm gonna fuck you. I'm gonna fuck you so hard that everyone inside will hear you scream." The thought of people hearing me, knowing what we were doing, had my heart racing. I wanted people to know. Just the idea of having an audience caused the dampness between my legs to spread. Luke lifted his lips to mine, leaving my breasts exposed, the cold air hitting them and making my nipples so hard, the feeling was almost painful. He trailed kisses down my jaw as his fingers worked my jeans, unzipping them and pushing them, along with my panties, roughly down my legs and to my ankles.

"Fuck." I heard Luke grumble, as he unzipped my boot and removed it from my foot, throwing it over his shoulder and pulling my right leg free of my jeans. I

47

unbuckled his belt, unconsciously running my tongue over my bottom lip at the feel of the thick leather in my hand. "That belt is gonna be on your ass very soon. You have been wanting it for too fucking long." I gasped, as he moved my hands and pulled the belt from its loops in one swift motion. Fuck, that was hot. Luke's jeans were opened and pushed down just enough to release that long, thick cock I loved so much. I whimpered with need at the sight of it. "Don't worry, babe. I'm fixing to give you all you can handle and then some." Luke grabbed my hips and lifted me, my legs going instinctively around his waist. My jeans and underwear hung from my left ankle as he pressed me against the wall and rubbed the head of his cock against my hot, wet flesh.

"Oh, fuck, Luke," I breathed; I looked down and watched, as he circled my clit with the head.

"Tell me you want my cock, baby," he whispered, his breathing was calm, but there was no mistaking the need in his eyes.

"I want your cock, Luke. I want you to fuck me." I gasped, feeling the build of an orgasm, as he continued to circle my clit.

"Louder." I looked up at him, not sure what he expected of me. Did he want me to shout it? Beg for it? He pulled away from me slightly, leaving my clit throbbing, anticipating his return.

"Say it louder, Dallas," he said, pushing back against me. I would have shouted it through a megaphone if it meant he would not stop rubbing against me.

"I want you. Fuck me, ple-," I screamed, my words replaced with a shocked moan of satisfaction as he sunk deep inside me. The feeling was so intense, and felt so good that my body completely relaxed, sagging against the side of the building causing Luke's grip to tighten on me. "Harder," I breathed, my eyes shut tight, as I blocked out everything but the feeling of him stretching me.

"I can't hear you, babe," he said, circling his hips, but not pushing deeper. Oh, fuck it. If he wanted me to scream and give the guys in the clubhouse a show, I would. The need for more of him, and the reassurance that they could only hear me, gave me the strength and confidence I needed.

"Harder! Fuck me harder!" I screamed, opening my eyes to see Luke's bottom lip disappear between his teeth. I don't know if it was a feral reaction, or to hide his smile, but he rewarded me with long, skilled, hard thrusts that had my vision blurring.

"Yes! Yes!" I panted, my voice carrying over the yard and echoing off the trees. I could still feel the steady thump of the bass, but my screams rang out over it. Luke drove deep, pulling my body on top of him, fucking me hard, just like I wanted. The heel of my boot dug into Luke's ass as I tried to push him further into me. With every thrust, he buried himself completely in me. His fast thrusts caused my orgasm to surface, giving my body no time to come down off the high I had when he was inside me. I came hard, screaming his name loudly. His pace quickened as he pulled me down harder, making the sound of our bodies colliding mirror the echo of my voice, which could be heard for miles. I felt myself building, even before he had milked everything out of me. His rough, calloused hands grabbed my bare ass, spread my cheeks open, and allowed the cold air to blast me, and the sensation caused me to explode around him once again. My hands squeezed his arms, my nails digging into his flesh through his thin white t-shirt. I was breathless, limp and sated, when I felt him still inside of me. His cock jerked as I felt his cum fill me, my shivering body finding comfort in his warmth. He withdrew, leaving me empty, and tucked himself back into his jeans, keeping my body pinned against the wall.

"I can't move," I whimpered. My body shook, as it took notice of the cold.

"Yes, you can, babe. Just put your clothes on, and then I'll carry you," Luke said through a chuckle. How did guys do that anyway? Does it not take everything out of them like it does women? He did all the work, yet he looked like he could run a marathon. Men must come with a built-in box of stamina that is used in times like this to completely refuel them. I unwrapped my legs from around Luke, allowing him to stand me up. I struggled with my jeans, as he went in search of my boot, which he had thrown in the heat of the moment. I pulled the other boot off, deciding that walking inside with only socks on was better than struggling with just one. After I had adjusted my clothes, and I looked somewhat presentable, Luke grabbed my hand and led me down the path to the house. As we rounded the corner, we came face-to-face with the PROSPECT cleaning the bikes. The look on his face let me know that he had heard, and quite possibly seen, everything that had just taken place.

Chapter 4

Dallas

"PROSPECT," Luke said, with a nod of his head as we passed.

"LLC," The PROSPECT answered, fighting a smile and avoiding my eyes. Part of me wanted to snatch that Red Bull from his hand and throw it at him. The other part was slightly thrilled at the thought of what he might have witnessed.

"Do you think he saw us?" I asked Luke, once we were locked away in his room.

"Nah, babe. He didn't watch," Luke said smirking.

"How are you so sure?"

"If he had, he wouldn't have been able to look me in the eye."

"Would you have been mad if he had?" I pressed, frozen to the spot, across the room from him. I watched as Luke removed his shirt, and revealed the bandages wrapped around his ribcage. He turned to me and raised an eyebrow, his smile curious.

"Would you?" I thought about this, as my head dropped to stare at my feet.

"I don't think so," I said weakly, my head still bowed in hopes of hiding the redness in my cheeks. I watched Luke's boots come into view as he stood before me. He lifted my chin with his fingers to meet his eyes, which sparkled with humor.

"Me either," He mouthed, before placing a kiss on the tip of my nose, and walking into the bathroom. I looked around the room and noticed that not one thing had changed since I left. My clothes still lay draped over the chaise lounge, and bulging out of open suitcases on the floor. I had practically moved in with him, but had not even put a dent in my closet back home. "Babe, you okay?" Luke asked, emerging from the bathroom, completely nude from the waist up. My eyes fell on the bruises that covered his side and I cringed. Surely, that shit had to hurt. I walked to him, snaking my hands gently around his waist and bending to kiss the swirling purple marks.

"Does it hurt?"

"No, babe. It doesn't hurt."

"It looks like it hurts."

"Looks can be deceiving. Besides, I took my medicine."

"What medicine?" Had Luke gone to the doctor, or had he swiped some pain killers from someone at the clubhouse?

"Your sweet pussy is my cure for everything." I smiled into his chest, I'm not sure why his words embarrassed me, but they did. A smug comment would have worked perfectly here, but instead I continued with the questions.

"Are you going to Lake Charles?" I asked, my grip tightening around him, unknowingly. I knew Brooklyn had been hinting about something, was that it? Was that what Red was hiding? Just the thought of her words had me wanting to stomp my feet and demand Luke tell me what was going on.

"You are just full of questions tonight," Luke said, pulling my arms from around his waist, so he could undress me. "Why do you ask that?" If I had not looked up, I would have never thought anymore about his question or the answer that he gave me, but when my head lifted, the impassive face he wore when he was hiding something was firmly in place.

"I overheard Brooklyn say something about us seeing more of them. What's going on?" Even though my voice was pleading, I knew he would not tell me.

"It's nothing you need to worry about, beautiful," he said, trying to appease me with a reassuring smile and an endearment.

"If it's about you, I need to worry about it. Just tell me the truth." I had pulled my body away from his. I didn't need him trying to avoid the conversation with his hands and mouth, which was exactly what he had planned. I watched as his tongue licked his bottom lip slowly, distracting me while he made his move.

"Oh, no you don't," I said, snapping myself out of my Luke spell and back to the matter at hand. I threw my hands up in front of me, and took a step back. I watched Luke's body sag with exasperation as he stared at the tops of my breasts. He had managed to remove my shirt and my bra, which lay on the floor at his feet. I knew I had the advantage, teasing him with the sight of my firm breasts and hardened nipples, but he would just have to endure it. "Tell me." I demanded, standing my ground, and placing my hands on my hips.

"It's nothing. Just club business. It doesn't concern you." I tried to hide my hurt, but Luke's tone was just a little too harsh for me to recover quickly. That one cut deep. I wasn't sure if he was doing it to piss me off, so I wouldn't ask questions, or if he was annoyed that I kept pressing the issue.

"No secrets, Luke. That's what you promised me. You said there would be no secrets between us, and now you have made me look like a fool." I watched as his eyes turned almost angry. His brow deepened as he opened his mouth to say something then quickly shut it again. He took a deep breath, trying to rein in his temper, and placed his hands on his hips, mirroring my stance. He squeezed his eyes shut, and lifted his face to the ceiling.

"How did I make you look like a fool, Dallas?" We were back to the formalities, and that was never a good sign. Babe, darlin', beautiful... Those were words that Luke used even when he was growing impatient. Dallas was the name he used when he was pissed, or trying to get a very strong point across. My bet was that he was pissed.

"Brooklyn and Red know what is going on. They tried to hide it, but I saw straight through them." I wanted to rat Red out, but I kept my mouth shut. "I am the President's ol' lady. Doesn't that mean something?" Luke's reaction was a huff and an eye roll, better than I was expecting.

54

"You gonna play the ol' lady card on me? Really? What's it been, Dallas? Twelve hours?" I knew Luke was still trying to avoid my question. I knew he was fishing for low blows to piss me off and shut me up. He was struggling with not telling me. I could see that he wanted to do so, but either he believe the truth would hurt me, or he thought I couldn't handle it. A small voice in the back of my mind was telling me he didn't trust me. Luke and I had been through too much to have trust issues, but it still made sense. I tried a different tactic, one that always seemed to have the best end result. I closed the space between us and stood on my toes to wrap my arms around his neck. His pleading eyes begged me not to ask, but I had to. I had to know what was going on.

"Please, baby. Just tell me. I can handle it. Whatever you tell me is just between us. I want to know what's going on. I deserve to know." I searched his eyes, watching as the pools of ocean-blue stared through me. I had covered all my bases. I had told him I could handle it. I had told him he could trust me, and I had let him know that I was deserving of the truth. When he brought his lips to mine and kissed me softly, I thought I had gotten through. I had beaten the truth out of him using my best tactical weapon. He was going to tell me because I was worthy of the information. His hands came to my face, brushing my hair behind my ears, as he kissed my forehead.

"It's nothing, babe. Nothing at all." I could feel his body tense as he forced the lie out of his mouth. His head rested on top of mine, as he held me close to his chest, probably in fear of me running. I closed my eyes and sighed in defeat. I wasn't sure what hurt more, that he had lied to me, or that he thought I was weak. I pulled out of his grasp and headed to the shower. I stripped my clothes off, not bothering to look at the wounded girl in the mirror. I stepped in, letting the hot spray of water cover my body, watching as it disappeared down the drain, and wishing my problems would wash away with it. A sudden wave of homesickness came over me. I wanted my house, my things, my dog... I wanted my old life. Maybe not for forever, but at least for a little while. I needed to be alone. I needed to process everything that had happened in my life over the past few days. I needed someone who might be able to shine some light on my fucked up situation. Someone not connected with the club. Two hours ago, I had thought I had it all. Now, I felt like I was on the outside looking in. Would I ever belong? Would they ever see me as an equal? Would Maddie ever be able to look at me, confide in me, and treat me the same way she did Red? Would Luke ever see me as the strong woman he could depend on like his other sisters? Or would I just be the woman he loved and kept locked away from harm and discomfort. I sobbed quietly, my salty tears mixing with the fresh water and sliding over my lips, giving me a taste of the pain I felt in my heart. Maddie was right. You can't be with someone who doesn't live this life. I thought I was different. I thought I was one of them, but I was just that girl that Luke fell in love with. *That girl* that Luke was paid to watch over. *That girl* that took up everyone's time. *That girl* that didn't read the fine print on the love, loyalty, and respect motto. That motto was true, but only applied to certain people. I was loved, because Luke loved me. They were loyal to me, because they were loyal to Luke, and I was a part of him. They respected me because I was the most respected man's ol' lady. I stepped out of the shower and came face-to-face with *that girl* in the mirror; the one that was not a member of the Devil's Renegades family.

Luke was sound asleep when I made my way back to the bedroom. This would be the first good night's sleep he had had in a while. He lay on his side facing me, a position that invited me to come lay with him. I couldn't leave him. I wouldn't. I was in love with Luke. He was my better, my other, half. Everything he did was to protect me. He couldn't control how the club treated outsiders any more than I could. This was a family that had been together a long time. Even the newest women had been around for over a year, which was the minimum time their men had to prospect. They were in the same boat as I was. The only difference was that mine was a kayak-that held one, and theirs was a pontoon-that held many. They were accepted because they had done their time, but even they were out of the loop on much of what was going on. Red was the queen in Hattiesburg, and Brooklyn was the queen in Lake Charles. They knew everything, and it was very apparent that they wanted *me* to know that *they* were aware of what was going on. I guess it made them feel powerful. As I crawled in beside Luke, letting him cradle me in his arms, another thought hit me. If I stayed around, which I knew I would, to what lengths would Red go just to prove that she was number one? Red was not the type of woman to back down from a fight, nor was she the type to accept second place. She would never let me be the leading lady in Luke's life, the truest sister to Maddie, or the best aunt to Logan. I shut my eyes, trying to enjoy the comfort of Luke's arms, hoping they were enough to push thoughts of Red and the club from my mind. I desperately needed a distraction. Tomorrow couldn't come soon enough. The job I regretted having to go to now sounded more appealing than ever.

"Pull the fucking trigger, Dallas! Do it now!" Frankie screamed at me from his place on the floor. He was on his knees, begging me to take his life. I didn't understand why he wanted to die so bad, or why he so desperately wanted me to be the one to do it. "Hurry the fuck up! She's coming!" Sweat poured from his face and I reached forward, wiping it with my hand. I realized then that it was not sweat rolling down his cheeks, it was tears. I touched his face again, removing the moisture, but before I could wipe my hand on my leg to get rid of it, he was covered again. "There she is! You are too fucking late! You are too late, you stupid bitch!" He was screaming at me so loud that I covered my ears with my hands, the gun falling to the ground with a loud thud. I watched as Frankie's eyes focused on something behind me, and I turned to see Red standing there with a piece of rope in her hand.

"Scream and I might let you live," she said, but her eyes were not on Frankie; they were on me. "Scream!"

I awoke with a jolt, my eyes trying to focus on my surroundings. The image of Red's gaping mouth demanding I scream was still visible in my head. My throat hurt, and it took me a moment to realize that I really was screaming. I clasped my hands over my mouth as the door to Luke's bedroom was thrown open and a herd of people pushed inside, with Red leading the pack. Her face was twisted in horror as she ran toward me. As soon as she was in reach, my hand lashed out and slapped her across the face, stopping her in her tracks. I only had a second to see the shock in her eyes, before she was not so gently pushed to the side, and Luke was in front of me.

"I'm here, baby. I'm here," he chanted, as he pulled me to him.

"What's wrong with her?" I heard Logan ask from the door. He was my undoing. I cried loudly into Luke's shoulder. I wailed like a wounded puppy as tears flooded my face, and my body shook. I took deep breaths, each one sucked in loudly and never enough to fill my lungs. The room was quiet now, except for my cries, Luke's whispers of "shhhh" and the sound his hand made, as he rubbed and patted my back.

Rub up. Pat, pat.

Rub down. Pat, pat.

Rub up. Pat, pat.

Rub down. Pat, pat.

I forced my mind to concentrate on the steady rhythm that flowed in time with his gentle back and forth rocking. I let his motions soothe me as I allowed all the events of the past few days to leave my body via a wail and a tear. My mind didn't need a reason for me to have a breakdown. It was long overdue. I didn't think about anything other than Luke's continuous pattern across my back, the rocking of our bodies and the whispers coming from his mouth. I cried for a long time. In this moment, I was making up for all the times I had held it in and stayed strong. Every bad experience in my life, every worry in my heart, and every horrible nightmare that had me waking up screaming was being dealt with. Sometimes I guess you just need a good cry. Even when my eyes were dry, my body was still and my breathing was normal, I let Luke hold me. I let him protect me from my fears and my past. My body was tired. My mind was a mess, and I felt myself slipping into a place where I longed to be. A place of peace.

Luke

Dallas was a fucking wreck. The nightmares, the kidnapping, the lies, the club... they had finally broken her. I wondered how long it would take her to deal with Frankie's death. She was just trying to be too strong, and trying too hard to prove to everyone that she could handle everything. My girl didn't like to show weakness, but this morning, she left nothing on the table. I held her, rocking her fragile body, as I let her fall to pieces in my arms. When she cried herself unconscious, I would be lying if I said I wasn't relieved. Women. Sometimes I guess they just need a good cry. Now I sat looking down at her, asleep and resting peacefully in my bed. Her eyes were red and puffy, her lips chapped and slightly parted. Yesterday's make-up still covered her lashes, a result of a shower that had been intended to wash away her worries, not the residue of the day's filth. She still looked fucking perfect.

It was almost ten. I needed to get up to see Lake Charles off, but I just couldn't take my eyes off of her. They would understand. I had been up early this morning. I had only had four hours' sleep, but it was still more than I was used to here lately. Before I heard Dallas' screams and came back inside, I had found Chris, the PROSPECT from Lake Charles, putting the finishing touches on the last bike when I had gone to the clubhouse. He had looked surprisingly bright-eyed. I knew this was a result of Red and her generosity. She thought she was smooth, but I wasn't stupid. He had refused her help, but she is a persistent bitch, and I bet he was thankful for that this morning. Tiny had been on the side of the building taking a piss, and had overheard their conversation. He later informed me that Chris had even tried to explain to her that he deserved it. When she countered, by telling him that he might wreck on his way home tomorrow if he didn't accept her gift of caffeine, he told her he would rather lose his life on the road than have to ride without his rocker. He was gonna make a great fucking brother.

A soft tap sounded on the door and I stood, holding my cramping side and wincing as I did. Fucking Charlie. I would say he would one day pay for kicking the shit outta me, but I wasn't gonna give myself any false hope. You can't fuck with the untouchable Charlie Lott. I pulled the door open, to find Red standing there with a plate of food and some juice.

"Thanks, babe, but I'm good," I said, offering her what I could manage in the way of a smile.

"You sure? I mean, I did set three alarms to get up in time to make this shit for everyone. The least you could do is try it, rather than refuse it, and make me feel like my entire day has been wasted." Red always had a way of making you feel like shit. I took the food from her hands, without another word. What was the fucking point? It wasn't like I could argue with that.

"Thanks, and sorry about earlier. I don't know why she did that." Dallas had slapped the shit outta Red. I didn't see it, but there was no mistaking the sound, or the huge red welt that still covered Red's cheek.

"It's cool. Bad dreams make you do bad shit. I know that all too well," she said, waving her hand dismissively. "Lake Charles is leaving. I'll tell them you said bye."

"They'll get it," I said in way of explanation.

"They always do." Red turned and sashayed away, her smart-ass remark not going unnoticed. I closed the door and placed the food on the dresser, taking the juice with me, as I joined Dallas on the bed. Ronnie was having some issues in Lake Charles. Territory issues, which always seemed to be the worst kind. A group of bikers who refused to abide by the rules and do things by the book had moved a chapter in. It had come to blows and word had it that they were bringing in reinforcements, trying to show the Devil's Renegades that they weren't scared. The Confederation of Clubs (CoC) was an organization built to unite Motorcycle Clubs (MCs). If you started a club, you went through the CoC. If you had a problem with a club, you brought it to the CoC. If you wanted respect, it started with the CoC. But there are always those motherfuckers who don't understand what being in an MC is really about. They didn't earn the respect of other MCs because they didn't want to live by the rules and follow proper protocol. Most of these guys were doctors, lawyers, and cops. They thought they were untouchable. They thought they could just show up in someone else's territory and take over. Well, that wasn't how shit worked. My Pops had sat on the board of the CoC. My club was built on principles formed by the CoC, and we worked our way to the top. It was a hard fucking road for my Pops, and it has been a hard road for me. He got us here and now it's my job to keep us here. When people see us, they stand in line to shake our hands. When we ride, we are always in front, and when someone fucks with us, we handle our business. Now, business needed to be handled, and I was stuck between a rock and a hard place. The last thing I wanted to do was leave Dallas. I knew she needed me now more than ever, plus I had promised I would not leave her behind. She was my ride-or-die bitch, and everybody fucking knew it. But I didn't want to uproot her, and make her come with me to Lake Charles for an undetermined amount of time either. I had just made her my official ol' lady. I could only give that patch to one woman, not that I had any intention of letting anyone else have it. Being an ol' lady was new to her, and after everything she had been through; a territorial war was the last thing she needed to be caught up in. I felt the bed shift beside me, and turned to see Dallas rolling onto her stomach. After she settled herself, I thought she would go back to sleep, but her eyes opened, searching until they found mine. She showed no emotion, just stared at me with those big green doe-eyes I had fallen for long ago.

"You feeling better?" Maybe that wasn't the best question to ask her right now. I actually sounded like a dick, which really wasn't out of my norm here lately. She nodded her head at me and continued to stare. I wondered if maybe she was suffering from temporary amnesia or some shit. "Babe?" I asked, feeling my brows knit together. Perhaps she was in shock.

"I'm fine," she said, her words coming out rough. I watched as she licked her lips. Fuck, she was sexy. I damned my growing dick to hell, and kept to the conversation.

"You sure?" I asked, not convinced. I watched as a spark flickered in her eyes, and she pulled herself to a sitting position. In times like this, I was a greedy bastard. It sucked to have Dallas hurting, but when she curled herself in my arms, it almost made it worth it. This time was different. There was a look about her, as if she knew she was about to receive some bad news, and had already accepted it. Instead of coming to sit in my lap or curl in beside me, she sat across from me. Not to be intimidated by a woman, I mirrored her position, sat cross-legged across from her, and looked her dead in the eyes. Now, would be a good time to tell the truth.

Chapter 5

Dallas

Me and my fucking meltdowns. What was wrong with me? Every time I let it all out, why did I feel like such a fool afterwards? Not saying that it wasn't much needed, but still. I hated falling apart and for the past few months of my life, that was all I had seemed to do. This shit was getting old. While I had laid next to Luke, pretending to sleep for the past hour, I had had an epiphany. Luke didn't fall in love with me because I was some weak woman who needed him. He fell in love with me because I was, well, me. I was a strong, independent, self-righteous woman, who didn't need any man telling her what to do or running her life. I always got what I wanted, and this time was no different. I was not intimidated by Red. She wasn't going to scare me off, and if that was her plan then she had better rethink it and consider who she was fucking with. I would no longer be that blubbering mess of a fragile human being. No, starting right now, I was going to be the woman that I knew how to be all too well. The Dallas Knox this cruel world had turned me into. Now, here I sat, on Luke's bed, watching as his acknowledgment of my independent actions surfaced in his brain. He clearly had something to say, and I knew it would not be good. I also knew that I would deal with it as best as I could, and if I couldn't, I damned sure wouldn't make the mistake of falling apart in front of him and *his* family, again.

"I don't expect you to tell me everything. That is not my expectation. What I do expect is for you to tell me things that concern me. I will not be a victim of Red's bullying, nor will I tolerate you keeping secrets from me that could affect us and our relationship. So, whatever you have to say just spit it out. And don't ever treat me like I am some hopeless, frail woman that you have to shelter from the world. You brought me here because you knew I could handle it. Don't fucking play these games with me, Luke. I'm not as brittle as you think." I felt my heart beating harder in my chest, as the words flew from my mouth. I knew Luke was trying to shield me, but damn that. And damn him for not having enough confidence in me to endure whatever he had to say. He seemed to enjoy my outburst, and fought hard to contain his smile. His lips twitched and he looked away, but I could tell it delighted him to know that I had not lost my touch.

"You are so fucking incredible. Do you know that?" he asked, smirking at me, causing my moment of pissed off boldness to disintegrate, like sugar in a hot cup of coffee. Why did he always have to do that to me? He knew he had me when my traitorous body relaxed in a sigh. "I don't want Red bullying you. I don't want any of the ladies to make you feel like you are less than they are. You are all just ol' ladies. Red sometimes acts as though she wears a patch herself, and I will make sure she knows her place before I leave." I felt a twinge of satisfaction, knowing that Luke was going to straighten Red out, but it was washed away at the word 'leave.' Not giving my brain enough time to process his comment, he continued, "Lake Charles is having an issue with a club. The club is big and has chapters in 47 states. They came in, trashed some bars, disrespected some citizens, and are making a bad name for MCs. We have fought like hell for the right to wear this cut, and we refuse to let someone take that from us. There is talk that this club is bringing in reinforcements, following an altercation they had with some of the guys. I need to be

67

there. Know that I want to be with you, but this is where I belong. There will be times when you can't come with me, Dallas, and this is one of those times." He was silently begging for understanding, but there was no need. I knew this was something Luke had to do and I had plenty to keep me busy around here anyway.

"I understand. This is what you need to do and I respect that. All I ask is that you be careful and come back home to me. In one piece," I added, watching as his eyebrows shot to his hairline. Clearly, he wasn't expecting that kind of response.

"That's it?" He asked, staring at me, with his face twisted in confusion.

"Do you want me to bitch and raise hell? Do you want me to cry and beg you to stay?" He was pissing me off with his need to have a negative reaction.

"No, I just assumed you would handle it a little differently." He still looked as if he couldn't quite believe I had taken the news so well. One step forward, five steps back.

"Do I want you to go? No. But, your club needs you and I respect that. So, either we can spend the next hour arguing about me not begging you to stay, or you can join me in the shower and fuck me like you are never coming back." Luke was off the bed and pulling me behind him as soon as the words left my mouth. Well, that worked. I was stripped, he was stripped and we were standing under a stream of hot water in record time. I barely felt the water on my skin before I was pushed up against the cold tiles and Luke's mouth was on mine to quiet my shocked gasp.

"I love you," Luke panted, taking my breasts roughly in his hands as he ground his hips into me. "I love you so fucking much." His need was powerful and contagious, and suddenly I couldn't get enough of him either. My fingers clawed at his back, bringing him closer to me, as I kissed him desperately, our tongues swirling together in a deep, passionate, untamed kiss that fueled our desire for one another further. "Fuck this," Luke said, pulling my bottom lip between his teeth, before plunging his tongue back into my mouth. My tongue met his greedily, punishing him for the seconds of time he was gone. Luke pushed the shower door open using his ass and backed out with me still attached to his mouth. He sat on the floor, pulling me with him and laid back, forcing me to straddle his hips. I moved my hips over his length, my wetness lubricating him as I rubbed my pussy over his cock, teasing my clit with each measured stroke. His hands gripped my hips, his fingers digging deep into my skin, causing a thrilling pain to climb up my sides. I lifted my body over him, tired of the distance between us, and positioned him at my entrance. I sank down onto him, feeling a wave of pure bliss, as he filled me completely. Our moans echoed throughout the bathroom, as I contracted my muscles around him, taking a moment to enjoy the pleasure of him being inside me. "Move, babe. You have to move," Luke gasped between his teeth. I relaxed my muscles, releasing the tight hold I had on him, and began to move up and down slowly. He watched as he slid in and out of me at a leisurely pace. I loved the feeling of control when I was on top. I knew it wouldn't last long by the feel of Luke's grip tightening on my hips. He hated not being able to control what I was doing. I stood suddenly, smiling at the look of confusion on his face and turned. I lowered myself on to him, using his legs for leverage. I began riding him, letting my ass do all the work as I kept my back arched and my head turned slightly to see him. I felt his hands grip my ass and his eyes got that sexy, lazy look as he watched my ass bounce up and down on his massive length over and over.

"Fuck, baby, you got a fine ass," Luke said through his teeth. I suddenly felt somewhat self-conscious of myself, due to lack of exercise and the fact that I had not been taking care of my body the past few weeks, as I once had. I used to visit the gym regularly, but with Luke, there was little time to spare. When I noticed the way Luke looked at me, full of need, want, and desire, it gave my self-esteem a boost, and I was no longer worried about what I thought of my body. If he thought I was fine, then that's all that mattered. His words fueled me, filling me with the desire to please him further. I picked up the pace, leaning forward slightly and arching my back, working my hips harder and taking him deeper. Luke sat up, pushing me forward only to grab my hips and slam me back on to him. I was no longer in control as Luke pushed and pulled my body, slamming me so hard onto him that I cried out. His legs disappeared from under me and my hands were forced to splay flat on the tiled floor as he positioned himself behind me on his knees and drove into me hard. I threw my head back, my damp hair a wild mess as it lay on my back. He grabbed it, wrapping the long strands around his hand and pulled. My head jerked back and I felt my forehead tighten as he pulled harder, sending an excited thrill that ran from the top of my head all the way to my soaking wet pussy. He slammed in and out of me, mercilessly. The feeling of him pushing deep inside me, hitting that sweet spot that made my toes curl, mixed with the blissful pain from my scalp, had me clawing at the bathroom floor, as I moaned in ecstasy. Nothing could ever feel better than this. I had never experienced something so powerful. No one could push me to my limits, or bring me to that thrilling destination of euphoria like Luke could. I never wanted him to leave me. I never wanted him to not be inside me. I wanted to glue myself to him and have that overwhelming feeling of completeness all the time. I wanted him to make love to me again, and again, and again, until we both passed out from exhaustion; only to wake up to him inside me, taking me, owning me once more. I wanted fatigue to be the only reason we stopped, and even then I wanted to lie on top of his body, covered in sweat, and listen to his heart beat through his chest. I knew my thoughts were not rational. I knew what I wanted was impossible, and I was in a delirious state, as a result of my sex-driven fantasies, but right now, in this moment on the bathroom floor, I couldn't give less of a fuck about anything, but him and me and this beautiful, seventh heaven we had created.

"Come, Dallas. I want to feel you come. Right. Fucking. Now." Luke demanded, enforcing each word with a hard thrust that had my knees trembling. With my hair wrapped around his fist, my head pulled back and positioned to look at him, and his cock constantly working that delectable spot deep inside me, I came hard. My cries faltered as he pumped into me. He released my hair from his grip and my head dropped, my body slumping immediately. I felt Luke pull out of me just before my back was graced with the feeling of his warm release. What I once thought would be disgusting was actually soothing as Luke's hands rubbed the results of his orgasm across my back as his large fist milked every last drop from him. "I already miss you," he said quietly, his voice barely audible

71

over my harsh breathing, and the sound of the shower. The steam from the hot water had engulfed the room, making it harder to catch my breath. I didn't want to think about Luke leaving. I still wanted to dwell in the serenity of the moment. I was pulled from the floor, and stood on my feet as Luke gathered me into his arms. He held me a moment, before leading me into the shower. Now that our session of intimacy was over, it was back to the real world and questions filled my brain as I laced my fingers through my hair, massaging the soreness from my scalp.

"How long are you going to be gone?" I asked, my eyes taking Luke in, as he soaped his body from head to toe. He looked to be in a hurry, but patiently waited while I soaked my hair completely, before stepping aside to let him under the hot spray of water.

"I don't know. I'll learn more when I get over there," he said, rinsing his body before grabbing my shoulders and turning me, so he could wash the remnants of his release off my back.

"Who else is going?" Surely he wouldn't go by himself.

"Me, Regg and Marty, but Crash and Kev will be in the area, just not with us. The others will stay here."

"Don't they have jobs?" I couldn't see him, but I was sure he was smirking. I could tell by the small laugh he let out through his nose.

"Their boss will understand." I turned around to see Luke smirking, as I assumed, and asked him the unspoken question with my eyes.

"They work for me, babe. At Carmical Construction and The Country Tavern," he said, proceeding to soap the front of my body as I stood there, wondering what to say to that.

"Isn't that a little weird? I mean, doesn't that cause conflict?"

"The club has part ownership in the bar and the construction business is booming right now, so it pays pretty well."

"But what if they wanted to do something else? Like, what if they wanted to work in the oilfield, or be a doctor or something? Is it mandatory that they quit their jobs when they become members?" I had never heard of a club working for their president's business or running a business themselves. But, then again, I didn't know anything about clubs until I met Luke.

"It's a free country, babe. They can do whatever they want, but why would they when they can do something they love in a business that benefits the club and allows them more freedom, more time to ride, and more time with their families? They don't all work for me, but the majority of them do." Well, when you say it like that, I guess it makes sense. But I wanted to know more.

"Explain, please," I said, focusing on Luke's face, as his skilled hands ran the length of my arms and down my sides.

"Regg is good with people. He helps with getting new contracts for the construction company. Worm used to drive a delivery truck, and is good with inventories. He handles all the beer and liquor orders for the bar. Tiny is our security guy, not only for the club, but the bar as well. He is over the bouncers, including their hiring and firing. Coon is good with money. So, he is the treasurer of the club and handles all the finances, which is pretty much a full-time job in itself. Marty, Boss Hogg, Scratch, and Bear are mechanics and keep our shit running. Trust me, there is always a bike that needs to be worked on, or an ol' lady's car, or a piece of construction equipment. Kev was the manager of a grocery store for years. He keeps the books on the bar, making sure we keep a good profit margin going. Octane is in the military. He has already been deployed four times, but works down at Camp Shelby full-time. He is a drill instructor and loves it. That's one of the reasons he isn't going, but if I needed him to, I know he would do whatever he could to make it happen."

"What is the other reason?" I asked, cutting him off.

"He has four kids," he said, simply. I didn't know if I should take that as meaning that something could happen and he didn't want to leave four kids fatherless, or that Juggs, Octane's wife, needed him at home.

"What about Crash and Buck?" I pushed the thoughts of Juggs being a single mother to four to the back of my mind, and concentrated on finishing our conversation. I didn't want to visit the dark place that housed all the "what ifs" in my mind. At least, not right now, anyway. Luke laughed a humorless laugh, and shook his head. Crash and Buck were young. Crash couldn't be much older than twenty-one or twenty-two, and Buck was twenty-five at the oldest.

"Well, let's see. Buck is a firefighter. He works forty-eight hours on, then seventy-two off, but has a pretty flexible schedule. Crash is a firefighter too, but he works a day shift of eight to five for a petroleum tank farm." I was missing the joke that was obviously there. There wasn't anything funny about being a firefighter. Hell, I thought it was a very admirable profession.

"How is that funny?" I asked, smiling, when Luke shook his head and smiled too.

"I lost a bet, so not only are they firefighters, they are also in charge of hiring the waiting staff at the bar." Luke laughed to himself as he turned the water off, and ushered us out of the shower. I remembered the bartender at The County Tavern that had waited on me was a man, but there had been a lot of women in miniskirts and tight tops that barely covered their chests running around with shot trays and baskets of roses.

"What was the bet?" I asked, laughing with Luke at the thought of the two guys getting one over on him. Luke didn't seem like the type of guy who would bet unless he was certain he could win.

"Not gonna happen, babe," he said, throwing a towel at me, and wrapping one around his own waist. "I got a few things to handle before I leave. Get dressed and I'll see you in a little while." He placed a quick kiss on my lips, and was gone.

I was dressed for business in a pair of black, wide-leg trouser pants, a black silk top, and my gold Prada heels to match my gold belt, bangles, and earrings. My hair was secured in a loose bun at the back of my neck and loose tendrils framed my face. My destination was Knox Companies and my goal was to resume my position as CEO. I needed an escape. I needed a distraction, and I was sure there was enough shit there to keep my attention for as long as Luke was gone. A commotion in the other room had me forgetting my appearance, and seeking out the voices I heard. I opened the door a crack, and although I couldn't see their faces, there was no mistaking Luke and Red's voices.

"I didn't say anything, Luke!" Red screeched, in an attempt to cover her ass.

"Yes, you did, but just enough to make her want more, then you shut her down like it was information that was only good enough for your ears. Stop trying to intimidate her. Just because Regg shares shit with you doesn't mean you can use it against others." Luke's voice was so strong and demanding that I actually felt bad for Red.

"I'm not trying to intimidate her. I was just preparing her for your news, because I knew it would come later than it really should. I thought if I let her know something was fixing to happen, she would bug the shit outta you until you gave it up."

"It is not your fucking place to decide when I tell *my* fucking business to *my* fucking girl."

"Oh, but it was my fucking place to inform her of how you followed her around for years and used your knowledge to persuade her to let you into her pants!"

"Enough!" I jumped at Luke's roar and felt my own self shrink at his deafening tone. I was sure Red was now a victim of Luke's death glare, and I silently willed her to shut her mouth. "I asked you to break the news to her, because I couldn't do it. I needed you to do that for me and you agreed. Not because you were supposed to, or because it was your job, but because you wanted to. Isn't that what you told me when I decided it was my place to tell her? You practically fucking begged me to let you do it. Why, Red? So you could watch her fall apart? What, do you get some sick satisfaction out of hurting people? From now on, you keep your mouth shut. If Regg shares something with you, you better take it for what it is; a privilege. He trusts you with that shit and has to vent to someone. That's why you are here. To support this club and my brother. That's the only fucking reason. You don't wear a cut. You won't ever wear a cut, and if I hear you leaking club information again, I'll cut that fucking ol' lady patch off your ass and burn it right in front of you. Loose lips sink ships, Red. Don't make your ol' man pay for your mistakes. I would hate to lose a brother 'cause his woman don't know her fucking place." I pushed the door closed at the sound of Luke's feet, and rushed back to the bathroom. I leaned against the counter, letting it support my weight as I let their conversation play over and over in my head. Was Red out to get me? Did she want to see me fail? I looked at my reflection one last time, before I pushed off the counter and let out a deep breath. I needed a drink.

Chapter 6

Red

I had been standing in the living room for what seemed like hours, staring at my feet and feeling like shit. I had just been subjected to an all-out LLC wrath; not my first and probably not my last. But this one was different. This time, I didn't have a leg to stand on. I couldn't blame Dallas for ratting me out. Hell, I expected it. What I wasn't expecting was for Luke to lose his shit on me. Thank God, Regg had already left and wasn't around to hear it. It was bad enough having Luke up my ass, the last thing I needed was trust issues with Regg. I heard Luke's bedroom door shut, and knew that the next face I saw would be Dallas'. I was sure she had heard everything. She came into view looking fucking stunning as always, and met me with a hurtful look that was like a punch to the gut.

"I told you that because I wanted you to ask Luke what was going on. I didn't want the club to suffer because he was too chicken-shit to open his mouth. When it comes to you, he doesn't think straight. It's like he only sees you. Not what's going on around him. Not what's happening in the near future, or what happened in the past; only you." There was no point in sugar-coating anything. She needed to know. "If I hurt your feelings or embarrassed you, I apologize. That was not my intention. I am not an idiot, ya know? I'm fully aware that I'm not a patch-holder, but sometimes ol' ladies see things the guys don't. Especially when it comes to women. Had I not acted the way I did last night, you would not have confronted Luke. If you hadn't, then he would still be trying to find a way to tell you he was leaving, and in turn he would be prolonging the ride, and putting his brothers at risk. He needs to be in Lake Charles. Not here with you." Maybe I was being a little too bold with that. I probably shouldn't have made it sound like Luke didn't know what the fuck he was doing, but it was the best way I could explain it. I watched as Dallas approached me. Her face was unreadable when she stopped only inches away from me. Even though she had to look up at me, it was me who felt intimidated.

"Luke is a grown man. He handles his club and his woman just fine. Stop trying to run shit, Red. Just because he doesn't do things the way you think he should, doesn't mean it's wrong. Shame on you for accusing your brother, the leader of this club, the man who you trust with your husband's life, of not thinking clearly because of a bitch. I'm not an idiot either. I know my place and it's always behind Luke. I suggest you find yours. Until you do, you better follow Luke's advice and stay the fuck out of our business and the club's business." Dallas walked off, leaving my hand twitching to slap the make-up right off her face. She was right and I knew it. I guess I had that coming. I knew Luke would never intentionally put the club or his brothers in jeopardy. I knew he wouldn't let a bitch, not even one as fine as Dallas, come between him and his club. I had let the stress of the past few weeks finally get to me. Where Dallas broke down and cried, I vented by acting like a bitch. Just the thought of Regg being gone for another undetermined amount of time had me blaming Luke for his absence. I needed Regg. I had become so dependent on him. He was my addiction. Even the high I used to get from cocaine back when I was at my worst had nothing on the high I got from Regg. I had let an addiction take over my life once again, and it had me lashing out at the ones I loved. I felt my demons resurfacing, and making me do shit I would regret. Thank fuck for Luke and Dallas, who had brought me back down to earth. Every ol' lady, at some point, had to be put in her place. Today must have been my lucky fucking day.

Dallas

I found Luke in the kitchen, making a meal out of last night's leftovers. I smiled brightly, as I climbed on the barstool across from him. My conversation with Red was not visible on my face, and neither was his. He looked just as happy as he had been the last time I saw him.

"You hungry, babe?" he asked, through a mouthful of food. I shook my head, my plans to have lunch downtown were the reason I had got ready so quickly. I would not ruin it over leftover barbeque and chips, although it did look quite tempting.

"I'm good. I'll grab something later."

"Glad to see you in such good spirits. Could it be because you're going back to work?" he asked, with a raised eyebrow. I shrugged my shoulders, brushing his comment off, while I grabbed my phone from my purse and switched it on. It had been off for over a week, and I dreaded seeing how many emails and phone calls I had missed. "Or is it because you talked to Red?" I stared at my phone, not looking at him. Had he eavesdropped on my conversation? Not that I could blame him. I had done the same thing.

"What did you hear?" I asked, attempting nonchalance.

"Everything," he said, propping his elbows up on the bar, and giving me a goofy grin. I rolled my eyes at his attempt to be cute, then turned my attention back to my phone. Without looking at all of the unread messages, I shot a text to Lindsey letting her know I would be there within the hour. "Don't be so hard on her." I snapped my head up at his demand. Was he fucking serious? He had just acted like a complete, over the top, mad man, threatening not only her, but her husband too, and he had the balls to tell *me* not to be hard on her. I scoffed. I couldn't even find words to spit at him. "She's only doing this to hurt me. She blames me for Regg being gone so much."

"Well, isn't that part of the life? She knew that from the beginning," I replied, not caring what her excuse was.

"Regg has been gone a lot lately. More than normal." I looked up, and he was giving me that expectant look. The one that told me I should know what he was referring to, without him having to actually say the words.

"Oh," I replied, realizing that *I* was the reason Regg had been gone so much.

"Yeah, so she gets a little out of line when he ain't around. She will be fine. I just don't want you thinking you can't trust her."

"Well, you sure sounded like you didn't." Fuck. Did I say that out loud? Luke didn't seem surprised at my words. I guess my eavesdropping wasn't such a secret after all.

"Not trusting her to not tell you something and not trusting her to tell an outsider club business are two different things. I gave Red what she needed, and that was a reality slap. The same as what you gave her, but without my hand." My face flushed when I remembered my

82

actions of this morning. She hadn't even said anything about it.

"Did she say something to you?" I asked. My eyes searched Luke's face and found nothing, but a smirk.

"She gets it."

"Gets what?"

"Bad dreams." Red has bad dreams?

"Babe, I gotta go. I'll call you when I get there. Keep your phone on you, always." He was really leaving. My good mood turned melancholy when I thought of how I would not see him tonight when I got home. "Stop it. Everything will be fine. Don't worry. I'll be back before you know it." I nodded my head in agreement, although my selfishness had me wishing I could have spent more than one night with him. Damn this other club. I would kill them myself if I had the chance. Luke was suddenly in a hurry, as he pulled me to him and kissed me hard. He released me all too soon, and I couldn't help it. I needed more.

"Another?" I asked hopefully, as I watched Luke grab his keys from the counter. He stopped in front of me, and smiled. His patience was no longer an issue.

"Anytime, baby." This time I was lifted onto the counter and he positioned himself between my legs, making us almost eye level. His hands came to my face and the next several minutes of my life were spent sharing an unhurried, lazy, passionate, kiss with Luke. When he finally pulled away, I sat staring at him, while his hands stroked my face. I memorized everything about him. From the way his ocean-blue eyes danced in his head as they scanned my face, to the way his hands felt while they were on me. "I'll come home. But until I do, remember I love you."

"I love you too," I said, still feeling his words seeping through my pores, and running through my veins, all the way to my heart. He pulled me into a hug, burying my face in his chest. I felt his lips on the top of my head, then I was pushed back away from him, and he was gone. I sat on the counter, dangling my feet, listening for the roar of his pipes. Eventually they came, and I strained my ears until I could hear him no longer. He was gone, but I couldn't dwell on that. By the 'OH THANK GOD!!' text message I had received from Lindsey, it seemed I had other things I needed to think about right now.

I pulled my Mercedes into my reserved parking area in front of my office building located in downtown Hattiesburg. The area was all too familiar to me, and as my feet hit the concrete sidewalk, I transformed from ol' lady to CEO in the small amount of time it took me to enter the office. Everything was just as I had last seen it, although it still took me a minute to adjust to the newly redecorated room. Lindsey's paintings hung on the walls, and I had that feeling of being home, once again. It wasn't cold and distant, like I had designed it. Now, it felt warm and friendly. Lindsey was seated at her desk, an abundance of paperwork stacked neatly in her inbox. She was so focused on her computer screen that once she finally noticed that I was there, she jumped at the sight of me, then shrieked as she pushed herself from her chair, and came running toward me. I caught her in my arms, her sudden attack nearly knocking the wind out of me.

"Oh, Dallas! It's so good to see you back! Look at you!" she said, beaming, and holding me at arm's length.

"You look radiant!" Lindsey looked pretty radiant herself. There was something different about her.

"Me? Look at you! What's with the dress and heels?" I asked, taking in her new wardrobe with approval. She wore a blue wrap dress with matching blue heels that I knew didn't come from Payless. I guess Lindsey was taking full advantage of her increase in salary.

"Oh, it's nothing. I just thought if I was gonna play CEO, I needed to look the part. It's really good to see you. I feel like I haven't seen you in ages. What have you been doing?" she asked, relief washing over me as I noticed she thought I had taken a vacation to spend my days having tons of sex with my new found love, rather than being held prisoner and shooting people.

"I've been traveling," I said simply. This appeased her and I was thankful that no more questions followed.

"Well, you ready to get to work?"

"More than you know." Truer words had never been spoken.

It was after four when I finally decided that food was something I could not go another minute without. I called Lindsey on her cell and asked her to pick us up lunch on her way back to the office. She was out running errands, and would be back within the hour. I had spent my day buried in paperwork, and going over contracts that would soon close. My email had yet to be touched, and my messages were still lying in a neat pile at the corner of my desk. I kicked up my heels, and leaned back in my chair, thumbing through the stack of small notes. Most of these consisted of communications from clients who refused to work with anyone but me, and one name stood out in particular. Mayor Kirkley. Just the thought of having to talk to him made me nauseous. Once I had learned that it was he who my father had paid to ensure the club protected me, my feelings toward him had changed. Knowing if I put it off any longer he would show up at my office, I picked up my phone and dialed his number.

"Well, if it isn't the infamous Dallas Knox," he answered, by way of a greeting.

"Paul," I said shortly, figuring formalities between us were no longer of use. Hell, the man knew more about me than I did.

"I assume Luke has informed you of everything."

"That he has, and I must say it came as a bit of a shock, although it shouldn't have. You always were a snake."

"Dallas, your words crush me," he said, with an exaggerated sigh. Prick.

"What do you want, Paul?" I asked, ready to end the conversation.

"You called me, dear."

"I was returning your call. I have about fourteen messages lying on my desk, each one more urgent than the last."

"Well, I just wanted to make sure you were still alive. You are running with a rough crowd now."

"Ha! I can assure you they are better people than you will ever be, you dirty, slime-balling, bastard." My overwhelming need to defend the club had me lashing out and resorting to name-calling. I heard his deep chuckle on the other end of the phone, and I could almost see him leaning back in his chair, with a satisfied smile plastered on his handsome face.

"I hope this doesn't affect our relationship, Dallas. It was just business. You, of all people, should know that."

"It's a little more than business when people's lives and futures are at stake," I spat at him. I wondered if he knew what had happened with Frankie.

"You're right," he said, his tone growing serious. "I never wanted you subjected to any danger. I was confident in Luke and the club. I thought they could protect you. Since you are still breathing, I'm assuming your father's money didn't go to waste."

"Speaking of which, are you still paying them?" I asked, thinking that if they were still receiving payment, then maybe it was me who should be in charge of handling it. That would get the Mayor out of my personal life for good.

"No, Dallas. I stopped paying them when you turned twenty-five. That was the deal." I mentally calculated the time. My birthday was less than a month away. I would be twenty-seven.

"Then why did they continue to stalk me? That was almost two years ago." My brain was in overdrive. I was twenty-six. Stacy would not benefit from killing me. The deal was, if something was to happen to me before I turned twenty-five, he would get the land.

"I'm a fucking mayor, Dallas. A business man. Not Oprah or Dr. Phil, but considering the shit you've been through, I'll tell you because it's obvious you aren't bright enough to figure it out yourself. Luke loves you. He fell hard for you. He did it because he knew he couldn't live with himself if something happened to you. Frankie was his fuck-up. He should have taken care of him a long time ago. Instead, he kept an eye out for you, even when he wasn't getting paid. You better be glad you have him. Frankie had a bounty on your head, girl. He wanted you dead and would have used any source close enough to you to get what he wanted. I hope that fucker is dead. If he ain't, you better watch who you let in. It's a tough world out there, and desperate times call for desperate measures. Frankie's got connections and he's got money. You'll do well to remember that."

"Let's say he is dead. Then what? Am I safe?" Maybe this wasn't a conversation that should be happening over the phone, but it was one that couldn't wait. If I was still at risk, then the people I loved were too.

"This is just my opinion, but a man like Frankie," he paused, and the silence was deafening. I already knew the answer, but I needed confirmation. "Just watch your back, Dallas. Men like him will stop at nothing to get what they want." I closed my eyes in defeat. The feeling of being safe and the thought of Frankie no longer being a threat had vanished completely. I said my goodbyes to Paul, noting the pity in his voice, as our conversation came to a close. I should have known that killing Frankie wouldn't be as simple as pulling the trigger. Even from the grave, he was going to haunt me.

I picked at my food, thoughts of should I or should I not tell Luke running through my brain, over and over. He had enough shit to deal with right now. I missed him, but the thought of him being away from me gave me a sense of peace. If someone did come looking for me, at least he would be out of the line of fire. As the evening descended, and the work I had laid before me became nothing more than words on paper, I decided to call it a night. I couldn't figure this shit out on my own, and my ally, Red, was no longer an option. I couldn't trust her enough with this information, although she was the one I knew could most help me. Lindsey appeared in the doorway of my office, looking just as tired as I felt.

"Wanna call it a night?" she asked, flopping herself down onto the leather chair in front of my desk. I nodded my head, still too deep in my own thoughts to speak. "You know, if you need to talk about something, I'm here. I know you better than anyone. This," she said, motioning with her finger between the two of us. "Hasn't really had time to bloom into a full friendship flower, but with a little water we will grow." I laughed at her metaphor.

"Friendship flower, huh?"

"Friendship flower," she mouthed, propping her feet on my desk and leaning back.

"What would you say if I told you that there are people who know me better than you?" I asked, mirroring her position by leaning back in my own chair, and crossing my ankles on top of my desk.

"First, I would say that is impossible. Nobody knows you. Second, I would ask where you got those heels because I love them."

"It's not impossible. Luke got paid to protect me from a man named Frankie the Cutter for five years. The jig was up when I turned twenty-five, but apparently, Luke had fallen for me from a distance, and continued to look out for me, even though he wasn't getting paid. Neiman Marcus."

"Who is Neiman Marcus?" She asked, confused.

"That is the store where I got the heels." I sat waiting for a reaction of surprise and shock, but instead got a knowing nod.

"I guess that makes sense. Frankie was the guy that attacked you. I heard his name dropped a few times that night at your house, but I didn't ask any questions. I was told by Red that I needed to be there, but only as moral support. If I needed to know any details it was up to you to tell me, not anyone else. So, I never asked. I was also confronted by Maddie who told me that everything was being handled, and there was no need for me to relay this information to anyone else. Her tone let me know that if I did, there would be consequences. It's a damned good thing I know how to keep my mouth shut," she said, a little accusatory toward them sharing the information with her.

"They didn't see you as a threat. You took over my company with no questions asked. I'm sure they kept an eye on you to make sure you wouldn't say anything. I guess they thought if I trusted you then they should too.

You don't seem very surprised at any of this new-found knowledge," I said, with a raised eyebrow.

"I'm not. Anyone can see the connection Luke has with you. I knew something was up when they all showed up to provide their support. No way could you become that big of a deal on your own. I knew that there had to be an underlying cause. I figured the club had something to do with it. You didn't seem to blame them, so I didn't either." Lindsey knew a lot about clubs, considering she had dated a man who prospected for one. He later left her once he became a member, but she learned a substantial amount of information the year she was with him. Even though her knowledge excused the nonchalance she showed, my need to get a reaction other than disinterest from her was growing.

"Maddie is my sister."

"What?" she asked in complete disbelief. Her stature had not changed, but I watched several emotions cross her face and smiled in satisfaction. I had known that would get a reaction.

"I was also kidnapped and held hostage for two days in Texas." I found the shock on her face comical. I fought hard to prevent a smile. I had gone this far, I might as well go all the way.

"I killed a man." This had Lindsey off her ass, and on her feet. Maybe I should have kept that one a secret.

"Are you fucking serious?" she shrieked, pacing the floor, crossing and uncrossing her arms over her chest, as she struggled to find words. I watched her reaction in silence, my face free of any emotion. If I saw that this was going to end badly, I would play it off as a joke.

"Why didn't you call me? I could have done something! Like been a lookout or some shit! What if you would have gotten caught?" I would not be telling Lindsey that it was just a joke. She would be the outside source to help me figure this shit out. A friend. A real fucking friend, who was willing to be my lookout and was downright pissed that I had not called on her for help. She wasn't judgmental or accusing. She didn't tell me I was a bad person. She didn't make me feel insecure about being the newest addition to the Devil's Renegades. I didn't have to share her with anyone else, or feel threatened by her position. She never hid things from me, or made me feel inferior. She was the only person in my life who had never lied to me. Now, more than ever, I was thankful to have her. "I want to know everything. I mean every-fucking-thing. All the good details. Don't leave anything out. My lips are sealed." She sat back down and ran her fingers across her mouth, as if she was zipping it shut, not that I needed the confirmation.

"You wanna go have a drink?" I asked, thinking even the most popular bars would give us some privacy, considering it was a Monday night.

"Hell, yes. I know the perfect place."

Chapter 7

Dallas

Lindsey's idea of the perfect place was none other than The Country Tavern, a bar where Luke and I shared our first encounter and was a business owned by the club. However, I didn't see anyone from the club as we made our way to the back patio, and found a seat. We placed our drink orders with the waitress, and no sooner had she left, than Lindsey was leaning over the table in anticipation.

"I guess the best place to start is at the beginning," I said, thinking maybe I should have ordered something a little more potent than a glass of wine. "Luke offered to take me to the beach one day a few weeks ago. As I was digging through his closet to look for my suitcase, I found a box full of pictures and information on me that dated all the way back to my days at Tennessee College. Of course, I lost my shit wanting to know where it had come from, and Luke took the easy way out, because he didn't know how to tell me the truth. He accused me of going through his shit, and told me to get out. I left, and that was the night I was attacked by Frankie." I paused when the waitress returned with our drinks. I eyed the cigarettes sitting on her tray and considered buying a pack, but she was gone before I could make my decision.

"Continue," Lindsey said, giving me her full attention.

"After I was attacked, Luke told me that he had been hired to protect me. I had decided that I didn't want a relationship full of lies, so I made my decision to let him go."

"But you didn't," Lindsey cut in. She took a big gulp of her wine, and shook her head apologetically. "Sorry. That's obvious. I just wanted you to know I was with you. Go ahead, I'll shut up," she said, gesturing with her hands excitedly, seemingly annoyed with herself for cutting in. I laughed, using the break in conversation to down my glass of wine. I turned around, and saw the waitress already heading back over to us. It was apparent that she didn't have much to do.

"Ready for another?" she asked with a bright smile. Thoughts of Crash and Buck interviewing her had laughter bubbling at the back of my throat.

"Can I buy a bottle?" I asked, while simultaneously thinking that at this rate I would never get the story out if I kept drinking this fast.

"We really don't sell it by the bottle, but you're LLC's girl, right?" she asked, her body relaxing, and her head tilting to the side as she eyed me curiously.

"Right," I confirmed, with a smile. "I don't need special treatment, though. Just bring us three glasses apiece and charge me for each individual one."

"That I can do. I can check with the bartender though, if you want me to," she offered, smiling sweetly at me. She may have just been being nice, but I could have sworn she was sucking up.

"No, really, it's not a big deal. Let's just keep me a secret and you just bring me the individual glasses."

Sheesh. Had I have known it would be such an issue, I wouldn't have asked.

"Okay, I'll be right back." She walked off, and I rolled my eyes at Lindsey's smile.

"What?"

"Look at you miss 'I'm LLC's girl.'"

"Whatever. Anyway, where was I?"

"You didn't let him go. You wanted to, but you didn't."

"Right, so during our conversation, he told me that Stacy was in line to get the land on Highway 98 if something happened to me. My dad had given it to the mayor, along with money, to ensure my safety. But, if something was to happen to me before my 25th birthday, then it would go to Stacy, leaving the mayor with nothing. I guess this was a way to ensure that the mayor kept his end of the deal. I'm sure my dad used Stacy because he was the closest thing to a son he had."

"So why twenty-five? I mean what's so special about that age?" Lindsey asked. I twirled my empty wine glass in my hand, as I contemplated her question.

"I don't know. Luke said my dad hoped to see that day, but didn't. This was all in place before anything happened to him. He was going to send me to live with my grandmother after my mother died. We always talked about me going to Tennessee for college, so I guess he just wanted to ensure my safety while I was in Mississippi and away at college. He couldn't watch over me from Atlanta, and maybe he thought that at twenty-five I would be married and living my own life, and that my husband could protect me."

"Or, he thought that would give him enough time to take your safety into his own hands and do away with the people that would do you harm. So, who was out to get you? The same people that killed your mom?" The waitress appeared at that moment and I hoped she had not heard our conversation. She seemed too focused on not spilling the six glasses of wine she carried for me to worry too much about it. I slipped her two one hundred dollar bills, waving her away when she started to inform me it was too much. Maybe the money would keep her out of hearing range. She gasped a few thank-yous, and I responded with a smile, willing her to just go away. She left, and I greedily took a gulp of wine and continued, considering Lindsey's insight.

"I don't know what was so special about twenty-five, but I'm sure both of our theories have some truth to them. Anyway, Frankie was the one who killed my mom. That leads me to my next story. Maddie is the result of an affair between my dad and a woman from Mississippi. A woman who was asked to abort her child, and, when she refused, was paid good money to keep it a secret. She also later married Frankie, who happens to be the only father Maddie ever had." I let my words sink in, as I downed my wine, and reached for another glass. "That's why Maddie hated me so much. I took the life that could have been hers," I said regretfully, still wishing things could have been different for Maddie.

"You said hated. That's past tense. I'm assuming you and Maddie have reconciled your differences."

"Only after we were both kidnapped by a man named Charlie Lott, who just so happens to be some kind of mob boss, I think. I'm not sure on that, but whoever he is, he is important and ruthless. Frankie owed him some money and he took Maddie when Frankie refused to cooperate. It just so happens that Luke found Charlie around the same time, and asked him for his help in finding Frankie. Luke used to work for Charlie, be his little errand boy or some shit, and when he quit, Charlie took it personally. So, when he grabbed Maddie, he grabbed me too. He made Luke decide which one of us he kept and I made Luke promise to keep Maddie. I felt like I owed it to her. He did, and I spent two days, which should have been a lifetime, with him." I reached for another glass of wine, welcoming the buzz that was forming in my brain.

"So how did you escape?" Lindsey was such a captive audience. I loved how attentive and observant she was.

"Somehow, I guess as a last gift to Maddie, Frankie offered himself in exchange for me. Charlie is known as a man of his word, and accepted the offer, but at a price."

"What was the price?" Lindsey spat impatiently when I paused. I downed my wine, trying to find the courage to tell her what had happened. It had seemed easy when I had mentioned killing someone earlier, now not so much. I stared at my empty glass, avoiding her eyes as I told her, my friend, what happened that day.

"The ultimate sacrifice." I grabbed the last of the wine on the table and took a long drink, draining half the glass.

"You are killing me here, Dallas," Lindsey whispered across the table, her wine glasses now empty as well. The waitress would be back any minute. As if my thoughts summoned her, she appeared. "We're good," Lindsey snapped before she could come to a complete stop at our table. I didn't look up from my glass, but I was sure the waitress was staring holes through me. I waited for her to walk off, before I continued.

"He said that the ultimate sacrifice was not giving your life for another. Once you die, you are free. It is the living who suffer, and suffering is a terrible thing." I placed my elbows on the table and leaned forward, focusing on nothing but Lindsey's big brown eyes. By the way they widened, I knew she knew exactly what my next words would be. "Taking a life is the ultimate sacrifice. My only road to freedom was through the hole I made in Frankie's skull. I killed him, Lindsey. I shot him execution-style while he begged me to spare his life. I pulled that fucking trigger, and even today, I don't feel any regret. I thought about what he had done to me, and the feeling was nothing compared to what I felt when I thought of him sacrificing the life of his own daughter to save his sorry ass. Had I not been there, had Luke not gone to Charlie for help, Maddie would still be in that man's custody. She would be away from her son, her life, her family, and no one would be able to save her from that. Now, I am stuck with his demons, haunting me from the shallow grave they threw that motherfucker in. Someone is out to get me. There is a bounty on my head, and I couldn't have prevented it even if I had killed him seven times over. I can't tell Luke, because he is in Louisiana dealing with serious club shit. I can't tell Red, because I don't know if I can trust her, and I can't tell Maddie, because I refuse to put her in danger again. So, what the fuck do I do now? How do I keep myself alive without hurting the ones I love?" I should have been crying. Tears should have been streaming down my face, blurring my vision and staining my cheeks, but as a result of my breakdown last night or the wine that I had consumed today, my eyes were dry. Lindsey placed her hands over mine, and cocked her head to the side with a small smile.

"You can't do this on your own. I'm here and I will help you, but you need your family. I don't know what Red has done for you to have trust issues, but I know that she cares about you. She wants to see you happy and who doesn't love a happy LLC? You need to talk to her, and Maddie is your sister. Your blood sister. Y'all have spent too much time being apart from one another. I think part of your problem with Red is that you are jealous of the relationship she and Maddie have. You have to remember that Maddie sees her as an equal. She doesn't know you well enough to have the same feelings for you that she does for Red. Give her some time. Maybe you need to get to know her. I mean really, how much about Maddie has *Maddie* actually told you? Talk to them and get their insight on how they think you should approach Luke with the situation. I would do one thing at a time. You need to get your mind off this shit for a little while. There is enough stuff going on at Knox Companies to keep you busy for the rest of the week. This weekend, have Maddie come over, and you two spend the day together. Get to know her. Then, reconcile your differences with Red. Even if it comes to blows, let it all out. I promise it will end on a good note." Maybe Lindsey really did know me better than anyone else. Her solution to my problem had me feeling better already. We hugged across the table, knocking over our wine glasses in the process, causing them to roll onto the wooden deck and shatter. We laughed, and I pulled another hundred from my wallet and dropped it on the table to cover the damage. I grabbed my purse as we hurried out, to avoid having to see our waitress once again.

I arrived at the office before the sun was up, and began sorting my emails. Last night's conversation had weighed heavily on my mind up until the point I had walked into my house. Just seeing the familiarity of everything and the smell of home put my mind at ease. Luke had texted late last night saying he was super busy, but that he loved me and would call me tomorrow. I felt guilty that I had no trouble falling asleep without him. It was like my need for him was drifting, until I woke up at three this morning, covered in sweat after dreaming about Frankie. He was not there to tell me it was okay, or hold me, and now I was fully aware of how dependent I had become on Luke. Usually, I wake from the dream and it fades before I fall back into a restful sleep, in Luke's arms. This morning was different. I couldn't shake it. I couldn't get the sight of Frankie crawling from his grave toward me out of my mind. If the dreams didn't stop soon, I would have to see a doctor. I thought back to how I never had them when I was with Charlie, and didn't start having them again until we got to Luke's. Was there a reason? I heard Lindsey's voice ring out over the office and looked at the clock to find it was already almost eight. I had been at work for over three hours. Where had the time gone?

"Well, look at you," Lindsey greeted, walking in, and placing a Starbuck's coffee on my desk. "I figured after last night you needed a pick-me-up. What's on the agenda for the day?" I loved how she was all business and didn't hammer me with questions on the holes in the story that I had shared with her last night.

"I've sorted my emails, responded to the ones that required it, and now I'm organizing a meeting with all the office managers and staff. I was looking over the contracts yesterday, and it seems we are being forced to drop prices on top-of-the-range properties, due to the market. I think we should just sit on them a while. We can afford it, and, although we will suffer a loss now, I feel like we will gain more by not selling them for less than they're worth. The market is in the process of a turnaround, but people are still milking it, trying to pinch every penny possible. But we don't deal with penny-pinchers. We sell high-end real-estate to high-end clients. Whatever happened to paying top dollar for things and using it as bragging rights? Where have all the rich people gone?" I asked, taking a sip of my coffee.

"Now it's cool to save money. Nobody wants high-rises in the city. They want small cottages in the woods. By saving on that, they can invest more money in charities and save the world operations. I'm telling you, this go-green shit is killing us. That and Pinterest."

"What does Pinterest have to do with anything?"

"I'm just pissed because I spent seventy-five dollars on this cool-ass necklace and Pinterest has a blog about how you can make your own for five bucks. Now, when I say 'hey look bitches, I can afford a seventy-five dollar necklace' my friends say, 'Yeah? I got the same one and I made it for five. You're stupid.'"

"That sucks."

"That's the story of my life."

"Well, I love your necklace and if it makes you feel better, I would have paid twice that for it," I said, thinking that I wish I had found it before her.

"So, the meeting is to inform everyone that we are not dropping the price?" she asked, pulling out her diary, and making notes.

"Correct. We are going to see if we can manipulate the system. It will take time, but I'm confident it will work. I'm also arranging a meeting with some people about that land on 98. Let me ask you something, how beneficial do you think a natural gas pipeline running through there would be?"

"I think it would be just as beneficial if it was moved a mile south. Even if they had to curve it around that one particular area. What is that? A square mile? Two, at the most? That place is really starting to take off. It would kill some of those businesses to be shut down, even if it was for just a few months. I know the gas company will compensate them, but it won't be enough. Think of Roman's Muffler Shop. If he is closed for three months, then his customers will find somewhere else to go. By the time he reopens, it will be another six months before he can regain his clientele, and even then it's not guaranteed." This is why I had hired Lindsey, because she was passionate about her job and people loved her.

"So, what do you suggest I do? The mayor will approve it. Hell, he pretty much already has. See, it won't hurt his business. He will be up and running for only a few weeks, before they offer him money and he will just sell out."

"Yeah, it won't hurt him, but what about the businesses in the surrounding area that will be affected? The ones that have been there for years? Just because it doesn't pass through that particular spot doesn't mean the re-route of traffic and cluster-fuck that comes with road construction isn't going to hurt them. I'm just saying." I watched as she wrote in her diary, noting that she looked like a schoolgirl with her hair in a ponytail.

"What if I put a school there?" I asked, thanking all that is holy that she had decided to put her hair up, or else the idea might not have ever occurred to me.

"A school? You can't just build a school," she said, shaking her head at my ignorance. I ignored the remark and chewed on the corner of my lip.

"What about an after-school kind of place. We can use it as a community project or something. We can let kids go there, even arrange public transportation for them." I was getting excited about the idea. Not that I really gave a shit about the program, but because I wanted to see the mayor fail.

"You would have to get that approved by the city and the mayor would never let that happen. He would find every reason possible to shut you down. The city wouldn't go for it. They would claim they couldn't afford it."

"Well, what would you do, genius?" I snap, immediately regretting my outburst. Shit, what had gotten in to me? Lindsey looked at me, with a raised eyebrow.

"I would convince him to invest in properties he couldn't afford to lose. Like a boutique that catered to the wealthy, an expensive spa, a celebrity-themed restaurant, and a popular coffee shop chain. Hattiesburg could use another Starbuck's. Target the business of the people that put him in office. They live in the elaborate subdivisions out there, anyway." She really was a genius. I was losing my touch. Lindsey's three weeks as CEO was really paying off.

"That just became top priority. Get me lined up with some investors. I want a meeting with someone from each business by Friday. Contact people from out of state, if you have to. Reassure people that they can't fail. Pitch them the pipeline proposal. Let them know that if it doesn't work out, they will be reimbursed once the pipeline takes over, and if it does, they will be more than compensated for the time their business is down. Send them appraisals of houses in the nearby communities. Assure them their targeted customers are in the same area. People will shop there just so others will see them. There are still people willing to pay top dollar for good quality products and envious friends who will go without lights to keep up with society. Wear that necklace proudly, Lindz. People who shop Pinterest are a dying breed."

Chapter 8

Dallas

It was another late night at the office, but the day had been successful. I had sent Lindsey home early, and told her not to return until next week. Joanna and Kylie, the assistants Lindsey had temporarily hired while I was unavailable, would be coming in to help out. Lindsey had done more than her fair share of work around here, and a vacation was much-needed, and well-deserved. As the day progressed, my thoughts kept drifting to Stacy and what had really happened that night in Tupelo. Did he really try to kill me? If so, why was I allowing him to keep his job? I had been avoiding the situation for too long, mostly in fear of finding the truth. Stacy and I had been close for many years. He was the uncle I never had. We had grown apart over the past few years, but I didn't believe he would ever be capable of doing something so terrible. If he had needed money, all he had had to do was come to me, and I would have given it to him. If Frankie did have a bounty on my head and had offered it to Stacy, the sum of money would have to be astronomical to make it worth his while. Was it out of greed? Was he jealous that he didn't inherit anything when my father died? Was I being selfish by just offering him a job at the bed and breakfast, or should I have offered to sell it to him? The Abbey was my business, but it governed itself. The only time I had anything to do with it was when I was in the area. I had never had any reason to intervene in the way they handled things. The business was old and simple, and made enough money to pay the staff and keep the place going, but not much more. It just didn't make sense.

I laid my head down on my desk, frustrated at myself for letting this go on so long. If he was a murderer, he could kill my staff. I thought of Gladene and Jackie, and the possible harm Stacy could cause them, and laughed to myself. Yeah, that shit would never fly. They were more capable of murder than he was. I could almost see Jackie trying to kill me. I was never really her favorite, but she had taken care of me and ensured I got help when I became ill. In the stack of messages on my desk there were several from them and Stacy, just checking in on me. The only person who knew about me being poisoned was Red. I had not even told Lindsey. I chewed on the end of my pen, my mind racing, as I planned my next move. Red was still on my shit list and I would die a thousand deaths before I called and asked her for help. Maybe one day, but not right now. I needed to work this out on my own, if possible. I looked over my desk, eyeing the cabinet across the room, which I knew was stocked with liquor. Maybe a drink would help me relax. I made my way to the cabinet, kicking my heels off as I went. I began pulling bottles from the top shelf, which was so high that I had to stand on my toes to reach it.

Wine?

Nope.

Crown?

Nope. More

wine?

Nope.

Scotch?

Scotch. The preferred drink of the almighty Mr. Charlie Lott. I missed Charlie. I looked around the room in a panic to make sure I was alone; afraid someone could have heard my thoughts.

"I can't believe I just thought that," I said aloud to the empty room. Had I lost my fucking mind? The man had kidnapped me! And my sister! And made me kill a man! He deserved it, yes, but still. As I eyed the bottle, I thought of the conversation we had while sipping a ridiculously priced scotch. I had poured my heart out to him, and he had listened with interest. I had told him everything, even about my near-death experience. He knew about Stacy. I grabbed the scotch and a glass, returned to my desk, and poured myself a generous amount. I was about to do the forbidden. Charlie had promised me a favor with no strings attached. I was about to take him up on his offer.

I located the card Charlie had given me, which I had placed in my purse without Luke knowing. He would kill me if he knew what I was doing. If I asked Luke what he thought about me reaching out to Charlie, I knew what his answer would be, 'Are you fucking crazy?' It took two glasses before I found the courage to pick up the phone. Even then, I replaced the receiver several times before I finally dialed his number. It rang twice before being answered by the very friendly voice I had regretfully grown fond of.

"The lovely Miss Dallas Knox," Charlie purred, causing my face to break out in an involuntary smile.

"Charlie. How are you?" I asked, kicking myself for not getting straight to the point.

"Well, I am delighted to hear from you. To what do I owe the pleasure of your call?" His voice was so soothing. *Think bad thoughts, Dallas. This man is not your friend. He had Luke beaten to a pulp, and threatened to kill him.*

"Charlie, do you remember our conversation that day? You know, when I told you about my life?" I sounded so stupid. I was tripping over my own words, and almost stuttering.

"I remember everything, Dallas." Of course he did. I had to get my shit together. *He may be sharp, Dallas, but you are too. Now fucking act like it.*

"I told you about a man named Stacy who could have possibly poisoned me."

"I have already confirmed that I remember everything. Is there a question there, Dallas? Or would you just like me to confirm that he was indeed a part of our conversation?" Well, fuck. I shouldn't have called. Charlie was not my friend. I did not miss him. He was just a mean man on a power trip.

"This was a mistake. I apologize for calling you. I hope I didn't impose." I took another sip of scotch, looking for a little alcoholic encouragement.

"Dallas, if you really thought calling me was a mistake you would have ended the call already, and you would not have assumed you had imposed unless you wanted confirmation that you didn't, therefore prolonging the phone call that you have apologized about, and

108

claimed was a mistake. If you have something to say, just say it."

"I want to know how much money you loaned Frankie, because I believe he used it to pay someone to kill me, and I think that someone might be Stacy." The words rushed out of my mouth. Charlie had that kind of power over me. Just the tone in his voice had me giving him exactly what he wanted.

"I never discuss business over a phone that does not belong to me, Dallas. Not that I would share information with you about another client, regardless of whether we are on the phone or not. Would you be opposed to dinner tomorrow evening?" Was he serious? The man had to be delusional.

"I don't think that's a very good idea," I scoffed. The chances of him actually releasing me without making me kill someone seemed pretty slim. This man could not be trusted.

"Are you sure? I can arrange to have you picked up and flown over here. You can even bring someone with you if you like." What? He wanted to send a plane to get me and fly me to fucking Texas? And bring along another fucking hostage? No way.

"Charlie, be reasonable. If you remember correctly, that didn't work out so well the last time."

"I thought everything worked out perfectly. I am a man of my word, Dallas. You are seeking information and it must be important for you to call me. You have one free pass. To use it so soon must make you pretty desperate. I will help you with whatever you need. Bring someone with you. Maddie, perhaps. There will be a car waiting for you outside your office at five tomorrow evening. I will have you home safely in less than twenty-four hours." I let out a surprised laugh with no humor, and struggled to find the right words to tell him to fuck off. Maddie? Really? He was gonna play that fucking card?

"Charlie, you're delusional. It's not going to happen. You can forget it," I countered, sitting on the edge of my seat awaiting his reaction.

"Yet you remain on the phone, knowing there is no other option. I will see you tomorrow, Dallas. Good night." I sat with the phone to my ear, trying to process what he had just said. Was it a demand that I go? Was he kidnapping me once again? Before I could stop my fingers, I was redialing his number.

"Yes, Dallas?"

"What if I don't come?" I spat at him. I was breathless, my heart hammering against my chest. I closed my eyes, praying his answer would be different from what I suspected it would be.

"Then you don't come. I want to help you, Dallas, but to do that we have to meet face-to-face. The decision is yours. There will be no hard feelings if you decline my offer. But if ever the day comes that you want my help, you will have to come and ask me for it. *Personally*. Good night, Dallas." There was finality in his tone that let me know that it would be in my best interest to not call him back. I hung up my desk phone and picked up my cell, mentally dying a thousand deaths. I needed someone. We would have to set our differences aside for now. Lindsey couldn't help me with this. I needed my sisters.

We need to talk NOW!! Be at Luke's in 20. Do not tell ANYONE!!

I hit send on the message and grabbed my purse, leaving in my office a half-empty bottle of scotch, a desk full of work, and any remaining sense, as I jumped in my car and sped off to Luke's to endure the wrath I was sure would come.

"What the fuck, Dallas?"

"Are you okay?" I felt a little guilty as I looked into the worried faces of Red and Maddie. They were in a panic, and I had not managed to get my shit under control on the drive over. I was quite a sight in my wrinkled skirt, and un-tucked blouse, with bare feet, a flushed face, and wide eyes. I resembled someone who had just been a victim of assault, and knew I needed to confirm that was not the issue, but I couldn't catch my breath. I began hyperventilating in the kitchen, letting Maddie and Red pull me to the table and soothe me. Eventually, I regained control, and took a sip of the water Red offered before I started talking.

"I'm fine. Nothing happened. Just a long day at work. No one attacked me." I watched, as they both sagged in relief. Maybe I should have called. "I didn't mean to scare y'all. I just panicked."

"It's okay. But next time, please call. A message like that followed by a you that looks like this, is a little much," Maddie said, gesturing her hands toward my rumpled appearance.

"Will do," I said, nodding my head.

"What's going on, Dallas?" Red asked, genuine concern in her lovely hazel eyes. It was good to see that she was not holding our spat from earlier against me. "Don't worry about earlier. I'm a bitch and I deserved it, but we will get to that later. What happened?" I had to work on not being so damned transparent.

"So, you know I have this issue with Stacy," I started, watching Red nod in acknowledgement, while Maddie looked between the two of us in confusion.

"Stacy poisoned her. When she was in Tupelo. Told everyone she had the flu. I found out through a friend. Nobody knows though," Red said quickly, informing Maddie, but keeping her eyes on me.

"I'm not sure if it was Stacy," I said, looking at Red, and ignoring Maddie's silent plea for more information.

"I am. Frankie confirmed it. Said he paid him to do it." I stared in shock at Red. I was so convinced that Stacy could not have done it, yet here was the proof.

"You can't believe anything Frankie said," Maddie added, looking at Red like she had lost her mind.

"What did he have to lose? He was going to die anyway. Why would he lie?" Red threw back at Maddie.

"To hurt Dallas. She apparently cares about Stacy or this wouldn't be an issue. Do you think Stacy did it?" she asked as if she didn't believe he had done, either.

"I don't think so. We are pretty close. That's why it doesn't make sense. If it had been before I was twenty-five, I would find it a little easier to accept, but that's not the case."

"Cause then he would have gotten the land, right?" Red asked, ignoring Maddie's pleading glare. "I'll tell you later, Mads," she said with a wave of her hand, as if it wasn't a big deal.

"Right. I need to know what happened and the only other person who knows the story, besides us, is Charlie."

"Charlie?" Maddie screeched, causing Red to shush her.

"Yes. Charlie. I told him about it and I know he could find out what happened. He loaned Frankie some money and I need to know if it was enough for Stacy to risk our relationship," I said, looking between Maddie and Red.

"You do realize that's not a strong enough reason to put yourself in danger. I mean, listen to yourself, Dallas. 'I need to know if it was enough money for Stacy to risk our relationship,'" Maddie said, mockingly. "That sounds fucking ridiculous. If you plan to go to Charlie to get something, you better have a better excuse than that."

"I need to know what happened that night. Charlie can find that out. I know it. I called him tonight."

"You what?" They both shouted, not caring who heard. Now, it was my turn to shush them.

"Shut up! Shit, tell the whole damned house, why don't you. Look, Luke can't know this. He would kill me and he has enough shit to deal with right now. Charlie will help me. I know it. There is only one catch." I tried to express the importance of talking to him, but knew I had lost them when they threw their hands up in the air and muttered 'I knew it.'

"What does he want? A fucking kidney?" Maddie snapped. I didn't blame her. Hell, she had been through just as much shit as me, and she thought he had killed the man she knew as her father.

"He wants to meet in person. And I want you to go with me," I said to Red, watching her head nod in agreement almost immediately. She didn't care if it was a bad idea, she was down for anything.

"Oh no," Maddie said, standing and waving her finger in the air between Red and me. "This shit ain't goin' down without me. If y'all goin', I'm fuckin' goin'."

"Maddie," I started, but was interrupted.

"Don't you Maddie me. I am goin', Dallas. I can keep my cool and not bring up old shit, but you two are not goin' alone." There would be no changing her mind. I knew that even before Red confirmed it.

"You are not going to talk her out of this," Red said, shaking her head in defeat.

"Well, I guess we are all going. I know he won't hurt us because-,"

"He is a man of his word," they both sang out, interrupting me. I guess Charlie's slogan was not one preached to only me.

"He is sending a car to pick us up at five tomorrow evening at my office. He will fly us over, and said we will be back within twenty-four hours, but," I said, emphasizing the stipulation by staring seriously at both of them, "nobody can know. It must be our little secret. It's only twenty-four hours, no one will even know we are gone." I left Luke's house with Maddie and Red's laughter still ringing loudly in my ears.

I was sitting at work, willing time to speed up. The day seemed to creep by, and the only thing I had to keep me busy was too important to half-ass. I couldn't work to my full potential when I knew that I would be on a plane to Texas in just a few hours. I had yet to hear Luke's voice, but was glad he was too busy to call. I was afraid that if I talked to him, I would give something away. Just as my shitty luck would have it, my phone rang around noon and it was Luke's name that flashed across the screen.

"Hey baby!" I squealed into the phone, forgetting my worries and focusing solely on him.

"Hey babe, look I'm sorry I haven't called. It's been kinda crazy the past few days." I melted at the sound of his tired, remorseful, voice and wished I was there with him.

"No worries, babe. I have had plenty to keep me busy while you've been gone," I said reassuringly.

"Stop stealing my word."

"What word?"

"Babe, babe. That's my word. It's what I do. Like the winks and finger-kissing and shit. That's mine. Get your own."

"Can I call you sugar?" I asked through the huge smile that was plastered on my face.

"Whatever makes you happy. I miss you." His voice was serious and low, letting me know that he was hurting without me, and that his boys were around so he couldn't shout it.

"I miss you too, Luke. Do you know when you are coming home?" *Please don't say tonight. Please don't say tonight.*

"It's gonna be a little while, babe. I'm not sure how long that is, but I'll let you know. I can't really say much right now, but I'll call you tomorrow and we can talk more. I gotta go babe. Tell me you love me."

"I love you."

"I know. I love you too. Stay out of trouble." The call was disconnected and I wondered if maybe he knew I was up to something. Why did he say that? I was being fucking paranoid. I needed to get my mind off Luke, and on Charlie, and my trip. I called for Joanna and she appeared, wearing a top so low-cut that it was hard to concentrate on anything other than her breasts.

"Joanna, I am not going to be here tomorrow. I have a meeting and will be tied up all day. If you need me, you can reach me on my cell." I wanted to add "and wear a fucking shirt", but I didn't. If I pissed her off, she might quit and I needed her here tomorrow. Kylie didn't seem quite competent enough to be left on her own, although at least she wore clothes that covered her.

"Will do. Anything else?" *Yeah, cover your ginormous fucking tits!*

"That's all." I stared down at my desk, busying myself with nothing until she left. This day could not end fast enough.

Maddie and Red showed up around 4:30, each carrying a small, designer, overnight bag that I was sure my father had paid for. I looked at Maddie, noticing how she tried to hide her nervousness by making meaningless small talk. I knew it was not the best time, but if anyone had to break the news to Maddie, I damned sure didn't want it to be Charlie.

"Maddie, I have something I need to tell you." I was so caught up in my own thoughts, that I didn't notice I was interrupting her and Red's conversation. Red seemed just as oblivious as Maddie, and I was sure she didn't know what had happened either. "I think you need to know what happened when Luke came to get me." Maddie's reaction was cautious, yet Red sat on the edge of her seat in excited anticipation.

"I think I can figure it out on my own. Dallas, I know Frankie is dead. There is no way Charlie let him live, but I don't need the details."

"I think you do," I responded, staring down at my knotted hands in my lap. It was now or never. This was my chance to tell Maddie the truth, yet I couldn't find the right words.

"Dallas," Maddie said in a tone that forced me to look at her. "If you really think I need to know, or if you want to prepare me because you are afraid I will find out once we get there, you can tell me. I know it wasn't easy for you, but he knew his fate when he made the decision to go." I looked at Maddie in confusion. Frankie chose to go?

"I don't understand," I said, looking from her to Red, knowing they were both fully aware of how the exchange had been proposed.

"Don't think he did it for me, or for you. He didn't. He chose to go willingly to Charlie because he knew he would die regardless. I'm sure he thought Charlie would keep him around and let him work off his debt. That was the only hope he had, so whatever happened, don't feel like it was too harsh of a punishment. Frankie deserved to die." Maddie had come to be at peace with the fact that the only dad she had known was dead. But would she be crushed to know that it was me who had killed him? Or would it even matter?

"Maddie, I killed Frankie." The words were out before I could stop them. One minute my brain was telling me to just spit it out, and the next minute, before the rational side could intercept, I had informed my sister of the worst. I watched her eyes widen in shock, then fall to her lap, with a sigh that had her shoulders slouched in defeat.

"Did Charlie make you do it?" she asked quietly, looking up at me with pity in her eyes. I nodded my head, trying not to show how little it affected me. The hardest part was telling her. She deserved more. She needed to know there had been more to it than what I had offered, but I didn't need her hating Charlie any more than she already did when we were about to be at his mercy. I opened my mouth to speak, but she beat me to it. "I hate that you have to live with that, but know that I hold nothing against you because of it. I couldn't imagine having to endure what you have been through. I'm glad you told me, Dallas, but I really don't want to hear anymore." Maddie offered me a small smile, her eyes pleading for me to just drop the subject. She was so strong. That was a quality that we both shared and had inherited from our father. I smiled back and was relieved when Red took the conversation in a different turn.

"Okay, so this is the plan. We are going to get just what we need and get the hell out of there. Ask your questions, but don't agree to shit. I mean it, Dallas. I don't care what he is offering." Red stood, grabbing her bag and slinging it over her shoulder as she pointed a long, orange, fingernail at me. Despite the cool weather, Red wore a sleeveless blouse that complemented her toned, muscular, arms. *Good thing our conversation had not come to blows.* She grabbed a leather jacket from the chair and pulled a cigarette from the pocket. "I'm going out to smoke. Y'all wrap this shit up. Don't get all teary eyed and emotional before we leave. In the words of my favorite dance teacher, 'Save your tears for the pillow.'" Maddie and I exchanged confused looks as Red left us, swinging her hips with enough exaggeration to break something.

"I'm sure she is quoting from some movie or T.V. show, she does that shit all the time. You ready?" Maddie asked, taking a deep breath, and gathering her stuff.

"Yeah, I guess," I said goodbye to Joanna, ignoring her low-cut top, and left before Maddie could make some snide remark. When we joined Red on the sidewalk, a black Lincoln Town Car sat waiting for us across the street. Charlie Lott was one confident son of a bitch.

Chapter 9

Dallas

The car took us to the Hattiesburg/Laurel airport, which was so small that the only plane that sat on the airstrip was ours. When we boarded, there was no doubt that Charlie had sent us his personal plane. It didn't even look like an airplane. It looked like the hotel lobby at the Roosevelt. Everything was lined in silver or gold, and the carpet that covered the floor was softer than any I had ever walked on. The chairs were not your traditional aircraft seats, but instead were wide, leather reclining chairs that swallowed you when you sat in them. I almost rolled my eyes at how ridiculous it was, but couldn't help but wonder if this was something I might want for myself. Red was taking full advantage of the bar, ignoring the man who stood beside it and who offered his help.

"Nah, I got it. Have yourself a seat. I'm sure you deserve it." The man straightened his back, looking perturbed at Red's comment, although he didn't say anything. Maddie was gushing over the lushness of the plane, while I sat completely at ease in one of the chairs. Luxury was not foreign to me, although this had to be the nicest plane I had been on. It was funny to watch the girls act like complete fools over it all, and attempt to play it cool when the pilot arrived to let us know we were preparing for take-off.

"Ladies, I hope you all are enjoying yourselves," the older man said, eyeing Maddie, appreciatively. I'd rip his fucking eyes out. Not that Maddie was helping the situation by wearing a dress that barely covered her ass, along with four-inch heels. She did look pretty hot. Red looked ever the biker bitch in tight jeans, heeled riding boots and a black, leather jacket. It was more of a designer leather jacket, but there was still no mistaking that she wanted people to gain an impression of who she was. I looked down at my own clothes and frowned, acknowledging that I had worn a very conservative business suit, much like what Charlie had bought for me. "We are about to take off, so I ask that you please be seated and fasten your seatbelts. I will notify you when it is safe to walk around." With one more full body glance at Maddie, he turned and left. I watched as the man behind the bar gently ushered Red toward her seat, although the look on his face let me know he wanted to push her. I laughed out loud at the thought.

"What's funny?" Maddie asked, taking the seat across from me and exploring the gadgets that controlled the built in massagers.

"Nothing," I laughed, as Red took the seat next to me and passed me a glass of something that I was sure would ease my nerves.

"Look, this shit is exciting to us. We are poor. Remember?" Maddie said, not bothering to look at me as she closed her eyes, and relaxed further into the seat. I chose to ignore her comment, and instead began mentally preparing myself for my re-acquaintance with the devil.

We landed at a private airstrip just north of Gonzalez, Texas; the same town Charlie and I had spent our time together. It came as no surprise to me that the car took us to the bed and breakfast we had stayed at before. The driver informed us that dinner would be in an hour and he would be back in 45 minutes to take us to the restaurant. We settled into our rooms and freshened up, unknowingly all presenting ourselves in similar attire. We all were dressed in little black dresses with killer heels, and looked as if we were going out for a night on the town, instead of a business meeting with a man that had brought turmoil to all of our lives. The same goal was in mind for each of us; we refused to be intimidated by Charlie. Few words were spoken as our nerves overtook us and we were ushered into the car. My heart beat rapidly in my chest as we pulled up outside a small Italian restaurant that was beautifully decorated with white lights and gas lanterns. We were led to the back of the restaurant to a round table that was set for five. We took our seats and ordered wine, the waiter informing us that our host would be here soon.

"You nervous?" Maddie whispered to me, her own nervousness evident by the way she clasped her hands firmly in her lap to prevent them from shaking.

"Nah. Everything is fine. You?" I asked, knowing she was aware I was lying through my teeth.

"I'm good," she said, fidgeting with the napkin in her lap.

"You two can lie all the hell you want to. I'm so scared, I might shit my pants," Red said, gnawing at her long nails, the consistent bouncing of her knee causing the tops of her breast to jiggle without her knowledge. I was just about to tell her when Charlie's booming voice caused all of our heads to turn. He looked stunning in a black tuxedo and neck tie. His fingers were littered with diamond rings and his hair was combed neatly, without a strand out of place. You could feel the power radiating from around him as he strode confidently to our table.

"What a lovely surprise. I will never know what I have done to cause the gods to shine down on me and bless me with three beautiful angels," he said, smiling brightly, and revealing two perfect rows of white teeth, that, at his age, had to be implants.

"They were probably scared of you," I heard Maddie mutter, as a way of explanation for the gods' behavior. I kicked her under the table and smiled brightly at Charlie; it came so naturally.

"Dallas, it is so good to see you again. You look as radiant as ever," Charlie said, taking my offered hand, and bending to kiss it. I smiled sweetly at him in my show of gratitude. "And this must be the beautiful, vibrant Red," he said, stepping past me to kiss the hand of a very star-struck Red. I watched as she batted her eyelashes, flattered by Charlie's compliment. Maddie looked at me, and rolled her eyes as Red flirted with Charlie.

"Well, it's a pleasure to meet you, Charlie. I have heard so much about you, but Dallas and Maddie failed to tell me how charmingly handsome you were." If there had been any food in me, I would have vomited all over the white linen table cloth. Red was laying it on thick. She was under Charlie's spell, and had forgotten who he really was.

I had been put under that same spell, so I was more lenient on Red; Maddie-not so much.

"Cut the shit, Red. We don't need his head swelling any bigger. Charlie, we came here for a reason. There is no need to wine and dine us. Dallas, tell him what you want, so we can get the fuck out of here." Red and I both looked to Charlie, awaiting his reaction on pins and needles. He was not at all affected my Maddie's outburst.

"Maddie, it is always a pleasure to see you, too. Would you ladies like to order?" Maddie's death glare had me re-thinking the veal cutlet I was craving. There would be no dinner with Charlie.

"Charlie, we have to get back. I would like to ask you some questions if you don't mind." The disapproval in Charlie's face had me wanting to shrink in my seat, but I stood my ground and my posture never faltered, as he considered my request.

"Ladies, how about you give Dallas and me a moment. The bar will be happy to accommodate your every need." I nodded to Maddie and Red, giving them the okay they needed to leave us. I watched them walk away, and as soon as they were out of hearing distance, I addressed the real reason I was here.

"How much money did you loan Frankie and do you think it was enough to convince Stacy to kill me?"

"I never discuss my business, Dallas. If you believe Stacy tried to kill you, then it should not matter how much money he was offered. If you have doubts about him, he must be guilty." Charlie was right. It didn't matter how much money was on the table. Did I really need a motive for him to kill me if I was going to accuse him of it anyway? This was the favor I was allowed, so I might as well be straight with him.

"I shouldn't have asked. You're right. I don't believe Stacy is capable of something like that, but money can make people do the impossible. I need to know what happened that night. Frankie told me himself that he tried to poison me, but I don't know how he went about doing it. He had to use someone to get close to me, and I had a drink with two people that night, Tammy and Stacy." I sighed, and took a drink of my wine, waiting patiently for the silence to be filled with Charlie's voice. It was so easy to talk to him. I felt like we were back at the bed and breakfast once again.

"Where did you have a drink?" Charlie asked, pulling his phone from inside the lapel of his suit.

"First with Tammy at Kingston's, then at the Abbey with Stacy, about two hours later." I watched as Charlie looked at his phone before placing it back in his pocket, and returning his attention to me.

"Frankie has a connection at Kingston's. My theory is that he paid someone to slip something in your drink and neither one of them were Frankie or Tammy. The payment was probably made in the form of drugs. My best guess would be crystal-methamphetamine, since that was Frankie's drug of choice. That should tell you what kind of people you are dealing with. You can request the footage from video surveillance from that night, but my advice would be to let it go. This person holds no ill feelings toward you, nor will you get any kind of satisfaction by eliminating them." I was flooded with relief, but kept my guard up knowing that Charlie had said this was his theory.

"What are the chances of you being right on this?" I asked, knowing Charlie didn't like to be doubted, but thinking that, in this situation, he really couldn't blame me.

"I'm always right, Dallas, but I understand that you need proof. You will have what you need before you leave tonight. While we are here, is there anything else you would like to talk about?" Was it just that easy? I started to question Charlie on just how he was going to retrieve that proof, but thought better of it. I didn't care how he got it, as long as he did so. I did have another question; one that Charlie couldn't possibly know the answer to, but into which he could give me some insight.

"The club was paid to protect me until I was twenty-five. Do you see any reason why my father would choose that particular age?"

"The contract your father had with the mayor was for two million dollars and a stretch of land valued at twenty million, with the increase in value estimated to range between thirty-five and fifty million over the course of ten years. The money was paid to Luke in increments of ten thousand dollars a week. There is absolutely nothing significant about the age of twenty-five, it just so happened to be your age when the money ran out." I sat in shock, staring blankly straight ahead. I couldn't believe my ears. Two million dollars? That sleazy son-of-a-bitch Mayor Kirkley. That was why he kept throwing out my age-he didn't want me to know the amount of money that was involved. Was that how much the club had made off of me? And the ol' ladies had the balls to give me shit about having to follow me around? "Dallas?" Charlie's voice cut into my thoughts, and I blinked rapidly, allowing my eyes to regain focus before I grabbed my wine to finish off the glass.

"Sorry. It's just taking me a minute to process what you are saying. How do you know all of this?"

"Once you shared your story with me, I took a further look into all of your problems. I was not sure if you would be able to follow through with my proposal, and I wanted you to have all your questions answered in the event you decided to stay with me." Was he really that confident in thinking that I would choose him over Luke? Did he really think I could not pull the trigger on the man that ruined my life?

"Well, as you can see, that was a pointless move." My liquid courage was kicking in, and I suddenly felt that although Charlie had the power to move mountains and shit, he still did not have power over me. It was a much better feeling than seeing him as my friend.

"Now there is the Dallas Knox, shrewd business woman I know. I'm glad to see you haven't lost your edge. As you know, this one is on me. I have more information that you might be interested in, but of course it comes at a price," he said, reaching into his pocket to retrieve his phone again. There was only one thing that Charlie could possibly help me with, and even that was not worth being in his debt. I needed to know if Frankie had contacted anyone else about taking my life. The mayor had said that Frankie had money and connections. Charlie was the best connection on offer, and money was something Charlie had plenty of. Frankie had also borrowed money from Charlie and refused to repay it.

"What kind of price?" I asked the question out of pure curiosity. There was no chance that I would take him up on it, but I had to know.

"First, I want to remind you of how thorough I am. I have just received confirmation that Frankie's connection was working the night you visited Kingston's. I also have video footage proving that your drink was prepared by an extremely nervous employee who fumbled with the small vial, and spilled some out before pouring the rest into your pink, fruity cocktail. It seems that person was your saving grace that night. If the entire vial had made it safely into your glass, you and I would not be having this conversation." Charlie was good. He had even told me the kind of drink I was having, so that I would not question him. Now that I knew, beyond a shadow of a doubt, that Stacy was innocent, I should have felt relieved and happy. Hell, I should go visit him. But the need to know what Charlie had to offer surpassed my need to express my happiness at Stacy's newly discovered innocence.

"The cocktail was quite delicious, even if it was supposed to kill me. 'Death by bartender's famous fabulous drink'; not a bad way to go." Charlie found much more humor than I did in my statement, but I joined him in his laughter, just to appease him. It was forced and he knew it. He was prolonging giving me the information I desired, and wanted the satisfaction of hearing me ask for it once again. "Okay, Charlie, I'll ask one more time. What is the price of the information that could be useful to me?" He smiled brightly, his eyes full of arrogant satisfaction.

"The ultimate sacrifice."

I nearly choked at Charlie's words. He had to be out of his fucking mind. I was not going to kill another human being, even one as sadistic as Frankie.

"Charlie, I'm not a hit man. The only reason I did what I did was because I had no choice," I said a little too loud.

"You always have a choice, Dallas. You chose the easy way out," he said, a cigar now dangling from the corner of his mouth.

"Easy? What the hell was easy about that?" He had forced me to kill someone, for crying out loud!

"Yes, I can see that you are having a very difficult time dealing with that." I shut my gaping mouth and avoided his stare. He was right. I was not struggling with the death of Frankie. It was probably one of the easiest things I had ever done. "I once referred to you as a soldier, Dallas. One who defends herself against her enemies, both foreign and domestic. You have something you want to ask of me. I can see the fear in your eyes. You are afraid that Frankie borrowed money from me to pay someone to take your life and even though he is gone, you are afraid that that person will still follow through on their promise." He knew. Charlie knew that I wasn't sure how, but I wasn't surprised either. He seemed to know everything.

"I won't ask you anything else. This conversation is over." Even though I spoke the words, I remained seated. He smiled at my feeble attempt to deny him.

"What is peace of mind worth to you? If you wish to leave without knowing, then by all means, do so. But, before you do, remember that I have the power to protect you, Dallas. While Luke is off fighting battles to protect his club, you have flown here to seek assistance from me. You know I am the only one who can help you. Why won't you let me?" I'm not sure if it was the mention of Luke's name or the unspoken accusation that he couldn't protect me, but I lost it.

"Luke doesn't need your help. I don't need your help. I came to you because you offered to help me and I would rather bother you than him. While you're out destroying people's lives, Luke is fighting hard to keep his and his family's whole. Trust me, his time is much more precious than yours. I don't need you, Charlie, I used you. Just like you have used so many others. Thank you for giving me exactly what I needed. Now, I can go back to living my life with people who care about me, and I don't have to worry about killing someone in return for their support." For the first time since I had encountered Charlie, I saw a genuine, hurtful expression cross his face. I'm not sure what part of my rant had affected him, and I wasn't going to stay around long enough to find out. I stood up from the table, turning my chair over in the process, and stomped off toward the bar, collecting Maddie and Red with just a look. If I didn't see his face for another three lifetimes, it would be too soon.

"What happened?" Red asked, once we were back at the bed and breakfast.

"Pack your shit. We are going home tonight," I said, throwing my clothes into my bag.

"Dallas, talk to me," Red begged, following me from the bathroom to my room. The ride here had been silent, but now we were alone.

"Stacy didn't do it. Frankie got someone at the restaurant to do it, but luckily they fucked up, and that's why I didn't die. He wanted more, but I wouldn't give it to him."

"How much more?"

"He wanted to share with me some valuable information and in turn he wanted me to kill someone for him. He did the same thing to Luke, using him as his personal hit man. He is a sick, demented, human being, and, thank God, we don't have to deal with him anymore. Now will you please get your shit together so we can go?" I asked, in a huff. Red didn't argue, and, within the hour, we were flying back to Hattiesburg.

Chapter 10

Dallas

I was in a shit mood the next morning at work, and Joanna and Kylie had avoided me at all costs. Lindsey had emailed me the list of investors that were interested in the new strip mall I was proposing. I sent the information over to the board for approval, knowing the mayor would be aware all too soon. He would take the bait, and soon the investors I had would be outbid by new ones that the mayor was backing. Ahhh, sweet victory.

"Someone is here to see you," Joanna announced, smiling like an idiot. Whoever it was must be hot.

"Send them in," I said, not caring to see anyone today, but knowing that now that they were aware I was here, I couldn't refuse them. I heard her heels clicking as she hurried off to get my guest, while I tried to make my desk a little more presentable.

"Babe." My head snapped up to find Luke standing there, wearing worn, ripped jeans, a black fitted thermal, and his thick, leather cut that had seen better days. He didn't look like the clean-cut Luke I was used to. No, this was bad boy, dirty-biker, Luke. And he was mouthwatering. He had not shaved, his jeans were filthy, and his boots were covered in dust. He looked huge and intimidating, standing in the doorway of my office. I was so shocked to see him that I couldn't find the right words to say or the will to move my feet to go to him. Noticing the darkness in his eyes, I knew that I was probably safer behind my desk. I swallowed and cleared my throat, hoping my voice would come out strong.

"Hey baby," I said, as if I had something shoved up my ass. It was too high-pitched and he knew I was aware that he was pissed. His nostrils flared at the sound of my voice as he stepped inside, and closed the door behind him.

"I sent Joanna and Kylie to lunch. I hope you don't mind." I shook my head, watching, as he slowly made his way to stand directly in front of my desk. He was too close. I could feel the anger emanating from him as I breathed deeply through my nose, trying to control my racing heart. He smelled like leather, and dirt, and Luke.

"Wh-what brings you here?" I stuttered, mentally cursing myself for being so easily intimidated. Maybe he just missed me and was pissed because Joanna had come on to him or something.

"I just wanted to see how you were doing. I wanted to make sure you were staying out of trouble." His eyes widened and his breath quickened as he spoke. Luke was fucking livid, and it was taking everything he had to keep himself in check.

"I'm good. You know, just work and stuff. Same ol' shit, just a different day," I said, with a small laugh, trying to convince him that I had been here since he had been gone.

"Really?" he asked, letting me know that he didn't believe a word I was saying. I didn't care. I would deny it to the bitter end.

"Mmm hmm." I couldn't speak. Hell, I couldn't move in fear that he would snap my neck if I spoke the wrong words.

"So, that couldn't have possibly been you that was seen boarding Charlie Lott's plane yesterday evening?" Motherfucker. I was as good as dead.

"Uh-uh," I responded, knowing I had been caught red-handed. Fuck, shit, dammit all to hell. I noticed the hold Luke had on each chair as he stood between them. His knuckles had turned white, and I was sure the expensive leather wouldn't survive much longer under his grip. In a flash, Luke grabbed one of the chairs and threw it across the room, as he let out a deafening roar. I screamed and jumped back in my chair, gripping its arms, and sliding back until I hit the wall behind me, watching as the sheetrock crumbled under the weight of the heavy chair that Luke had thrown as if it weighed nothing.

"Why the fuck would you go to him?" Luke yelled loudly enough that I was sure the windows would shatter from the boom of his thunderous voice. I shook my head, scared of what would happen if Luke didn't get his temper under control. *Speak, Dallas! Say something!* My subconscious screamed at me, but I couldn't find my voice. "After every fucking thing he has done, you are just going to hop on a plane and fly across the country to see him?" Luke asked, or more like screamed, at me. He was now leaning over my desk, shouting at me, his voice coming out as a snarl.

"He gave his word," I said weakly, wishing I had chosen to keep my mouth shut.

"I don't give a fuck about his word!" Luke barked in my face, sending the papers flying off my desk with a flick of his hand. He came round closer, and I cringed under his approach.

"Luke, you are scaring me," I said, trying to force my chair back further, but going nowhere.

"You need to be scared," he said, his voice a low growl, as he gripped the arms of my chair and brought his face frighteningly close to mine. His deep breaths flowed from his flaring nostrils. He looked and sounded like a bull ready to attack, and I was the matador dressed in red. "I made a four-hour ride in less than two to get here to give you a piece of my mind, and you are going to listen. I don't care what your problem is, if you need something, you call me. Not Regg, not Red, not Maddie, and definitely not Charlie fucking Lott. Now, you are going to tell me exactly what the fuck was said while you were there, and so help me God, Dallas, if you leave anything out I will tear this whole fucking office to pieces and lock you in my house until I get back. Now, start. Fucking. Talking." Oh fuck. I was too scared to tell the truth, and too scared to lie. Maybe if I kept my mouth shut he would leave me alone. "Talk!" he snapped in my face, and although I might not have shit my pants, I suddenly had diarrhea of the mouth.

"When I was in Tupelo I didn't have the flu. I was poisoned. I thought it was Stacy. Charlie found out it was Frankie who paid the waiter with drugs to put arsenic in my drink. He messed up, and didn't put in enough to kill me, just make me sick. I didn't want to bother you and Charlie said he owed me a favor, but I had to see him in person 'cause he refuses to talk on a phone that doesn't belong to him."

"Is that all?" Luke asked, after a moment passed. Without hesitation, I responded.

"Yes." Liar. But thank God, I had answered fast enough that Luke didn't find any reason to question me.

"You could have been killed. You could have been hurt. You could be halfway across the country right now, and I wouldn't even know it. Not only did you endanger your life, but Maddie and Red's too. The only reason Regg isn't here is because I knew if I told him he would likely kill you for putting Red through that shit." Damn. I was glad Regg didn't know. For some reason, I was sure he would be a lot more violent than Luke. "Get up." I looked at Luke to find his tone was deadly serious. I shook my head. No fucking way. "I said, get up." I shook my head again, afraid of leaving the safety of my chair. "I've had a really fucked-up day. I'm tired, and mad as hell, and have a long ride ahead of me. I think since you are the cause of it, you owe me something." I saw the angry, feral need in his eyes and suddenly, I was happy Luke was pissed. I was about to be subjected to one of the greatest punishment fucks in history. "Don't get too excited, babe. You won't benefit from it," he said, catching that gleam of hope in my eyes, and snatching it back out of my reach. There was nothing that could happen with Luke that I wouldn't benefit from. But, if it made him happy to believe that, then I would let him. I managed to frown and make it look genuine as Luke moved back, allowing me to stand. "Lean over the desk," he demanded and I smiled to myself, thinking how wonderful this was going to be. I had never been so thankful for skirts in all of my life. I leaned over the desk, giving Luke a tease by shaking my ass at him. Bad idea.

138

"Ouch!" I yelled, my back straightening, and my hands flying to my ass, as I rubbed the spot where his hard hand had just landed.

"Bend over, Dallas," he said, his voice not holding even the slightest hint of remorse. I leaned across the desk once more, forgetting about my stinging backside as his hands gripped the hem of my skirt and brought it up around my waist. I felt my panties being tugged down my legs, and I widened my stance to accommodate what I knew was coming- a big, hard cock that was sure to send me to that perfect oblivion where nothing mattered but him and me. I heard his huff of laughter through his nose, and knew he was smirking. I was glad that he was finally showing an emotion other than anger, although I was clueless as to what was so funny. I heard the sound of his belt being unbuckled and my body broke out in goosebumps. Fuck, I wanted to see it. I wanted to watch him as he lowered his zipper and freed himself, but the sound of the zipper never came. Instead, I heard the sound of his belt being removed from its loops. Was Luke going to get completely naked? I felt his hand firmly on my back as I felt him move to the side of me. "I once told you something, Dallas, and today is the day I make good on my promise. You practically begged me to spank you, and I let you know that I only gave out spankings in the form of punishments. When I leave from here, I will be sure that you rethink your decisions to double cross me." I struggled against the weight of his hand as I tried to lift myself from the desk. This was not happening. I was his lover, his ol' lady, I was a fucking CEO. I was not going to be spanked like a child in my own office. I had never had a spanking in all of my twenty-six years, and I wasn't going to have one now. I heard the belt before I felt it. It cut through the air, leaving a whistling sound in its wake. The pain was excruciating as I yelped and began to struggle harder against Luke's hold.

"Stop, Luke. I fucking mean it. Stop, right now." He answered with another crack from his belt that landed hard on my ass, taking my breath from my lungs, and causing tears to prick the back of my eyes. "Dammit Luke! Stop!" I screamed in anger. This wasn't just unnatural, it was fucking ridiculous!

"Not gonna happen, babe. At least, not anytime soon." By the tone of Luke's voice, he was still pissed, and I knew there was no stopping him. I heard the belt once again, as it sliced through the air and landed on my ass in a stinging smack that forced another yelp from my mouth. Another, and another, and another, and I was squealing, begging for his mercy. My words fell on deaf ears, as my tears soaked my face and my desk. He continued with his vicious spanking, which I was sure would result in me sleeping on my side for weeks. He was angry, too angry to be touching me. My voice was hoarse from screaming. My make-up was smeared from crying, and my desk was covered in tears, spit, and snot. There was nothing pretty about this situation, and although my ass was taking the pain, it was my pride that was the most hurt. Eventually, Luke stopped. My hands remained balled into fists and my body stayed tight, anticipating another blow that didn't come. When Luke's calloused hand rubbed the raw and beaten flesh of my ass, the feeling was not nurturing and comforting, but revolting and painful. When I tensed at his touch, his hand stilled but remained. I was still begging for him to stop, even though he had.

"Dallas." This time I heard the remorse, but it was too late. He had stripped me of all my dignity as I lay in shambles across my desk. Luke was right. There was no cuddling or feelings of butterflies, only a whole lot of pain and discomfort.

"Just leave," I whispered through my hair, which was splayed over my face, blocking the view of my surroundings. I didn't expect him to follow my wishes, but he did. I stayed in the position he had left me in until I was sure he was gone then I stood, wobbling slightly on my weak legs. I lifted my feet out of my heels and headed to my private bathroom to survey the damage. I gasped when I shut the door and my behind came into view in the full-length mirror that hung on the back of it. It was not pink and rosy, but welted with deep red stripes that were beginning to purple around the edges. I sank to my knees and cried harder into my hands. How could anyone do this? How could I ever get past it? I wished Luke had told Regg, I would rather have suffered death at his hands than be subjected to Luke spanking me with his belt, an idea that I had once found appealing. I heard my office door being opened and silenced my tears, not wanting Joanna and Kylie to be the least bit aware of what had just taken place. I pulled myself up, using the sink for support and removed my panties from around my ankles. I grabbed the hem of my skirt, easing it down over my ass, wincing as the material made contact. I did my best to fix my make-up, and smoothed my hair back into place. If they asked, I would just say I was having a bad day. I opened the bathroom door to find an expressionless Luke propped up against the edge of my desk.

"You can't imagine what I have been through today. All I knew was that you had boarded Charlie's plane, but were back in Hattiesburg safe and sound. I knew you were not hurt, but just the thought of you seeing him did something to me. Dallas, he is not your friend. He is not someone you can confide in or trust. But, I would be lying if I said he wasn't different with you. I don't know what happened when he had you for those two days, but whatever it was gave him hope. He wants you, Dallas. He is drawn to you and will do anything to have you. A man like his is used to getting what he wants. I can't let that happen." I stared at Luke, wondering where he was getting this information. Charlie wanted me? That wasn't possible.

"Maybe he is my friend," I said weakly, my voice still hoarse and unfamiliar to me.

"Charlie doesn't have friends. He has people he hates and people he employs, but with you there is more. He likes you. I've never seen him look at anyone, woman or not, the way he looks at you. It's as if he thinks he has some connection with you. You can't give a man like Charlie false hope." I walked past Luke, and winced as I leaned down to grab my purse, struggling as I stood, then remembered my heels. I contemplated leaving them there, but Luke reached down and grabbed them before placing his hand on the small of my back, and guiding me toward the door. I should have resisted. I should have told him to just leave me alone, but I didn't. I couldn't. As much as I hated him at this moment, I loved him a hundred times more. I had missed him, and having him here reminded me that I did not need Charlie in my life. Maybe what Luke had said was true, and Charlie really was infatuated with me. I didn't need him thinking I had feelings for him, or that I needed him. Not only did it give him false hope, but it gave him the wrong impression. We met a wide-eyed Joanna and a drooling Kylie at the door, and before I could speak, Luke handled the situation. "Dallas fell. I think she sprained her ankle so I'm taking her home." The girls didn't answer, only gaped and nodded their heads as Luke graced them with his smile. My limp was not exaggerated as Luke led me to the passenger side of the car, and opened the door for me to get in. I just looked at him, wondering if maybe he had lost his fucking mind. I would rather walk home than ride on my ass. He leaned in, whispering in my ear and I could hear the regret in his voice. "Crawl in and lie on your side, babe. Let the seat back first." He pulled away, acknowledging the girls still on the sidewalk with a flick of his eyes. I reclined the seat back and slid in, hissing through my teeth as the fabric of my skirt stretched across my ass, and rubbed roughly against the sensitive flesh. Luke gracefully seated himself next to me and sped off, being extra careful to not sling me around too much. I couldn't look at him. I didn't want to, and I damned sure didn't want him to see my agony. Although if it made him feel worse, then he deserved it. I turned over, tears pricking the back of my eyes as I did, but I would be damned if I shed a single fucking salty tear in front of him. I leaned the seat back more, finding myself lying almost flat in the most comfortable position possible.

"I want to go home," I said, letting him know that I refused to go to his place.

"I know, babe."

"And don't call me babe. You can't beat me like that, and then think you can just call me babe and make it all okay," I snapped, letting him know I was still angry. My emphasis on the word "beat" was overstating it, but I didn't care. He didn't respond with words, only a sigh. I closed my eyes, and somehow managed to let sleep find me. It was a welcome escape from reality.

I woke up while Luke's arm was snaking its way around my waist. He held me close to him, as he struggled to lift me from the car without hurting me. Yeah, good fucking luck with that. I let him carry me when I should have walked. It was hard to refuse Luke when I had been away from him for so long. I noticed the door of my house had already been unlocked and propped open as his long strides led us all the way to my bedroom. He sat me on my feet and steadied me, before reaching around and locating the zipper on my skirt. The front of his body was pressed up close against mine and I inhaled deep, inviting the scent of him into my nose. Damn, even dirty he smelled good. Manly. Not like cologne or freshly laundered clothes, but like a man who had been working all day. I felt him lower the zipper of my skirt and tensed in anticipation of the discomfort, but Luke took that time to bury his face in my neck and run his tongue across my earlobe, taking my mind off of the pain. When my skirt hit the floor, Luke removed his head and stepped back, undoing the buttons of my blouse slowly.

"Can I fix you something to eat?" he asked, his way of apologizing, I'm sure. I would never hear the words, and he was fighting hard to not show how badly he regretted what he had done.

"No. I just want to take a shower." I pushed his hands away from me and proceeded to undress myself in front of him. Once my shirt and bra were removed, I turned, giving him a full view of what he had done as I walked to the bathroom. When I looked up at his reflection in the mirror before me, I saw that his hands were rubbing his face in frustration. He turned his back to me and kicked at the air, bringing his hands to his hips in fists and throwing his head back to stare at the ceiling.

"Dallas, I shouldn't have hit you so hard. I was too mad. I should have waited till I had cooled off some." There was no apology. He didn't say he shouldn't have hit me, only that he should have waited until he wasn't quite so angry. Yeah, that's a good way to have me forgiving you, LLC. Good job. I ignored him, turning in the mirror to check myself out and gasped. My wide, shocked, eyes met Luke's lamenting ones in the mirror for only a moment before I turned my attention back to my very unfortunate buttocks. The welts were not only red and swollen, but badly bruised in a dark purple color. There were even a few tiny beads of blood in one area, where the flesh had been hit numerous times, and the skin was broken.

"How could you do this to me?" I whispered, rubbing my fingers lightly over the bleeding area, removing the few droplets and looking at them more closely, as if they might not be real. Luke didn't answer, but couldn't stay away. Even when I tried to push him away, he didn't leave. He turned me away from him, and inspected me closer. I felt humiliated. Mortified. Ashamed. This was so degrading that I couldn't even make eye contact with him.

"What can I do to make you feel better?" Still, there was no apology from Luke. I stood there with my back to him, observing the wallpaper designed in perfume bottles as I let the rational side of my brain be heard. *Did I deserve this? What would I have done if Luke had betrayed me? If Red had received the same punishment would I have found it demeaning or deserving?* I would probably have found it comical, just like I was sure she would when she found out. The reality was, I had got on a plane, with no regard for myself or the people I asked to go with me, to meet a man that had once kidnapped me and my sister. He had also had my husband beaten, forced me to take the life of another man, and just so happened to be the most powerful, evil person I had ever encountered. I was deserving of so much worse than a wounded ass. Luke didn't owe me an apology because I wasn't worthy of one. If I thought this was bad, I was sure that what Luke had endured when he found out was much worse. I took a deep breath and met Luke's eyes in the mirror.

"Maybe I just need some lotion or something. It's not that bad. Just that one part, but it should heal by tomorrow." My acceptance of Luke's punishment and the understanding of why he had done it caused his whole body to relax. He kissed the back of my head with a sigh, and reached for the bottle of Jergens that sat on the counter, pumping a generous amount into his hands before leading me back to the bedroom. I lay across the bed on my stomach as Luke rubbed the cool lotion into my skin in the gentlest manner possible. Soon, the strokes of his hands were less uncomfortable and more soothing. Then, he began stroking lower, his fingertips brushing lightly over the lips of my pussy, making my back arch every time he did. I spread my legs slightly, allowing him better access as he began frequenting the area more and more. The slight discomfort coming from my behind, mixed with the feel of his fingers rubbing the outside of my smooth lips had a fire building inside me.

146

"Fuck," he whispered, when his finger slid between my thighs to find me wet and ready for him. He pushed it deeper, my hips rising to more easily accommodate his finger, which slid in and out of me with ease. I pulled myself up to my knees and buried my face in the mattress, giving him the full view of my hot, wanting pussy that clenched his long, skilled finger with each stroke. His finger was removed, and I moaned as he replaced it with his mouth, stroking my inside walls with his velvety, smooth tongue. He licked his way up, stopping to run his tongue over that forbidden, tight place that seemed to relax when his mouth found it. He placed kisses across my bruised bottom, tender ones, with just a hint of tongue then followed each kiss with a light blow of air that left goosebumps in its wake. "Please, Luke." I begged, knowing he knew just what I needed.

"I shouldn't be rewarding you, baby," he said, kissing his way up my spine.

"Then give me a punishment fuck." That wasn't a reward. Well, it was but he didn't need to know that.

"Are you sure?" he asked, the slightest hint of humor in his voice as he teased me with his torturous tongue.

"Yes," I said, breathlessly. I would rather take another beating than have to go another minute without his cock buried inside me. He pulled my earlobe between his teeth before getting off the bed. I scrambled up onto my hands, worried that he was leaving, but he grabbed my ankles and pulled, forcing me back onto my stomach, and dragging me toward the end of the bed. My pulse raced with excitement. Adrenaline pumped through my veins as I lay trembling with pure exhilaration, anticipating his next move.

"On your knees, Dallas," he demanded, his dark bedroom voice full of authority. I pulled my knees apart, pushing myself up at a leisurely pace, but only after I remembered the current state of my ass was probably not as appealing as it usually was. I waited for Luke to rub the head of his cock over my entrance, tease me while he told me how hard he was going to fuck me, but he had another idea in mind. He grabbed my ass cheeks, separating them roughly, causing me to hiss from the shock of the pain, before ramming deep into me, not stopping until his hips collided with my ass, leading me to let out an involuntary screech.

"You still want it? Or have you changed your mind?" Luke asked, not treating me to a delicious circle of his hips or a soothing hand across my stinging ass. It took me a minute to decide. The sensation of him being inside me was more pleasurable than the pain of the punishment fuck, but would it get worse? Would he deliver more aching pain than gratifying pleasure? Was it worth the risk of not knowing? *You bet my bruised ass it was.* I nodded my head, turning it to mouth at him the words he desired with a smile, and earning me a smirk from my deliciously sexy, belt-whipping, intoxicating, dirty-boy, biker.

"Fuck me." I was treated to deep, hard thrusts that came fast and unforgiving, causing me to wince when his body collided with mine, and whimper with want when he pulled away. It was everything I wanted, and everything I didn't. The pain was agonizing, but the pleasure... the pleasure was bliss. My moans were foreign to my ears. An assortment of numerous feelings and emotions were released from my body in an audible pitch that was unnatural, and unlike anything I had ever heard. Luke pummeled my fatigued body with no remorse or regret, unknowingly giving me exactly what I wanted, the roughness of his drives in and out of me pleasing me more than any love-making we had ever shared. I came hard, listening to Luke groan his approval at my release. I could almost hear his chest swelling with pride and conceit at his accomplishment. My man knew how to fuck me, and in his own way, he was showing me that he was all I would ever need. He stilled inside of me, with a deafening roar that matched my own screaming moans, as his pulsing cock milked the last of my orgasm from me.

We were lying naked in bed, me on my stomach and him on his back, finding comfort in the silence. We both knew our time together was fixing to end. Luke had to go back to Lake Charles, and we were not sure when he would return.

"Is there something you want to tell me, babe? Are you worried about something?" Luke asked, turning his body over onto his side, and tucking my hair behind my ear. I did, but he had so much to deal with already. The last thing he needed to be worried about was my assumptions that someone was out to get me. "Dallas, if I couldn't handle you and the club I wouldn't have you both. If there is something you need, then I am the man you talk to. But I can't help you if you don't tell me." I studied his eyes, which were pleading with me to be honest. This is what Luke did. He was my protector. Why couldn't I let him do his job?

"You just have so much on you. I don't want to be a burden," I said, my voice barely audible, and weak.

"Dallas, don't you give me that shit. You're not a burden. You are my girl, my love, my property. It's my job to protect you, and it fucking hurts to know that you don't trust me with that. Have I not proved the lengths I will go to make sure you are taken care of?" *Great, Dallas. Hurt his feelings and take his pride, why don't you. Oh, and while you're at it, grab his balls.*

"It's not that I don't trust you, Luke. It's just that you have already sacrificed so much for me and now your club needs you, and I don't want to be the reason you can't be with them," I said, swirling my finger over his chest, and using my eyes to will him to understand my point.

"You need to stop fucking listening to Red. Do you think you are the only one of the ol' ladies with problems? Every man in this club has had to deal with shit. Just because I have shit going on with the club doesn't mean I can't take care of you too, babe. I need you to trust me and tell me what's going on."

"I'm afraid there's someone out there who wants to kill me," I blurted, my lip shaking as the realization of my words hit home. When I had spoken to the mayor, it hadn't hit me. When I had talked to Charlie, my safety was the last thing on my mind. Now that I had confessed my darkest fear to Luke, it occurred to me how serious this situation was. I could lose my life. Before, I didn't have time to prepare for it. Now that I was almost positive it could happen, I freaked out.

"Babe, no one is going to hurt you. What makes you think that?" Luke asked, running his finger over my trembling lip, and catching a stray tear with his thumb.

"Frankie hated me, Luke. What if he set something up before he died? What about the guys who were with him?"

"Dallas, if anyone wants to get to you, they're going to have to come through me. Don't live your life in fear. There's no one looking for you." Luke offered me a reassuring smile, and I nodded. I trusted Luke, and if he said no one was looking, than no one was. He would protect me, just as he always had. I was going to be okay.

Chapter 11

Luke

I spent the night with Dallas for two reasons, one I didn't want to leave her upset and two, I needed her just as much as she needed me. I didn't want the company of any other woman, although it was offered to me every day. Lake Charles had some fine bitches that were willing to warm my bed with no strings attached, but I couldn't do it. I only wanted one bitch warming my bed and sucking my cock, and it just so happened that I loved her, so it made it easy to turn down other women. I had panicked when I had heard that Dallas had been on board Charlie's plane, but my panic was soon replaced with pure fucking anger when I found out she was home and safe. I let Ronnie know I would be back in the morning and took off, leaving him shaking his head and muttering how I needed to put my ol' lady in her place. How could Dallas be so stupid as to go to Charlie, and what the fuck made her think she could get away with it? She needed to be taught a lesson, and since I wasn't a man who put my hands on a woman, I had to find a way to let her know I was tired of her shit. Spanking her brought out my dominant demons, but at least I got my fucking point across. I only wished that I had cooled down a little before I had done it. But thank fuck she got the fucking picture. Now, she was freaking out about someone being after her, and it took all I had not to tell her the truth. I had to convince her everything was fine to keep her away from Charlie and to keep her from living a life of fear, when in reality, she should be. There was someone out there who was looking for Dallas, and I knew it just like I knew her pussy was the sweetest I'd ever tasted. It was something I thought about every day, but I would never let her know that. Charlie wasn't the only man with connections, but I was sure his were better than mine. The phone call I knew I was going to have to make to him made me sick to my fucking stomach, but it had to be done. I would pay whatever price necessary to protect Dallas, and the penalty charged would not come cheap.

"Luke." Charlie offered, as a form of greeting. Fucking arrogant pig-headed motherfucking bastard.

"Charlie."

"Is this about Dallas' visit, or her problem?" Asshole. He was hoping I didn't know about her little journey to Texas.

"My problem." Dallas didn't have problems. I didn't want him thinking that I was asking for help for her. It was me to whom he would be offering his services.

"I'm in Hattiesburg," he confirmed. I already knew that, but I wasn't going to tell him.

"Good. Meet me at my office," I demanded, and hung up the phone. Charlie didn't like being told what to do, but for Dallas, he would do just about anything. He had called me the day I had left for Lake Charles, asking how she was doing. Something Charlie never did. She had unknowingly connected with him, and now he felt that she was important to him. Another reason for me to hate him. Of all of the fucking women in the world he picked mine to fall for. Biggest mistake of his pathetic life.

My office was located in a place away from the hustle and bustle of downtown and uptown Hattiesburg. It was in a shit community and only the locals knew it existed. Perfect for a man who wants to be left the fuck alone. Charlie, or should I say Charlie's fucking puppet, pulled his town car up to the curb, and I fought hard to not tackle him and pummel his face with my fist when I saw him step out of the car. I shook his hand, neither of us very happy about the exchange, but it was a show of respect that was demanded on both our parts. We walked into the office, and he took a seat in one of the chairs in front of my desk, while I took the other. In Charlie's eyes, this was a smart move. He didn't like to feel as if he wasn't the one in charge, and I was surprised he didn't take a seat in my desk chair, but, again, it was a show of respect.

"Who is he and what does he want?" I asked, cutting all the bullshit and getting straight to the point.

"Wouldn't you like to make small-talk first? I'll start. You didn't hurt Dallas for coming to see me did you?" he asked, threatening me with his tone, and the iciness of his stare.

"Only in a way that made her come around my fat cock. Now, who is he and what does he want?" I watched Charlie shift in his seat. Good. I had struck a nerve.

"You sure are bold, Luke. I once had a man's tongue ripped out for talking to me like that. Very bloody experience, but one neither he nor I will ever forget." I took a deep breath, and checked my temper. I didn't need to get on Charlie's bad side. At least not right now.

154

"If you are asking if I put my hands on her, then no, Charlie. I would never hurt Dallas in that way." Only with my belt, I thought cockily. My dick twitched in my pants at the thought of her perfect ass bent over her desk, and it was my turn to shift in my seat.

"Well, that's good news. For everyone," he concluded, the meaning underlying his words letting me know that he would have killed me had I have hurt Dallas. "I will tell you what you need to know, but it is me who takes him out. Not you or your club. Or Dallas," he added, reassuringly. "I feel like I am owed that."

"Then why are we here? If you know who he is, and where he is and you want to take him out, why don't you just do it?"

"Dallas needs a man who can protect her. Obviously you are that man, so now it's your job. You intercept him and I'll handle it from there," he said, as if the answer was obvious. He seemed hurt, and I fought hard not to smile at the middle-school crush this grandpa had on my girl.

"Okay, so how am I supposed to do that?" I asked, wishing he would just give me what I wanted and get the fuck out.

"I suggest you bring her to Lake Charles with you. Wait until the weekend so you don't make her suspicious and then send her away when I give you his whereabouts. She has a business meeting scheduled in Atlanta on December 15th. Keep her with you until then, and I'll make sure he is in the area during that time."

"Why don't you just tell me now and I'll take care of it. There's no need to prolong this," I said, wondering how Charlie could benefit from waiting.

"All in good time, Luke. All in good time."

"I need more than that," I snapped, stopping him from standing and leaving.

"This man owes me a favor. I plan to make sure he follows through with it before I kill him." He left my office, leaving me with a feeling that the favor that was owed consisted of taking my life.

Dallas

I had driven Luke back to my office, turning on my side as much as possible; the pain of my ass reminding me that this time when he left, I would not be doing anything stupid. Instead of returning to work, I had agreed to meet Maddie and Red for coffee to fill them in on Luke's surprise visit. I was dressed in sweats and a hoodie with my hair piled on my head, and no make-up. They took in my attire, and immediately knew that I had had a long night.

"Well, by your disheveled look and your slight limp, I would say Luke fucked you half to death." Maddie said, once I took a cautious seat with them.

"Something like that," I responded, taking a sip of my coffee. They wanted details, and I didn't want to give them any.

"Soooooo," Red said, looking at me expectantly.

"He was pissed. Very pissed. He threw a chair across my office," I said, concentrating on my steaming coffee in an effort to ignore the pain of my ass. Maybe that would be enough to pacify them.

"Shit. Is that all?" I looked up at Red. I wondered if she knew what Luke was really capable of. She seemed to know him better than the rest of us. I looked between them, wondering what their reaction would be if I told them everything that had happened. Would they be surprised? Mortified?

"Yep. That's it," I lied. I couldn't tell them. I just couldn't.

"Liar. Come on, tell us what he did," Red pushed, intent on knowing exactly what had happened.

"What does Regg do when he gets super mad at you? Like, what would he have done if he had found out you went?"

"He would have killed me," Red said simply, with a shrug of her shoulders.

"Seriously, Red. What would he do?" It was my turn to press her for information. Maybe Regg was a spanker too.

"I don't know. I don't even want to think about it. But if you tell me what Luke did, then maybe it will give me insight on what to look for in the future," Red suggested, with a wink. Oh, what the hell.

"He spanked me," I said, trying to avoid their gaze, but found my eyes flicking from my coffee to their faces.

"He what?" Maddie asked, seriously thinking she had not heard me right. Yeah, Maddie. I fucking said it.

"He *spanked* me." This time I met their gazes, and while Maddie continued to look confused, Red had fully processed what I had just told them. I looked around the coffee shop, embarrassed, as Red almost fell out of her seat laughing. Fucking bitch.

"Are you fucking serious?" she asked, with a laugh. I just glared at her, and she lost it again. "You *are* fucking serious!" I gave her about ten seconds of glory before I decided to shut her up.

"Yeah, funny huh?" I asked, faking laughter. She nodded, her face beet-red from laughing so hard. "That shit's just too good not to share, huh?" I continued to fake my laughter as she nodded more, unable to catch her breath enough to talk. "So good that maybe we should tell Regg." Red sobered immediately, and the begging began.

"I'm sorry. Shit. It's not funny. I mean it is, but I won't laugh anymore. Don't tell Regg. He really will kill me." She was breathing hard, reaching out to lay her hand on my arm, hoping the gesture would emphasize that she meant her words. She was struggling to keep a straight face, but I knew she didn't want to face the wrath of Regg.

"So you are saying he *spanked* you? Like, with his hand?" Maddie asked, oblivious to Red's laughing, and my empty threat. She really didn't seem to get it.

"Yes, Maddie. But he used his belt." This earned me another snicker from Red, which she tried to cover up with a cough.

"It's not funny dammit. That shit hurt," I said, crossing my arms over my chest, and rolling my eyes at them. I should have kept my mouth shut.

"Hey, look on the bright side. At least you still have your teeth." Red's comment was serious, but by the looks of all the ol' ladies, none of them had been subjected to physical abuse.

"Now that you've said it, I can see Luke doing that. I mean he has always had some dominant tendencies. He likes control, he gets what he wants, and he has that aura about him that screams 'I'll fuck you till' you pass out.'" Maddie noted, her brain finally recognizing the information and sorting it, delivering a reasonable explanation for Luke's actions.

"He did that too. He's pretty good at this thing we call a punishment fuck," I informed them, glad that I had got this shit off my chest. "But y'all don't tell the guys, okay?" I asserted, knowing I would be the laughing stock of the clubhouse.

"Hell no," Red said, zipping her lips.

"Not in a million," Maddie added, shaking her head, confirming that she would keep her mouth shut. It was nice to know I could trust these two. This would be our little secret.

I didn't think about Charlie, or the information that he had offered to share with me, for the rest of the week. I focused on work, the daily calls I got from Luke, and building my relationship with Maddie and Red. Red had explained her outburst, and her reasons for it, to me over drinks the other night. We had gone to The Country Tavern, where she ran karaoke on Thursday, Friday, and Saturday nights.

"I used to be a dancer." Those were the words she chose to start our conversation. It took her a few minutes to elaborate, because she had to announce the next singer, leaving me time to consider her comment. I never would have guessed it, but it wasn't too hard to believe. She definitely had the personality and build. Her arms and legs were toned and muscular, and even in her late twenties, Red had a killer body. "That's what I was doing when I met Regg for the first time," she continued once the singer was set up and killing me with a rendition of Bobby McGee. "I saw him come into the club a few times with Luke, but we never spoke. He was a big flirt, and quite a hit with all the girls. I was at a bad place in my life, and didn't have time for him, or anyone else for that matter."

"So you have known Luke for a long time?" I asked, knowing they had a history, but not sure how far it dated back.

"Oh, yeah. We grew up together. He always knew he wanted to be a biker, and me," she paused, smiling as her mind flooded with old memories, "I wanted to be on Broadway." I noticed the sparkle in her eyes as Red left me and went to a different place, one that she must have dreamed of for many years.

"What stopped you?" I asked, smiling at her reaction to her dreams as if they were my own.

"Cocaine." My smile died, as Red shrugged, unaffected by her reason or my reaction. "I was an addict. I didn't have a home growing up with two loving parents and a house full of siblings. I was property of the state and spent my entire childhood in the system. I bounced from foster home to foster home. That's how I met Luke. I was placed with a family when I was fourteen and they were wealthy, like Luke's family." I watched as Red stopped our conversation to congratulate the horrible singer before playing a setlist consisting of three line-dancing songs, prompting every girl on the patio to get up and dance, leaving her and I to continue our conversation without interruption. "They sent me to the same private school Luke attended. He might have been raised rich, but that boy was hood, giving us something in common. We would

161

meet every day after lunch, and smoke a cigarette together. He was the perfect athlete with the good looks and charm, and I was the poor little orphan girl without a real family. He never let anybody fuck with me, though. Even after I fucked up my chances with a good family and they sent me back, he stayed in touch. I would go hang with him at his Pop's shop and watch him work on motorcycles. He shared his dreams with me and I shared mine with him. We were best friends. Life worked out for Luke, but not so much for me. He tried to save me, but I was hell-bent on destroying my life. Then, one day, I almost did." I watched as she struggled with her emotions. Red was opening up; she was showing me a side of her I had never seen. It was hard to watch her go from the hardcore, fun-loving Red, to a broken girl who had nothing. "I was dancing at this nightclub on the coast, making damned good money, catering to high-end clients. The problem was, I was using my hard-earned money on dope when I should have been saving for college. I took too much one night and it almost cost me my life. Luke took me in, treating me to his style of rehab, and that's when I found Regg. I pushed him away at first, but eventually I let him in. Now, he's all I have. I mean I have the club, but Regg is what wakes me up in the morning. I go to sleep just because I know it's his face that will fill my dreams. Once an addict, always an addict, Dallas. Just because I don't snort cocaine or shoot up doesn't mean I don't get high. I'm high on Regg. I traded cocaine for a six-foot, blonde-haired, baby-faced boy with a Harley, and a smile that can light up my darkest day. So, you can see why it bothers me that Luke has something to focus on other than his brothers. I know Luke would never let anything happen to them, or he would die trying. He is a great brother, leader, and friend. It's just easier to focus

162

the blame on someone. And that someone just so happens to be Luke. I don't like Regg being gone, but I would rather go back to being a drug addict, all alone with no one to care whether I am alive or dead than to ever see anything happen to the people I love. That includes you." She leaned forward, poking her finger into my shoulder, so that there was no mistaking to whom she was referring.

She smiled and let out a deep breath, fighting hard to keep her tears at bay. The conversation was over, and, although our trip down memory lane had ended, our journey toward the future, and our promising lifelong friendship, had only just begun.

Friday, Maddie had come to spend the day with me and I was glad I had taken Lindsey's advice to find out more about Maddie from Maddie's point of view. Our conversation had started when memories of her own mother were triggered once I showed her the hope chest full of things my mother had left for me.

"I was born Candice Madison Pittman. I was nicknamed Maddie by Frankie, who refused to call me Candice because it reminded him of a stripper that stole his wallet named Candy." Maddie laughed, and I joined her, my memories of Frankie not as pleasant as hers, but even I found humor in him saying that. "My mom didn't like it at first, but it grew on her eventually. She was such a romantic," Maddie said, pausing to look at a picture I had of my mother and father kissing. "She would always read these books with these heroes that rode white horses and shit, and tell them to me as bed time stories. Frankie wasn't around much, so most of our time was spent with just the two of us. When she died, Frankie tried hard for the first few weeks, but he couldn't handle it. I hardly saw him after that. I spent my life with the club, looking up to Red and Luke. Red was a junkie, and Luke was always going on runs, working hard trying to prove himself. I spent a lot of time with Pops, and they all tried like hell to shield me from the life, but it found me and I welcomed it." She turned her head, dabbing at the corners of her eyes with her fingers to stop her tears, as she struggled to continue. I knew this was painful for her. Talking about her mother was bad enough, but Brooklyn had shared with me a small bit of her story, and I was aware of what was to come. We were sitting on my bed, our backs against the headboard, with a box of old pictures strewn out around us. When she gathered her composure, her eyes landed on a picture of me and my ex-boyfriend Sam, sharing a kiss on the beach. "That's when I met Brett," she continued, as I remembered that Brett was Logan's dead-beat father that was no longer in the picture. "He was such an asshole." Luke's signature smirk had rubbed off on Maddie and she wore it well. "I was such a fool. I just wanted someone who would spend time with me, and show me a little attention. Luke hated him from the first time he met him. Every time Brett left, Luke would say, 'He's a piece of shit, Maddie. You are too good for him. I don't like the way he looks at you.'" I laughed at Maddie's impersonation of Luke. It was actually pretty good.

"Sounds just like him."

"I wanted Luke's attention. Negative attention was better than no attention, and I got plenty of it when I started seeing Brett. When Luke told me I couldn't see him anymore I rebelled. I knew I didn't love Brett, but I didn't care. Then I got pregnant. Luke was furious at first, but then he told me that he would help me take care of the

164

baby, and I didn't need Brett. But Luke was so busy with the club that he wasn't there all the time, and I began to get lonely. He called to check on me, but that was about it. When Logan was born, Luke was at the hospital, but so were Frankie and Brett, so it was a little awkward. Luke didn't stay long, and I was on my own again. The calls from Luke came less and less. He still cared about me, and was worried, but I was living my own life with a baby and Brett, and Luke was doing his own thing with the club. Then Brett lost it one night. I had Logan in a high-chair in the kitchen, and I caught Brett and his buddies smoking dope in front of him. I later found that they had been blowing it in his face, but at the time I had no clue. If I had, I probably would've tried to kill him that day. When I started screaming at Brett, he snapped. He had slapped me around before, but this time was different. He wouldn't stop. Luckily, we were living in a cheap apartment, and the walls were so thin that the neighbor heard the baby crying later that night, and came over to check on me. She beat on the door, but I was unconscious. Soon the police came and I was admitted to the intensive care unit, and Logan was placed in foster care. When I finally did wake up after being in a coma for three days, the only person I wanted was Luke." Maddie opened her mouth to continue then shut it, her dark memories taking her far away. She turned her head to me, her eyes brimming with tears that were threatening to spill out over her long lashes. "When Brett was beating me, Dallas. When I knew he wasn't going to stop until I was dead, I didn't cry for help. I didn't scream for someone to call the police. The only person I screamed for was Luke." I felt like vomiting at her words. I had done the same thing. I had screamed for him over, and over, and over. Then later when I was angry at him, I had told him what I had done. No wonder it had hurt him so bad.

Not only did he feel like he had failed me, but the memory of him failing Maddie was thrown back in his face. "When I saw his face in that hospital room, I knew my life would never be the same, and neither would his. I believe everything happens for a reason, and I thank God that Brett did that to me. If he hadn't, Luke might not have ever quit doing the shit he was doing." She wiped her eyes, taking a deep breath then blowing it out slowly, nodding her head as if she was having a mental debate and had found a side to agree with. "Shit changed after that. Luke found me an apartment and set me up with a job as a secretary for his father. I got Logan back and Luke's nanny became my new best friend. She took care of Logan while I worked and got back on my feet. Luke took the club in a different direction. He used the money your father had paid him to protect you to invest in the bar. He got his own shit together, and started working for his father, becoming a partner in almost no time at all. Everything was perfect, and then Luke saw you that night in the bar and couldn't resist you. I knew when Red called me and said the two of you had left together that nothing would be the same. I expected the worst and got the best." She nudged her shoulder against mine, and I found the opening I needed to ask her the question that had been gnawing at me since this conversation had started.

"So, when did you find out about me?" I asked, hoping she would give me the whole story so I didn't have to keep questioning her. I knew it was a touchy subject.

"When the mayor called Luke. He and I had become extremely close, and while the other guys had ol' ladies, Luke had me. We were closer than siblings, and, after what I had been through, Luke never let distance come between us. He told me, and, at first, I was excited.

166

Then I learned that I couldn't say anything because I couldn't blow the club's cover and let you know what was going on. I became extremely jealous of you, not because I was in love with Luke or anything, but because I didn't have his undivided attention. He was still there for me, and we were still close, but he was falling for you and I could see it. When you started coming around, I hated you. I hated the way you looked, I hated that you had years of memories of time spent with my father, I hated that you were all the women ever talked about, and I hated that Luke was in love. I tried to make you jealous, I even tried to turn everyone against you. I never should have done that, Dallas, and I apologize. When we were in the back of that van, all I could think was that I had spent the short time I knew you constantly pushing you away when I should have been getting closer to you. I thought I might never see you again. It almost killed me. But now that I have you in my life, I never want anything to come between us again. I want to know everything about you. I want to get to know you, and I want Logan to know you. Promise me you won't let anything or anyone come between us." I looked into the shining eyes of my sister, silently thanking her mother Rebecca for choosing to keep her, so that I could spend the rest of my days making her happy, then I uttered those two little words that held more guarantee than any I had ever spoken.

"I promise."

Now, it was Saturday night, I was at home, in my robe, sipping a glass of wine, and delighting in the feeling that my life was in a good place. Luke and I were good. I held no hard feelings against his harsh punishment, the

167

reminders of which were healing quite well. It had taught me three things: One, Luke had a dominant side; two, I knew what the punishment would be if I crossed him, which I never planned to do again. Ever; and three, in no way, would I, nor could I ever, be submissive. This wasn't entirely true, considering the submissiveness I was subjected to as an ol' lady. Red and I had also resolved our problems, now that I was aware that her insecurities had absolutely nothing to do with me. She was not trying to reign over me, or make me feel insignificant when it came to Luke or the club. And then there was Maddie. My sweet little sister, who had my temper, our father's grit, and her mother's charm. No one was trying to kill me, Charlie was a distant memory, and construction was going to start next week on my new project that would result in the takedown of Mayor Kirkley. I had a meeting in two weeks in Atlanta, with an investor who was willing to expand his business to Hattiesburg, and I would be lying if I said I wasn't ready to get back to my old hometown, even if it was for only a few days. The only thing that could make this night any better would be if Luke were here. I picked up my cell, deciding to send him a message to let him know I was thinking about him. Chances were he wouldn't respond, but he would see it sometime tonight and give me a call in the morning. I still wasn't sure how things were going over there, or the details of the situation, but he had assured me every time we talked that everything was going fine.

Just wanted you to know that I was thinking about you! Can't wait to see your face!! I love you :)

My phone vibrated almost immediately, notifying me of a message.

Really? I was just thinking about you too. I'm tired of us being apart. Pack a bag and come stay with me.

Seriously?

I sat staring at my phone, willing it to notify me of his response.

Seriously babe.

My face broke out into a smile, as my fingers worked feverishly to respond.

How long? The weekend?

I should call him. If he could text, maybe he could answer. I dialed his number, finding myself listening to his automated voicemail after the second ring. I frowned at my phone, pleading with the phone gods that his cell had not gone dead. My prayers were answered when his text came through.

Can't talk babe. Sorry. I don't want you for 2 days. I want you for 2 weeks. You think I would miss your birthday?

He had remembered my birthday. I melted into my chair, smiling at the thought of him being in a crowded place with a million things on his mind, yet he had not forgotten my birthday.

When can I leave?

I sat tapping my finger on the couch, waiting for his reply. I hoped he said tomorrow. I couldn't wait much longer to see him. When I felt the vibration again, I hesitated, hoping he wouldn't make me wait out the weekend.

I'm hoping you already have.

Chapter 12

Luke

"Is she coming?" I took a deep breath, trying not to jump across the table and snap the neck of the man I fucking hated. I looked up, to find Charlie waiting very impatiently for my answer.

"Yeah, she's coming."

"Good. At least she will be safe." It would take less than three seconds for his eyes to roll back in his head and him to vanish from my life completely. That included the time it would take for me to get across his desk, and put my hands around his throat. I hated this fucking game. Charlie was going to make me wait before he told me where Crazy was. Crazy was one of Frankie's guys, and had assisted in assaulting Dallas by hanging her in a barn, stripping her, and putting his filthy fucking hands on her. My jaw clenched, and my fists tightened, at the thought of him hurting her. The motherfucker would pay. He was also the man who Frankie had paid a million dollars to kill Dallas. My plan had been to kill Crazy, once I had located him, but that had all turned to shit when I found out he was working for Charlie. The motherfucker was so protected that nobody could get to him. Not even me. Charlie claimed he wanted revenge for himself, but what he really wanted was me at his mercy. He wouldn't hurt Dallas, personally, but if he ever cut Crazy loose, there was no telling what *he* would do.

"Why are you so obsessed with Dallas?" If the question pissed him off enough to kill me, then so be it, but I wanted to fucking know. I watched as Charlie considered lying, but for some reason, decided to tell the truth.

"I've asked myself that question more times than I care to count. I don't know if it is her, or the fact that she belongs to you, which makes me so anxious to have her in my life, but the need is there. I just want to make sure she has the best life possible."

"She does. Trust me." Charlie laughed and I wanted to take advantage of his gaping mouth, and shove my fist into it until he choked to death.

"Trust you? I will never trust you, Luke. I will never trust in you to provide her with the things she needs like I can."

"What does she need? Safety? Is that what you're referring to?"

"Her safety is not an issue. There is one man who wants her dead, and he can be taken down by any man in your club with bare hands. It is her future that I am concerned about. What kind of life will she have running with a group of dirty bikers like yourselves?" I closed my eyes tight, telling my mouth to stay shut before I asked any questions, or made any assumptions. Charlie would go to the ends of the earth to get what he wanted, and it didn't matter how low he had to stoop to get it. But I couldn't keep quiet. I had to fucking know, and even if he didn't answer, I would know the truth by his body language.

"Why would a man like Crazy take money from a man like Frankie and decide to follow through on his promise? Why wouldn't he just take the money and not risk losing his life when he knows if he comes after Dallas that I am going to be waiting?" Charlie's posture didn't falter and his eyes gave nothing away, but that split-second pause told me everything I needed to know. I stood up from my chair, knocking it to the floor, as I placed my hands on the table and leaned close to Charlie's face. I could see his goons coming toward me from the corner of my eye, but I didn't fucking care. "You motherfucker." I spat at him, barely getting the words out of my mouth before I was pulled back and someone's arm was wrapped tightly around my neck. I didn't fight back because there was no need. I couldn't win. I trained my eyes on Charlie, daring him to look away while I threatened him with words that held so much promise, even he looked a little worried. "If so much as one hair on her fucking head is harmed as a result of your little game, I will slice you from ear to fucking ear with the dullest knife I can find. If you want a fucking war, then you got one."

"Get him out of here," Charlie demanded, tearing his eyes from mine, as he gestured with his head toward the door. I was dragged out the side of the building and pushed into the alley, while Charlie's goons surrounded me, waiting for me to fuck up and make a move. I stood my ground, looking at each of them knowing that I was once in their same shoes. I had been one of Charlie's goons, too. It had not been easy and any man with a conscious was usually found dead or not found at all. The ruthless ones were the only ones who made it out alive. I was sure my voice fell on deaf ears that didn't give a shit as to what I had to say, but they were gonna fucking hear it.

"This woman is innocent. You want to fuck with me or my brothers, that's fine. We have all fucked up

173

somewhere along the way, so we deserve it. But that woman has been nothing but a victim. She has been through hell and I did my fair share of dragging her there, but him," I motioned toward the general area of Charlie, thankful that I couldn't see his face through the brick wall that separated us, "he is going to fuck up and when he does, she is going to die. If that ever happens, you remember my face 'cause it's the last one you'll ever fucking see." I wanted to hit something. I wanted to kill all of them, and I was sure I could do it without breaking a sweat. I straddled my Harley, my hands shaking with anger and adrenaline as I squeezed the clutch and turned the throttle, leaving the pathetic motherfuckers that were lucky enough to live to see another day in a cloud of black smoke.

I was in the clubhouse in Lake Charles, sitting at the bar twirling my beer bottle between my fingers. I had taken a long ride when I had left my meeting with Charlie, letting the wind and my steel horse help clear my head. Frankie had borrowed money from Charlie, but it had absolutely nothing to do with Dallas. There was a million dollar bounty on Dallas' head, but it was Charlie that was offering it, not Frankie. Charlie was right, there was only one man that wanted Dallas dead and it was him. The catch was that he didn't want to kill her, he wanted to save her. He wanted to set Crazy up, then barge in at the last minute to rescue Dallas from her attacker. He wouldn't kill me because he knew that Dallas would mourn my death, taking away precious time that could be used on him. He wanted to make me look like the bad guy. I wasn't sure how, but I knew it was going to happen. Charlie knew I was onto him, so he would most likely either speed up his plans or change the game. But I had an ace in the hole. I didn't want to use it, but I knew I didn't have a choice.

Dallas

I was sitting outside Luke's, honking the horn impatiently, while Red and Maddie dragged their asses out. When I had called to tell them I was going, they had informed me that they were going too. I had assumed they had been asked, just as I had, but, chances were, they were just going to show up unannounced, and make their presence known, whether it was welcome or not. I asked Red if she wanted me to pick her up at her house. Her response was that she was at Luke's. Funny. Did she ever go home? As they piled into my car, carrying more shit than they could use in two weeks and stuffing it into every available space I had, I decided now was as good a time as any to ask the probing question.

"Why are you two always at Luke's?"

"Because," Maddie started, pausing to shove one of her many suitcases behind my seat, "Logan loves Nanny and refuses to go home most nights. And Red is always there, so I have someone to talk to." Well, her excuse made sense. I turned to Red, finding her struggling with the buttons to adjust the seat to her liking. It took a couple of minutes before she was satisfied, then she turned to me, finally noticing that I was watching her.

"What?" she asked, her head snapping between me and Maddie, whose head was perched between the two front seats.

"The question was: Why are we always at Luke's?" Maddie informed her, placing her chin in her hand, and looking expectantly at Red. I guess she had never thought to ask either.

"It's boring at my house. There's always something going on at Luke's, and when Regg ain't home that's where I stay. Is that a problem?" she asked, daring either one of us to say it was.

"I think the big bad Red is scared to stay by herself," Maddie teased. I snickered, as I pulled out of the driveway to start our long journey to Lake Charles.

"I'm not scared to stay by myself." Red snapped. "I just don't like it," she added, avoiding us both as she flipped down the mirror to check her appearance.

"Pussy." Maddie said, in a huff, not believing Red's excuse in the least.

"One more time, Maddie. Call me a pussy, just one... more... time." Red exaggerated her words, giving Maddie plenty of time to rethink her decision about name-calling. Silence filled the car and through the rearview mirror I watched Maddie hide her smile with her hand. Red sat with knowing satisfaction at the reason for Maddie's silence, and even though the feud was funny to me, my mouth remained closed. I turned up the radio, to hear Macklemore and Ryan Lewis serenade us with "White Walls." Maddie sang along, offering us her own remix, which I never would have caught had I not have been paying attention to how well she could sing.

"I got that off black Cadillac, midnight drive. Got that gas pedal, leaned back, taking my time. Red is a pussy, roof off, letting in sky," I couldn't contain my laughter, as I fought hard to keep the car between the ditches.

"I heard that," Red snapped, clearly not going to follow through on her unspoken promise, only leading

Maddie and I to laugh harder. This was going to be a long ride.

"I gotta pee." Maddie whined, once we had been on the road for no more than an hour.

"Well maybe you should have thought about that before you ordered that big kidney infection when we stopped to get gas," Red snapped, jerking her head towards the now empty 44oz cup that sat between our seats. My stomach already hurt from laughing too much at the two of them and their constant back and forth shit-talking, which ranged from Red being referred to as a pussy, to Maddie being accused of licking one. I took the next exit, finding a nearby gas station to allow Maddie the opportunity to relieve her bladder and me to get something sweet. Red wouldn't admit it, but I noticed that she also took full advantage of the stop, loading up on beef jerky and Mountain Dew. I was the first one out of the store and noticed that my car had a few admirers, which wasn't out of the norm. What made this time so unusual was the fact that they were bikers.

"What's a pretty girl like you doing driving a fast car like this?" A guy who favored Marty in looks asked. I smiled sweetly at him in response. It was nice to see a group of people who shared the same love and respect for riding and brotherhood as the Devil's Renegades did.

"Her ol' man bought it for her," Red said, walking up and gracing them with her own smile. I shot her a questioning glance, but remained quiet. "We don't ask questions when we are told what to do or given

178

something. We just appreciate it because they give it to us. Property of Devil's Renegades, Enforcer Regg," Red said, introducing herself, not by her own name, but by her husband's. "This is Property of Devil's Renegades, President LLC." She put her arm around my shoulder, and I offered them a weak smile, confused by the way this conversation was going. By the look on the guys' faces, they didn't seem very impressed by our titles. "Sorry to rush off, but we have to get going." Red made her way to the passenger side of the car, while I followed suit and slid behind the wheel, the man in the black and white cut barely giving me enough room to squeeze by. As we sat in the car, both of us in silence waiting for Maddie to return, the group of men seemed to grow. I was getting a little nervous when Maddie finally made it out the door and approached the vehicle with caution. She avoided the stares and comments thrown at her, and pushed her way through the crowd and into the car.

"Leave, Dallas. If they don't move, run their asses over," Maddie said, as she looked over her shoulder and out the back window. I started the car, putting it in reverse and easing back, forcing the men to move out of the way. When we were safely back on the interstate, I let out a breath I didn't realize I had been holding.

"What the fuck was that?" I asked, looking between the rearview mirror at Maddie, over to the passenger side of the car at Red.

"That was the infamous Metal and Madness Motorcycle Club." Red said, pulling her phone from her purse and firing away at the keys in a text message.

"And?" what did it matter?

"And they are the reason our boys are in Lake Charles. I saw Idaho, bottom rockers. What did you see Maddie?" Red asked, waiting on her reply before she finished her message.

"Same." Maddie replied simply, leaving me wondering what in the hell they were talking about.

"Hey!" I snapped, aggrieved that they were speaking as if I wasn't in the car. "Speak English."

"The bottom rocker they wear tells us what state they are from. These guys were from Idaho, which tells us that their threat to call in reinforcements wasn't bullshit." Well, that made sense.

"What was up with the way you were talking to them?" I asked, realizing how close I had come to be too friendly.

"When someone from a club addresses you, always refer to your ol' man. When you introduce yourself, unless you want to be friendly, never let them know your name, just your ol' man's title and that you are his property. We showed no form of disrespect and we didn't lead them on. Never lead them on. You don't want them thinking your man ain't givin' it to ya good enough at home." Wow. This club shit was a lot more complicated than I had thought. The idea of me being addressed by another club never even came to mind. "That's why we wear property patches, to avoid shit like this. But, we can't wear a property patch everywhere we go," Red said, her frustration getting the better of her, as she pulled out a cigarette and lit up. I started to say something about her smoking in my car, but then Maddie lit up too. Who was I

180

to crush their spirits at a time when a cigarette was much needed? The rest of our ride was made in silence, all three of our heads spinning with thoughts of what would happen when the Metal and Madness MC came face to face with the Devil's Renegades.

It was after two in the morning when we finally arrived at the clubhouse located in the middle of Lake Charles. It was once a building that housed several offices, but was now the property of the Devil's Renegades, Lake Charles chapter. Even though the outside still looked like that of an office, the inside had been transformed to look similar to the one in Hattiesburg. Pool tables, couches, and a bar long enough to seat twenty, filled the front area. Behind the cinderblock wall, at the back of the building, were rooms where the club stayed when they couldn't go home, or where other chapters were housed when they were in town. Behind that was the meeting room, where church was held, which was equipped with a long table, a lot of chairs and shadow boxes filled with fallen brothers' cuts. When we walked in, I was surprised to find the place packed with people. Women danced on the bar, men gathered in circles talking, and the music was almost deafening. Maddie and Red left me to fend for myself as they floated around the room like social butterflies, reacquainting themselves with the ol' ladies. My eyes scanned the room, looking for those ocean-blues I had not seen in several days.

"Hey baby." I turned to the familiar sound of Ronnie's warm voice greeting me. He stood tall, his legs bowed and a Bud Light dangling from his ring-clad fingers.

"Hey, Ronnie!" I eagerly accepted his hug, and was flooded with warmth as he kissed my cheek. There was something calming about his presence.

"Luke is around here somewhere. Come on, I'll help you find him." I followed Ronnie as he made his way through the crowd at a slow pace. My eyes were constantly searching; looking twice at every orange and black cut to be sure I didn't miss him. I was so busy searching that I had not noticed Ronnie had stepped around a man blocking our path, until I ran into the back of him. The impact was so hard and sudden, that I felt myself falling back before his powerful hand grabbed my arm to hold me upright. My eyes dragged up his huge frame until they found his face, which was hard as steel, much like the rest of his body. This was the guy people pictured when they put a face to the word "biker." He was more than intimidating, he was downright fucking scary. He wore a hat just like the one Luke often wore; black and turned backwards, with the letters DFFD stitched in orange on the back panel. His French Fork goatee was long and dark, and the whites of his eyes were slightly bloodshot, while the irises were a dull cornflower blue. His thick neck was covered in tattoos that laced through one another, creating a beautiful design that disappeared under the collar of his black t-shirt. I envisioned them continuing down his rock hard body, past his navel and to his V that I would have paid good money to see. I swallowed hard at my perverted thoughts, not believing that this man that oozed bad-boy, biker, killer, womanizer, fighter, thug-life, gangster, and panty-wetter all wrapped up in one, could have such an effect on me. I looked down at his hand, which still had a firm grip on me, and noticed the tattoos continued down his arms and to the tips of his fingers. I

182

wasn't sure if I was fascinated by him, scared of him, or turned on by him, but I was going to convince myself that I was scared. I had to be. Why else would my heart be hammering so hard against my chest that the sound of the music couldn't even overpower it?

"You LLC's girl?" he asked, and I shrank at the sound of his booming voice. Yep, definitely scary. I scanned his cut to confirm that he was a member of the Devil's Renegades and that he was also the Sergeant At Arms. I could have guessed that one. The man could kill someone just by looking at them, I was sure of it. Instead of closing my mouth and standing up straight, I remained in the position of a wounded, frightened animal, and just nodded my head.

"Who the fuck is your friend?" I tore my eyes away from Mr. "I can snap your neck with one hand," and found myself staring at a very beautiful, very intimidating, very pissed-off woman, whose attitude was perceptible in her stance and voice. "Who the fuck are you?" she asked, not giving the man next to me a chance to answer. I took in her appearance, from the black and orange bandana she wore over her dark hair, and the extremely large diamonds that dangled from her ears, to her perfect, bulging breasts and skin-tight, ripped jeans. Even if she wasn't such a bitch, I still wouldn't like her.

"She belongs to me." Luke said, appearing beside me. When my eyes landed on him, thoughts of Mr. and Mrs. Evil Biker disappeared, as did the hand on my upper arm. Luke was shirtless and sweaty, and looked like he had just finished fucking every woman in the room, and I didn't care. Any woman who failed to at least try was a fool in my book; not that they had a chance in hell. Now I was sure of the reason for my irregular heartbeat, thundering against my chest louder than the music. It was because of the Adonis that stood before me. Luke's hair was getting long. It was probably long enough for me to wrap my fingers around, a theory I would test soon enough. His breathing was harsh and deep, causing his chest to heave out at an intake of breath, and his nostrils flare on the release. His body shined, the sweat glistening on every visible part of his exposed, tanned skin. The veins in his arms were big and thick, protruding from his biceps and down his forearms. His abs rippled across his stomach and couldn't have been more perfect if they had been spray-painted on. When his tongue darted out of his mouth and across his bottom lip, moistening it before pulling it between his teeth, I lost the ability to breathe. Motherfucker. How had I survived without him? How had I allowed him to be away from me? I was in a fog, watching Luke's lips move as he spoke, imagining what they would feel like on my pussy. When his eyes were right in front of mine, blocking my view of his chest, they moved again and I realized he was talking to me.

"Huh?" I asked weakly, my mouth dry from gaping open for so long. I quickly shut it, licking my lips as I tried to figure out what he had repeated for me, so I wouldn't look like such a love-struck fool. I had nothing. He had repeated his words to me, and still I had no idea what he had said. Between the awe I had experienced at meeting Mr. Mean, and the sight of a half-naked Luke, I had lost all sense.

"Babe," Luke said again, a little louder, gaining us the attention of a nearby crowd of guys.

"What?" I asked, giving him an annoyed look. Damn him for fucking up my ab-watching.

"I want you to meet some people. Officially." Oh. Luke placed his hands on my shoulders, turning me back around to the couple whose faces of hate had turned to faces of smirking amusement. Was the smirk a biker thing? I forced a smile on my face as I stood up taller; trying to reclaim what little dignity I had left after my public eye-fucking session with Luke. "Dallas, this is my brother Shark, and his ol' lady, Chi Chi." I placed my hand in Shark's, making sure my handshake was firm, as I figured his would be. Instead, he clasped my hand lightly, leaving me looking like an idiot as I squeezed the shit out of his fingers, with an overachieving firmness. The gesture earned me a friendly smile, and a small nod of respect. Chi Chi on the other hand, had a smugger smile, as she all but curtsied in sarcasm, leaving my opinion of her where it had initially stood, with a few new additives; jealous, evil, bitch. They didn't speak to me, but stayed around, trying to form their own opinion of me as I was introduced to the other people in the group. "I know you have met Mary," Luke said, gesturing toward the petite woman with beautiful, silver hair that fell to the tops of her shoulders.

"Hey girl," she said, stepping forward, and surprising me with a hug that I returned awkwardly.

"And this is her husband, Big Al." I had seen Big Al at Luke's, but had not had the opportunity for proper introductions. Where Luke was country, Big Al was anything but. His flat bibbed hat, long silver chain and Louisiana accent was a perfect concoction, making him a biker with a hint of street thug. His warm friendly smile was welcome, and I graced him with my own, as he wrapped me in his arms in a comforting hug. I eyed Mary when he pulled away, hoping she didn't take offense to our hands-on exchange, but she was too busy engaging in conversation with other people; a lot of other people. A throng of others had joined us and consisted of nearly everyone in the clubhouse. "This is my brother Kyle and his wife Katina." Kyle was a man of few words with a very shy demeanor. His eyes were kind, and his smile warm, but he seemed a little nervous. Katina, on the other hand, was the complete opposite. Her flamboyant behavior consisted of a squeal, an exciting smile, and a big hug. Her long brown hair fell virtually to her waist, and its sweet scent overwhelmed my nostrils, just as it engulfed my face when she pulled me to her. Like her husband and many of the others in the Lake Charles chapter, her skin was tanned, and her accent thick. I laughed at her welcome response and accepted her hug. "And I'm sure you remember PROSPECT Chris, but you will address him as Chris." There was a hint of warning in Luke's voice, but I ignored it, as I smiled encouragingly at a very nervous, stuttering Chris.

"De-Devil's Renegades PROSPECT Chris, Lake Charles, Louisiana." Big Al clapped him on the back in approval, which only lasted a split second before someone hollered for a prospect, and he excused himself. I saw Katelan looking uneasy and out of place nearby, and started to make my way over to her, but was stopped by Mary.

"She is a PROSPECT's wife. You are the President's ol' lady. Let her come to you." Gone was the sweet, fun, Mary and in her place was biker Mary, who was very intimidating, even though I had to look down to meet her gaze. If she had been about a foot and a half taller, my blood would have run cold at the look she gave me. I started to protest. I wanted her to know that I had once felt like an outsider myself, and that I felt sorry for Katelan, but Luke grabbed my hand and led me away.

"Come on, babe. I'll show you where we are staying." I followed Luke through the mass of people, and down a long corridor lined with doors that led to private rooms. At the end of the hall, we stopped in front of a wooden door with the word 'PRESIDENT' carved into it in a very neat script. I looked behind us, and the door across from ours had the same engraving.

"Is there something special about this room?" I asked, remembering all of the other doors were not labeled.

"Not really. It has a door that leads outside and a bigger bathroom, but all of the rooms are more or less the same." Luke's breath blew through my hair, sending shivers down my spine, as he leaned over me to open the door. Inside was just as I had imagined it. In many ways, it was very similar to the rooms at the clubhouse in Hattiesburg. The walls consisted of light brown paneling, with posters of motorcycles, women in bikinis, and a reaper scattered across them. Thin, black carpet lined the floors, and in the middle of the room sat a queen-size bed, with no headboard or footboard, just a frame that kept the mattresses off the floor. The door that led outside was metal, with a slide bar lock that could only be opened from the inside. A small desk with a worn chair and a lamp sat in the corner next to Luke's bag.

"Yo, LLC. I got your ol' lady's shit." I heard someone yell from outside the door. Luke opened the door, revealing a grinning Possum, holding my bag in one hand and a drink in the other. "I figured she might need this after that long-ass ride with Red and Maddie." I smiled at him as Luke took my bag, and stepped back so that I could hug Possum. "Good to see you made it, baby."

"Thanks, Possum. And thanks for the drink," I said, taking it from him without question, and taking a sip. "Margarita. It's delicious." I licked the salt stuck to my top lip, before taking another drink.

"Thank Regg. He loves this shit. I don't know why he can't drink beer and liquor like the rest of us. All he needs is a little umbrella and a girdle, and I would swear he was a woman." Possum laughed as he talked, and I found myself laughing too, yet mine was of the mental image I had of Regg in a girdle.

"Thanks, brother. I'll see you in the morning," a smiling Luke said, from behind me.

"Why don't you have a shirt on?" I asked, as Luke shut the door. I didn't really believe that he had been fucking every woman in the bar, but now that we were alone, I wanted to know.

"I was working out," he said simply, throwing my bag down next to his, and fumbling with something on the desk. I drank in the sight of Luke and noticed that, he had indeed been working out. Perfection. That was the only way to describe Luke when he stood before me in ripped jeans that hung low on his waist, a muscular back and sweaty, messy hair. "I have been listening to this song everyday and each time I did, it made me think of you, and all the things I was going to do to you when I got home."

188

Luke said, turning toward me, as the music to a song I had never heard filled the room. "But, since you are here, let's see what *this* house is made of." My breath caught in my throat as Luke sauntered toward me, his eyes half closed, and full of possessiveness. I watched as he observed me in leggings, an oversized sweatshirt that hung off of one shoulder, sandals, no make-up, and my hair piled high on my head in a messy bun. I knew I looked ridiculous. There was nothing sexy or hot about my outfit, yet by the look in his eyes, one would think that I was dressed in lingerie. He stood before me, his eyes appraising my body, worshiping each fully clothed part with just a look. His hands slid up my arms and to my neck, as he turned my head slightly and brought his lips to mine, giving me a slow, lazy kiss. He began to turn me in a circle while kissing me. We were dancing to the music, my feet moving to follow his lead effortlessly. Instead of feeling that fire ignite, I felt that somatic sensation that only he was capable of giving me take over. I felt treasured by the way he kissed me, as if he had all the time in the world to make me feel loved. He broke the kiss, pulling away from my mouth long enough to pull my shirt over my head, before wrapping his hands around my waist and pulling me back to him, continuing to lead me in our circle of dance which reminded me of how romantically sweet Luke could be. My head lolled to the side, as he showered my neck in kisses and unclasped my bra. My nipples hardened immediately, and I released an audible sigh as I basked in the pleasure of the feel of his naked chest against mine. His mouth made its way down my neck, to the hollow of my throat and across my collar bone, before continuing its way between my breasts, down to my stomach and my navel. When he dropped to his knees before me, kissing along the edge of my pants across my stomach, I realized that this was an intimate side of Luke that I had yet to experience. Sure it was great when he made love to me and fucked me into a haze of dizziness, but Luke's intimacy was something that made me feel cherished, and loved, and like I was the only woman in the world. I felt... precious, as if there was nothing as valuable to him as me. I looked down at him as my hands caressed his soft, damp hair. I watched as he pulled my sandals off, then ran his hands back up my legs to grip the hem of my pants and slide them down, kissing the exposed skin as he went. The music stopped then started again playing the same tune. I was glad he had placed it on repeat. I loved the way the music flowed so perfectly with Luke's actions. I was left standing in nothing but a pair of black panties that Luke took his time to remove, being sure to kiss each place he revealed in appreciation, with a light touch of tongue and two full lips. When I was completely naked and showered in his kisses, when not a single inch of my body was not tingling from the feel of his lips, he carried me in his arms and laid me down on the bed, gently removing his arms from under me as if I were porcelain, and he was afraid he might break me. He stood tall over me, his lips parted, his eyes shining, and a look of admiration on his face while he took in all that was me, as I lay completely nude before him. I watched as he took his time removing his jeans first, then followed this by taking off his black boxer briefs, which were stretched across the swelling that was continuing to grow inside them. Luke knelt on the bed, kissing the inside of my thighs as he positioned himself between my legs. His mouth avoided the center of me that craved him, in turn, devoting his attention to the areas that were usually forgotten in the heat of the moment. I wanted to squirm under him. I wanted to beg him to take me, but I knew that this was something so much more. Something I

190

desired and didn't even know. This was something I needed, a show of intimate affection from the man I had given my heart to. When Luke made his way to my face, tears pricked the back of my eyes at his words, as he rubbed my hair, and spoke so softly to me that I was sure his tongue had turned to satin. "You are the reason I live. You are the reason I get up every fucking morning of my life. There is not one thing you could do to make me love you less, or make me want you more. I feel you, Dallas. I feel you in places inside me that I didn't know existed. You are just as much a part of me as the heart that beats in my chest keeping me alive and on this earth another day. Each day I love you is a day I will never regret. Everyone receives a gift that's worth dying for at some point in their life. Dallas, you are my gift." The sincerity in his words was almost too much. I felt like Luke was saying goodbye. I felt like there was something he was trying to tell me, but knew that he couldn't. My thoughts were washed away that night, replaced with the feeling of bliss as he made love to me, passionate love that was so amazingly intimate that, as I fell asleep in Luke's arms with the lyrics of Eric Church's "Like a Wrecking Ball" playing in my ears, I felt him in places I didn't know existed either.

Chapter 13

Dallas

Something woke me only a couple of hours after I had gone to sleep. I looked out the window to find it still dark outside. Luke's side of the bed was empty, and a sudden feeling of uneasiness washed over me. I heard the sound of a thud, followed by the sound of chains rattling and sat up, listening harder to see if I could figure out where the noise was coming from. The sound came again, and I turned my head to the right, to find the door leading outside unlocked. I grabbed my sweater from the floor, pulling it over my head, and stepped into my leggings. I walked to the door, not giving myself time to be nervous or scared of what I would find, and pushed it open. It was the early hours of the morning, and I saw Luke dressed in basketball shorts, tennis shoes, and no shirt, hitting a punching bag. He didn't seem to have any set strategy, which told me that he was not working out, he was venting. Something was on his mind, and he was trying to clear his head by beating the shit out of some imaginary person. I watched him for a minute, as he bounced lightly on his feet, hammering away at the bag, as it swung from side to side. We were in an alley between two buildings, and I noticed the area was filled with grills, tables, workout equipment and a dumpster. A tall, iron gate sealed off both exits, and kept it clear of any traffic. A large street lamp hung on the side of the building, casting an eerie glow over the alley.

"Luke," I said, getting his attention immediately. He turned to look at me, not moving or speaking, just staring at me across the dimly lit street. "Everything okay?" I asked, wishing I could see his face better. He was breathing heavily, his shoulders rising and falling, while his hands stayed at his hips. Was he pissed at me?

"Yeah, babe. I'm okay. Just go back to sleep. I'll be there soon," he said, his breathing irregular and harsh.

"You know, we can talk about it. I know something is bothering you. You can tell me." I expected his response before I received it. At times like this, Luke was very predictable.

"I'm good. I'll be in soon." He had still made no effort to come to me, and I was frozen in place as well. I wanted to go to him, but something told me to just give him some space. I walked inside, my mind spinning as to what could be wrong. He had asked me to come, and had made love to me, and then I find him outside only hours later, venting about something he was refusing to talk about. I wasn't surprised or pissed that he wasn't sharing, but, after his speech, I was worried. I didn't like the way he was talking as if he might go away and never come back, and wanting me to know just how much he loved me. I crawled back into bed, fully clothed, despite the stifling humidity, and curled up facing the door. I would know when he came through it, and I refused to fall asleep until he did. What couldn't have been more than five minutes had passed when Luke made his way inside, securing the door and going straight to the bathroom, without a single glance my way. I heard the shower start, and something came over me.

"Fuck this." I said to the empty room, stripping off my clothes, as I headed to the bathroom. I opened the door, just as he was stepping into the shower. "Don't shut me out, Luke. Tell me and let me help you deal with this. That's what I'm here for." I wasn't demanding or desperate, but encouraging. He observed me for a moment as if to see if what I offered was the truth. I stood there patiently, waiting for him to decide if this was something he knew he could trust me with. Finally, he took a deep breath and nodded, gesturing with his hand for me to join him. I waited for him to start the conversation as he allowed me to stand under the streaming water, before changing places with me. We bathed in complete silence. I would not push him on this. If he wanted to talk he would, but I refused to beg him to do so. This was something he was going to have to do on his own. If I wanted him to tell me, I would have to wait until he was ready. It was evident that it was weighing heavily on his shoulders, whatever it was. After our shower, I followed him into the room to retrieve my bag, but he stopped me by placing one of his own shirts over my head. He took the towel from my hands and tossed it on the floor, before pulling me to the bed and placing me so that I was lying on top of his chest. I was finally accepting defeat, and was ready to go to sleep, when at last he spoke.

"We have two weeks together before you leave to go to Atlanta. I want to enjoy this time with you. There may be some shit that goes down with this other club, but we aren't too threatened by them, so even if it does, it shouldn't be that big a deal. I'll tell you what's going on, but only when you need to hear it. Right now, let's just enjoy the moment. I've never had two full weeks with you without some crazy shit happening. You don't worry, and I won't worry. Deal?" Just the thought of two weeks with

Luke without interruption was enough to make me agree. He said he would tell me, and although I wanted to know now, I would wait. I was sure he would find some way to keep my mind busy enough to forget the anticipated news.

"Deal. No work, no worries, and no bullshit. Just us." I agreed, sitting up so I could see his face.

"I can't guarantee the no bullshit bit. I'm sure something fucked up will happen, but it won't be between me and you. Now, go to sleep. I'm tired as fuck, and I need you beside me." He didn't have to say it twice. I fell asleep on Luke's chest, with thoughts of us being together overshadowing the dark thoughts of what he had to tell me, which were not too far away in my mind.

I woke to find Luke sound asleep next to me. The worry and strain of the previous night was still evident on his tired, peaceful face. I decided to let him sleep in, and pulled myself from the bed, making sure not to wake him. I crept to the bathroom to freshen up, grabbing my bag on the way. The weather in Louisiana was just as difficult and crazy as it was in Mississippi. The humidity was unbearable, even though it was November. I chose a black t-shirt and gray yoga pants in the hope of hitting the clubhouse gym before Luke and I started our day. I pulled my tennis shoes from my bag, and tiptoed out of the room in search of coffee.

The corridor was quiet, but once I hit the main room, things were in full swing. There was not a man in sight, but every ol' lady and a few stray women from the previous night were cleaning up, and the smell of strong coffee was in the air.

"Hey, baby!" I heard Brooklyn yell at me across the room. I smiled at her, giving her a small wave, as I made my way to the bar where she was cleaning. "I didn't get to see you last night. I'm glad you're here." Before I could take a seat, she had a hot cup of coffee laid out for me, and a warm hug waiting. I leaned across the bar, melting in her arms, which swallowed me up me in a motherly hug. She looked amazing, as she always did. She wore a Harley Davidson baseball cap over her long hair, yoga pants, and a tank top. Her face was made-up completely, and she looked like she had been up for hours.

"Good morning to you. Thank you for the coffee." I said, sitting and taking a sip.

"You're welcome, baby."

"Is there something I can do?" I asked, feeling silly for sitting on my ass while everyone else was cleaning.

"No no. We got it. Enjoy your coffee. We're almost finished anyway."

"I was thinking about hitting the gym in a few. Is that okay?" I asked, watching Mary and Katina from across the room, as they did back flips over the couch.

"We do yoga the mornings we're together. It helps us clear our heads. You want to join?" Brooklyn asked, taking a break and propping herself up on the bar while she lit a cigarette. "She is gonna break her neck. Look at her! She is too little to be doing that shit." We watched together, as Mary got a running start to jump backwards onto the couch. I turned to see Brooklyn doubled over in laughter. There was something amazing about the way she laughed, it just pulled you in and soon I was laughing too.

"Morning," Red greeted us, taking a seat next to me on the bar stool, and leaning her head on my shoulder.

"Good morning, Red. Long night?" I asked, thinking that she and Regg had probably had a very interesting night filled with hot sex, considering they had been apart for so long.

"No, I'm just not a morning person," she replied, leaning over the bar to give Brooklyn a kiss on the lips, as she accepted her coffee with a sigh. "Brooklyn's coffee is sure to cure any hangover and give you some pep in your step." I nodded in agreement, and we clinked coffee cups, before taking another appreciative sip. I looked back across the room, to find Chi Chi sauntering in, wearing a sports bra, and yoga pants that fit her like a second skin. "Chi Chi is so fucking hot," Red said, following my gaze. I rolled my eyes, knowing she couldn't see, but forgot that Brooklyn could, earning me more booming laughter from her.

"Got some competition?"Brooklyn asked through her laughs. Was I intimidated by Chi Chi's looks? Every woman in the bar was appealing, so why did she get under my skin so much.

"It's because she reminds you of yourself," Red said in my ear, answering my unspoken question.

"I am nothing like her," I responded, locking my eyes on Red for the first time. She wore no make-up and her face looked fresh and young. I noticed her freckles, and bright red eyelashes. If I wasn't sure it was her, I wouldn't have recognized her. "Stop staring. It's rude," she said, turning back to her coffee.

"Red is self-conscious about her freckles. I think they're cute," Brooklyn said, giving Red a wink.

"I like them," I said, trying to convince Red that she had no reason to feel uncomfortable.

"Fuck y'all. Are we gonna work out or what?" Brooklyn laughed again, and I joined her, as Red stomped off.

"I love fucking with her. It's funny as shit to see her get so worked up over something so silly." The other ladies had made their way to the bar, and I greeted each of them with a hug, except for Chi Chi, who sat too high on her horse for me to reach.

"Yoga! I just love yoga. It cleanses the body and relaxes the mind," Katina said, as she walked off in the same direction as Red.

"So does an enema, but you don't see me sticking one up my ass every morning." The room erupted into laughter as Punkin graced us with her presence, and her wonderful choice of words. While the rest of us were dressed to exercise, Punkin wore jeans and a sweatshirt, full make-up, and earrings that looked like peppermints.

"Are you not joining us, Punkin?" I asked, as we made our way out the side door and into the alley.

"I'll get y'all some water when you pass out from a heat stroke." She replied, lighting a cigarette before giving me a hug. Outside, a large mat covered part of the street as everyone took their places. I chose last, considering I was the newest, and wished I had chosen to go first. The only spot left was the one next to Chi Chi, and I would rather have stabbed myself in the face with a fork than have to sit next to her. But, I took my seat as if it didn't bother me, noticing by the snickers coming from Red and Brooklyn that I was set up. Bitches.

"Punkin, hit play, please," Brooklyn said, prompting Punkin to hit the play button on the small CD player before taking her seat beside it. A warm, encouraging voice filled the air as we were told the position to assume to begin the exercise. Only ten minutes in, and Red was talking, interrupting the silence.

"I was thinking. If we did this everyday for the next few days, when we go out for Dallas' birthday, I'll be loose."

"You're already loose." Mary said, causing everyone to break position, so they could laugh.

"Al has a big mouth," Red threw back, encouraging the rest of us to cheer her on, and pump Mary up for a comeback.

"I'm here! I'm here!" Maddie said, as she burst out the door and ran to take a seat beside me. "What did I miss?"

"Mary said Red was loose and Red said her husband had a big mouth. Now we are waiting on Mary to throw something back at her," I explained to Maddie in a rush of breath, as I held the plank position.

"I got one for you, Mary," Maddie said, assuming the same position as everyone else in the group. "Red is scared of the dark."

"Maddie I will come over there and punch you in the fucking vagina if you don't shut up," Red said, as we changed positions, with a laugh.

"I can't hear the fucking tape!" Brooklyn snapped, looking around to see everyone moving.

"Locust position."

"Thanks, Punkin!" Brooklyn yelled from the back of the room. "I could hear if you bitches would shut up." Another round of laughter and then silence, for about five minutes.

"How much longer we got? I'm ready for a cigarette," Red complained.

"Here honey. I have one," Punkin offered, standing and making her way to Red.

"Punkin don't give her a cigarette. We doin' yoga," Katina said, on a huff.

"Says the only fucking non-smoker out here," Brooklyn added, agreeing with Red that it was time for a smoke break.

"Dallas don't smoke." Katina threw back in defense.

"Hell, yes she does." Punkin said, walking in between all of us, as her cigarette dangled from the corner of her mouth. "Don't ask me how I know, 'cause I won't say a damned thing." I laughed as the CD ended, prompting everyone to act as if we had just done a two-hour workout instead of one lasting only twenty minutes. I was feeling loose, not in the same way as Red, and was ready to lift some weights, when my nemesis decided to announce the same thing.

"I'm gonna hit the weights for a little while." Fucking bitch. Did I have to like her? I would just have to wait until tomorrow to workout. No one paid Chi Chi any mind as she left the group, until a shirtless Luke walked out the back door.

"Does he not own a shirt?" Maddie grumbled, prompting every eye to turn to look at him.

"Hell, I'm glad he don't own a shirt. I like seeing him half-naked." Brooklyn said, giving Luke a very appreciative eye.

"He ain't got shit on Possum," Punkin added. I looked at her to find her deadly serious, and I smiled. It was nice that even after all they had been through, she still found him just as attractive as she always had. I turned my eyes back to Luke, watching with burning fury as he assisted Chi Chi with bench-pressing. Surely she wasn't hitting on him? Shark would probably kill them both. His name definitely suited him. When her weights were situated and she was on her back lying under them, she gave Luke a nod and before he turned to leave, he leaned down placing his hands on either side of her face and kissed her. I was on my feet and walking toward them before I knew what was happening.

"Forehead! Forehead!" I heard Red yelling, as she grabbed my arm and stopped me mid-stride. "He kissed her on her forehead. It's just a show of love, nothing more." Red was worried, as she should be. I was sure the look on my face was murderous. Red's yelling had drawn the attention of everyone in the alley, which now consisted of not just the ladies and Luke, but Shark, Ronnie, and Possum as well.

"You got a problem, Dallas?" Chi Chi called from her position on the bench about thirty feet from me.

"Let it go, Dallas," Red warned in my ear, but my mouth had another idea.

"As long as you keep your fucking hands off my ol' man there won't be a problem." My hands were fisted at my sides, my breathing calm and my voice deathly. Where had this possessive side come from? Or had it ever left? Chi Chi stood, walking toward me with a murderous look of her own. Bring it on bitch.

"So, I can't touch your ol' man, but it's okay for you to eye-fuck mine?" If my cheeks had not already been red from anger and my previous workout, my blush would have given me away.

"Ok, girls. That's enough." Brooklyn said, walking between us and stopping Chi Chi in her tracks. I saw Luke in the distance, his face devoid of any emotion, as he stood with his arms crossed.

"Naw, Brooklyn. If she has something she wants to say, then she needs to fucking say it. Seems like we are going to be spending a lot of time together, so we might as well get this shit out in the open." Chi Chi said on a daring smile.

"Oh, don't you even!" I snapped, my voice now just below a yell. "You have been a bitch to me ever since I got here."

"What the fuck do you expect when I walk up and see some bitch I don't know gawking at my man like she wants to lick his fucking nut sack? You think I didn't notice that shit?" She was right, and I would have reacted the same way, but I was pissed and it wasn't *me* we were talking about-it was *her*.

"Your man has a pretty powerful fucking presence, if you haven't noticed. But even when you found out who I was you still treated me like I was some outsider." My defense was weak, but it was all I had.

"Because I don't know you, bitch." She said slowly, clapping her hands together on each word for emphasis. I would not look like a fool in front of all these people.

"Well, maybe it's about time you got to know me. You want to clear the air? Here's your fucking chance." I said opening my arms, offering her the fight I knew she wanted.

"Dallas," Brooklyn started, trying to reason with me. The look of warning in her eyes was telling me that Chi Chi was not a bitch I should fuck with. I had taken an ass whoopin' before, I could do it again.

"Let 'em go." Luke called from behind them. "They're too fucking much alike. That's the problem. Y'all want to handle this shit like men, go ahead, but when it's over, it's over. The next one that says a cross word to the other will have me to deal with." Luke's tone was stony and serious, as he spoke to us from a distance.

"I got twenty on Chi Chi," I heard Mary call from behind me.

"Bitch, please. I got fifty says Dallas walks away with a full head of hair," my cheerleader, Red, added.

"Enough." Ronnie said, causing all eyes to turn to him. He stood with his arms crossed, mirroring Luke's stance from the opposite end of the alley. "This ain't something you should be rooting for or against. This is two sisters who may not share a bond, but will soon, and who have differences that are apparently so fucking bad that it has to come to blows to solve it. I ain't never in all my life seen two ladies act like the two of you. Sisterhood is a special thing and y'all are willing to fuck that up 'cause you're too damned much alike and can't get along. But, y'all wanna duke it out, fine. But you heard Luke and I stand behind my brother. When this shit is over, it's over. Finished." I felt a sharp pain in my gut as a result of Ronnie's speech. I had disappointed him, as had Chi Chi, and it showed in her face just as it did in mine. Luke was disappointed too, but somehow it hurt worse coming from Ronnie. Would my pride allow me to let it go? Would Chi Chi's? Or would we have to do this because neither one of us would ever respect the other if we didn't. I sized her up as she stood in front of me. She was a couple inches taller than me, but not much. We were about the same weight and built almost identically. Chi Chi took care of herself, just as I did, and she seemed to have a reputation for fighting, which let me know that I wasn't dealing with an amateur. I wasn't scared of her, but should I walk away and save face with the men who allowed us to be a part of this club? I would not back down. I couldn't. No matter the cost.

"You are not my sister," she said, closing the short distance between us. I kept my stance casual, but my guard up. "But only because I don't know you and you haven't earned that title yet. I'm willing to give you a chance, but you are going to have to prove to me that you are more than that arrogant bitch I was when I first entered into this lifestyle. I won't disrespect you, but I will not tolerate you being disrespectful to me. I am going to walk away because I love my husband, and I respect this club. Nothing more and nothing less. There ain't a man out here who can make it without a good woman behind him. LLC is a good fucking president, so is Ronnie. Brooklyn is a hell of an ol' lady. She has stepped up and taken responsibility for her sisters, just like her husband did for his brothers when he became president. If you want to set a good example to your sisters and play that role as president's ol' lady then you better step the fuck up, 'cause you got some big shoes to fill if you ever want to be half the woman she is." Chi Chi stepped around me, leaving Luke as the only thing in my line of sight. No one had heard what she had said, but the silence was deafening, and the tension was thick, as everyone anticipated our next move. I turned to see Brooklyn wrap her arm around Chi Chi as she whispered something in her ear then released her to a very proud Shark. Ronnie stood stone faced, as Shark led Chi Chi inside. His eyes then turned to me as he spoke.

"Y'all get dressed, and let's go get some breakfast." I had never felt so low in all of my life. The disapproval in Ronnie's face cut straight to my heart, leaving me feeling like I had let him down. Being in a head-on collision with a Mack truck couldn't have felt worse. Thank God for Red, and her ability to turn any awkward moment into a fun one.

"Yes! Breakfast! Oh thank God, Ronnie. I could see my ribs." Ronnie broke eye contact with me to lean back with a laugh, as his eyes landed adoringly on Red.

"Don't worry, sugar. I ain't gonna let you starve." I watched as he slipped his arm around her shoulder, and led them all through the door and back into the clubhouse. I stood, staring at the closed door as if I were a kid who had just been put in the corner. I was embarrassed, heartbroken, and alone. It was the most awful feeling I had ever experienced.

"Ya feeling like you lost your best friend?" Luke asked from behind me. I nodded, my eyes still focused on the closed door. "Wishing you'd done something different?" I nodded again, feeling my eyes burn, as tears formed at the back of them. "Is the shame so heavy in your chest that you feel like an elephant is sitting on it?" This time, the tears spilled over my eyes as my bottom lip involuntarily poked out, trying to stop the sob that was soon to come. Luke wrapped his arms around my waist and kissed my neck, resting his chin on my shoulder, and following my gaze to the closed door. "That's good, babe." I turned into his chest, letting my tears fall freely, as I searched his eyes for reason.

"How is that good? How can anything about this feeling be good?" I asked, choking back another sob. Luke smiled that unbelievably handsome smile that said he was proud of me, although he had no reason to be.

"Because it means you care."

Chapter 14

Dallas

I stood in the bathroom, practicing my happy face, which I would have to force on once we joined the others for breakfast. I wanted to stay home and shield myself from the disapproving eyes of Ronnie, and the rest of the club. I didn't mind if the ladies found my actions wrongful, it was the brothers that I didn't want to hate me. Why? I had no idea. Luke said it was because I cared, which I did, but proving myself to them was going to be hard. How would I ever convince them that I could act like a good sister and be someone they could confide in and depend on? The women knew what I was going through because they were, well, they were women. We all had that ugly bitch lurking inside us somewhere, and she often reared her repulsive face at the most unwelcome and awkward moments; usually when we were surrounded by people to whom we were trying hard to prove our loyalty.

"Ready, babe?" Luke asked, peeking round the bathroom door.

"I don't want them to hate me." I pouted, looking at my reflection in the mirror. I might have looked like a biker chick in my black long-sleeved shirt, studded belt, tight jeans, and wedged, thigh-high riding boots, but I damned sure didn't act like one.

"They don't hate you, babe. We have all let one another down at some point. Look on the bright side," I eyed him incredulously, biting my tongue to keep from asking what the fuck was bright about any side of this scenario. "You could have refused to back down and forced Chi Chi to settle your problems right there and then, but whatever she said to you convinced you that it was best to leave things as they were. No one is going to hold it against you. Stop beating yourself up." I sighed in frustration at Luke's obvious lack of knowledge. "I know, my words don't help, but you will get over it babe, and so will they." Okay, so maybe Luke did have knowledge, but it still didn't help with my frustration. Panic filled me as I remembered something much more important than the club hating me.

"I forgot my cut," I whispered to Luke, my eyes the size of saucers, as I started to lose my self-control. How could I be so stupid to forget it? My first ride would be without the weight of my leather, and I might as well have been naked.

"Babe," Luke said calmly, but I didn't have time for calm.

"What am I going to do? They're going to think I'm an idiot."

"Babe,"

"I don't want to go. Tell them I'm sick." I couldn't go out with all of them. No fucking way. I would just change clothes and take my car. No one would expect me to wear a black leather vest with my blue sundress with the brown, braided, leather belt. That would be like a slap in the face to Dolce and Gabbana.

"Babe," Luke said, a little louder this time, pushing his way into my thoughts.

"What?" I snapped, wanting to scream bloody murder until his smirk disappeared. I was at my wits end, and was just fixing to open my mouth to release a blood-curdling scream, when he dangled my cut in front of my face, waving it from side to side on the tip of his finger. Relief flooded me, and I almost hit my knees. "Oh thank fuck, Luke." I said, eyeing the beautiful patches that covered the back.

"Don't thank fuck, whoever the hell that is. Thank Luke. I'm the one who brought it for you." I kissed Luke's smirking face and pulled back, rewarding him with a smile reserved for his eyes only. "There's my girl." His girl. That would never get old. "Okay, let's go," he said, hurrying me, as I grabbed my black leather, cross-body Balenciaga bag. Here goes nothing.

We entered the bar area of the clubhouse to find everyone waiting for us. Just fucking great. I expected an eye roll, and a sigh from each one of them, but they greeted us, everyone hugging Luke good morning, while the ones I had not seen hugged me. Big Al walked up, punching the air before he hugged me, earning him a humorless look from me that just made him laugh harder.

"I'm gonna nick-name you Tyson." He said, oblivious to Chi Chi and Shark, who stood within hearing range of him. Hell, maybe he *was* aware of them, and just didn't give a shit.

"You are a little small to have a nickname like Tyson," came a deep voice from beside me. I looked up... and up some more to find the face of a man I recognized as Brayson, or Brad, or something like that. I gave him an apologetic look, and he smiled in return. "Devil's

Renegades Sergeant At Arms, Bryce. Good to see you again, Dallas."

"Bryce. Right. Sorry, I'm terrible with names. It's very good to see you too." Bryce was a monster in size, with fingers so huge there was no way he could pick his nose. He looked so much like the wrestler The Big Show that he could easily have been his twin brother. Where Shark was the Sergeant At Arms that screamed 'killer,' Bryce was the one that whispered 'peace.' Luke had informed me that the Sergeant At Arms was in charge of the club's security and the protection of the president, and Brooklyn had told me that although one would think a Sergeant At Arms was supposed to just kick ass first and take names later, he actually needed to be level-headed, and must avoid confrontation at all costs, yet be prepared to meet confrontation head-on with an iron fist if need be. My guess was that Bryce was the peacekeeper who tried to reason with people, and Shark was the one they called when reasoning was no longer an option, not that Bryce looked like he needed any kind of reinforcements. I was sure he could take on the whole city of Lake Charles without breaking a sweat.

"Y'all ready?" Ronnie asked, his voice rising over everyone else's.

"Yes!" Red agreed in excitement, causing Ronnie to laugh that breathy laugh I loved. Well, used to love. Now it pained me that it wasn't me who would be making him laugh anytime soon.

"I got some sausage for you, baby, if you that hungry." Regg said with a smile, and when my eyes found his face, it was looking at mine. "Hey, darlin'," he said, his thick country accent pouring out like warm honey. Well, at least Regg still loved me. "Don't hit me," he added, pulling his hands back when he got close.

"Ha ha ha." I said, narrowing my eyes at him, but unable to hide my smile. Big Al must have thought that was the funniest shit ever, since he was doubled over in laughter. I'm glad at least someone was finding humor in my turmoil. Regg hugged me hard, then wrapped his arm around my shoulder, as he led us out the door and to the bikes.

"Ain't nobody tried to kill you lately? Well, other than Chi Chi," he added with a laugh. I ignored his last remark.

"No. Not lately."

"Well, shit." I slapped his arm playfully. "What? There ain't ever a dull moment around you." I rolled my eyes at him, but what he said held so much truth that I actually felt guilty. He felt my tension and squeezed me tighter. "Just kiddin', babe."

"You sure are a funny fucker today." Luke said, coming up behind us. Regg winked at me, but didn't say anything, as he walked off toward his bike to join Red. I followed Luke to his bike, taking my helmet from his hand and putting it on, waiting for him to mount. I looked down at the perfect line of bikes that were in order of officer positions. It started with Ronnie and Brooklyn, then Luke and myself, Possum and Punkin, Big Al and Mary, Bryce, Shark and Chi Chi, Regg and Red, Kyle and Katina, Marty and Maddie, and finally Chris. My eyes swung back to Marty and Maddie, who nobody seemed to notice were riding together, other than me. Everyone wore full-face helmets and drove black bikes. I wasn't sure if that was mandatory, or just the way it had happened to play out. Luke patted my leg, letting me know he was ready for me to get on, and I stepped on the foot peg with my left foot, and slung my right leg around the back of the bike. I was getting pretty good at this. The bikes were cranked in the same order they were parked, starting with Ronnie. No one turned their bike over until the one to their left did first. We pulled out onto the busy side street, the pack riding so close that traffic was forced to stop to let everyone out. I held on tight as we rocketed down the road, surpassing the speed limit before shifting out of third gear. Cars seemed to move out of the way when they saw us coming. When we passed a business or a residence where people were outside, they stopped and watched until we were out of sight. I felt superior, important, and intimidating as we flew through lights; although they changed in the middle of the pack, everyone surged forward. We stopped at a busy intersection that was a four-way stop sign, forcing us to remain patient as the cars slowly moved in front of us. Luke adjusted the volume on the radio, that sat inside the big, black fairing on the front of the bike, allowing Bon Jovi's 'Wanted, Dead or Alive' to rattle the windows on the car in front of us. How fitting that this song was playing. I caught a motion out of the corner of Luke's rearview mirror and found Red flailing her arms around like she was flying. I tapped Luke's shoulder and pointed, and he just shook his head as his abs flexed under my hands, letting me know he was laughing. I looked over at Brooklyn to find her studying her fingernails, and Ronnie bobbing his head in rhythm with the music. My grip tightened as we made it to the stop sign, and before Luke could put his feet down, we were off again. Ronnie led us up a steep hill to a restaurant that served breakfast twenty-four hours. Once the bikes were parked, everyone who smoked pulled out a cigarette and lit up, while we talked about the ride. I watched as all the women, except Mary, gathered together, while the guys did the same. Mary was wiping down the bike with a towel, and I started to ask if I should do the same when Red chimed in.

"She does that shit. Now, we will all have to hear the guys bitch about how we should be a little more like Mary." I watched as Mary flipped her the finger, as she continued to remove any dust from the bike.

"What were you doing flailing your arms around?" I asked Red, trying to smooth my hair down and get rid of my terrible case of helmet-head. The humidity made it impossible to make it even resemble something presentable, but all the women seemed to have the same problem.

"She does that shit," Mary said, walking up, and throwing Red's words back at her. "She's always singing and dancing, acting like some crazed idiot." This time it was Red's turn to flip the finger, as everyone started to slowly make their way inside. The restaurant housed booths large enough to sit four. Brooklyn, Red, Maddie, and myself sat in one, while Mary, Katina, Chi Chi, and Punkin sat in the other. A waitress approached, passing us to go to the guys. Luke sat on the outside of the booth, making him her target. When he flashed her his million-dollar smile, she all but melted into a pile of mush on the floor. She wore her hair in dreads, her nails long, her skin tanned, and her tits falling out the top of her shirt. Red started to strike up conversation, not realizing what was going on because her back was to them.

"Shh!" I said, in a whisper, grabbing her hand to halt her speech. Her eyes followed mine, as did the other ladies', as we all sat and watched the scene unfold.

"Hey handsome," the waitress said, dragging her long fingernail down Luke's arm. I felt my whole body still. I didn't know this woman. She didn't know me. She might think he was single. I didn't care. I wanted to rip her fucking finger off, and throw it in the deep fryer.

"Hello, Renee. It's a pleasure to see you, as always." Renee? Always? A pleasure? He knew her? I felt a hand on my shoulder, and turned to see Punkin poking her head between me and Maddie.

"You want me to shank her? I can kill that bitch with this spoon, and she won't ever know what hit her," she said, loud enough for the guys in front of us to hear, prompting them to burst out in fit of laughs disguised as coughs. I didn't acknowledge Punkin, but seriously considered her offer when I watched Renee run her hands through Luke's hair.

"It was a pleasure, wasn't it?" I started to get up when Brooklyn spoke.

"Yo, bitch. We would like some service if you are through fucking with my sister's ol' man. Can't you see the bitch has a property patch? Do you not see that big fuckin' LLC on the front of her vest?" I could have kissed Brooklyn for this. At the sound of her voice, the waitress dropped her hand from Luke, but the smile remained, as she leaned down on the table, taking their order. Regg seemed to be

214

loving the voluptuous breasts that all but fell in his lap, but Red didn't seem to care. She looked up to see me watching her, and gave me a quizzical look.

"What? That bitch's balls ain't big enough to touch my ol' man. If she wants to pour those fake-ass titties out for him to look at that's fine, but if she lays a hand on him I'll cut that bitch up in her own restaurant and place her in her own fuckin' cooler, and burn this motherfucker down with her in it." I sat in shock at Red's outburst, which was loud enough for everyone, including Renee, to hear.

"Shut up, Red," I heard Regg say, from two tables down.

"I got my point across, though." Red said, her voice lower this time, but loud enough so that Regg heard once again. Damn, he had some good ears.

"Last warning. Shut your fucking mouth." I had never heard Regg take that tone with anyone, and, as if he had slapped her mouth shut, Red's lips closed immediately, as she scanned the menu. When Renee finally made it to our table, her enthusiasm was less than barely there, it was non-existent.

"Ladies," she greeted us, shortly. "What can I get you all to drink?" We all ordered something different, not purposefully, but I was glad we were making her job a little harder. I watched her scurry off, giving our ticket to a young girl who looked scared to death, before heading to the back.

"So she owns this place?" I asked, remembering Red's rant.

"Yeah, but when the guys come in here she always waits on them. Especially if Luke is around," Maddie said, as I felt a commotion under the table. Someone had kicked her for opening her mouth.

"Oh, really? Do her and Luke have a history?" I attempted nonchalance, but nothing got past these women.

"Dallas, do you really want to know?" Brooklyn asked, giving me that face that said I didn't.

"Yes, I want to know. Luke knows everything about me, so why can't I know about him? I'm not gonna hold it against him. It was in the past." The chatter among the guys had picked up and everyone, other than the four at our table, was unaware of our conversation.

"Sometimes she comes to the clubhouse for entertainment," Brooklyn said shortly, hoping that would be enough to appease me. It wasn't.

"What do you mean entertainment?" I asked, wondering if she was a stripper or a dancer.

"She's a dick-sucker. A pass-around. A clubhouse whore who tends to the single guys while they are away from their current pussy project." Well, I definitely wasn't expecting that, and my face showed it.

"Hey, you said you wanted to know. Now you do. Be careful what you ask for. If you're asking me, you're gonna get that shit straight. I tried to dissuade you, but you just had to know." Brooklyn was right, as always, and from now on, I would keep my mouth closed, and my inquiring mind quiet when she warned me to.

216

"What's a current pussy project?" Maddie asked, entering the conversation, and steering it away from Luke and Renee."

"You know, when they don't have a girlfriend or an ol' lady. Instead they have a go-to girl. A booty call." Brooklyn explained. Luke had a pussy project? Was she from Hattiesburg? Did I know her?

"Stop it," Red said, snapping her fingers in my face. "You're going to drive yourself crazy with this shit. He's a man. He was a single man for a very long time. He fucked people. Get over it."

"This is true, Dallas. If it makes you feel better, you were fucking people too. Hell you were looking for a one-night stand when you found Luke." Maddie said, never looking up from her phone. Out of sheer curiosity, I looked over to see Marty's head down too, and he was also looking at his phone.

"Maddie, do you always ride with Marty when they go places?" I asked, finding an opportunity for privacy, while Red and Brooklyn were engaged in a conversation of their own.

"Yeah. Even when he was prospecting and we were going somewhere local, Luke would let me tag along with him."

"Don't you think that shows that he trusts him?"

"Of course he trusts him. If he didn't, he wouldn't have let him patch out."

"Patch out?"

"Get a full cut. Become a patch-holder. We call it patching out."

"Oh, well have you had a chance to spend some time with Marty since you have been here?" Marty had not been around until this morning, and even then, we had been too busy for me to say hello. If I didn't know any better, I would think he'd been avoiding me.

"Why do you think I was late this morning?" She gave me a wicked smile and I laughed, just as the waitress returned with all of our drinks.

"It's okay, honey. We don't bite. We just don't like your bitch of a boss," Red whispered to her. She let out a nervous laugh, fumbling for her guest-check pad in her apron.

"How will the tickets be divided?" She asked, struggling to remove the cap off of her pen. Were we that intimidating? Or had she been witness to Red's death threat to her boss?

"All on one," I said, without hesitation. "But don't tell the guys that right now. Just say that we told you how to divide them." She nodded in agreement and I ordered, ignoring the stares from the women at my table. When she left to wait on the others, I could no longer avoid them. "I fucked up this morning. I let my temper and my jealousy get the better of me and took it out on a patch-holder's wife. The least I can do is buy all of you breakfast for putting up with that shit first thing this morning." This seemed to mollify them, and the stares disappeared. We ate our breakfast with no more drama, bullshit, or Renee. It was the first time I had been out with all of them that things had gone so smoothly. Other than the shit that had happened when we first got here, it was perfect. When the waitress brought the check, she practically dropped it and ran. We laughed at her retreating back, knowing that she was afraid of the outcome once the guys realized I had paid.

"Be sure to leave a good tip," Brooklyn said, as I pulled my credit card from my wallet. I motioned for the waitress, and she looked as if she was going to pass out.

"I always tip good, but why do you say that? She did a good job, but she wasn't outstanding. Hell, she was practically scared of the guys," I responded, finishing in just enough time for her to retrieve the check and card, and leave again.

"That's why," Brooklyn said, pointing to the frightened waitress. "Any time you are in a town that one of your brothers lives in, always tip good so that if your brother was to have a meal there, he will get good service. She might be scared now, but if you leave her a fat enough tip, she will gladly wait on them again, and soon she will realize that they aren't gonna rape or kill her. Then she tells her friends how these guys aren't so bad and society has a chance to form an opinion of them based on experiences, not on what T.V. and other media say about them." I had just been taught one of my most valuable lessons. I could never imagine one of my brothers being mistreated in a restaurant, just because they wore a cut and rode a Harley. When the waitress returned, I thanked her for her services, with a smile. Paying the two hundred dollar bill for my family to eat was easy. Leaving a two thousand dollar tip was even easier.

"Thank you, Dallas. That was great." Marty said, coming up to hug me and giving me a kiss on the cheek. "Sorry I haven't had time to say hey. I was busy last night and running late this morning." I didn't lead him on to think I knew anything, I just smiled, and brushed it off with a wave of my hand.

"Not a problem. I was really tired by the time we got there," I said, pulling my sunglasses over my eyes. Luke walked up, pulling me into his side, and kissed the top of my head.

"Thank you, babe. It was great. Sorry about that shit." I had forgotten until he brought it up. Great job, Luke. I kept my mouth shut, in fear that if I opened it, I would cause more problems. I didn't need that today.

"Well baby, you definitely know the way to a man's heart," Ronnie said, giving me his grin, and letting me know all the transgressions I had committed earlier were now forgiven. "I love you, baby. I'd do anything for you, just like I would for any of the others." I found my face buried in his chest, as he held me close and kissed my hair. I inhaled the scent of him; that delicious leather mixed with cigarette smoke.

"I love you too," I mumbled into his cut, hiding my smile. When he released me, I wanted to jump up and fist-punch the air, but thought better of it. Shark had not spoken to me, and neither had Chi Chi, but no one else seemed angry or disappointed in me anymore. Two out of seventeen wasn't very bad odds.

Chapter 15

Dallas

The rest of the day went better than I could have ever expected. Luke and I spent the majority of our time lounging around in our room. We watched a movie, took a nap, and just enjoyed our time alone with one another. Later that evening, as the sky had just began to darken, Luke's phone notified him of a message. Without leaving the bed to retrieve it, he looked at me with regret, obviously knowing what it already said.

"I gotta go, babe. We are gonna hit a few bars around town, and see if we run into these guys."

"What are you going to do if you see them?" I asked, snuggling closer into his side.

"We're going to talk," he said slowly, as if he was developing the lie as he spoke.

"Talk?" I gave him that incredulous look that said I didn't believe a word he said.

"Yes. We're hoping that will resolve the issue."

"You're hoping, but you doubt it will." He smiled at my uncanny ability to see through his words.

"You've been hanging around the ladies too long. You observe and over analyze too much." His smile faded to a look of defeat. I watched as the sorrow showed in his eyes. "I wish it was that simple," he said, running his finger across my lip. "I just don't understand why we have to go to great lengths against people of our own kind to get our point across."

"Your own kind?" I thought they hated these guys. I had been told more than once that Metal and Madness were nothing like the Devil's Renegades.

"Usually, we're fighting against society for our right to wear our cut. Now, we're fighting against a brotherhood. These are a group of guys who ride Harleys like us, are a fellowship like us, and have a relationship like us. They are going about it the wrong way, but in the grand scheme of things, they are bikers too." I climbed on top of him, straddling his waist as he lay under me on his back, running his hands up and down my thighs. I was wearing his t-shirt and nothing else, and by the feeling of his hardness between my legs, he liked me that way.

"Well, you try to talk to them. Do your best to make them see things from your point of view. If it doesn't work out, or if it creates a war, at least you tried. Don't be so hard on yourself, LLC. You're a great leader, a great brother and you're good with people. You will find a way to make this work so that it benefits you both." I was proud of my pep talk, although I was sure it wouldn't do much good.

"Thanks, babe. Now, get your fine ass off my cock before I fuck you and make everyone late." He grabbed my hips and threw me off him, not giving me the chance to remove myself. I landed on my back with a bounce, and before my back was back on the mattress, he was between my legs and moving the hair out of my face. "Kiss me," he whispered, his eyes lingering on my lips. I pulled his head to mine, my fingers tightening around his short locks and slid my tongue through his full, smooth lips. He thrusts his hips into me, the hardness of his cock pushing through his thin shorts and against my hot center that was wet and ready for him. All too soon, he pulled away, leaving me lying in a breathless heap, full of need and want.

"Just a quickie," I suggested, closing my legs trying to find a hint of a release.

"No such thing with you, babe. If I get started I won't want to stop. Here's an idea, play with yourself while I get dressed." I gasped at him in astonishment at his absurd request.

"I most definitely will not," that is, not until you leave. Masturbation was something I was perfect at, but I preferred to do it alone, and in the dark, without him watching me.

"Come on, babe. You know you want to," he said with a smirk, as he removed his shorts and left me with an eyeful of him in a pair of tight, grey boxer briefs. How did he keep them from cutting off circulation to that huge dick he housed in there? "Please?" he begged with an exaggerated pout, sticking his lip out.

"No." I said firmly, wishing he would hurry up and leave so I could get to business, or stay and finish the business himself. He walked back to the bed, kneeling before me as he pulled my knees apart, running his finger between my lips and to my entrance, then repeating the motion. My eyes rolled back in my head and my back arched involuntarily at the feel of his touch. He slid his long, middle finger inside me, treating me to a delicious fingering as my hands grabbed the hem of my shirt and pulled it up, revealing my breasts. I covered them with my hands, giving them a light squeeze before I pinched my nipples, arching my back again, as the sensation of what I was doing to myself and what he was doing to me took over my body's movements. He grabbed my right hand, pulling it down to place it on to my pussy. I instinctively found the small nub that was throbbing in anticipation of my touch. I moved my fingers in a circular motion, applying just the right amount of pressure in just the right spot to bring me to that orgasm I longed for. I felt Luke shift as his finger was pulled from inside me, but was too deep in the moment to care, as his words caressed me just as his finger had.

"That's right baby. Play with that sweet pussy for me. I love watching you like this, pleasuring yourself. Just like me, you know just the right places to touch to send you over the edge. When I get home tonight, I am going to fuck you again, and again, and again. I'm going to start from your toes, and lick all the way up to your neck, stopping at your sweet pussy so I can get it wet and ready for my big cock-" I cut off his speech with my moans, as I let his words and my fingers bring me to that seventh heaven I refer to as orgasm central. That beautiful place that washes all sense of reality from your mind as it is replaced with a mind-blowing sensation that is the best ten seconds of your day. My body relaxed, sinking further into the mattress as I came back to reality from my orgasmic state of "I don't give a fuck." When my eyes fluttered open with a smile, I found a fully dressed Luke, standing before me, smirking in victory.

"You're an ass." I muttered through my smile, pulling my shirt down and crossing my legs.

"I am a very happy ass who will be readjusting his cock all night when he thinks of the last time he saw you." He leaned down and kissed me sweetly, rubbing his thumb over my jaw as his hand held my neck. "I love you, babe. See you when I get back."

"I love you, too. Be careful." He gave me that stomach-flipping smile, and I gave my vagina a mental high five for turning our nervous, sorrowful Luke into a relaxed and happy one. He left and I lay in bed, waiting for the sound of his bike. When it came, along with so many others, I got up and put on some presentable clothes to go see what my crazy sisters had in store for tonight.

"It's poker time. You in?" Red asked, as soon as I walked into the main room. I laughed at the green visor she wore in an attempt to look like a dealer from the 19th century. A round table was set up in the middle of the room with nine chairs gathered around it. Ashtrays, poker chips and beer bottles littered the table, at which Red, Chi Chi, and Katina were already seated. I saw Punkin and Mary dragging an ice chest toward us, while Brooklyn lined the bar with junk food and Maddie pulled a trash can next to Red. Katelan was behind the bar assisting Brooklyn, looking as nervous and out of place as always. God bless her, but I would heed Mary's advice and let her come to me first. I didn't want the girls jumping down her throat for not addressing me properly. "Dallas." Red said, snapping her fingers in the air to get my attention. Geeze. Her voice was enough. Red had the ability to get everyone's attention with that big mouth of hers.

"Yes, Red. I'm in."

"Good. It's a twenty dollar buy-in, with the option to buy-in again as many times as you want. House rules, which are slightly different. You can find them behind the bar. No big blind, little blind, no max on the raise and a dollar ante. Three-card poker and you match the pot if you lose. If everyone folds, the dealer takes the pot. The pot can get big, so if you don't have enough cash we do accept payment in the form of jewelry, and there is an ATM beside the bar." I swung my head toward the bar in disbelief. Who the hell let them put an ATM in the clubhouse? I stared at the lighted machine, pointing my finger at it, and giving Red a disbelieving look.

"They have an ATM?" I asked, as if I still needed confirmation that it was really sitting there.

"So it seems," Red said slowly, looking at me like I was stupid.

"I mean I know it's there, but how in the hell did they get an ATM?"

"We stole it," Chi Chi said, her face straight, and her tone serious.

"Oh," I muttered, unsure of what to say to that.

"We didn't steal it," Mary said, slapping Chi Chi on the arm. Chi Chi's smug smile lit up her face, as she put her lips to her beer to control her laughter. "This is a legit business. It's a pool hall for members only. As you can see," Mary said, gesturing with her hands around the room. "We are the only members." Now that made a little more sense.

"Y'all come on." Red called impatiently. I ran to my room, digging my wallet out of my purse, and grabbing a couple of twenties. I wouldn't need any more than that. I heard a light knock on the door and found Katelan standing there, blushing as if she had just seen me naked.

"Sorry to bother you. I wanted to introduce myself properly." I smiled at her as I motioned for her to come in, while I shoved my wallet back in my purse and threw it on the dresser. She stuck her shaking hand out to mine, and I took it, finding her hand clammy and warm from nerves. "Devil's Renegades Prospect Chris' wife, Katelan, Lake Charles chapter."

"Say that five times fast." I said with a wink, which made her relax a little. As I started to say my name, I froze. I had never introduced myself before. The lost look on my face made her smile as she, the wife of a PROSPECT, helped me, the ol' lady to a president, introduce myself.

"Property of Devil's Renegades President, LLC, Hattiesburg chapter." She said with a whisper.

"Right. I don't say my name?" I asked confused.

"It depends on how cordial you want to be. Like, I am a potential sister, so I am assuming I am not a threat to you, and since we are going to be getting closer over the next year, you would probably want to tell me your name. I say over the next year; that's if he makes it." She didn't sound as if she doubted his ability to make it, just informing me that she wasn't assuming he would. I liked that. This girl knew her shit.

"Okay, so hi, I'm Dallas, property of Devil's Renegades President, LLC, Hattiesburg chapter." I bit my

227

lip and held my breath awaiting her confirmation. She smiled and made a slight bow.

"Nice to meet you, Dallas." We laughed together, and I knew Katelan and I were going to get along just fine.

"I have another question," I said, still holding her hand in mine. "Why didn't you introduce yourself as property?"

"Because I'm not property. I'm Chris' wife. He is a not a patch-holder, so therefore he can't have any property in the club. I won't get a patch, or any kind of recognition as part of the club, until my husband becomes an official member. Then he will have the option to make me his property."

"Which he will," I clarified, although she didn't seem to need confirmation.

"First, we have to get him patched in," she said, in a rush of breath. Her husband's prospecting period was taking its toll on her, too.

"He will be fine. You playing poker?" I asked, finally releasing her hand, so I could put my hair up.

"No. I'm just gonna watch," she said, watching me as I piled my hair on my head.

"You should play. It will be fun." I wanted to encourage her to participate and be a part of the group. What I would have given to have that year to bond with the club, instead of just being thrown in and given a title.

"I can't. But I don't mind. I'll be y'all's errand girl." She smiled at me, reassuring me with her eyes, and I heard her silent plea to just let it go. I wondered why she didn't want to play. She never said she didn't know how, just that she couldn't.

"Hey, ya coming?" Maddie asked, barging into my room and going straight to the bathroom.

"Yeah, I just need a mirror." I followed Maddie into the bathroom, leaving Katelan, who busied herself with making my bed. I started to tell her to stop, but she seemed to need to do something to make her feel worthwhile. "Reckon something is wrong with Katelan?" I whispered to Maddie, as I fixed my hair in the mirror.

"What do you mean?" she asked, unconcerned.

"Well, I asked her if she was going to play poker and she said "I can't." Not like she didn't know how, but like maybe someone didn't want her to."

"It's probably the money, Dallas. Hell, prospecting is expensive. You're always on the go, and most of your free time is spent with the club. Between work, a mortgage, a car note and all that other shit you have to pay for to live in this world, I'm sure money is tight." Maddie joined me in the mirror, as she attempted to fix her own hair, which looked just as messy as mine.

"Yeah, but it's only twenty dollars," I said, finding Maddie's excuse for Katelan's behavior a very poor one.

"To you, Dallas. To most people that's groceries or a half tank of gas. Not everyone was born a millionaire."

"But the club has money," I argued, letting Maddie's comment about my financial upbringing go in one ear and out the other.

"The *club*. He isn't a member of the club. He is *prospecting*. If a brother falls on hard times, the club helps him out. If a PROSPECT falls on hard times, he's shit out of luck. If he didn't have his finances in order then he shouldn't have joined. I'm not saying they are poor or broke, I'm just saying that times are hard right now. I overheard Brooklyn say that they just bought a two hundred dollar tire. Again, that ain't a lot to you, but when you makin' three fifty a week, that can put a hurtin' on ya." I'd never had money issues, so they were something very foreign to me. I'd dealt with people who worked for me and had asked for advances, and I'd never really had any compassion for them. Now that I saw the sacrifices Chris and Katelan were making on the club's behalf, it made me more aware of how serious the issue could be. I knew that in the end, they would get much more in return and it would be worth the struggle, but it never occurred to me how much prospecting affected the lives of the people involved. Sacrifice was one of the things PROSPECTs needed to help prove their loyalty. It would be much easier if there wasn't so much at stake, such as your family, your finances, and your life, therefore proving that this is something they must really want if they were willing to risk the things that held such high importance in the everyday life of everyday people. I wanted to help Katelan, but I didn't want to offend her, and I didn't want anyone to know what I was doing. I was sure Maddie would keep her mouth shut about our conversation. I would not make Katelan feel like a kept friend, but I didn't want her to miss out on this bonding opportunity either. Sure, she could visit from the sidelines, but if she participated, she would gain so much more. I found Katelan still tidying my room when I emerged from the bathroom.

"Katelan I really want you to play." She started to open her mouth, but I shut her up by continuing. "It's no secret that I come from money, but know that is not what this is. I'm not here to hurt your pride or make you feel like you owe me something, I'm offering my help because I wish someone had offered it to me." Her face became puzzled, as she tried to process what I said. I took a seat on the bed, patting the spot next to me, indicating that she should join me. She sat down, and I looked into her big, blue eyes as they appraised me with caution. "I didn't have the same opportunity you do. I was thrown into this life without the chance to get to know anyone. I felt like an outsider for the longest time, and I am just now finding my niche. As you can see, Chi Chi and I are still on the outs, and I haven't had the time to really connect with anyone other than Maddie, Red, and Brooklyn. Chris is making sacrifices, as are you, so that one day you will gain so much more than you have put in. But remember, you are forfeiting a lot too, and deserve to let your hair down every once in a while. If you don't connect with these women, his whole prospect period will be a waste. Trust me. You will find yourself hating the club and this life. You will start to see Chris in a different light as one of *them* instead of your husband. To be a part of this club, you have to participate with the club. And besides, you don't want to miss out on all the fun shit." She dropped her head and smiled, considering my words. Finally, she let out a long breath, and nodded.

"Okay, Dallas. I'll play." I wanted to hand her some money, but she stood, pulling a twenty from her pocket. "But I'm only buying in once."

"Deal. Oh, and Katelan," she stopped and turned, looking over her shoulder at me. I fidgeted with my hands, trying to muster up the courage to beg for her silence.

"Don't worry. I won't say anything. We have to look out for each other, right?" She gave me a wink, and I smiled gratefully. My embarrassing moment of not knowing how to introduce myself would remain a secret.

Chapter 16

Dallas

The game had started and Red dealt the cards like a pro, slinging them around the table, so that they landed perfectly in front of each of us. Even though she held the title as dealer and wore that hideous green visor, she dealt to herself and I, as well as everyone else, eyed her when she won the first nine dollar pot, as a result of a king high flush-one of the best hands you could get in three card poker.

"You're fucking cheatin'," Mary accused, matching the nine dollar pot along with Katina, Brooklyn, and myself.

"Well, I didn't have shit, so I don't care if you cheated or not." Punkin chimed in, throwing her cards on the table.

"I didn't cheat. It was just a lucky hand," Red said in defense, while piling up her nine dollar win. It wasn't the amount of money on the table, it was the title of poker queen that really mattered. I wanted to win.

"I say everyone deals their turn. Throw that little plastic dealer chip you got there in the trash and pass the cards to the person on your left." Brooklyn said, not accusing Red, but not happy about losing almost half her chips on the first hand. Everyone agreed, and Red passed the cards to Chi Chi, who sat on her left, with an eye-roll. The pot was now thirty-six dollars, and whoever lost would be going to the infamous ATM, or taking off some earrings; everyone except Red, of course. I was dealt a low straight and stayed. Everyone had folded except me, and now the decision was left up to the dealer. If Chi Chi folded, I would win, and everyone would ante up another dollar. If she stayed and lost, she would owe thirty-six dollars, as would I if it was me who lost. I kept my face blank, as Chi Chi stared at me from across the table. There was more to this particular stand-off, than there would have been to any other. One of us was going to lose and whoever that was, would rather lose to anyone at the table than to each other.

"I'm considering staying with cowboys, because there's not too much that can beat them." I knew what she was doing. First, she used slang terminology like "cowboys" instead of "kings" to see if she could throw me off, hoping that I didn't know what that meant. Second, she never mentioned they were a pair, so she was trying to convince me that she had three of a kind, which was the best hand you could get in our house rules of three-card poker. Third, she was trying to get a reaction out of me, which she didn't. According to the house rules, if you and the dealer are the only two who stay, you have the option of folding. Yeah, that wasn't gonna happen. I would lose to her before I folded.

"Three little ol' kings don't scare me. If that is in fact what you're holding. I'm in." Everyone was quiet as they waited for Chi Chi, who had yet to determine whether she was in or not. I just wanted to let her know that I wasn't going anywhere, no matter her decision.

"I never fold a winning hand." Chi Chi said, with a smirk, as she laid her cards down for me to see. I looked at her two, three, four off-suited hand, and couldn't help laughing.

"It's got to be divine intervention," I said, with a smile, as I laid out my two, three, four off-suit for everyone to see. Laughter filled the room as everyone bore witness to the two identical hands that fate had dealt us.

"Fair enough, Dallas. Fair enough," Chi Chi said, dividing the chips, and pushing mine to me with a nod of truce, and for the first time, I finally saw a glimmer of light at the end of our friendship tunnel.

It was after midnight, everyone was drunk, and we were all half-naked. After finding the ATM machine empty, and realizing that none of us wore any jewelry, we had succumbed to gambling with our clothes. Many of us had bought in twice, and a couple three times, bringing the chip total to almost three hundred and sixty dollars. Everyone was out except me, Chi Chi, and Katelan. All of my chips were on the table, along with Luke's black Nike shirt and my favorite Victoria's Secret silk pajama pants, leaving me in my bra and panties, which had gained compliments from everyone-including Chi Chi. Katelan was the chip leader, leaving her with only her shirt left to remove, which read "Support Your Local Devil's Renegades", making it a pretty valuable bargaining item. Chi-Chi sat in nothing but panties, giving up her the rest of her chips, along with a pair of flannel pajama pants, a white t-shirt and her "favorite motherfucking bra", or so she claimed. Now we were all subject to her firm breasts, which she didn't even try to hide. I shuffled my cards in my hand, looking around the table as I did. Not a soul, other than Katelan, wore a shirt. Mary had even lost her underwear, which was now hanging from the light over the table, a donation from Brooklyn for all to see. Mary had expressed how happy she was that at least they were cute, and we had all agreed. Katina had passed out, in the chair, lucky enough to still have her pants, but I was now the proud owner of her shirt. Punkin sat with her arms across her chest as if she were cold, but refused to be a 'pussy' and put her shirt back on. That gained her a cheer of laughter, and a shot of tequila, which led to all of us taking shots, hence the drunkenness. Red, like Katina, had only lost her shirt, which was now tied around Punkin's head. She said it was to keep her ears warm, but we knew it was a show of victory. Maddie and Brooklyn were both out of the game, but both had been wearing pants, until Brooklyn took hers off for a side bet that Maddie's final hand would win. When Maddie had lost, Brooklyn had demanded that she remove her pants too, due to the fact that she had a shitty hand and had led her on to believe it was actually a flush, when in reality there was a diamond fucking up the heart trio. Now they waited in bras and panties in anticipation of how the game would end. Katelan was the dealer, and had agreed to stay. Since two of us had stayed with the dealer, we were not given the option of folding.

"Well, ladies. What's it gonna be?" Katelan asked, slurring, oblivious to the house rules. She had never been in a situation in which she had to be reminded of them. Chi Chi looked across the table at me, with inquiring eyes. She had been in Katelan's shoes at one time too. She knew the struggles and hardships that came with prospecting, and I knew that she had a plan once she knew Katelan wasn't aware that we were not allowed to fold. I held an ace high flush in my hand. By the way Chi Chi had been playing cards all night, I knew she had to have something similar to be so confident in such a large wager. Katelan,

236

on the other hand, was completely unpredictable. She would stay on a pair of twos or a straight flush, no matter the cost. If she had a pair or better, she was playing. So far, she had gotten lucky, and it wasn't because we were cutting her any slack. I wanted Katelan to play, so she could socialize and interact, but I wanted to walk away the winner, as did Chi Chi. But this was an opportunity for me to not only help Katelan financially, but also to give her the spotlight, even if it was for just one night. My pride would suffer, but I was beginning to care less about my pride, and more about the people I liked, and she fell into that category.

"Katelan," I said, turning my eyes from Chi Chi's to Katelan's, which were glassed over in her alcohol-induced state. "There ain't no fucking telling what you have in your hand, and I would rather fold than lose to you. I'm gonna let you and tits over here battle it out." I threw my hand down, making sure they were lost in the discarded pile, and grabbed my beer, downing the last swallow.

"There's one down. Chi Chi, you gonna stay or you gonna fold? It's up to you." Brooklyn said, lighting a cigarette and leaning up, putting her arms on the table.

"I want to stay, but," she said quickly, leaning up and glaring at Katelan. "I'm like Dallas, but I'm not gonna be so nice about it. I ain't gonna lose to no PROSPECT's wife and have to walk out of here without my balls. I would rather fucking fold." Chi Chi threw her hand down, and sat back with her arms crossed.

"Well, all I got to say is that this PROPSPECT'S wife is the proud owner of your favorite mother-effin bra." Katelan threw her hands up in a happy dance, giving

237

Brooklyn a high five, and soon she was joining Katelan in her celebration dance, while the rest of us wondered if Katelan had really just said 'mother-effin.'

"So, what did you have?" Maddie asked, walking up behind Katelan and giving her a congratulatory kiss.

"Not shit. I bluffed 'em with an Ace high!" Katelan squealed, still dancing in her seat.

"Well ain't you happier than a pig in shit. Hell, I could have beat that and I wasn't even playin'," Punkin added, passing out beer to everyone at the table.

"I'm proud of you," Brooklyn said in my ear, coming up behind me and wrapping her arms around my neck. I arched my head so she could see my questioning look. "Maddie told us she explained to you about Katelan and why she was so hesitant to play." I had never been so happy that Maddie had opened her mouth.

"Thanks Brooklyn. That means a lot coming from you." Chi Chi came to sit beside me, and nudged her shoulder with mine.

"I had an ace high flush," she said, with a smile. I grinned at her.

"So did I." She threw her head back and laughed. "You know," she said, gaining her composure, and turning serious, "Shark and I had it rough when he prospected. It nearly ripped us apart because I refused to give these girls a chance. I'm glad I did, and I'm glad you're here. Thank you for what you did for Katelan. I know it took a lot." I knew she was referring to my stubborn pride, and not the money and clothes that were on the table.

"Not as much as it once did," I said honestly, enjoying the feeling of elation that had overwhelmed me when I saw how happy Katelan had been to win.

"That's good, Dallas. That means this club actually means something to you."

"So I have been told," I responded, happy that Chi Chi and I were now working with a fully lit tunnel. In the words of Lindsey, our friendship flower was starting to bloom, but the light in our tunnel was busted and our friendship flower wilted, as the sounds of bikes approaching rang loudly in our ears.

"Oh, fuck." Punkin said, jumping from the chair and scrambling around for her shirt. We were all in a drunk, naked frenzy as we ran around the table trying to find clothes.

"Punkin, give me my fucking shirt!" Red yelled, chasing Punkin around the pool table.

"Not till you find mine!" she replied, holding Red's shirt securely on top of her head. I stopped my run to hold my side, which was in pain due to my laughter. Mary shook Katina, scaring the shit out of her, and causing her to flip over the poker table and scatter beer bottles everywhere, when she jumped up in a panic.

"Shit, fuck, dammit!" Maddie squealed with a laugh, as she jumped over the rolling bottles. As they rolled around the floor, I watched as Punkin stopped dead in her tracks, her look serious and almost angry.

"I just about pulled my fucking back out dragging that trash can over here and y'all didn't even use it," Punkin said, pointing to the empty trash can.

"Punkin, you carried the fucking cooler," Maddie informed her, as I hit my knees trying to see through my tears of laughter to gather the beer bottles.

"No shit? Well hell, y'all know I be forgetting," Punkin said, as she dropped to her knees with Red's shirt still securely wrapped around her head.

"What in the hell is goin' on?" Silence descended, as we all stopped and looked to Ronnie standing in the doorway. Here we were, half-naked, on our knees in a destroyed clubhouse, trying to clean up the havoc that we had wreaked. I was expecting Brooklyn to come to our defense and placate a very confused and amused Ronnie, but it was Punkin who spoke.

"I didn't do shit, Ronnie. It was all them."

We were ushered to bed, leaving the mess for poor Chris to clean up. Once Luke had me alone in the bedroom, I attempted a sexy strip tease that had him laughing and shaking his head.

"Are you gonna take advantage of me?" I slurred, hoping like hell that he would. Every drunk girl's fantasy was to be fucked senseless by a sexy biker until she feel into a restful sleep, as a result of her orgasmic oblivion.

"No, babe. Not tonight." Luke was lying in bed on his back, his arms behind his head, enjoying the show.

"What in the hell do you mean? You promised you were gonna fuck me like forty times." Luke laughed, patting my spot beside him in the bed, trying to encourage me to lie down. I collapsed next to him, completely naked as my head spun, and I laughed out loud, remembering the events of the night. "Ya know, Chi Chi ain't so bad once you get to know her."

"Is that so?" Luke asked, pulling me across his chest, so he could stroke my back.

"Mmm hmm," I said, my eyes fluttering closed as Luke rubbed me, the feel of his fingers rubbing circles on my back was so relaxing that I found myself drifting.

"I'm glad you had fun tonight. You still up for forty rounds of sex?" I ignored his comment, wishing I had the strength to tell him to fuck off. He took my silence as all the answer he needed. "That's what I thought."

Chapter 17

Dallas

"Dallas. Baby, wake up." I opened my eyes to hear Luke shuffling around the room. Why was he whispering? And why was he moving around the room in the dark? "Dallas, come on. Get up." Luke said, gently shaking me, as my eyes focused on him in the dark.

"What's going on?" I asked in a whisper, my voice still thick with sleep. Luke didn't answer me, just pulled me up and threw a t-shirt over my head in record time. I sat, while he pulled a pair of shorts up my legs, then grabbed my hand, dragging me through the door and down the hall. My feet moved fast, trying to keep up with him, while my mind was still trying to wake up. My mouth was dry, and my breath tasted horrible. "Luke," I started, as I stumbled over my feet.

"Shhh," he replied, grabbing my arm to hold me up when I almost fell. Why didn't he just carry me instead of dragging me behind him? He opened a door and pushed me in, turning me so I was facing him, although I couldn't see a damned thing. "Stay here. No matter what, you stay in here. I'll be back in a few." He let go of my arm and pulled the door closed behind him, leaving me alone in what? A closet? I heard a noise and saw a small flicker of light illuminate what I now knew was the bathroom located off the main room. Maddie and Red said next to one another, propped up against the bathroom stall looking just as shitty as I felt.

"What's going on?" I asked in a whisper, taking a seat between them. My brain had still not had time to panic or worry, it was still half asleep.

"Fuck, I don't know." Red said, not seeming to care too much. "My head is fucking hammering, and if someone is here to kill us, I hope they take me out first." I sobered a little at her comment.

"Kill us?" I asked, a little too loudly, earning myself another shhh from them both.

"No one is gonna kill us. It's just a precaution. There are two vans parked across the street, and someone triggered the silent alarm on the back gate," Maddie informed us. She lit a cigarette, blowing the smoke out in a long breath.

"How the hell do you know?" Red asked, her grumpy tone and nonchalance about the possible danger of the situation getting on my nerves.

"Unlike the two of you, I demand to know what is going on when I am dragged out of bed in the middle of the night." Well, at least one of us had enough sense to ask.

"Where is everyone else?" I asked, now noticing that the room should have been full. There were only three of us when there should have been nine.

"They went home. A lot of them have to work tomorrow. Only me, you, Red, Luke, Marty, and Regg are here. Everyone from out of town. I'm sure the other guys will be here soon." Just then, the door opened, startling all of us, even Red.

"It's just me, girls," Marty said, from the door. "Big Al, Shark, and Bryce are on their way, but until they get here and we know what's going on, y'all need to stay in here."

"Oh for fuck's sake Marty," Red said in a huff, wide awake now that she had had the shit scared out of her. "Can we please just go to bed?" I prayed that he said no. If this was the safest place to be, then this is where I wanted to stay.

"No, Red, and quit bitchin'. It's only for a little while."

"Thanks Marty," I said, giving Red a look, although she couldn't see it. "We'll be fine. Don't worry about us," Red huffed, but kept her mouth shut. Marty started to leave and I melted when Maddie spoke.

"Be careful," she said quickly. I knew she wanted to go to him but couldn't.

"I will, babe," he said, before leaving us alone once again.

"Well ain't y'all just sweet," Red said, and I started to slap the shit out of her, but Maddie had it covered.

"If you got something to say bitch just say it. If not, shut the fuck up. I hate when you get drunk and pissy. You're gettin' on my nerves with that shit," Maddie snapped, and I could feel the anger radiating off her and filling the room.

"I'm sorry. I'm just being a bitch 'cause my head hurts. It's like fucking pounding, man. I don't know what's wrong," Red said, her voice holding just a hint of apology.

"Well maybe you shouldn't have drunk so much," Maddie muttered, Red's apology not being accepted in the least. The door opened again, and our heads snapped up as a large dark figure approached us. I tensed, the feeling of dread pumping through my veins, as I opened my mouth to scream at the intruder.

"Here, baby." I recognized Regg's voice and nearly pissed my pants in relief.

"Fuck you scared me," I said, holding my chest and feeling my heart beat hard against it. Regg handed something to Red, who fumbled in the dark, thanking him in a rush of breath once she had it in her possession.

"I brought y'all a bottle of water." Regg said, handing me and Maddie bottles of water that we both greedily accepted.

"Can we turn the light on?" I asked, thinking how much easier it would be if we could see, and it would keep us from panicking when they barged in.

"Can't. The power is out." I looked up into the darkness, expecting him to answer my unspoken question, but then remembered he couldn't see me.

"Why?" I asked Regg, who stood looming over us.

"They must have shot out a transformer, 'cause the whole street is out of lights. Probably hoping it would kill the alarm, but the dumbasses must not be up-to-date on technology. Even the worst criminals know that alarms are backed up by a battery pack." Shooting out a transformer was a pretty extreme measure to take. They must have really wanted to get to us.

"Gotta go. Y'all good?" We assured him we were fine and he left, giving Red a quick kiss first.

"What did he bring you?" Maddie asked Red, after we had all consumed almost all of our water. Shit, I was thirsty.

"Headache meds," Red replied shortly, curling up, and using my leg as a pillow. I began rubbing her head, knowing that she must be in some sort of pain to be so indifferent about the situation, which was clearly a very serious one. Maddie leaned her head on my shoulder again, and I placed my head on top of hers. I wasn't worried about Luke, he could take care of himself, and I wasn't worried about the intruders because Marty and Regg didn't seem too bothered by them. I felt safe here. I knew these guys wouldn't let anything happen to us. Maddie and Red knew it too. How else could they sleep in a time like this? I closed my eyes, listening to Maddie and Red's relaxed breathing. Not only had I learned that I cared about the club, but, as I joined my sisters and fell into an unconscious state, I knew that I had now learned to trust them.

"Get a shovel and help me dig!" Red snapped, the long t-shirt she wore covered in mud. She was drenched in water, barefoot, and her hair was stuck to the side of her face and neck. I picked up the shovel without question,

digging into the soft ground in the middle of the woods, while the rain poured down on top of me. "You have to dig faster. We have to hide the body before the cops get here." I saw headlights in the distance, closing in on us slowly. I began digging faster, sticking the shovel in the dirt and throwing it over my shoulder. We were getting nowhere.

"We need some help!" I screamed at Red, panicking that we would be caught if we didn't hide the body that lay next to us wrapped in a white sheet. The headlights were closer now. They must have been driving through the woods. "Get Maddie!" I yelled, looking around, trying to find her. "Maddie!" I screamed, waiting for her to emerge from behind one of the tall trees that littered the woods.

"Maddie? She can't help us now," Red said, constantly shoveling dirt from the shallow grave we had dug. Was Maddie hurt? Was it so bad that she couldn't lift a shovel?

"Where is Maddie? What's wrong with her?" I asked, the car headlights that were once in the distance now upon us. Red stopped what she was doing, a look of devastation on her dirty, wet face.

"Whose grave do you think this is?"

My eyes flew open to find Luke squatting in front of me. His face looked concerned, as he wiped the sweat from my head and spoke softly to me. I looked around, searching for Maddie in my lethargic state. She, along with Red, Marty, Regg, Big Al, Bryce, and Shark stood behind Luke, eyeing me with concern. The lights were on and blinding as I sat on the floor, propped against the wall trying to calm my harsh breathing and my racing heart. I stared at them all, wide-eyed trying to wash the horrible image of Maddie wrapped in a white sheet from my mind.

"Luke, she needs a doctor," Red said, coming up behind Luke and placing her hand on his shoulder.

"Dallas," Luke said calmly, trying to claim my attention, which was now on Big Al's face. He looked at me with pity, and I wondered if Luke's brothers were aware of my nightmares.

"This is happening too much. Does she talk about it?" My eyes swung to Maddie, who stood chewing her lip next to Regg. Luke shook his head, and I realized that they must think I was still asleep.

"I can hear you," I said, my voice so low that I could barely hear it myself.

"What did she say?" A confused Shark asked Marty, who answered with a shake of his head and a shrug of his shoulders. Luke started to answer, but I beat him to it.

"I said," my voice a little louder and clearer this time, "I can hear you." No one said anything, just stood there still staring at me. Was there something wrong with me? Why were they acting as if they hadn't heard me? Or did they just not have anything to say? I looked at Luke, finding his blue eyes wide and full of agony. Maybe a change of subject was in order. "Did y'all find the guys?" Luke gave me a small smile, rubbing my hair, and placing his palm on my cheek.

"Everything is fine, babe. You don't need to worry about that right now. Let's take a walk, okay?" Luke pulled me to my feet, wrapping his arm around my waist.

Everyone stood around nervously, as if I might collapse to the floor at any moment. That's when I noticed I was not in the same place I had been when I fell asleep.

Luke

"How did I get here?" Dallas asked me, her pale face was twisted in confusion, as I led her away from the bar and outside to get some fresh air. Talk about a fucked-up morning.

"I carried you here from the bathroom. You started fighting me, so I sat you down. Your screams had everyone running to see what was wrong. Sorry about the audience, but they were worried." Marty and Regg knew Dallas suffered from night terrors, but it was something new for Shark, Big Al, and Bryce. It was a scary thing to witness that was for damned sure.

"Oh," Dallas replied simply, looking up at the sky, which was beginning to lighten. It was Monday morning and a hell of a start to the new week. My first thought was that Metal and Madness had taken a bold step and tried to break into the clubhouse. So, I was more than surprised to find Charlie's goons as the culprits. They had been sent to make sure Dallas was still here, and since Ronnie had taken Dallas' car to ensure a very drunk Brooklyn got home safe, they thought she might have left. He could have just fucking called, but Charlie had a way of doing things, like breaking into the clubhouse and blowing up fucking transformers, just to show me that he could. I walked with Dallas down the alley behind the clubhouse until we reached the gate, then turned and walked back toward the entrance to the main room. She looked calmer, but whatever dream she had had was still very clear in her mind. Her brows were furrowed, as she tried hard to shake the mental image, which I knew she couldn't clear from her head.

"Dallas, I need you to tell me about these dreams," I said, stopping her and pulling her face up, so I could look into her troubled eyes. Fuck, she was beautiful, even at her worst. She didn't want to tell me, but I needed to know. I needed to know that she could deal with this and get past it, because I had something I needed her to do. A mission that would require her to be mentally stable enough to perform. "Tell me, baby. Please." I asked her softly, reassuring her with a kiss. That worked.

"Red and I were in the woods and I was helping her dig a grave. When I asked where Maddie was, so that maybe she could help us, she said 'whose grave do you think this is?'" That was some serious shit. I rubbed her hair, pulling her into me and just holding her close. What the fuck was I supposed to say to that? My poor girl was suffering from nightmares because of the shit she had been through. Shit that I could have prevented and hadn't. I had demons of my own I was still having to deal with after her assault from Frankie and then his death. Not a day went by in which I didn't wish I could have done something different to prevent it from happening.

"Dallas, no one is gonna hurt Maddie. She's fine. And no one is gonna hurt you." They were shit words with a shit meaning that wasn't doing shit to make her feel better, but it was all I had. Reassurance was all I had to offer, yet I had failed her before, so why should she trust me now?

"Tell me what happened," she said, her voice muffled by my chest.

"Maddie said you were moaning in your sleep, shaking and mumbling. When she tried to wake you, you pushed her away. She came and got me, while Red stayed with you. When I got in there, we had just got the generators running and the lights were on, and I could see you sweating and pale. You looked sick. I tried to carry you back to bed, but you started fighting me, so I sat you down. You woke up stunned, and it took a few minutes for you to respond to me. That's why we thought you couldn't hear us." I wrapped my arms tighter around her, remembering that sick feeling in my gut at the sight of her lying there unconscious and shaking.

"That explains the lights." She mumbled, leaving me confused.

"What lights?"

"In my dream. I kept seeing lights and I thought it was the police coming." I pulled Dallas away from me, staring into those huge green pools that were tired and sad. She offered me a small smile, as she stood up straighter and took a deep breath. I saw that spark in her eyes, and I knew she would be fine. These dreams were fucked up, but if that was the only side effect after everything she had been through, then I guess she was doing okay.

"Let's take a shower. I want to take you somewhere." She nodded her head, and hand-in-hand, we went back inside. Everyone was at the bar drinking coffee, and I started to assure them everything was fine, but Dallas and her mouth had their own plan.

"I'm good. Just a little fucked up in the head. Don't worry, Shark," I watched Shark's eyebrows lift as she addressed him. Of everyone here, I think he felt the most uncomfortable about this morning's events where Dallas was concerned. "It was just as good for me as it was for you, but next time leave those vibrating anal beads at home." Dallas never slowed her pace as we passed through the main room, leaving everyone in laughter and one badass motherfucker blushing.

"You look fucking hot, babe." I said to Dallas, who wore leather pants, thigh-high leather riding boots, and a leather corset. I felt my dick twitching in my pants at the sight of her. She had asked me where we were going and I told her we were taking the bike. That was all she needed to know. When she asked how she needed to dress, I told her sexy, which she looked no matter what she wore. But this time, Dallas took it up a notch. Good thing we weren't going out in public, or I would have had to break fucking necks for looking at her. That was the only downside to having a woman as fine as her. I threw on some jeans and a t-shirt, grabbing my cap and cut, not giving a shit that she looked like a goddess, while I looked like a thug. Fuck it. By the way her eyes appraised me, I knew it didn't matter what I wore. My girl knew what I could do to her, and she wasn't going to find anyone who could do it better. I gave her a smug smile, letting her know I was on to her eye-fucking. How a motherfucker like me wound up with a girl like her, I'll never know. All I knew was that I loved her, and I still got that tingling in my gut at the sight of her looking at me like she could eat me alive. I cleared my throat, feeling like a sap for being so deep inside my own mind and grabbed my dick, making sure my manhood was still there. "Get your shit, so we can go." I was such a

253

smartass, but I felt my nuts drop a little as I said it. Sometimes a man has to be a man just to prove to himself that love hasn't turned him into a poetic, love-struck pussy.

Chapter 18

Luke

I took Dallas out to Ronnie and Brooklyn's for the day. They both worked full-time, but had taken the day off, due to the late night we had pulled, and to have some time to visit. Brooklyn was the only one aware of my plan to take Charlie down and outsmart him, and was going to help me assess Dallas to see if she was capable of doing her part. I trusted Brooklyn's judgment, and if she thought Dallas could handle it, then it would be a go. If not, then I would have to resort to plan B, and plan B sucked ass. Ronnie and Brooklyn lived in the country, in a house that made you feel as if you were home every time you walked inside. Of course, it was them that made you feel welcome, but something about their place made it even better. Maybe it was Brooklyn's cooking or Ronnie's shop filled with Harleys, or their little mutt dog named Dawall that brought a smile to my face when we pulled up, whatever in the hell it was, it made me feel good. We walked onto the covered back porch to find them seated at a table with a breakfast fit for a king laid out before them.

"Hey brother," Ronnie said, standing to give me a hug and then Dallas.

"Damn, girl!" I didn't have to look to know that Brooklyn was referring to Dallas' outfit, but I did, just so I could see it one more time. The cut Dallas wore with my name on it made her outfit that much more appealing to me, and I sat down so Brooklyn wouldn't call me out on the bulge in my jeans. "You look fucking hot!" Dallas winked at her in response. I loved how confident she was. Most girls would require either more convincing, or would blush with embarrassment, but not mine. She knew she was fucking smokin', and her smile showed that she was happy someone had noticed. "Sit down. I made you a southern breakfast with a touch of Cajun. You'll love it."

"No doubt about that, babe. Everything Brooklyn cooks is fine," I said, loading up my plate with eggs, bacon, biscuits, and Brooklyn's famous Cajun gravy.

"I love it when good-looking men flatter me." Brooklyn said, pouring me some juice before treating Dallas to a mimosa.

"I think we're doing a good job at making our presence known." Ronnie said, getting straight to business as we ate. That's why I loved my brother. He was just as passionate about the club as I was.

"I agree. We're gonna hit the local spots all week and not give 'em any down time. It won't be long before we show up in the same place. I got the word out to some of the bar owners. They're gonna give us a call if they see them." There wasn't much you could do when someone came in and you couldn't find them. Lake Charles was a big town and although we had connections and a big club of our own, it seemed we kept missing them.

"Oh, we'll find them eventually. Don't worry about that. They can't hide forever, but I'm sure they're just waiting for their reinforcements." Ronnie said, as I felt Dallas looking at me. I turned to find her silently observing our conversation.

"I got Kev and Crash still on the road, checking out some places north of here. They have seen one or two on the road, but I told them not to pursue 'em." I turned back to Ronnie after giving Dallas a wink, and watching as she melted in her chair. Yep, I still had it.

"Oh, no. We don't need 'em doin' that. Just tell 'em to keep an eye out. They will fuck up soon enough."

"So, Dallas, what's Luke getting you for your birthday?" I looked at Ronnie, as he tried to fight his smile by shoving a forkful of eggs into his mouth. If I thought my leg could reach, and I could do it discreetly, I would have kicked Brooklyn under the table. She knew I had not gotten Dallas' birthday present yet, and she was letting me know just how shitty she thought it was. It was her subtle, Brooklyn way.

"Oh, I don't know." Dallas said, blushing and playing with her food. I gave Brooklyn a face that said "that's what you get" when she realized that her comment had made Dallas uncomfortable. But it didn't faze Brooklyn.

"Well, I think he should get you a car or a big flashy diamond. Or a kitty cat." Bitch. She knew I hated cats. And of course, Dallas turned into a drooling mess over the mention of a fucking pussy.

"I love cats!" She announced, looking at me hopefully.

"No fucking way, babe." I said, shaking my head as I looked to my brother for help. He nodded at me and his face turned serious.

"Alright now, Brooklyn. That's enough." I smiled like an immature prick at Brooklyn's scolding. We just had that kind of relationship. "You know he can't get her just one kitty cat. It would be lonely." Brooklyn laughed until tears rolled down her cheeks at her victory, while an oblivious Dallas looked on and smiled in confusion, her mind filled with thoughts of two little kittens playing in my fucking front yard. Shitting and pissing on my shit. Clawing my fucking Harley seat. Just the thought of one of them furry bastards climbing on my bike had me seeing red.

"You ain't gettin' no fuckin' cat. You might as well get that shit out of your head," I said to Dallas, who pouted. She poked that fucking lip out, and I wanted to cave right then. I pushed my chair away from the table, standing and looking down at Ronnie and Brooklyn's laughing faces and Dallas' exaggerated pouting one. I had to get away from this table before I did one of two things, choked Brooklyn, or asked her to find Dallas a kitten. My money was on the latter.

Plan A involved Dallas having a gun. She needed to know how to shoot, just in case she found herself in a situation she couldn't get out of. I figured that if she practiced over the next week and a half, she'd be ready. I walked her down to the river behind the house, where Ronnie had set up a shooting range. Behind the targets across the river was a huge bluff, so shooting someone accidentally wasn't an issue. He had rigged up a pulley that could go back as far as one hundred yards, depending on how far away you wanted your target to be.

"Okay, babe," I said, pulling my Beretta M9 from under the back of my shirt. "We are going to start at close range. Hold the gun like this," I said, holding the gun in my hand and showing her the stance she needed to take. I turned to look at her and found her looking at me like I was crazy. "I just want to show you how to shoot. I thought it would be fun." Shit. Had I freaked her out?

"Luke, I know how to shoot a gun." All chicks said that.

"I'm sure you do, babe, but I want to show you the proper way."

"Give me the gun, Luke." She said, as if my lecture was boring her.

"Babe, let me show you first." She gestured with her hands for me to go ahead, and I shot her a warning look. She rolled her eyes, and I was tempted to throw her ass in the river. So I could see her in leather. Wet. And shivering. I could warm her up. By taking her clothes off. I bet her nipples would be hard as fuck. I could warm them up with my mouth, along with other parts of my body. Like my cock. In *her* smart mouth. She let out an impatient breath, and I was snapped back to reality. I seriously needed to get my shit together. I showed her how to hold the gun, informing her of the safety, and how to load one in the chamber. She stood listening, completely uninterested in anything I had to say. That pissed me off. "Here," I said, holding the gun by the barrel in my hand and offering it to her. "Since you're so fucking smart, you do it."

"Thank you." She replied in that smart ass tone of hers, greedily grabbing the gun and mirroring my stance. I had set the target ten yards away. If she had to shoot, it would be at close range. She squeezed off five rounds without even flinching. I didn't have to pull the target in to know she had delivered five perfect head shots. Without looking at her gloating face, I moved the target back five yards just because I was an ass. I crossed my arms, waiting for her to continue to show her skills, hoping like hell she would miss. Again, she squeezed off five rounds, and this time, I retrieved the target to find five perfect neck shots. Ha! She missed. "I shot him in the neck so that you wouldn't say I missed. His head is already almost blown off." I would be lying if I said it didn't get under my skin that she was good. I would be lying if I said I wasn't proud either.

"Who taught you to shoot like that?" I asked, praying to the gun gods that she wouldn't say an ex-boyfriend.

"My ex," she said simply, and I wanted to kill someone. "I'm kidding." She said, laughing at my murderous glare. "You're such a *man*." I ignored her comment. Our shooting session was over.

"Let's get back," I said, grabbing her hand in mine.

"Baby. Don't be mad at me." She whined, her voice laced with laughter and amusement.

"I'm not mad," I said, acting like a stubborn kid. She was killing me. My balls were now non-existent.

"You're better than me. I'm sure of it." I stopped in my tracks, smirking at her lying face. She didn't believe that in the least. I grabbed the gun from my back, changing out the clip with the spare I had in my pocket. I loaded it and eyed in on the target that was now about 40 yards from us. I fired ten perfect shots into the chest of our paper villain. She couldn't see if the target had been hit from where we were, but I knew I hadn't missed. I turned and started walking back toward the house. "Aren't you gonna see if you hit it?" Dallas called from behind me.

"Nope," I said as I kept walking. I knew she would stay behind and look. And when she did, she would know for sure who was better. I took the small hike back to Ronnie and Brooklyn's house alone, with a smirk on my face, and a pair.

Dallas

"Well I'll be damned," I muttered, looking at the paper that was now home to ten, perfectly delivered holes in the heart of it. What was it with men and their pride? Luke had gotten pissed that I knew how to shoot. I knew he was proud, but mad because he wasn't the one to show me how to do it. Fucking caveman. I was surprised he didn't carry around a big stick and grow his hair long. I found him in Ronnie's shop, shirtless, and squatting beside one of the many bikes inside. I eyed the tribal tattoos on his arms as his muscles flexed while he tinkered with the motor. I pulled my eyes from him, refusing to get lost in the sight of his half nakedness and searched the room for a topic of conversation. "Is this a Harley?" I asked, eyeing one that sat low with a huge tire on the back. It was painted black, with chromed-out Ape Hanger handle bars, and looked beautiful and manly at the same time.

"Yes, babe. It's a Harley," Luke informed me, acting as if the answer was obvious.

"I wish I knew something about bikes just to piss you off," I mumbled to myself, but Luke was closer than I thought and heard my every word. He had deserted the bike he was working on and was now at my side.

"Have a seat," Luke said, unaffected by my words.

"What?" What if I broke something or messed it up?

"Sit," Luke commanded, pointing to the seat on the bike. I did as bid and straddled the seat. "This is the throttle." Luke said, pointing to the handlebar before placing my hand on it and covering his with mine. I pulled back, feeling it twist in my hand trying to ignore the closeness of Luke's body, and the sexiness of his voice. My arm was stretched out, causing my leather corset top to ride above my belly button. "This is the brake and the other is the clutch," he said, moving my hand to pump the brake. He released my hand, dragging his fingers down my arm slowly, leaving goosebumps in their wake. He threw his leg over the bike, straddling it and facing me before placing his hands on my waist and lifting me, pushing me back further on the seat. I leaned back against the cool fender as he grabbed my left leg and positioned himself between my thighs. "The greatest thing about this bike is that it's the perfect height." My breath caught in my throat as his hips pushed into me, treating me with the feel of his rock hard cock against my leathered crotch. "You have the perfect amount of leverage to get just the momentum you need," he said coolly, pushing against me deeper.

"Is that so?" I asked breathlessly, enjoying my lesson.

"Do you want me to fuck you on this bike, Dallas?" His words caught me off guard. They were so forward and to the point, just how I like them.

"Yes," I said, with a relieved sigh. I thought he was just teasing me before, but now I knew he would deliver.

"I know you do," he said, his voice filled with arrogance. He released my leg to unzip his pants and free himself. I moaned at the sight of him, thick and hard and all for me. He grabbed my pants, and I lifted my ass so he could peel them off of me. Instead of removing them, he slid them just low enough to expose what he needed, leaving me restrained and my legs forced to come together. He draped them over his right shoulder, before guiding himself inside me.

"Yes!" I said, as he sank into me. I was immobile. I couldn't move an inch due to my position and my clothes, leaving me at his mercy.

"This is gonna have to be quick, babe," he said, hammering inside me as he grabbed my hips and pulled me to him. I couldn't get the right angle for him to hit that spot that would have me coming in minutes. As I tried to move my legs, I felt his grip tighten, forcing me to stay still.

"Luke," I said, distressed at the situation. He felt so good inside me, but I knew I would never reach that climax in this position. I needed to open my legs. I needed to arch my back. I needed more.

"Talk to me, baby," he said, his thrusts becoming more urgent and his breathing ragged and fast.

"I need to move. I can't come like this." I wished I could take back the words as soon as I said them. How could I have been that forward and honest? And selfish? It wasn't always about me.

"You don't trust me?" Luke asked, his voice calm, unlike his movements. What? Of course I trusted him! But this wasn't about trust. It was about me coming apart beneath him. It was about me having an orgasm on Ronnie's motorcycle. It was about my juices soaking into the thick leather on the seat and possibly staining or even ruining them. How dare he think this was about trust. It was about me getting mine, him getting his, and Ronnie wondering why the fuck his bike smelled like sex. I closed my eyes, trying to force all thoughts from my mind other than him inside me. I was trying too hard to concentrate on my release that I wasn't even enjoying the moment and what it had to offer. Luke, noticing my despair, or proving his loyalty, moved his hands from my waist and grabbed my ankles, pushing my legs over my head as he repositioned himself and began driving into me again, making me cry out on contact.

"Yes! Fuck yes!" I said, my voice loud enough to prompt Luke to place his hand over my mouth.

"Okay baby, now you can scream all you want." I don't know if it was his command, the challenge to see how loud my screams could get with his hand muffling them, or the feeling of intense ecstasy as Luke pounded relentlessly in me, giving that delicious spot all the attention it had been deprived of, but I screamed. My screams thrilled Luke, and he let me know it. "That's right, baby. Let me know how good it feels when I fuck you with this cock." I moaned against his hand, letting his dark, beastly voice and his expert, assured movements push me into the climactic state that had my eyes rolling into the back of my head. When Luke stilled, I felt the warmth of him engulf me as he stayed buried deep inside me. "Motherfucker," he groaned, and I agreed with a nod, finding the bike becoming rather comfortable. "Come on, babe." Luke said, pulling out of me and pushing my pants up my thighs before anything he had left inside me had a chance to run out onto Ronnie's seat.

"Now?" I asked, with a whine. Why couldn't we just stay here?

"Yes, beautiful. Now," he said, lifting me from the bike and swatting my ass to encourage me to walk. I was fully sated and sleepy. I just wanted a nap. He grabbed my hand to lead me out of the shop, stopping at the door and turning to me to fix my unkempt ponytail. "Babe, could you try and look a little less fucked?" Luke asked, with a smirk as he dressed himself. I rolled my eyes at him and smoothed my clothes and hair, placing a smile on my face to appease him. It worked. We walked inside and I began cleaning the breakfast dishes, while Luke went in search of Ronnie. Brooklyn joined me soon, and by the look on her face, I was not the only one recently fucked, and in need of a nap.

"So how's shit going baby?" Brooklyn asked, once the dishes were cleaned and we were seated in the living room. Brooklyn sat in an overstuffed camouflage recliner and I lay sprawled on the couch petting little Dawall, who had taken a liking to me.

"You know, for the first time in a long time it's going really good. No one is out to kill me, I'm not surrounded by people I don't trust, and Luke and I get closer every day." I scratched Dawall's ears, as he sat on my stomach, his eyes getting heavy much like mine.

"What if there was?" Brooklyn asked, her legs crossed, as she sat with a cigarette dangling from her fingers.

"What do you mean?" I asked, not looking too much into her question.

"What if there was someone out to get you or some shit came up, like more drama. I mean, there is

266

always a chance with this life and with Charlie still out there," she said, her eyes appraising me. I shrugged my shoulders, still not worried about her inquisition.

"Charlie is not a threat to me, and even if he was, we would deal with it like we always do. I'm not some weak woman who can't handle her own, but when I need someone I know Luke will be there. Not much scares me anymore, and if it ever comes to a war with Charlie, then I will fight just like I know Luke will. Life is too short to not fight for the things we love. If anyone tries to take my happiness from me then they are gonna have a helluva time getting it."

"Good answer, baby. Good answer." Brooklyn said, dropping the subject, and turning up the volume on the T.V. The conversation was over, and sleep was in my near future.

Chapter 19

Dallas

My nap was fabulous and so was the ride home. I found out why Red stretched her arms out and moved with the bike to the tune of the music. It was relaxing and liberating. I felt free, and if I closed my eyes, it kind of resembled flying. It was mid-afternoon when we arrived back at the clubhouse to find Red, Regg, Marty, and Maddie playing pool. Luke informed them they were leaving at five, and the girls suggested we find something to get into ourselves. Luke didn't like the idea, and suggested we found something to do around here if we were still planning to go out tomorrow night.

"Why?" Red whined, but changed her tune when Regg gave her a look that told her to shut up. "Okay," she said in defeat, not bothering with anymore questions.

"I'm sure you three can find something to get into around here," Regg said, enjoying his moment of authority. I fought hard to control my laughter, as Red stood behind him and rolled her eyes. Everyone else was at work or at home with their kids and back to their normal lives, while we were forced to stay inside the clubhouse, which was not built to entertain three, young women who were itching to go out.

"So what are the plans for tomorrow?" I asked Maddie, who sat perched on the pool table trying to ignore Marty as he pulled his t-shirt over his head revealing his abs before the one he wore under it was pulled back down to conceal them. She ignored me or didn't hear me, but Red answered my question excitedly.

"It's a surprise! And you are gonna fucking love it!" She said, clapping her hands and bouncing around like a child.

"She's gonna love it or you're gonna love it?" Regg asked, trying to steal Red's glee, but she wasn't having it.

"*She's* gonna love it," Red said, still grinning from ear to ear.

"Who all is going?" Luke asked, half-interested, as he thumbed through some papers that lay strewn on the bar.

"All the girls," Red said, dancing over to Luke and eyeing what he was doing, then dancing away when he gestured with his hand for her to get lost. Wherever it was we were going, it made Red very happy. Almost too happy, and it showed on Regg's face.

"Where they going?" Marty asked, looking at Regg's perplexed face and smiling.

"Amateur night," Regg said in a huff.

"Dammit baby! Hush!" Red commanded, her hands flying to her hips as she glared at Regg, who just shook his head. Amateur night? For what? Luke laughed, finally getting the joke and pointed at Regg from across the room.

"You're gonna have to keep your shit together," he warned with a smile. Everyone laughed, but me and Regg;

me because I had no fucking idea what they were talking about, and Regg because he didn't find it very funny.

"Well y'all ain't going. It's just the girls," Red informed them, this time it was her who sent Luke a look of warning.

"Oh, I'm going," Regg said, and the fight was on.

"The fuck you are! We are going to have a ladies night out. There are only women there Regg, so don't go giving me that lecture and shit." Red snapped, her face turning red with anger, and I felt like it had a lot more to do with something that wasn't being said, rather than actually going out.

"I ain't giving you no damn lecture. I'm just telling you that if you plan to get on a stage somewhere then I'm gonna be there to make sure nothing happens," Regg said, but I could already tell some of the fight had gone out of him. Amateur night must have been at a club, and he knew Red would want to dance.

"Nothing is going to happen. I'm just going out with my sisters to have a good time. Stop treating me like I am that same coke whore you met ten years ago. I haven't danced in years, and I have no desire to. You of all people should know that." Red was pissed, but she was hurt too.

"Baby," Regg said, regret filling his voice. He knew he had cut her deep. Apparently this was a recurring thing with these two. Regg didn't have time to finish what he was saying before Red stomped out of the room and toward the back, leaving him trudging behind her like a whooped puppy.

270

"I tried to tell him," Luke said, shaking his head still eyeing the papers on the bar.

"Red misses dancing," Maddie said, from beside me. "She loved to dance and Regg has been known to make her feel like shit about it. The problem with Red is that she gets lost in the moment and Regg is afraid that she will relapse like-"

"Shut up, Maddie. That's not your story to tell," Marty said, standing before us, and glaring at Maddie.

"What? That's her sister. She can know," Maddie said in defense.

"If Red wants her to know she will tell her. You need to keep your fucking mouth shut." I had never seen Marty be so demanding. It was kinda sexy and he was hella scary, causing me to shrink at his words, and they were not even directed at me.

"You are such a fucking asshole," Maddie said to him, and again I felt as if her words were referring to another time and another place. There was so much malice in her voice that there was no mistaking her anger. She was not joking, and everyone knew it.

"Maddie!" Luke roared from across the room. Maddie's face turned ashen, as Luke stalked toward us. Oh fuck. Maddie had screwed up this time. Red could talk to Regg that way, because he was her husband. I could talk to Luke that way, because he was my lover, but Maddie and Marty were nothing, as far as Luke knew. Here she was, a little sister to the club, being disrespectful to a patch-holder. "What the fuck is your problem? Don't you ever speak to another member of this club like that again."

Luke was so mad he was shaking. His finger was in Maddie's face, and although I felt the need to protect her, I remained quiet. This was the LLC they had warned me about-the one who didn't tolerate bullshit or disrespect from any bitch when it came to his brothers or his club. As bad as I felt for Maddie, I felt even worse for Marty who stood behind Luke wanting so bad to say something, but couldn't. Or I thought he couldn't.

"Luke, that's enough brother," he said to him, his voice coming out strong and confident. Maddie and I both nearly died at the exchange.

"No, it's not enough. She fucking knows better," Luke seethed, still keeping his eyes on Maddie. "Maddie, I'm warning you," Luke started, but stopped as his eyes fell to the hand on his shoulder. He closed his eyes and took a deep breath, trying to rein in his anger. "Marty."

"Luke," Marty said, cutting Luke off once again. If a banner had fallen from the sky along with a stream of confetti and balloons, Luke wouldn't have gotten the message any clearer. When the realization of what was going on slapped him in the face, I lost my ability to breathe. Luke's eyes darkened and he turned ferocious. He walked away from Maddie, shrugging off Marty's hand as he left. The nearest thing that wasn't nailed down was the round table we had played cards at. Luke grabbed it with his hands, slinging it across the room, with a deafening snarl. I jumped, as the table clattered to the floor, leaving Luke in search of something else to throw. Next came chairs, which he sent flying across the room, yelling and cursing, before turning back to face Marty who now stood between us and Luke. Regg came running into the room, assessing the situation and staying neutral, but I knew when he found out what was going on, he would side with Luke.

"How long?" Luke growled, shooting daggers at Marty. I held my breath, praying that Marty would think of a good lie to save him.

"Long enough," Marty replied, without the slightest hint of worry or regret in his voice. I felt Maddie melt next to me, and I was sure if I looked at her, she would just be a big pile of mush.

"Did you not think that was something I would want to know?" Luke asked, his voice thick with sarcasm.

"With all due respect Luke, it's none of your business who I see," Marty replied. Regg jerked his head to Marty, in surprise.

"Oh fuck," he said, rubbing his hands down his face. Yeah, Regg. Shit just got real. Luke laughed without humor, as he shook his head at Marty's response.

"None of my business, huh?" Luke said, still smiling in disbelief. "She is my fucking business!" He suddenly yelled, causing me to jump. Maybe I should say something. Maybe Maddie should. I looked at Maddie as she chewed on her lip, clearly thinking the same thing I was. I nudged her, and that was all the encouragement she needed.

"Don't I get a say in this?" she asked, jumping down from the table, and standing next to Marty.

"Sit the fuck down Maddie and stay outta this," Luke snapped, and this time it was Marty who sent chills down my back with just the tone of his voice.

"Watch how you speak to her, brother. I won't tell you again." I knew Luke. I knew Luke like I knew myself. I recognized shit that a lot of people didn't, so when that sparkle of recognition formed in his eye, I knew he was impressed with Marty's boldness. I just hoped it worked in Marty's favor.

"Tell me what that 13 on your cut stands for, *brother*." Luke demanded, his hands fisting at his sides. I figured he would find something else to throw any minute. Marty must have been thinking the same thing, because he stuck his arm out in front of Maddie, pushing her behind him. Luke's nostrils flared at the exchange, and I wondered if it was because he touched her, or because Marty thought Luke would actually hurt her. Either way, it pissed him off even more.

"M is the 13th letter of the alphabet," Marty replied simply, and Regg actually smiled a little. I didn't get it, but apparently the answer was what Marty had been trained to say in front of other ears. It held a different meaning inside the club.

"I helped you sew that motherfucker on!" Luke yelled from across the room. He was angry, but he was also hurting. He felt betrayed, and he had been. This time when Marty spoke, it was a plea for Luke to understand. He realized, just as I had, that Luke felt as if he had been cut deep.

"Luke, I never lied to you. I love her, man. I was just waiting for all this shit to be finished before I told you." Luke was getting antsy. He was moving around too much, and I was afraid it was fixing to come to blows between him and Marty.

274

"You should have told me. I fucking told you she was off limits," Luke said, his lip curled up, as he breathed deep through his nostrils. He looked like a raging fucking bull ready to attack. I had seen that look once before, right before he bent me over my desk and beat the shit outta me.

"You can't run my life, Luke," Maddie said, her voice soothing, begging Luke to understand. Luke pointed his finger, fixing to lay into Maddie, when Regg interceded. He knew, just like I knew that if Luke said something to Maddie, Marty was going to say something to him, and there wouldn't be enough time for us to get out of the way before the fighting commenced.

"Luke, let's take a walk," Regg suggested, holding his hands up to Luke in surrender. He should have just taken off his white shirt and used it as a flag.

"I don't want to take a walk," Luke said, looking over Regg's shoulder at Marty.

"I'm telling you that we're going to take a walk," Regg demanded, getting directly in front of Luke's face, and blocking our view of him. Oh shit, now Regg and Luke would fight. Then Marty would jump in. Then me, Red, and Maddie would be the only ones that would try and get them to stop. But that didn't happen. Surprisingly, Luke listened to Regg, and turned to walk out the side door into the alley.

"Cat's outta the bag now," Red said, walking in and taking a seat next to me on the pool table.

"I'm so sorry," Maddie said, looking up at Marty with tears in her eyes.

"Don't be. It was time he knew," Marty said, taking Maddie's face in his hands and kissing her so lovingly that Red and I both sighed as we leaned against one another. "I'm gonna go get a shower. Don't worry, he will cool off. He just wants the best for you."

"I'm gonna go talk to him," Maddie announced, as soon as Marty left the room.

"Oh, no," Red said, jumping up and blocking Maddie's retreat. "Just leave him alone. He's pissed, Maddie."

"I think she should go talk to him," I said, standing next to Maddie in her defense.

"You two," Red said, swinging her finger between the two of us, "are suicidal idiots." I rolled my eyes at Red's remark and walked with Maddie outside to find Luke lifting weights, while Regg stood beside the door.

"How is he?" I asked, watching Luke bench press the heavy bar filled with weights as if it held feathers instead of metal.

"Pissed. But he is just mad at himself. He told me if he wasn't careful you two would end up falling for each other," he said, addressing Maddie. "It was bound to happen as much time as y'all have been spending together. Don't be hard on him," Regg said, looking at Luke protectively. "He just wants what's best for you, Maddie." I smiled, but Maddie rolled her eyes, these words having been said to her twice in a matter of minutes. My guess was she would be hearing them again very soon. I walked with Maddie over to Luke, not really feeling as if it was my place, but my sister needed me. I would tune out the conversation once it started. Or at least that's what I told myself. Hell, I wanted to hear it just as bad as Red, who I knew was listening through a window somewhere.

"Luke," Maddie said cautiously, as we approached a sweaty, shirtless, still-pissed Luke. I was glad I had come. While Maddie fidgeted with her hands, trying to find the right words to say, I used mine to wipe the drool that was running down my face at the sight of him. "I know you don't like it, and I know it's because you felt like we lied to you, but that's not the case." Maddie paused, waiting on some acknowledgement from Luke that he had heard her, but he continued lifting as if we weren't even there. Maddie swallowed hard and looked at me. I gave her a reassuring smile and nod, and she stared at her feet as she continued. "He's so good to me," she said with a smile, her eyes becoming dreamy, as they had when she had first told me about him. "For so long, I looked at him as just a friend. But after Texas, I came home and he was there. He listened to me and understood me. I've always had you for things like that, but with everything going on, I didn't want to bother you. Luke he makes me feel like I'm important. He makes me feel like you did, but we have that connection, ya know? I know you want more for me, but *he* is my more." At this, Luke stopped, replacing the bar, but keeping his hands on it as he stared at them. I watched his stomach, as it retracted with his deep breaths. I pulled my eyes to his face to see it looking impassive as Maddie's words continued. I knew he was listening, but he didn't want to. "He loves me and he loves Logan. I know this like I know you would give your life to save me from another disaster like Brett. Luke, I wouldn't take the risk of losing you if I wasn't sure that this was what I wanted. I love him." Luke's eyes swung to Maddie for the first time since she had begun speaking. Maddie continued, ignoring Luke's stare and lost in her own little world, as if the words she had just spoken made her realize how true they were. "I love him more than anything. I don't care that he's not a doctor or a lawyer, or that he probably loves his Harley more than he could ever love me. All that matters is that I love him and for a long time, I didn't even know it, but now I do. I love him, Luke. *I love him.*" I smiled at Maddie, whose look of elation caused my stomach to swarm with butterflies, and my heart to swell with pride. My little sister had finally found happiness. I would kill Luke if he fucked this up, but when I turned to him, he was sitting up, eyeing Maddie with a smirk.

"That much, huh?" he asked, as she nodded her head vigorously while her tears streamed down her face. Maddie squatted between Luke's knees, taking his hands in hers.

"I can't do this without your blessing. Please don't make me choose, because I would be lost without either one of you." Just like I did, Luke knew that the girl who sat before him was a girl in love, and she would leave Luke and this life for a shot at her own happiness.

"I won't let you go Maddie," Luke said, tucking a strand of hair behind Maddie's ear. "And I won't stand in the way of your happiness. I'm not saying I like it, but if it's what you really want, I'll try to deal with it. If you love him, then love him fiercely. That man deserves that kind of love, and so do you, my Maddie." Luke leaned forward, taking Maddie's face in his hands as he kissed her forehead, leaving me a crying fucking mess as the scene unfolded. I heard a sniffle and turned to see Red standing outside the door to mine and Luke's room. I knew she would be watching. Nosey bitch. She just couldn't help it. I was glad we were staying in tonight. A chick flick was in order.

Chapter 20

Dallas

The three of us, Maddie, Red and myself, were lying in mine and Luke's bed, sniffling and snorting at one of the sappiest chick flicks I had ever seen. Nicholas Sparks definitely knew how to make a girl cry. The guys had left around five, and no sooner had they left, than we had jumped into bed to begin our movie marathon. Luke had yet to speak to Marty, but he didn't kill him either, and that was progress. Regg expressed his relief that the fight was out of Luke by grabbing a bottle of Jack and turning it up, not even bothering with a glass. I got out of bed, choosing another movie for us as, my stomach grumbled in complaint.

"Y'all hungry?" I asked the two saps lying in bed covered with tissues.

"Starving," Red said, which wasn't unusual. She was always hungry.

"Yeah, me too," Maddie added, her permanent smile still as fresh as it had been when she'd uttered the words, "I love him."

"I'll order pizza." I walked into the main room, flipping on lights as I did, and found the number for a local pizza joint behind the bar. I ordered a large pepperoni and cheese pizza for delivery, and they let me know they would be here in thirty minutes. I skipped back to the bedroom, where the pajama party looked more like an ICU waiting room, with snot rags, covers, and red, crying eyes. Everyone wore their significant other's t-shirt instead of pajama tops with their pajama shorts, leaving our tanned legs exposed and a topic of conversation. I looked at Maddie's legs, which were considerably darker than mine and Red's. "Maddie, do you tan *every* day?" I asked, causing all six eyes in the room to fall on Maddie's legs.

"Not every day, but most. I have a tanning bed at home. Luke bought it for me for Christmas last year," Maddie said, propped up on her elbows, while she turned her leg examining it.

"He bought you a tanning bed?" Was she serious?

"Yeah, I had been wanting one so he got it for me," she answered, with a shrug. I would have thrown a jealousy fit had she and Marty not confirmed their love for one another earlier.

"I want a tanning bed," Red said with a pout, holding her leg up to Maddie's in comparison.

"Why? It ain't like you're ever home to use it," Maddie said, with a laugh. "Albino," she added, and I laughed too, making sure to shield my legs from Maddie's eyes. If Red were an albino, then so was I.

"Don't be trying to hide, Dallas. Your tan is shit too. For November, we all have pretty good tans." Red said, and I had to agree. Maddie was an exception, but when we were forty, she would look like leather, and Red and I would still look youthful... and very white. A bang on the door sounded, and I took off to get the pizza. As I ran through the main room, a thought hit me. It had not been anywhere near thirty minutes. I did a one-eighty, and hightailed it back to my room, to find Maddie and Red still talking tanned legs, when I entered.

"That's not the pizza. Can't be," I said, my breathing coming fast from my sprint and my sudden nervousness.

"Well, let's go see who it is," Red said, clambering off the bed. I turned leaving her searching for something, as Maddie and I made our way back to the door. "I'm coming, wait!" Red said in a whisper, as we slowed for her to catch up. I made it to the door first, making sure the light outside was on as I unlocked the deadbolt and cracked it open, but Red grabbed it, pulling it open wide and glaring at the man who stood there. He looked nervous and fidgety, and I knew he was up to no good.

"Can I help you?" I asked, stunning him with my million-dollar smile. He took the three of us in, nothing but t-shirts and legs.

"Yeah, I was looking for directions," he said, looking around nervously.

"No you fucking ain't. Tell whoever that is down the street that if he wants to send a lookout, he needs to send someone who isn't an idiot," Maddie snapped, causing the guy's face to whiten. I stood between Maddie and Red, wondering how in the hell they were staying so cool about the situation. What if he had someone with him? It wouldn't take much for them to push their way inside.

"I-I don't know what you are talking about," the guy said, with a nervous laugh. He reached up to run his hands through his greasy hair and I noticed the track marks on his arms. He was doing this for dope.

"Look, tell your informant that there are three women alone in the Devil's Renegades clubhouse, so if they want to ambush it, now is the time." I wanted to look at Red and mouth to her, "are you fucking crazy", but I kept my eyes forward and my face impassive, although I was anything but.

"You're a brave little bitch," the guy said, his lip curling, revealing a set of rotten teeth.

"Do I have something to be scared of?" Red asked, holding the door open wider, as if she were inviting him in.

"Yeah, me," he said, looking like he wanted to take a step inside, but thinking better of it. "And my friends," he said, with a smug smile.

"Really? Well I have two sisters and a nine with ten shots that says I'm the baddest motherfucker on this block. You want to test that theory?" Red asked, staring the guy down while I fought hard to control my laughter. There was absolutely nothing funny about what was taking place, but just hearing Red talk like she was in some action movie had me nearly dying.

"That's enough Red, I got it," Chris said, emerging from the side of the building and shooting Red a glare. He might have been a PROSPECT, but if he was here under his superior's orders to protect us, then he would do so at all costs. And Red knew that. She gave him an apologetic smile, and closed the door, leaving Chris and the junkie outside, alone.

"Are we just gonna leave him out there?" I asked Maddie and Red's backs, as they descended down the hall.

"Yep," they replied in unison. I caught up with them and stood in the doorway of my room, while they piled back onto the bed without a care in the world.

"But were there really people watching?" I asked, straining my ears for the sound of gunshots.

"Nah. Luke called and said a guy was coming by to get directions. He said to let Chris handle it, but I knew Chris was out back walking the perimeter, so I thought we could have a little fun," Red said, lighting a cigarette.

"Y'all could have told me. Bitches," I added, turning my back to them to as I grabbed my wallet for the pizza guy.

"Then it wouldn't have been fun. Don't worry. Luke will chew my ass when he gets here and you will get all the pay back you want when he does."

"Will he really chew your ass?" I asked, memories of earlier today reminding me that Red really didn't want to piss Luke off.

"Probably not, but I was hoping it would make you feel better." She and Maddie shared a laugh, as I walked down the hall to answer the door to the pizza man. I pulled open the door and found Chris standing there, holding my pizza in one hand, and his key in the other.

"I could have got that." I said, taking it from him, with a smile. "Is anyone outside?" He looked behind him then back at me, confused.

"No. Just us," he said, as the pizza man sped off in his small car. I opened my mouth, and began screaming bloody murder.

"Help! Help!" I screamed, beating on the wall and turning my head toward the hallway to see Maddie and Red come barging out so fast that they ran into each other as they hit the wall across from my room. I closed my mouth and smiled, as Maddie flipped the light on and Red scanned the room frantically, her hands waving a gun around looking for the intruder. Chris stood next to me, his gun also drawn, as he scanned the room for my imaginary culprit, too.

"What's wrong?! What's wrong?!" Maddie screamed in panic, her eyes searching as she stood behind Red, who still held then gun toward the bar, with shaky hands.

"Gotcha," I said, with a smile, leading Maddie to nearly faint with relief and Red to go fucking nuts.

"I almost shot you, Dallas! Just fucking then. I almost pulled the trigger! What if one of the guys had been in here! Are you crazy?" she asked, but I knew she wanted to laugh. I pulled the clip from the gun she held from my back pocket and smiled. "Dude! That was good. You are good," Red said, laughing and pointing her finger at me. Maddie joined in, and I bowed and curtsied in front of them, while they extended their arms singing "hail Dallas."

"What the fuck is going on!?" Chris exploded from beside me. I jumped at his voice and stood stock still as he stood before us shaking with anger, his arms still extended with his gun in his hands. "You bitches are gonna drive me fuckin' crazy!" he yelled to the ceiling, placing his gun in his belt and grabbing from the floor the pizza I had dropped in the moment. "I'm taking this," he said, pointing at each of us, and giving us a look that said if we argued he might shoot us. He stomped through the room and out the side door, slamming it behind him. I looked at Maddie and Red, and the three of us burst out laughing. We had become delirious from cabin fever, and it was the greatest fucking thing ever.

Luke didn't wake me when he got home, but sometime during the night, I realized the arms that held me were not Maddie or Red's. When I snuggled closer to him, absorbing his warmth, he squeezed me tighter and kissed my hair. I fell back into a restful sleep, and woke the next morning to find him gone. I pulled myself from bed, heading straight to the shower in hopes that it would wake me up. When I stepped out, I found Luke standing there seemingly nervous as he fidgeted with something behind his back.

"Hey baby!" I said smiling, leaning up to give him a quick kiss.

"Hey beautiful. Happy birthday. I got you something," he said, his huge smile replacing the nervous look he wore only seconds ago.

"Is it a kitten?" I asked excitedly, clasping my hands together as I beamed at him.

"No, babe. Not a kitten." He presented me with an envelope, and I eyed it warily, while he watched with so much excitement and anxiety that I thought he would snatch it from me at any minute, and open it himself. I opened the envelope slowly, just because I'm a bitch and I knew a kitten couldn't fit inside, and pulled out a plane ticket. To Fiji.

"I promised you a trip to the beach," he said, once again nervous now that I had it open, and had not given him a reaction. Thoughts of Luke and I on a beach, alone, for any length of time had excitement bubbling inside me. Thoughts of kittens fled my mind, and all I cared about was seeing him shirtless, and devoting all of his time to only me, on a beach, in fucking Fiji. A slow smile formed on my face and, at Luke's obvious reprieve, it turned into that heart-stopping smile reserved only for him. I jumped into his arms with a squeal, allowing him to spin me around the room in celebration.

"I love it! I love you!" I said with a laugh, my cheeks hurting from my permanent smile. I jumped out of his arms in search of Red and Maddie, ready to share my good news. Everything was perfect. This would be my best birthday yet, and we had a long night ahead of us.

"So Luke didn't kill him?" Katina asked, as she straightened another lock of her long hair. We were crammed into the bathroom of the clubhouse, getting ready for our night out to celebrate my birthday, all nine of us. Brooklyn, Mary, Katina, Punkin, Chi Chi, Maddie, Red, Katelan, and myself were all dressed in sparkly attire. Red and Maddie had chosen my outfit, which had resulted in a tiny scrap of gold, sequined material they called a dress. It was strapless, barely covered my breasts, and came just below my ass. Luke was going to have a heart attack when he saw it.

"Nope. It's all good," I replied, darkening my eyeliner.

"I can see how he would be pissed, though," Brooklyn added, looking gorgeous in an orange, sequined dress that fell off her shoulders, and stopped just above her knees.

"But it really is none of his business," Maddie said, reaching across the sink to dig through my makeup bag for some lipstick. "I mean, he can't judge every guy I see just because he wears a cut. Luke wears one too for fuck's sake." Brooklyn shot her a look that said, "The hell he can't", and Red agreed, rushing to swallow her drink, so that she could verbally express her opinion.

"Look, I think if anyone can judge a man because of the lifestyle he chooses it's Luke. And he promised that anyone who laid their hands on you would have him to answer to. And we all know what answering to Luke can entail. From beatings to a meeting with the Reaper, and everything in between. Even spankings," Red added, as she looked over her glass at me with a wink.

"I seriously doubt Luke would spank someone," Mary said, with a laugh, as she stood two inches taller in her back heels, which matched her black mini dress.

"He spanked Dallas," Red said, putting all of my business out on show. Again.

"What?" The girls asked in unison, every eye turning to me for confirmation.

"Thanks a lot Red," I mumbled, avoiding everyone's stares as I applied mascara to my long lashes.

"Oh, wait. I have to hear this," Chi Chi said, squeezing her way into my personal space, sure not to miss anything.

"I am not discussing it. End of." I would not share that humiliating moment with these women. No fucking way.

"Hey!" Maddie snapped, forcing us to turn to look at her standing in the center of the room with her hand on her hip. Maddie's dress was a deep blue that perfectly matched her eyes. Her blonde hair was styled impeccably on her head, and her long, tanned legs put everyone in the room to shame. "Y'all are acting as if we are just talking about some guy. This is Marty. Not some punk off the streets. It's his brother. The man he trusts with his life, and the life of the ones he loves. How can you all act like we're dealing with some kind of fucking outsider when in reality, we're talking about one of our own." Maddie was right. And by the look of guilt on everyone's face, they all knew it too.

"Maddie, baby," Brooklyn said, her voice calm and motherly, as she went to stand beside Maddie and wrap an arm around her trembling shoulder. "We're not saying it's right, we're saying that Luke was justified in what he did. He chose to take a different route and for that we are proud, but can you blame him for worrying? He knows first-hand what happens in this life. He has been like your brother for years. How many times have you cried on his shoulder? How many times was he there for Logan because he knew he needed a good man in his life?

289

Remember honey, it's not just you anymore. Luke is looking out for both you and Logan, and when someone comes in and wants to take over and be the sole protector of the two of you, he wants to ensure that the man is capable and willing. Of course he trusts Marty, but at the end of the day, he knows Marty better than all of us. He remembers how Marty ran away from his past love when he thought he wasn't good enough. Luke doesn't want him to make the same mistake with you. Plus, it would be very difficult if something were to happen between the two of you. I couldn't imagine this club without you or him, but the truth is, if you two split, we are going to lose someone we love very much. And who do you think the weight of that burden is gonna fall on? Be glad you have a man like Luke to look after you and protect you, even if it is from his own brother." We all stood quietly, hanging on to Brooklyn's every word. I knew it was difficult for Maddie. I knew that even though Luke and Marty would be okay there would still be times when Luke had a tough time dealing with it. But if anyone could handle the pressure and patience it took to deal with what was to come, it was Maddie.

We were crammed into Katelan's SUV, which comfortably seated seven. Considering there were nine of us, we were packed in, lying on top of one another. Katelan was going out with us tonight, but she would not be drinking. Chris would be tagging along, to keep an eye on us, and the guys were not too far away. I was happy to see Chris well rested, and wanted to tell him I had requested his nap to earn me some points to help smooth out my actions of last night. It was not necessary. When I approached him to apologize, he simply held his hand up and told me he understood, and actually thanked me for not shooting him. Bless his little heart. Luke had approved of my dress, and I wondered how I had gotten away with it when Maddie informed me that the club we were attending was only open to women on Tuesday nights. It gave women the opportunity to see if a career in stripping or pole-dancing was something they were interested in, without the prying eyes of men there to judge. Everyone looked absolutely beautiful in their sequined dresses, but it was Punkin who nearly took my breath away. She looked amazing in a silver, floor-length gown that had one long sleeve that covered her right arm, leaving her left arm bare. She had shocked us all when she had walked in with jet-black hair, courtesy of Red and a mix-up at the local beauty supply shop. Apparently, they didn't wait on Punkin in a timely manner, and when she had asked if she had to steal something to get some fucking service, they rewarded her with the wrong color dye. Well, the joke was on them. If their intentions had been to make her look bad, they had failed miserably. She looked marvelous from her head to the bottom of her dress, until she lifted it to show us that she wore combat boots on her feet. Her answer to her wardrobe malfunction was simple; if someone needed the shit kicked out of 'em, she could do a lot more damage with boots than we could with heels. I liked her way of thinking.

Instead of dinner out, Katelan would be driving us to the home of the last original member of the Devil's Renegades. I had never heard of the man, and was anxious to meet him. As we all piled out of the car and into his home, I had no idea what to expect, but what I got in return was so much more than what I ever could have hoped for.

"Come in, come in." A raspy voice greeted as a man held the door open for us. I was the last of the ladies to enter with Chris on my heels, as I came face-to-face with Devil's Renegades Rick. "Well, I'll be damned," he said, his eyes appraising me with approval. "You're so much more beautiful than LLC gave you credit for." I blushed as I observed him. He was shorter in stature, but his figure was stocky and hard. He wore glasses on his face, and a black goatee, with traces of gray, lined his mouth. He looked handsome in jeans, boots, and a button down and smelled of tobacco and aftershave; his scent reminding me of my father's.

"It is a pleasure to meet you, Rick. I'm Dallas." I said, giving him that smile that earned me one in return.

"Yes you are," he said, kissing my hand then tucking it into his arm to lead me inside. "The ladies are helping to prepare dinner. I hope you all don't mind, but I have been a little under the weather." When he said ladies, somehow I assumed he was talking about women other than the ones I saw. Rick was the Hugh Hefner of the Devil's Renegades, and beautiful bunnies littered his playboy mansion. The house we were in seemed small with all of the people inside it, but I knew it had to be pretty big to accommodate all of us. Old pictures of the club's past and newest members hung on the wall. Leather furniture covered the living room, and the biggest fucking T.V. I had ever seen in my life sat mounted above a massive fireplace. I watched in awe at the half dozen women who made their way around the house wearing rabbit ears, high heels and tails on top of their tiny, pink thongs. Their large, perfect breasts stood to attention as they scurried around, making sure everyone was comfortable and seated at the huge dining room table that sat twelve. The entire first floor of the house was open for viewing, and I looked up to find the upstairs open as well, with a balcony that overlooked the bottom floor. The place was a dream home for house parties. Rick led me to the table, seating me to his left then turning to greet Chris. Brooklyn sat across from me to his right, and I leaned up to look down the table to find everyone at ease as if they had been here a million times. Even Katelan didn't seem to feel out of place. "Ladies, tonight I am treating you to a Devil's Renegades special. Pops and I created the perfect gumbo back when we were room-mates before this all started." I smiled at the man beside me. His voice was low and strained, his raspy tone something I was falling in love with. I was sure it was a result of years of living the good life of booze, women, and smoke. Now that I had met him, I couldn't imagine ever having a different image of him in my mind. When a beautiful, blonde bunny appeared and refilled his glass, he thanked her with a kiss and a promising smile, leaving her gushing as she scurried off, but not before he smacked her ass. His eyes followed her, until he seemed to remember he had company. "We were living in a small apartment, both of us working as mechanics in an old shop. Back in those days, everyone rode a Harley. You didn't have these rice burners and mopeds and shit. You had an American bike or nothing at all. So, work was always plentiful. But we spent our nights at strip-clubs and parties, spending all our hard-earned money on booze and ass when we should have been investing in our own business." He paused as we were served bowls of steaming gumbo, with a side of French bread. I waited patiently until everyone had their meal before I placed my napkin in my lap, ready to dig in. I looked up to see everyone grabbing hands and I followed suit, placing mine in Rick's, who sat to my right, and

Mary's, who sat to my left. I wasn't shocked that we were saying grace, but I wasn't expecting it either. I bowed my head as Rick blessed our food, his choice of words making me smile as they warmed my heart. "Father bless this food and the lovely, delicate hands that helped to prepare it. Thank you for blessing me with such beautiful company and may their time spent here be well served. I pray that you bless this beautiful creature whose hand I hold in mine with twenty-seven more wonderful years, and may the majority of them be spent in the fabulous life of our MC. Help us to keep the rubber down as we ride for our brothers who live, and honor the ones who have gone. Amen." A chorus of "amen" was heard around the table as I gave Rick's hand a squeeze, and I smiled in thanks at his mention of me in his prayer. I took my first bite of what would be many of the most delicious gumbo I had ever tasted.

"Shit this is good," Chi Chi said, before taking another bite and closing her eyes with a moan. We all agreed and Rick smiled at our enjoyment.

"I'm glad y'all like it. So," he said, continuing with his story. "Pops and I had been around MCs all our life. We decided to form one of our own, and we found the biggest, baddest motherfuckers around to form our posse. See, big, strong tough guys is what we envision when we think motorcycle club, but some of the best brothers come in a pint-size package. We finally got a crew together that had everything we desired in brothers; loyalty, honesty, and trust. He didn't have to be big and bad, he just needed to be willing to give his all for his brothers. We found that in the first five; Pops, Gill, Tony, Carl, and myself. We were unstoppable. We turned this town upside down, and soon we had chapters in three different states. We ran the biggest illegal operation this state has ever seen. There were women everywhere, money grew on trees, and the highest respect was paid to anyone who wore our patch." Rick paused, taking a sip of his drink. He took his time continuing, as if he was searching for just the right words to say. I continued to eat and drink, looking at him from time to time during his story, until he spoke again. This time, my gumbo was forgotten, and my attention was focused on nothing but him. "Then there was Luke." My eyes found his as he smiled, a memory from far back held his attention as he laughed to himself. "Luke was the one I knew would either be the downfall or the success of this club. He was so passionate about it. He never once gave up, even though his Pops put him through hell trying to persuade him to take a different route in life. When a man does time for a crime he commits then in turn creates a life where crime is the sole benefit of his life, it's one thing. But when he sees his grandson, a boy he loves and wants to succeed in life, following that same path of destruction it's another. Pops never wanted that life for Luke. He didn't want to live knowing his actions were ones that Luke would follow, creating a cesspool that would be passed down from generation to generation. But I," he said, pointing his finger at himself as his eyes locked on mine, "I had faith in Luke. When shit got really bad, he realized he had to make some changes, and he did. He had business sense and smarts that the other guys and I only dreamed of. He found a way to make peace with our connections, and pulled the club out of its illegal ways and into the path of what was right. When the club realized the hit it was going to take, they voted against Luke's efforts. They had got accustomed to the life of a constant heavy cash flow, and an easy ride. That's when Luke used his own money to float the club. He drained every dollar he had from his savings and his father's investments for his future. He took the risk of losing everything he had to save the one thing he loved from self-destruction. That's when I learned that it's not the cut who makes the man, but the man who makes the cut." You could have heard a pin drop in the room, as Rick grabbed my hand across the table. "You got a good man, darlin'." He looked around the table at the ladies who sat there, making eye contact with each one. "You all do. Gone is a time when MCs were outlaw bikers who broke the law, raised hell, and stepped on anyone they could to get up the ladder of success. All that remains from that time is this old man with a lot of good memories of the way things used to be. Those days were the good ones, and damn how I miss them, but the future of the Devil's Renegades will now live on for generation after generation, and we have your good men to thank for that. Of course, they wouldn't know shit if it wasn't for an old-timer like myself." We all laughed, tears rolling down our faces, and not one of us caring if it ruined our makeup. We finished our meal with light conversation, laughter, and good company. When it was time to go, we were all kissed on the lips as Rick bid us goodbye with a host of sexy women surrounding him. Once in the car, I waved my final goodbye to the man who had left me with a new outlook on Luke. If ever I had been blessed, it was with the gift of Devil's Renegades President, LLC.

Chapter 21

Dallas

The strip-club was packed with women of every age and size, but it was us who were the belles of the ball. Our entrance couldn't have been grander if we had been surrounded by white doves in our sequined dresses, which covered every color of the rainbow and then some. The place was huge, with a stage that covered most of the floor, and had at least ten poles scattered across it. In the center, one pole reached all the way to the second story, where private dances were held. Neon lights illuminated us, as they blinked in time with the strobe lights that hung from the ceilings. A long bar lined with stools sat against the side wall, with mirrors that ran the length of the wall behind endless bottles of premium liquor. Men who resembled Chippendale dancers wore black slacks, suspenders, and a black bow tie; each of them muscular, tanned and extremely good-looking. Their chests were broad, and their abs rippled down their stomachs. Red got a tray of shots delivered to our table; the girls had gone all out for me and had reserved us a section in the area that was reserved for VIP members only, which consisted of a half-circle booth that wrapped around a table at the front, stage-center. Music blared from the speakers, as we gathered around the booth with me in the middle. Everyone grabbed a shot and it was thrown back in honor of my birthday. Within seconds of our empty glasses hitting the table, they were filled once again by a good-looking Italian man named Greg. Greg informed us that he would be taking care of us all night, and that whatever we wanted would be provided to us upon request. This prompted Brooklyn to run her fingers down his chest and grab his crotch, leaving him smiling and promising her that his cock was available too. He then informed us that if we would like to dance, all we had to do was sign up and they would usher us backstage, where we had full access to the dressing room and the outfits that it contained. I quickly busied myself to avoid his stare. I knew he was addressing me and assuming I would be the one dancing. Red saved me by assuring him we would not be participating, but that we appreciated the offer. We ordered drinks and sat back to relax before the show, which was due to start in about thirty minutes. By the time the first dancer took the stage, we were all feeling the buzz as a result of several shots, and strong, mixed drinks.

"She should have stayed her fuckin' ass at home," Punkin said, referring to the woman on stage, whose feeble attempt at dancing had us all laughing.

"Punkin!" I admonished, feeling sorry for the poor woman, although my laughter continued as she busted her ass trying to look sexy in platform heels that stood six inches high. "That's why they call it amateur night. There aren't any professionals here."

"There is one," Punkin said, pointing at Red with her long fingernail. I rolled my eyes at her comment. Red might be good dancer, but I doubted she was a professional stripper. "Well, I ain't doing it, anyway. I told Red I'd hold the camera."

"I'm with you," I agreed, lifting my glass in the air for Greg to refill it.

"What you want to hold the camera too?" she asked, her mouth twisted in annoyance. I guess Punkin didn't want to share her chance at being a photographer. I laughed, as she chewed the side of her mouth, trying to calm her frustration. She had been incarcerated for too long.

"No, Punkin. I meant I ain't dancing either." I patted her leg, giving her a huge smile of reassurance. This seemed to pacify her, and she gave me a small, apologetic smile. We all clapped as the lady left the stage, shouting words of encouragement at her as the next dancer came out, stopping to give her a hug. The chorus of "Shots" by LMFAO rang through the speakers, and Greg presented himself at our table holding another round of shots and performing a dance on Brooklyn's lap, as we all danced in our seats with our hands in the air. Katina took the tray of shots from Greg as he lay on the table and spread his legs, placing one shot glass at a time between them on the table. Brooklyn all but pushed us out of her way to straddle him and reach between his thighs to retrieve her shot with her hands behind her back. She stood there a minute, dancing over him with her dress hiked up her thighs, as she wiggled her ass in his face. We all took turns, except for Katelan, who stood beside us cheering us on with a glass of water in her hands. Chi Chi, Mary, and I formed a train over him, as we danced and pushed our faces between his legs one at a time, downing the shot that seemed to burn a lot less due to the numbing sensation I was experiencing from all of my previous drinks. Red and Maddie faced one another, as they sat on top of him and placed their shots in each other's cleavage. Punkin stood and grabbed a shot from the tray Katina still held and threw it back, before returning to her seat, not at all worried about the half-naked man that lay before us. When he got up from the table, he grabbed the tray from Katina, taking the last shot and holding it in his hand, before discarding the tray by throwing it to the floor. We watched and cheered in amazement as he bent Katina over the table and jerked his hips against her ass in rhythm with the music. He kept his hand on her back as he made his way around the table to stand in front of her, putting his crotch in her face. He proceeded to stick the shot in the waistband of his pants, and we all screamed our approval as Katina took the shot, making sure to run her tongue from his navel to the glass before taking it in her mouth, and throwing her head back in a seductive manner. When the song stopped and Greg left, we collapsed back in our seats, laughing, as we all fought to give the best re-enactment of Katina's sexy pose.

"Oooh ooh!" Red said, jumping up and down in her seat to get all of our attention. "Dallas you're up in fifteen. Let's go get you ready." I paled at her comment, looking around to see everyone grinning at me. "Come on!" Red urged. I laughed in her face as I shook my head and sat back.

"Red I ain't gonna do that shit," I said, watching Mary laugh hard at my response, her small body falling over in Chi Chi's lap. She was piss drunk, but, hell, which one of us wasn't.

"Dallas!" Red whined, her attempt to pout only making me laugh harder.

"Hell no. I can't do that," I said, gesturing with my hand to the poles on the stage.

300

"You don't have to use the pole, just dance." There was no way I was getting up there. I shook my head, draining my glass and lifting it in the air, as I swayed without intending to, and hiccupped.

"You pussy. I should have known you would be too scared," Red said, daring me to prove her wrong.

"I'm not a pussy, Re-ed," I said, rolling my head and sucking my teeth, while I snapped my fingers in her face with my free hand. I slammed down my glass and stood, wobbling slightly, but was assisted when a strong hand grabbed my arm to steady me. I turned to see Chris standing there, his eyes laughing, although he didn't utter a word. Had he been there the whole time? "What do you think Chris?" I asked, turning on my heels and facing him. "Do you think I'm a pussy?" he fought to contain his laugh, but there was no chance of him hiding his smile.

"I'm just here," he offered, taking the easy way out. But I wouldn't let him.

"Come on, Chris," I said, playfully punching his arm and nearly falling on my face as I did. "What ya think?"

"I think you're drunk," he said, his arms clasped in front of him. He leaned in as if to tell me a secret, but everyone at the table heard what he said. "And a pussy."

"Red, I don't think I can do this," I said, my stage-fright so bad that I thought I might vomit. We were backstage, and I was dressed in a ridiculous plastic outfit with a teeny, nude bikini underneath. The idea was for me to strip down to the bikini and give the appearance that I was naked, but my privates would be covered. Or at least that was the plan. "I don't know why I let you talk me into this," I said, taking deep breaths trying to remain calm.

"I didn't. I believe it was you who dragged me back here. And for what? To prove to a PROSPECT that you weren't a pussy? You're pathetic. And very hot in that nurses' outfit. Here, drink this." She shoved a glass in my hand, and clinked it with hers. I downed the shot, which was so strong it nearly took my breath away.

"What the fuck is that?" I asked, wiping the remnants from my lips.

"*That* is liquid encouragement. Here, take one more." I looked at her as if she was crazy. "Oh stop, you've had fifteen fruity shots that can hardly be considered hard liquor, and five mixed drinks. If you were really drunk, you wouldn't be freaking out right now. Take the shot." She pushed it into my hand and I downed it, knowing that I would probably need ten more just to get through the next ninety seconds.

"Arrgghh!" I said through my teeth, as the liquor scorched my throat and burned the inside of my stomach.

"Okay, you're up. Just work the pole in front of our table. Remember, it's your birthday, have fun!" Red blew me a kiss and I caught it, slapping it against my ass cheek, as I peeked through the curtains at the audience. The alcohol was already taking effect as I felt my body loosen and my mind relax. When the announcer called my name, I stepped through the curtain and hit the stage, full of confidence. My girls stood front and center with fistfuls of one-dollar bills, screaming my name while Chris stood

302

behind them, looking very pleased with himself. Asshole. When Def Leppard's "Pour Some Sugar on Me" filled the room, I transformed from the nervous girl who had stood backstage to the baddest bitch in the room, or so I thought. I got lost in the moment, as I used the pole to grind against, forgetting to strip through the first half of the song, until I looked to my sisters to see them making motions that signaled I should rip my shirt off. I grabbed the center of my shirt, which was held together by Velcro instead of buttons, and positioned my fingers to pull it apart in an attempt to look very sexy, during the climax of the song. But the damned thing was stronger than I thought. My dance went to shit after that, and when the song ended, there was not a one-dollar bill on the stage. Even my sisters refused to tip me. I walked backstage fully clothed, and had to have Red help me with my pathetic outfit.

"I was terrible!" I laughed, as Red quickly removed my outfit with no problems.

"No you weren't," she said, helping me back into my dress.

"Yeah you was," a voice said with a snicker. She had tried to conceal it, but I knew by the way she reacted to our gaze that she had intended for us to hear.

"Hey, bitch. Why don't you keep your comments to yourself," Red snapped, her temper flaring as a result of too much alcohol, and her possessiveness over me.

"Bitch, I can say what I want to. I run this motherfucker." The girl was tall, her legs going on for days. Her skirt was so short I could see the cheeks of her ass, and her miniscule tube-top was just a thin piece of material that was just wide enough to cover her areolas.

"Ohhh, okay," Red said, turning to me, feigning interest. Like she actually gave a shit who this girl was. "So you're Lonnie. Now I see it. You do look a little butch. I'm pretty sure that's a penis between your thighs." This time, I did snicker.

"Bitch, what you laughing at?" she snapped. I guess she thought she could pick on the little one. Wrong.

"I will beat your ass with her," I said, my voice slightly slurred, as I jutted my thumb at Red.

"Really, Dallas? That's all you got?" Red asked, forgetting our confrontation for the moment to scold me on my pathetic comeback.

"Yeah," I said, with a defeated sigh. "I'm pretty drunk."

"You can't dance and you can't talk shit," the skank who supposedly "ran shit" said, counting off each of my shortcomings on her fingers.

"Look chick," Red started, as I stood next to her with my arms crossed, nodding my head to stress the importance of her words. "We're here to have a good time. It's her birthday and she danced for fun, not for tips. So, I would really, really appreciate it if you would just, shut. The. Fuck. Up." *Go Red, go Red, go Red.* I chanted in my head, as Red pulled us away from the woman before she could respond. We made it to the table just in time to see top cunt take the stage. Red fought hard to control her anger, but I could tell the girl had gotten under her skin. I made a point of ignoring the girl and engaging in conversation with everyone, including Red. It seemed to be working until the bitch on stage walked in front of our table and threw a wad of ones at me.

"Here, ho. Bye ya'self some lessons."

"Oh hell, naw!" Brooklyn said, standing and walking to the stage. "Bitch, we'll fucking kill you!"

"Yep. That's possible," I added, standing and nodding in agreement with Brooklyn's threat. "We do not fuck around. Nope. Not us." I wobbled on my heels, trying to look intimidating, but in my inebriated state, I was more comical than threatening.

"Well why don't we take it to the stage?" the girl asked, now through a microphone. Who the fuck had given her a microphone? I looked around, to find Chris on the phone. I was sure he was calling for back-up.

"Pussyyyy!" I whispered, loud enough for him to hear. He responded by giving me the finger, and I clutched my chest to feign a broken heart, which earned me a smirk. The crowd had grown louder, and I turned to see everyone cheering in favor of a dance off. I cheered too, throwing my fist in the air and screaming with the rest of the fools in the building.

"Would you sit down," Mary said, with a laugh, as she pulled my arm to bring me back to my seat.

"You fuckin' up, girl. That's all I'm sayin'," Punkin yelled to the woman on stage.

"Yeah? Well what you gonna do about it combat boots?" the girl shouted into the microphone, earning her a round of ooohs from everyone in the club, including myself. Katina shot me a warning with her eyes and I shut up, grabbing another drink off of a waiter's tray. When he started to protest, I informed him I was VI-mothafuckin'-P. He walked off with a shake of his head. I guess I told him.

"That's it!" Maddie yelled, standing on our table and hushing the crowd with just her voice. "Red, get on the stage," she commanded, without making eye contact with her.

"Maddie!" Red snapped, in a hushed voice.

"What? You're our only shot!" Maddie replied, stepping down from the table as we all leaned in, while Maddie gave Red a pep talk. "Do you really want us to look like fools?"

"No." Red said, her voice defeated. The amount of liquor we had consumed was absurd, impairing our judgment, and making all of us act completely out of our norm.

"Where is that fiery red-head we all love?" Katina asked, ignoring the impatient crowd as they all stood fist-pumping the air, and chanting.

"Red, baby," Brooklyn said, handing Red a shot and putting her arm around her shoulders. I waited for Brooklyn to give Red the reassuring speech I knew she needed as Red eyed her thankfully, assuming Brooklyn understood why she chose not to dance. "Get your fucking ass on that stage." Well, so much for reassurance and understanding. I was so 'Team Brooklyn' as I nodded, agreeing with her demand.

"If you don't, I'm gonna stomp that bitch to death with my boots," Punkin added, propping her foot on the table and revealing her black boots, which were laced up her ankles.

"Red, Red, Red, Red," Mary began to chant, and soon the entire bar was calling Red out.

"I fucking hate y'all." We cheered, as Red downed the shot Brooklyn handed her and made her way backstage. I clambered up on the table in front of our booth, using Brooklyn's shoulder to hold me up. Once I was up there and steady, she and Maddie joined me, while Katelan, Katina, Mary, Punkin, and Chi Chi stood on the booth behind us.

"Look behind you," Maddie said, signaling toward the door with her head. I turned to see the Devil's Renegades standing at the door, looking intimidating as hell with their arms crossed and faces serious. I frowned when I looked at Luke, hoping he wasn't mad at me for being so drunk. I mean, it was my birthday after all. When his eyes found mine, he gave me a wink and a smile, and as I lifted my arms to give him a little dance and show off my dress, I lost my balance and nearly fell off the table, taking Brooklyn with me. It took every ol' lady in our group to steady us back in position, and when I looked up again, all of the men were fighting hard not to laugh. All but Regg, who stood directly behind us looking nervous as hell. I was not the only one looking at the hot bikers lining the back wall. Every horny woman in there gaped at them with open mouths. There wasn't a dry pair of panties in the house, and my sisters and I held smug smiles because we knew that it was us they would be going home with. Everyone cheered as Gabby, or so the announcer called her, took the stage wearing a black, leather vest and shorts. I booed her, alongside my sisters, before the music even started. When Nelly's "Hot in Here" blasted through the speakers, I couldn't help but dance to the music. Maddie grabbed my arm, and shook her head at me and I stopped, frowning as I watched Gabby work the stage like a pro. Everyone cheered, as she stripped down to her nude underwear and swung around the pole, smiling as if she knew she had already won. She never made it all the way up the pole, but made pretty good work of the part she used. Plus, that was a long way up there. It must just be for decoration. The strobe lights flashed around the room as everybody moved in tune with the music, while Gabby entertained the shit out of them. When the song concluded, ones were thrown on the stage and she sashayed off with her hips in full swing. I looked to Brooklyn, my lips pressed in a thin line.

"She was good," I shouted in her ear, already accepting defeat. Brooklyn threw her head back and laughed at me, lighting a cigarette before she spoke.

"You ain't seen shit, baby girl," I dug my ones out of my dress, ready to throw them at Red to make her feel better, although the bitch hadn't given me shit when I danced. But I hadn't been in a competition, and it took a lot of guts to get on stage and dance against someone who actually knew what they were doing. The lights dimmed, and the strobes were turned off, as a single spotlight hit the center pole. The announcer welcomed Red to the stage and we screamed our asses off, waiting for the music to start. When it didn't, we finally shut up. Once the room was quiet, a song began to play and I recognized it immediately. "Gorilla" by Bruno Mars was a slower tune, one that is sexy and sultry with a good tempo, and, after watching the music video, I had to agree that it was a great song to strip to. Red walked onto the stage in a red, satin, spaghetti-strap nightie that was super short, but covered her. Her long, red hair flowed down her back as she walked around the pole slowly, as if to get a feel for it. When the light caught her just right, I got a glimpse of her face. Her eyes were closed and it was as if she had tuned out everything, but her and the music. When she lifted her arms and swung around the pole, her short skirt fanning out around her, I thought she looked beautiful. The move didn't require much skill, but Red did it with grace, and I was glad she was playing it safe. She twirled around and around, her legs stretching out into a split, until she sat on the stage in front of us, her head hung as her hands slid from the pole, down the sides of her neck, down her waist and over her thighs until they lay splayed on the stage in front of her. I thought she was quitting. I figured she had given it all in her one good move, and she had even surprised me with the splits thing. I gave her an E for effort and we would love her just the same. But Red's timing was perfect, and just as the chorus started, her head snapped up and she became a vixen before our very eyes. I stood in awe, one hand holding onto Brooklyn's shoulder for support, while the other held a fistful of money. Red drew herself up on her knees and began crawling toward us, as we all looked up at her speechless. Her gaze held that of someone who stood behind us and I didn't have to guess who it was. I wanted to look, but I couldn't peel my eyes away from the girl on the stage, who rolled onto her back, lifting her long, shapely legs in the air and crossing her ankles. Her arms splayed at her sides and her back arched off the stage, giving us a look at her face, which held emotions of pain and pleasure. The pole was positioned right between her legs, and her next move had her pulling herself to her feet for only a moment before she was climbing. Her ankles wrapped around the pole as she pulled herself up with her arms, then came back down on a slow twirl, her arms extended and her head dropped back, so that her hair hung freely. This time when she hit the stage, it was on the words "bang bang", and that's exactly what Red did.

"Fuck me," Maddie muttered as Red did just that to the stage. My mouth hung open as she made love in front of a room full of viewers. Her face showed it, her moves showed it, and I was sure if the stage could talk he would ask for a cigarette. At some point during her escape from reality, Red became almost angry. Gone was the slow love-making, and in its place was raw, hardcore fucking. It was as if she was demanding more attention from her imaginary lover when her skilled moves became more aggressive as the song intensified. She took her frustration out on the long, silver pole, caressing it one moment then acting as if it had slapped her the next. When she grabbed it and began climbing, locking her ankles and pulling herself up, causing the muscles in her arms to flex and really show her strength, I was expecting her to go halfway and then spin back down. What I didn't expect was to have to hold tighter to Brooklyn, so as not to lose my balance, while my head leaned further back to watch as she made her way to the top, two stories up. Everyone held their breath, as Red let go with her hands, and fully extended her body, starting her descent upside down at a leisurely pace. When Red's satin gown slid over her head and fell through the air, revealing her lacy black bra and matching

310

black lace boy shorts, the crowd went wild. Her arms hung lifelessly in the air as she depended on her crossed ankles and six inch stilettos, which were wrapped around the pole, to keep her from falling on her head. Before she hit the bottom, her hands found the pole once again as she unlocked her ankles and flipped, landing on her feet. She walked across the stage, her legs crossing in front of one another, as she lifted her finger, pointed over my head and lip-synced the words "you and me baby we be fucking like gorillas", before throwing her head back and hitting her knees. All the emotions that were heard in the lyrics were felt by Red, as her fists knotted in her hair for a moment before she released it to rub her hands suggestively down her body, her eyes never leaving Regg's. She stood and walked back to the pole, taking one last walk around it, just as she had when she had first come out, before posing beside it as the song came to an end. Everyone screamed and money littered the stage, while Red stood breathing hard, her focus on her man not faltering, even in all the commotion. Regg walked in front of us, and Red met him at the edge of the stage. He lifted her from it and every word that wasn't spoken was heard loud and clear. When they shared a kiss so sweet it made all our hearts melt, I was afraid the moment would call for all of us wanting to abandon one another to be with our men. But trust Punkin to ruin it, and get us back on track.

"I thought Red was a dancer," I said to her, as she joined me on the table where I now stood alone. She handed me a shot then leaned in close, so she could be heard over the crowd.

"Hell naw. She was a stripper. Hey, can I tell you a secret?" Punkin asked, her face serious as she chewed on her lip. I gave her a smile and put my hand on her shoulder in reassurance.

"Of course."

"I'm not sure, but I think I just cum."

Chapter 22

Dallas

"But I wanna ride with you," I whined to Luke, as I jumped in his arms and wrapped my legs around him.

"Babe, you ain't riding with me in that fuckin' dress," Luke said, with a laugh. He had retrieved me from the table I had been standing on and him, along with the other guys, had led us out of the crowded bar and to the parking lot. He sat me down, having to pry me from around his waist, and kept a firm hold on me until my wobbly legs finally managed to hold me up. I looked around the parking lot to find Mary and Katina in their own little world, as they attempted to re-enact Red's performance.

"Get in the damned car," Big Al said, holding the door open for Mary, who stopped to grind against him before entering. He rolled his eyes and looked at Luke, not hiding his impatience. "I've already held her hair once this week, while she puked her fucking guts up. I ain't doin that shit again." Luke's body shook with laughter, as he turned me toward the car to climb in behind Mary.

"Yeah, fuck you will," he said, leading Big Al to laugh in agreement.

The door was closed and we were all crammed in, our dresses now soiled with liquor and sweat, and not one of us giving a single fuck about the way we looked. Katelan got behind the wheel, and looked in the rearview mirror to get a headcount. Brooklyn sat in the front seat, while Punkin and Katina claimed the two captain chairs in the middle, and Mary, Chi Chi, Red and Maddie sat on the third row bench seat, leaving me on my knees on the floor between Punkin and Katina.

"Give us some music Katelan," I said, as she pulled into traffic. I held tight onto the arm rests beside me, trying to keep from falling over as she took a sharp right and gassed it. "And slow the fuck down. You tryin' to kill me?" Everyone was talking at once, and I was trying to listen in, but Punkin held my attention as she slid a bottle of birthday cake vodka from her purse, which looked more like a diaper bag. There was no telling what was in there and if I were to find out, it would probably make me an accessory to a crime.

"Happy birthday honey," she said, the wrinkles at the corners of her eyes becoming even more visible, as her smile stretched across her face. "We didn't get you a cake, so I stole this from the bar. Brooklyn helped by distracting Greg while I slipped back there and got it." I had never been more proud to have such skilled thieves as sisters.

"Awe! Thanks guys!" I said, hugging Punkin then leaning to the front to give Brooklyn a kiss on her cheek, as I clutched the bottle of vodka tightly to myself.

"Open it up!" Katina demanded, sitting on the edge of her seat and steadying me, as I struggled to get the lid off. I took a pull then passed it around, until everyone had a drink.

"Music Katelan!" I reminded our very nervous driver, who was trying very hard to pay attention to the road instead of what was going on behind her. She hit the preset station for rap and hip-hop on her satellite radio, and YG's "My Nigga My Nigga" boomed through the speakers. "I fuckin' love this song!" I shouted, fighting for my voice to be heard over the carload of singing women. Everyone danced and sang along, even Punkin sat bobbing her head to the music. The song was our own testimonial to each other. We would ride for each other, die for each other, and wouldn't go in and leave one behind to fend for themselves. We were a team, and through the song lyrics, we let each other know it. When the song ended, Chi Chi hollered from the back for Katelan to turn down the music.

"Okay, I got a question," Chi Chi said, as soon as the volume was muted. I lifted the armrest on Punkin's chair and she scooted over to accommodate me, so I could look at Chi Chi, who was obviously about to ask something important. "Did Luke really spank you?" the silence was deafening as everyone waited for my response.

"Yeah that motherfucker spanked me. I couldn't sit on my ass for the rest of the day." I grumbled, just the reminder of the way it had felt giving me chills. The laughter in the car rattled the windows, as I opened the vodka to take another drink.

"That's fucking crazy!" Mary said, her voice telling me that she didn't really believe my words.

"Well, it happened. He took off his belt, bent me over my own fucking desk, and spanked me," I said, fighting to keep my balance.

315

"Hell, he could spank me," Brooklyn chimed in from the front. I shook my head vigorously, my eyes growing wide and serious.

"Don't say that, Brooklyn. It was bad." She nearly expired at the seriousness of my tone. "Go ahead, bitches. Laugh it up. But there ain't nothing funny about gettin' a whippin'."

"So what did you do?" Chi Chi managed to ask through her laughter.

"I fucking cried!" I answered, finding that they were getting too much enjoyment out of my story, as I watched tears of laughter fall down their faces.

"No," Chi Chi said, shaking her head, her words hard to understand, due to her laughter. And my current state. "I mean, what did you do for him to spank you?" I sobered somewhat at her comment, the laughter dying as everyone took in my face of regret.

"I'll tell you what she done," Maddie offered. My spirit fell at her words. I had not planned to tell them about my trip to see Charlie. That would be something they would all have a hard time forgiving me for. "She stripped for him." Everyone laughed and the crisis was averted. She shot me a wink, and I mouthed a silent thank you to her. The party continued until the vodka was gone, and we were back home safely.

"My head is killing me," I mumbled into my pillow, as I buried my face deep inside it to keep the sunlight out of my eyes. "Please turn off the light." I didn't even know if

Luke was in the room, but if he was, I hope he heard my plea.

"Light's out babe, but I can't prevent the sun from rising," Luke said, his voice coming out refreshed and awake.

"You haven't even tried," I complained, knowing it was impossible, but just wishing he would do something to make my headache go the fuck away.

"Why don't you come shower with me?" Luke asked, running his hand up the back of my thigh and under my panties. I didn't respond and he kept rubbing, massaging, and kneading my ass, thighs, and calves.

"Oh shit that feels good," I moaned into my pillow, as he took my foot in his hands and began applying deep pressure with his thumbs. My heels looked killer last night, but I was paying for it today. I squeezed my eyes shut before lifting my head to flip my pillow. The cool material against my warm, clammy cheek along with Luke's skilled hands massaging my feet was pure bliss. I lay there lifeless, allowing him to cater to me as if I were a queen and him a peasant. The only acknowledgement I gave to reassure him I was alive was a grunt or a moan every now and then. When his hands left my body, after about twenty minutes of pleasuring it, I grumbled in complaint. I knew it was a bitch thing for me to do, but it was the day after my birthday, that should count for something.

"Okay, babe. Come on and get up. It's already two in the afternoon and the guys are gonna want to leave around five." Two o'clock? Had I really slept that long? I thought back to last night and remembered that once we had gotten back to the clubhouse, it was already after three in the morning and I didn't pass out until around five. Shit. It would take me forever to get back on a normal schedule.

"I can't, Luke," I whined, earning me an exasperated sigh from my man, who I was sure looked sexy as fuck this morning.

"Babe," Luke started, but I cut him off.

"My head hurts too bad. I can't even open my eyes. That sunlight is blinding." I felt Luke's arm around my waist as his hand came between my face and the pillow, covering my eyes. He assisted me out of bed, pulling my back to his front when I was on my feet, and guided me to the bathroom with his hand still securely over my eyes. Once we were in the bathroom and the door was closed behind us, Luke released his hand. The only light came from a nightlight that served as a scent warmer, and which cast a very dim glow around the room. My eyes would adjust eventually and it would be perfect, just like Luke.

"Better babe?" he asked, gathering my wild hair into his hands, and holding it up off my neck.

"Much better. You're perfect." He kissed the back of my neck, before releasing my hair and turning me to face him.

"You, Miss Knox, are wearing entirely too many clothes." I looked down at my thin, tank top, which barely covered my navel and the small scrap of black panties I wore. Luke must have removed my dress because last I remembered, I had still had it on. He grabbed the hem of my shirt and I lifted my arms over my head, allowing him

318

to rid me of my clothes. He then hooked his thumbs into my panties, dropping down on one knee as he slid them down my legs. Once I was completely naked, I expected him to lead me into the shower. What I didn't expect was for him to bury his face between my legs, sending my nerve endings into a frenzy, as his tongue began its slow torture in circular movements around my clit. My body jerked in response to his touch, and my hands flew to his hair, which was now long enough for me to pull.

"Fuck!" I let out breathlessly, my headache forgotten and my mind focused on nothing but the way his mouth felt as he kissed, licked, sucked and blew his cool breath on my warm, aching center. He knew just the right places to tease me, prolonging the inevitable. I knew a mind-blowing orgasm was in my near future, but he stopped the moment my climax started to build, applying lighter pressure and moving his mouth to accommodate a different part of my sensitive flesh. I wasn't sure if he was preparing me for something more, making sure I was wet, ready and full of need before he gave me his thick cock, which I knew was hard and anxious to be inside me, or if he was teasing me only to shatter me to pieces and watch me fall apart, as he worked me to my full potential before allowing me to come all over his beautifully wicked mouth. My knees went weak as my fingers dug deeper into his scalp, earning a shocking, electrifying sensation as he placed my throbbing clit between his teeth, giving it a slight nibble before releasing it to continue his torture. My moans and pleas for more echoed off the walls of the small bathroom and my fingers cramped from being knotted in his hair. My breathing was ragged and staccato, and my legs were trembling, the muscles begging for relief from the strain of holding me up when my body wanted to collapse. When I thought I could take no more, when I knew that if I didn't get that release that I had come so close to, but was yet still so far away, he stood, bringing my legs around his waist with one hand while the other supported my back. I was carried from the bathroom, back to the fully lit room where we slept. My eyes squinted as they fought to adjust to the light, but when Luke laid me on my back and slid into me with ease, nothing else mattered.

"Baby, you feel so fuckin' good," he said, working me slowly with painstakingly deep thrusts. I admired his face, his lips slightly parted, coating my face in his cool, minty breath, his ocean-blue eyes shining even at half-mast, and the small furrow between his brows. The feel of Luke stretching me, burying himself completely inside me, slightly circling his hips as his body connected to mine on each drive, was soothing and delicious. But when he lifted my leg, pushing it so that my knee was in my chest, and his drives became forceful, pummeling, plunges the feeling inside me intensified. His pace quickened, the head of his cock hitting that sweet spot inside me, and escalating my senses to a new height. The position was almost painful, but the tiny ache I felt when he reached that peak inside me was overpowered by the astonishing sensation of all that was him. It wasn't just the area deep inside me that sparked when he touched it, or the tingle I felt when he rubbed against that wonderful cluster of nerves as he rotated his hips. It was everything; the way his eyes closed as his emotions claimed his face when I squeezed him or moaned his name, the way his veins bulged in his neck to accommodate the blood that rushed through them to get to his rapidly beating heart. It was the tattoos on his arms and how they stretched across his massive biceps as they formed an intricate pattern all the way to his wrists. Or maybe it was the way the muscles in his stomach constricted, showing me those perfectly toned abs every time his body arched to deliver me that next plunge, which could be the one to send me into that orgasmic abeyance. Whatever was causing me that tingle in my gut, those butterflies in my stomach, and that fulfillment in my heart was because of one man. One man who I'd rather die than live without. One man who made days that were not even my birthday special for me. One man who I know I would go to the ends of the earth for, and one man I had given everything to. As I shattered into orgasm, my body pulsating and contracting around him, I held my eyes open so I could see that one man who made my life worth living. That one man who owned my heart and soul: Lucas Lorn Carmical.

I was showered, dressed, and holding my nose as I chugged the drink Brooklyn assured me could cure any hangover. It smelled like motor oil and fish guts, but at this point, I would try anything. Luke's good afternoon love-making had cured me temporarily, but as the day progressed, the shit feeling I had had when I woke up returned. It was ten minutes after five and the guys were planning another night out. This time, we had been invited to ride along since we were going to Wawee's, which was a local spot that the club often frequented. Of course, on the night we actually got to ride, the temperature decided to take a nosedive into the low forties. I was dressed as warm as my wardrobe allowed, wearing two pair of leggings, skinny jeans, thigh-high boots, three shirts, a leather jacket, and my cut. Chi Chi assisted me with my bandana, which was over my ears in an attempt to keep them warm. Southerners thought anything below sixty degrees was cold, so tonight was considered freezing to us, and our destination was about a thirty minute ride away. Doing the math, ninety miles an hour in forty-two degree weather equaled too fucking cold.

"Let's go," Ronnie announced, as he stood there in leather from his head to his toes. I didn't ask, but I was sure he had to special order his chaps to accommodate his long legs. We walked to the bikes in silence. Every ol' lady was feeling the side effects of last night. I had not seen Red or Maddie all day, until about fifteen minutes ago when they had come trudging into the main room, begging Brooklyn for her miracle concoction. The guys, on the other hand, were taking full advantage of the silence by constantly talking and laughing extremely loudly, punishing us and our throbbing heads as a form of payback for having to take care of us. Everyone was present except for Katelan. It was not unusual for a PROSPECT's wife to not be present on any ride, unless it was a family affair or a situation like last night. Luke said PROSPECTs had enough to worry about, and throwing a wife into the mix just complicated shit. I could see how that would be a problem with a troublemaker like myself, but Katelan actually knew how to act when she went out in public. We pulled into traffic and took off as if we were running from the cops, which I didn't doubt, and I held tight to Luke, using his body to shield the freezing wind that seemed to cut through my layers of leather and clothes all the way to my skin. Luke was kind enough to turn on the radio and soon favorites of mine and his were blasting through the speakers. Classic country hit after classic country hit played, ranging from Vern Gosdin's "Chiseled in Stone" to Johnny Paycheck's "Old Violin". I let the music take me

322

away, singing the lyrics to myself as we flew down the highway. Before I knew it, we were pulling into Wawee's and by the way Luke's body tensed, I knew something was wrong. I peeked my head around his wide shoulders and found the parking lot lined with over sixty bikes. A wave of uneasiness washed over me, as Luke turned off the bike's engine, leaning up to allow me to clamber off, before gracefully dismounting himself. A group of men gathered in a crowd in the center of the parking lot, forming a circle around someone or something.

"That's Mike," Luke said, more to himself than anyone else. "Stay here." He commanded me, walking behind Ronnie, as the entire club walked over to join the mass of men in leather.

Chapter 23

Dallas

"I'm not stayin' here," Brooklyn snapped, falling in behind our men. I stood there, watching in horror as she stomped off. Soon, everyone was following Brooklyn's lead and although I had been told to stay, I joined them. As we approached, I recognized the black and white patches the men wore, with Metal and Madness stitched boldly across the back. In the middle stood a man who wore a different cut from the Devil's Renegades, but the colors were the same. He stood tall and proud, without the slightest hint of fear on his face. To say he was handsome was an understatement.

"Before you open your mouth, I want everyone here to know that I am willing to die for this cut. Right here tonight." My heart stopped at the mere thought of Ronnie being subjected to danger. I watched the anger radiate from him, as he continued his speech. "Your club has been coming into my town and ruining the relationship we have worked to build with this community our entire lives. I don't give a fuck if there are five hundred of you motherfuckers, I will fight until I don't have a breath left in my body, as will my brothers, to protect what we have. So, if you think bringing in reinforcements from all across the country is gonna help save your ass, then you're wrong. We may go down tonight, but you can rest assure that at least half of you motherfuckers are going down with us." At Ronnie's words, my nervousness dissipated and was replaced with pride; the kind that straightens your backbone, and allows you to lose all sense of reason and logic to defend what makes you who you are. This

324

club had made me who I was and now our odds were looking better. Judging by the looks of my sisters, our army had just doubled. "Now you have traveled a long way to say something, so speak your fucking mind." My eyes stayed trained on the man leading the pack, who I assumed was the president of the chapter. I later found out that he was the national president, the top of the food chain, and every piece of shit in the parking lot behind him derived from the same basket as this one bad apple.

"First of all, I don't know what you mean when you say we have ruined your relationship with your community. I don't see how that's possible. How can a few men destroy in less than a month something that you say you built in a lifetime?" The man waited for a reply, his stance casual and non-threatening.

"Your men came into my town and trashed bars, disrespected civilians, and intimidated everyone they came into contact with. Half the places we were once welcome now have signs that read if you wear a cut, you can't come in. Now when we go somewhere, we are under the close watch of everyone who isn't family. We don't need that kind of heat on us. Like I said, we have fought very hard to earn the trust of the people in this town, and you should know how difficult that is to do." The man's face transformed from impassive to incredulous, as he eyed Ronnie, his mind battling whether he should believe him or not. He yelled a name and a man from the back of the crowd reluctantly came up front.

"Do you have any idea what this man is talking about?" his eyes never left Ronnie's as he spoke; waiting for an answer that would prove Ronnie wrong, yet by the look on his face, you could tell he already knew the truth.

"I mean, we didn't trash no bars. Lopair got a little rowdy one night, but what was I supposed to do?"

"Fucking stop him. Apologize to the people you disrespected, and deal with your man when you got out of the public eye," Luke snapped, his voice so deadly and threatening that it took the man a moment before he could reply.

"Look, I'm my brother's keeper," the man replied, his defense weak and unconvincing to Luke, who fired back at him on a snarl.

"I'm my brother's keeper, too," he said, pointing to a large, round patch on the front of his cut that said it just as plain as day in orange and black. "But you can bet your ass if one of them steps out of line that I handle it, so my club doesn't take the fall for it. That's what a brother's keeper does, he protects him even if it's from himself." The man had no response, and I knew Luke wished he did. He was itching to put his hands on him, as was everyone else in the club. If these guys didn't shut up soon, all hell was fixing to break loose.

"Tell me what we can do to make it right," the leader said, hoping for a truce that I was afraid wouldn't come.

"Leave. Get the fuck outta my town and go find another one to fuck up," Ronnie said, his tone letting the man know the offer was not negotiable. But the man pressed on, hoping to settle the problem with a different alternative.

"This is a big town. Can it not accommodate the both of us?" His voice was not hopeful or pleading, just straightforward, and without emotion.

"I think you already know that answer. If you're smart, you'll leave. If you decide to stay, you better build a fucking army 'cause I'm gonna make it my mission to take you down. We don't tolerate disrespect from anyone. We don't give a fuck how untouchable you think you are." I knew Ronnie was referring to the fact that the majority of their club consisted of lawyers and cops. They figured they could do whatever they wanted and get away with it, but in this town, it was the outlaws who ran the streets. Not some pencil pushin', divorce attorney or cop, who lived on a median income and whose highlight of the day was writing traffic violation tickets. No, this was biker world and nobody knew it better than our guys. Anyone could ride a Harley and slap a patch on, but it was how they conducted themselves while wearing it that made the difference between us and them. The man studied Ronnie for a long time. I don't know if he was weighing his options, or waiting for one of our guys to make a move, but when he finally did speak, I was relieved. He closed the small distance between him and Ronnie, stopping a couple of feet from him when Shark and Bryce stepped out from behind Ronnie and halted the man with a look.

"I am Metal and Madness National President Jock, and on behalf of my club I want to apologize for the disrespect and inconvenience some of our members have caused you. I can assure you that it will be dealt with." Ronnie didn't stick his hand out to Jock and Jock didn't offer his hand to Ronnie. He just turned and walked back to his club, signaling with his hand for everyone to get ready to leave. We stood and watched until the last bike was gone and the sounds of the pipes were far in the distance.

"I'm glad y'all showed up. Hell, I was thinkin' I was gonna have to have all the fun myself," the handsome man who was already there when we arrived said, his face breaking out into a smile revealing a perfect dimple in each cheek. I heard Red sigh next to me and found her eyes filled with lust, as they raked down the man's tall, muscular body.

"That Dallas, is Malfuctional MC President, Magic Mike." I followed her gaze and watched as Mike hugged each of the men, and then made his way over to the ladies. Red nearly took everyone out, as she reached to wrap her arms around Mike's neck. "Have mercy I have missed you!" Red squealed, stopping to grab Mike's shoulders, biceps, and forearms with a squeeze. "Fuck," she said, shaking her head as if to clear her thoughts. There was no telling what was going on inside that head of hers.

"Red, you lookin' fine, and you still crazy as hell," Mike said, before giving the other ladies a hug. When he got to me, he stuck his hand out and I took it with a smile. "Malfuctional MC President Mike."

"Dallas, Property of Devil's Renegades President, LLC." When I introduced myself, like a fucking pro, the expression on Mike's face turned to surprise, as he looked at the vest I wore for confirmation.

"I'll be damned. Well Dallas, it is a pleasure to finally meet you." He said, his eyes sparkling with amusement.

"Likewise," I said, with a nod. Our attention was drawn to the small SUV that barreled through the parking lot, coming to a screeching halt in front of us. A pretty brunette emerged from the car, her face filled with panic and worry as she appraised Mike for a moment before clutching her chest in relief.

"Oh thank God," she said, running and jumping into his arms. I took in her outfit, consisting of a hoodie and pajama pants that were stuffed inside a pair of snow boots. She grabbed Mike's face and kissed him before gathering Brooklyn and Red in a hug, hurriedly talking to each of them. "I was sitting at home when I got a call from the bartender to tell me that Mike was surrounded by Metal and Madness in the parking lot. I just threw some shoes on and jumped in the car." She hugged the other girls, everyone telling her she looked beautiful even in her scruffy attire. She walked to me and stuck her hand out, her eyes wild and crazy as she came down off the rush of adrenaline. "Angela, Property of Malfuctional MC President, Magic Mike."

"Dallas, Property of Devil's Renegades President, LLC," I said, smiling to myself. I was now two for two. Her eyes drifted to the patch on the front of my cut in disbelief, just as her ol' man's had.

"Holy shit," she said, staring at me. "I'm sorry," she shook her head, pulling her out of her state of shock. "It's so good to finally meet you, Dallas. I'm excited to see the girl who stole LLC's heart in the flesh. For a little while, I thought you didn't exist."

"Well, here I am," I said, with a laugh, unsure of how to respond to her comment.

"Ladies, it's so good to see you all, but I have to get back home. Dallas, it really is a pleasure to meet you." We waved goodbye, as she found Mike before getting back into her vehicle and leaving. We crowded into the bar, and as Big Al announced that the first round was on him, all the ol' ladies groaned in unison. Not only were our nerves frazzled and stomachs rolling with soured liquor, now we would have to play babysitters to a bunch of grown men who we were sure would drink themselves stupid in celebration of regaining what was rightfully theirs.

Now that the issue in Lake Charles was solved, there was no need for the Hattiesburg chapter to hang around any longer. The next day, started with a teary goodbye as we prepared to leave and head back to Mississippi. I would miss my sisters, but they assured me they would keep in contact, and I promised the same in return. Maddie was anxious to get back home to Logan, standing impatiently at the door, as I gave a second round of hugs out before finally joining her and Red in the car. The bikes took the lead as we barreled down the interstate with no regard for the speed limit. The ride was long and quiet, as we all lost ourselves in our own thoughts. Mine drifted back to the first night I had arrived in Lake Charles and the mood I had found Luke in. He had promised that when this was all over he would tell me what had been weighing on his mind. As we neared home, I become more anxious about what he had to say. By the time we made it to Luke's, I was a nervous wreck.

"Everything okay babe?" he asked, eyeing me cautiously as we sat at the kitchen counter. We had said our goodbyes to everyone, and now Luke and I had the house to ourselves.

"You told me you would tell me what was going on after the shit with Metal and Madness was over," I reminded him, not elaborating further, because I didn't feel there was any need to do so.

"I told you I wanted to enjoy two weeks with you," he corrected, standing on his toes to reach the back of the cabinet, searching for what I knew was his hidden stash of junk food.

"Cut the bullshit Luke and just tell me what's going on," I said, exasperated. I was tired of playing the waiting game with him. Luke took his time, analyzing me from across the room, as he shoved into his mouth a cookie he had retrieved from the back of the forbidden cabinet.

"Charlie Lott has offered one million dollars to a man to kill you." *What the fuck*? My breathing ceased, my body stilled, and my heart went into overdrive at his words. He watched me closely, letting my new-found knowledge sink in, before he continued. "He doesn't really want to kill you, he just wants someone to abduct you so he can come in and save the day in the hope it will be enough for you to want to be with him." I sat in shock, listening to words I knew had to be true but were difficult to actually believe. "Dallas, I have a plan, but I'm gonna need your help. You think you're up for it?" This part was easy to comprehend, easy to believe, and even easier to answer.

"Absolutely."

Chapter 24

Dallas

I woke suddenly, finding that the room was cast in pale lighting from the flickering T.V. I had been dozing in and out of consciousness over the past few hours, a result of exhaustion from my struggle against waterboarding. I shivered at the thought of it, my movements waking me completely, and reminding me I had a job to do. I didn't know how much time had passed, all I knew was that it was now dark outside. I had been left alone for the rest of the afternoon and I didn't know what time the goons would be back. Step one of my mission was to get captured. Step two was to call Luke when my captors left the room. I was assured the phone lines would be working, I just had to make sure I got to the phone without getting caught. If in the event I couldn't get to it, the plan was over. I had until midnight, and, by the lack of noise from outside, I might already be too late. I swallowed hard, my throat dry and scratchy, as I prepared myself for the five-foot journey to the phone. I sat in the chair, my pants soiled from my own urine, and my t-shirt covered in dry vomit. My hair was wild and untamed, damp strands sticking to my face and neck. I scooted my chair, moving only an inch, thankful for the thin, worn carpet. I pushed forward, letting the memory of Luke's voice invade my head as I remembered how he had trained me. When he had talked me through my mission, he had transformed from my lover to my teacher.

"You're going to be scared. You're going to think of all the things that will go wrong, but you have to stay

focused. You're the only one who can do this Dallas. When you feel like giving up, dig deep and find the will to survive. Think of the sacrifices you've made. Let the priceless memories of the past few weeks flood your mind and fuel your drive. When they leave you alone, get to the phone. You will likely be restrained, but they will want to talk to you so I'm guessing you'll be in an upright position. The room is only ten feet wide. You should be able to get to the other side. If you can't get there, be patient and stay still. You have until midnight and then you're outta there. You can do this, baby. I wouldn't put you in danger if I thought you couldn't handle it. But, Lord knows it kills me. If I could trade places and do it myself I would. Now, put your game face on, and remember how much you have to fight for."

I made it to the phone, letting Luke's words overpower the pain in my chest, as I pulled against the restraints and the dryness in my throat, which craved a drink of water. The time on the phone read 11:52. I had eight minutes. I pushed my tongue between my lips, stiffening it as I hit the speakerphone button. I sighed in relief as the loud dial tone filled the room. I punched in the number I had memorized, with my tongue moving slowly, so as not to mess up. It rang once before I heard Luke's voice.

"Dallas?" he asked, hopefully. I felt tears spring to my eyes as he spoke to me.

"Yes," I said, with a croak, my voice coming out rough and dry.

"You okay?" me being hurt had not been part of the plan. Luke had been sure that Charlie would not let any harm come to me, as had I. I guess we had both been outsmarted. I didn't want Luke to know what had happened, not right now. He needed to believe all was well. I knew if he found out he would call the whole thing off, and our one shot would be ruined.

"I'm fine," I said, straining my voice so that I sounded more like myself. "I dozed off. My mouth is just dry." What I would have given for one of Punkin's peppermints.

"You're sure?" He asked, his voice sounding worried.

"I'm sure. We don't have much time," I said, turning my head to look at the door as I spoke.

"Just a few more hours, baby. Do you remember what to do next?" His voice was hesitant and I envisioned him pacing, running his hands through his hair, and wishing we'd never done this.

"Yes, I remember. I'm gonna hang up now. I'll see you soon." My words sounded promising, but I wasn't sure how much truth they actually held.

"Yes you will. I love you, baby," Luke said, his words just as promising and determined as mine.

"I love you too." I stuck my tongue out and hit the speaker button, ending the call because I knew he didn't have the strength to. As I scooted back across the room, my heart hurt for Luke. I couldn't imagine the willpower it had taken for him to let me do this. He was my protector, the one who had saved me time and time again, yet he was the one who had coached me on how to save myself. I made it back to the center of the room between the two beds, my chest burning from the pain my lungs had endured earlier today. It took a while, but eventually, I calmed down. I was alert, aware, and ready when the door was opened almost an hour later, and the three goons, dressed head-to-toe in black, entered.

"How you feeling, Dallas?" The man asked, turning on the lamp beside the T.V.. I ignored him, my eyes following his every move, as he walked across the floor to take a seat on the bed beside me. I wished he would remove his mask so I could see his face. I tried hard to remember his voice, but it didn't sound familiar to me. "Ready for round two?" he laughed at the look of panic on my face. I shook my head, unable to stop the movement as terror filled me. Just the thought of being subjected to his waterboarding torture had my heart racing and tears pricking the backs of my eyes. "I'm only kidding. That was fun, but I have something different in mind." I watched as his head moved up and down my body, taking me in with lust-filled eyes. He didn't seem to care how I smelled or what I looked like. I closed my eyes, letting Luke's words fill my mind once again.

"You shouldn't be subjected to any harm, but if you are, don't panic. Move your body, so that you can feel that piece of steel digging in your back. If they want to hurt you, they will have to untie you. When they do, as soon as your hands are free, you reach behind you and pull out that M9 and don't think twice. Aim at their heads and pull the fucking trigger. I know you can do it. You have already proven you're a good, fast shot. Before their bodies have time to hit the floor, you call me and tell me it's over then you run. I will meet you, just like we planned. I'm counting on it not happening. Charlie's interest in you is the only reason I'm doing this. He wouldn't tolerate anyone hurting

you. But, just in case, you remember: Your life is the only one that is important. Don't let them touch you, Dallas. You kill them. Kill them all."

"Phone." One of the goons announced, handing the cell phone to the man sitting beside me.

"Yeah. Yes, sir. As you wish. I'll see you then." The goon snapped the phone shut and handed it back, never taking his eyes off of me. I stared at the T.V. screen, trying to ignore him. "Now, why would the man who hired me to kill you want to see you one last time?" the guy asked, tapping his finger on his chin. "Is it because he just wanted to pay me to capture you so he could kill you himself? Or is it because he wanted to use me to make the kidnapping, then kill me, and kill you himself? Do you know the answer?" I closed my eyes, my tears flowing down my face, as the man realized he had been played. How could Charlie have been so stupid? He was not an amateur. He should have known better. "Why do I feel like you were in on this little set up?" I kept my eyes closed, refusing to look at the betrayed man. "I see, well," the man said, standing up from the bed. I opened my eyes, watching him as he walked across the room, popping his knuckles and stretching his neck. "The joke is on y'all. You're gonna die today, Dallas Knox, and I'm gonna take my five hundred grand and forget the other half was ever offered." He walked back over to in front of me and leaned down, putting his face very close to mine, as he held onto the arms of my chair. "I am gonna pour water over your face, until you drown, then I'm gonna cut your tongue out, like I should have done when I had the chance." The man removed the ski mask revealing the face I feared was beneath it. Crazy stood there, the tattoos that crawled up his neck to his jaw were in plain sight, and a dreadful reminder of the last time I had seen him. I stared at him, my eyes wide with shock and brimming with tears, my nostrils flaring as my breathing accelerated, and my mouth releasing the slightest whimper as it dropped open in horror. "Dennis!" the man snapped, causing me to jump in surprise. I looked over his shoulder as the man removed his mask and I remembered him as the one who had broken into Luke's house, suffered at the hands of Luke's iron fist, and grew excited and hard at the thought of touching me while he assisted in my assault at the hands of Frankie. "You recognize these faces?" Crazy asked, motioning between himself and Dennis. "If you don't, we're about to refresh your memory. We're gonna relive that scene in your barn, but this time *I* will be in charge. We gonna tie you up, wet you down, fuck you dry, then kill you. And baby," he said, his dark eyes filled with hate and evil as he ran a finger down my cheek. "There won't be anyone to save you this time." I began sobbing, begging for them to stop. I pulled against my restraints, screaming in the man's face, prompting him to throw his hand over my mouth in an attempt to shut me up. "Jeff, get the gag!" Crazy yelled, and I stilled on his words. My sobbing stopped and my screams ceased, my flawless acting skills no longer needed as the name I had been waiting to hear was spoken. I looked into the eyes of Crazy, the look of victory in my own eyes registering on his face as I smiled underneath the weight of his hand. I watched as he stood and turned, reluctantly pulling his eyes from mine to land on that set of ocean-blues I loved so much.

Chapter 25

Dallas

"Where is Jeff?" Crazy asked, his hands in the air as a result of Luke's gun, which was pointed at his head.

"Right where I left him, but don't worry, you'll be seeing him soon enough," Luke said, motioning with his gun for Crazy and Dennis to move to the other side of the room. Jeff, my ex-lover that Luke later found out was working for Frankie, was the flaw in Charlie's plan that had given us the opportunity we needed to intercede. With a little bit of persuasion, Luke had convinced Jeff whose side he needed to be on. Jeff apparently felt terrible about what had happened to me and was willing to do whatever he needed to help. A gun shoved down his throat was also a factor in his decision, but regardless of the reason, Jeff accepted Crazy's offer to assist in capturing me, and kept us informed of their every move. As they had walked from their vehicles to the outside of my room, Luke had simply walked in behind Dennis, rather than Jeff. The darkness and location of the hotel made the exchange work in our favor. Once I heard Jeff's name, it was all the confirmation I needed to know that the switch had been made. Had it not, plan B would have taken effect, and it was much more risky than plan A.

"So, what happens now?" Crazy asked, his hands behind his head as he glared at Luke.

"You have two options. With the first, you might have a chance to live. With the second, I kill you," Luke said with a shrug, feigning disinterest either way.

"Well it looks as if I don't have a choice," Crazy answered, his voice laced with malice, as he looked into Luke's eyes. This was the part we feared most; whether Crazy would actually follow through or if he would kill me just because he could. Because of that, Luke sweetened the deal.

"When Charlie Lott walks through that door, kill him," Luke said, spitting Charlie's name as if it left a bad taste in his mouth. "Don't ask questions, don't wait for introductions. Just shoot him dead. He will possibly have three men with him. You have to take them out as well." Crazy laughed at Luke's offer.

"Why the fuck would I do that? I'd be signing my own death warrant. Nobody can just kill Charlie Lott," Crazy said, looking at Luke as if he had lost his mind.

"You've already signed your death warrant, which brings me to the second part of my first offer. If you succeed in killing Charlie and actually walk out of here alive, and Dallas is unharmed, I'll help you disappear. With a lot of money."

"How much money?" Crazy asked, the offer on the table sounding more appealing now that he knew he didn't have a choice.

"Ten million dollars," I said, with a smile, watching as his face held recognition of our earlier conversation when I had offered him that to not torture me. It didn't take long for him to answer, which was great considering time was not of the essence.

I was still tied to the chair, still covered in vomit and still sitting in piss when another episode of "Golden Girls" came on. This time, I was gagged. After Luke left, Crazy made it his mission to make me as uncomfortable as possible. At least he used a bandana and not duct tape. I was lost in my own thoughts, remembering the promise Luke had made to me as we had said our goodbyes the day I left for Atlanta. We were going through everything once again and when we discussed him leaving me here after making Crazy an offer, I knew it would be difficult for him to endure.

"When you come into that room, no matter the state I'm in, you have to play it cool. Whatever he says to me, whatever he does, you can't lose it. If you kill Crazy, all of this will be for nothing. We need him. If everything goes according to plan, you walk out of that room and don't look back. This is what you have trained me for. It's what we have spent days preparing for and I'm ready. I'm going to need you to trust I can handle it. I know it will be hard. I know you will want to take me with you, but you can't. Don't say goodbye, don't kiss me, don't look at me, and don't you dare fucking change your mind. Luke, promise me that you will leave, and promise me that you will be waiting for me when this is all over"

"I promise."

Luke had fulfilled his promise, and had left without a single glance in my direction. I knew when he had walked out of this room and left my fate in the hands of Crazy, a little piece of him had died. I almost wished he could have traded places with me, not because I wanted him subjected to harm, but because I knew the turmoil he endured in walking out was worse than any physical punishment. We had already lived through that once before when he had chosen Maddie to go with him, and had left me in the hands of Charlie. To do it twice was almost too much for one man to take...Almost. Good thing Luke was not your average man. The flash of headlights bouncing off the walls in the room notified us that Charlie had arrived. He was right on time, according to Crazy, and I hadn't expected any less of him. Crazy stood next to Dennis across the room, both of their hands behind their backs, as they held tightly to their guns and prepared for battle. I had been moved as far back as possible, leaving me pressed up against the night stand between the two beds, out of the line of gunfire. Hopefully. I was breathing hard, my eyes dry from them being open so wide, watching the door and waiting for it to burst open and the firing to begin. I started to hyperventilate. My body got that feeling you have when you are at the top of a rollercoaster, the slow climb causing the nerves inside you to build until you reach the top, where there is no turning back. The descent is slow at first, but then it free-falls, and your heart drops to your stomach, making bile rise in your throat, as your mind diligently attempts to prepare you for the worst, and you come face-to-face with what you are convinced is death. When the door swung open, two men entered and without question, opened fire on Crazy and Dennis before they had time to react. The sound of the bullets exiting the silencers on their pistols was louder to me than if they had been shooting without them. As I watched Crazy and Dennis' lifeless bodies fall to the floor, I knew that sound was one I would never forget. My body heaved, trying to rush air into my lungs, which at this point was like breathing through a straw. I took loud, quick breaths in through my nose, my tongue pushing against the bandana in the hope of removing it, so that I could breathe. Charlie walked in behind the men, straightening the cufflinks on his customary black suit as his eyes surveyed the room. When they landed on me, he frowned, and I knew he was very displeased with my appearance. He quickly walked over to me, untying the bandana from around my mouth. As soon as it was removed, I began sucking large amounts of air into my mouth, trying to accommodate my aching lungs, as I continued to hyperventilate. The tape around my waist was cut and Charlie grabbed my head, gently pushing it me between my legs while he gathered my hair in his hands. Once I was somewhat calm, I sat back in the chair, eyeing the three men in the room. I recognized the tall, dark-skinned man who was always with Charlie and one of the goons that had assisted in my previous abduction.

"Dallas," Charlie said, his voice soothing, as he sat on the bed next to me. I pulled my gaze to him, regret so evident in his face that I almost felt sorry for him. "I am going to cut the tape off you, and see if I can rub some feeling back into your limbs." I nodded in acknowledgment, as Charlie freed my hands and ankles, which were taped tightly to the chair. He grabbed my arm, stretching it slowly and rotating it, causing me to whimper as a result of the pain and relief I felt from the movement. He kneaded my arms with his firm, skilled hands before making his way down to my wrists, and then my fingers. I watched as he slowly worked me, bringing life back into my arms. When I could flex my fingers on my own, he dropped to one knee in front of me to begin the same motion on my calves.

"I'm dirty," I whispered, embarrassed as recognition of my disgusting soiled state registered on his face.

"This wasn't supposed to happen," he said, taking in my filthy clothes and rancid odor. My bottom lip jutted out, involuntarily trembling as the shocking events of the past twenty-four hours finally took their toll on me. I had a plan to stick to. I couldn't break now. My condition was supposed to be beneficial to my mission. Part of the plan was to make Charlie realize what he had done was a mistake, but as I looked into his eyes, filled with pity and remorse, I couldn't help but ask the question that burned at the back of my mind.

"How could you do this to me?" I asked, with a sob, as he knelt at my feet. His white hair was perfectly parted, his suit creased to perfection, and his scent was cool and refreshing, while I had been forced to undergo the most traumatic form of torture and was left praying for death, as I sat bound to a chair in the remnants of my anguish. "You did this," I said gesturing down my body as my sobs intensified at his guilt-stricken face. "And for what? To try and prove that you're what's best for me? Do you know what they did to me?" this time Charlie's eyes dropped from my face, and focused on my feet as he removed my shoes and began massaging them. "Do you know?!" I shouted, springing forward in my seat to get closer to him. He looked away, avoiding my stare, but he couldn't block out my voice. "They tortured me! Th-They held a towel over my face and tried to drown me! I've had to sit in my own fucking piss for twenty-four hours, while you were sitting on your royal fucking throne!" I was crying, screaming, begging him to understand what he had done. As my words penetrated his brain, the images he created to match my story replaying in his mind over and over, his expression became angry. Gone was the look of remorse, and in its place was cold fury.

"Luke never should have left you like this." The slight widening of my eyes at his comment confirmed his accusation. "I'm not stupid, Dallas. I knew Luke had gotten in touch with Jeff and I knew what his plan would be before he concocted it. He is a fool if he thought for even a minute that he could outsmart me. I am the Alpha and the Omega, Dallas. I am the beginning and the end. God himself doesn't even reign over me. Luke is a fucking idiot to leave your fate in the hands of someone as unstable as Crazy, and, because of that, look what you have been through. Those people are savages, Dallas," he spat, standing and stomping around the room as he continued his rant, fueled with rage and hate. Just the sight of him made me sick. He was responsible for this, yet he blamed Luke. "Luke Carmical will never amount to more than what he is; a pathetic waste of air that rides a Harley and plays in the minors. I own the fucking world, Dallas. I have it at my fingertips. The people you have been slumming it with are here for only one reason, because people like me need to step on them to get to the top. So, you tell me now Dallas, in the game of life, who will you choose? Who will win: A man who can give you the world on a silver platter, or a man who can only make false promises, while he drags you from one disgustingly contaminated clubhouse to another?" I looked at Charlie, who now stood several feet from me. His words had cut me deep and it was like salt in the wound, as I played them over and over in my

344

head. I knew he was aware of Luke's plan, we were counting on it. I also knew how much he hated the club, only because they posed a threat to him, and the truce he had made long ago wouldn't allow him to do anything about it. The terms he used when he spoke of my family only made my decision easier. I was once like Charlie. I had believed that I was on top of the world, looking down at the people below me, silently thanking them for allowing me to use their lives as stepping stones. But one thing I was not guilty of was blasphemy. Charlie felt superior to God. He considered himself untouchable even by the Almighty himself. He had evaded the inevitable for years, but this time divine intervention would make its presence known in the life of Charlie Lott. If he wanted to portray the role as Alpha and Omega, then I would introduce him to the angel of death. As the cold metal of my gun filled my hand, I answered his question right before the back of his head exploded, as the bullet flew through his skull.

"Luke wins."

Chapter 26

Dallas

It took a moment for the goons to realize what had just happened. As they watched Charlie's body collapse to the floor, I took the opportunity to train my gun on them. This was something I had not mentally prepared for, but I let Luke's voice guide me, even though he was miles away.

"If you have to pull your gun, fire. Don't ever show it unless you plan to use it. If you do, get out of there as fast as you can. Even in the worst parts of town, someone will report gunfire. Keep your mind focused on your target, but once you squeeze that trigger, it's over and you need to focus on your next move. You can do this, baby. Now, shoot the target and move to the next. Don't let anyone or anything distract you. Stay in the zone and stay in control."

"I'm going to walk out of here now," I said, standing on my wobbly legs, forcing them to hold me up. "I suggest the two of you do the same. Don't follow me and don't come looking for me. If you aren't aware of Charlie's orders about excluding me from harm, then I suggest you get acquainted with the man who is now in charge." The black man eyed me warily, wondering how I was aware of such confidential information. "To answer the question that you refuse to ask, Charlie is the one who shared that useful piece of information, and it was a fatal mistake." Charlie had informed Luke that no matter my transgressions, his army had specific orders that no harm was to come my way. He forgot to add a clause that stated it was null and void if I took his life. Like I said, divine intervention.

"It was a fatal mistake, and a very stupid one. As Charlie's second, I can assure you that no harm will come your way. You are free to go Miss Knox." I took a second to wipe my fingerprints from the arm of the chair, before I made my way to the door. The men stepped aside and I nervously walked past them, afraid that the goon who looked quite pleased to now be running things might not be as faithful to his word as Charlie had been. When my feet hit the concrete sidewalk, I stuffed my gun in the back of my pants, pulled my hood up over my head, and attempted to run as fast as my stiff muscles would allow. There were no cops in sight as I looked around nervously, having to remind myself of my next plan of action. I was not in the clear just yet. I had to get away from the scene and meet Luke before a certain time. If I was not at his hotel by noon, he would come looking for me. The last thing we needed was for him to be seen anywhere around the scene of the crime. I was thankful for the thunderstorm that was brewing. The light shower of rain was helping to wash the grime from my body, as I hobbled down the block, keeping my head down as much as possible as my eyes focused on the stop signs in front of me. I would not get sidetracked. I would not allow my mind to think of anything, but my next move. I was to go to the third stop sign and turn left. The light shower became a heavy downpour as the heavens opened, and the flood gates were released. The sounds of sirens in the distance helped to urge my stubborn muscles to work harder, so I could move faster. By the time I rounded the corner at the third stop sign, I was running. My feet splashed through the puddles of water as the cold, hard rain beat down on me. In a matter of minutes, I was running down the stairs of the subway station and out of the rain. I found the ladies restroom on the right and ran inside, going to the fourth stall to find it occupied. I waited patiently, keeping my head down, so as not to draw attention to myself. I counted to ten in my head, remembering Luke's words as I began to feel anxious.

"Don't allow yourself time to think. When you find yourself in a situation where you have to wait out some time before your next move, do something simple that doesn't require a lot of focus. Say your ABCs or count to twenty. Repeat this until you can move forward. If you think, you will get upset- allowing time for panic to set in. If you've made it out of the room, you're on the homestretch. Don't fuck it up over something stupid. Be patient. Keep your head down and don't do anything to draw attention to yourself. If you engage in conversation with someone, it will throw you off. Ignore people. It's a big city. They are used to it."

When the door to the stall finally swung open, I waited for the woman to leave, before stepping into the stall and locking the door behind me. I squatted down, finding the loose tile behind the toilet and removing it with ease. Inside the hollow space was a small, black bag about the size of a clutch purse. I opened it, my eyes ignoring everything else in the bag as I searched for the key with the yellow tag. I found it, flipping it over to find #19 inscribed on it, and zipped the bag, placing it into the front pocket of my hoodie as my hand clutched tightly to the key. I replaced the tile and exited the stall, avoiding the mirror that lined the wall in front of me. I walked back up the steps leading to the main road, and took a right, walking quickly until I was forced to stop at an intersection. *1 2 3 4 5 6 7 8 9 10 11 12 13 14 15,* as soon as the crosswalk signaled for me to go, I was off again. At the second intersection, I took a right and shielded my eyes from the rain as I looked up. The balconies overlooking the street confirmed I was in the right place. Number nineteen, third door on the right, was my next destination. I pulled the hand that still clutched the key from my pocket, and inserted it into the lock. I stepped inside, locked the door behind me, and went in search of the bathroom, as Luke's voice reminded me of why I was here.

"Your goal is to not leave a trace. We don't want any stones unturned. The chances of you being tied to this are slim, but we aren't taking any chances. You want to distance yourself from the scene, get rid of anything that can tie you to it, and make sure you have an alibi as to where you were. You own an apartment in Atlanta. Make sure they know you are there. Keep your voice calm, make the call and create the problem. Be sure to do or say something familiar, use the tone of voice you would if the problem had actually occurred, but don't say too much. Get to the point, get off the phone and remember, once you hang up you only have fifteen minutes."

I pulled a hand towel from beneath the sink, threw it in the toilet and flushed, holding my breath until the toilet became clogged, and water began filling up the bowl. I walked to the kitchen, retrieved the phone from the wall, and made a call to the maintenance office.

"This is Dallas Knox," I said, my voice coming out strong, confident, and laced with the slightest hint of bitchiness. "I have an appointment to show one of my apartments and I walked in to find the bathroom flooded. Something seems to be lodged in the toilet. I'm going to need someone here to fix it. I have already turned the water off and cancelled my showing."

"Yes, Miss Knox. We will get someone on that right away."

"While you're at it, call me a taxi. I have scheduled to show another property while you fix the problem here."

"Yes, ma'am. I apologize for the inconvenience. We have you scheduled for a twelve o'clock showing. We should have performed a final sweep. It must have been overlooked."

"It's fine. Just get someone up here after I leave."

"Yes, ma'am. Your taxi will be here in fifteen."

I hung up the phone without a goodbye, something I was known for, and headed back to the bathroom. I trudged through the growing puddle of water, grabbing a washcloth on my way to the shower. I opened the curtain and wrapped it around the pole so it would not get wet. I removed my filthy, wet clothes and turned on the water, being sure to use lukewarm as not to fog up the mirror. I took several gulps of water, soothing my dry throat and quenching my thirst. I scrubbed my body with the washcloth, using the shampoo that was used as a display for soap. By the time I counted to 150, I was clean. I stepped from the shower, into the running water that was now flowing into the hallway. I grabbed two towels from the cabinet and used one to wipe the remnants of water from the shower, making sure to wipe down the shampoo bottle as well. I grabbed my clothes, replaced the curtain, turned off the water to the commode and made my way to the bedroom, drying my feet before I entered. I pulled the large duffel bag from under my bed and threw on an outfit consisting of a clean pair of jogging pants, hoodie, and tennis shoes. I flipped my head over, piling my hair into a wet ball and stuffed my wet clothes, towels, and washcloth in the bag before throwing it over my shoulder and walking back to the front door. I threw the hood over my head, opened the door, and stepped back into the rain, before sliding across the seat into the taxi that waited for me.

"Where to ma'am?"

"Windsor Bed and Breakfast."

"Yes ma'am."

"How long before we arrive?"

"We should be there around noon."

At 11:59 we turned onto the street leading to our destination and I had a wad of twenties in one hand and a key to "The Sunset Lodge" in the other. Once the car had stopped, I handed the money to the man over the seat and stepped out into the pouring rain, which impaired my ability to see. I ran down the cobblestone walk ways, eyeing each wooden sign that was perfectly placed in the flowerbed outside each individual cottage. By the time I made it to the room, I feared I was too late. As I turned the key to unlock the door, I prayed that he was still here.

Inside the beautiful room that was decorated in light, pastel colors, I found Luke sitting on the edge of the enormous bed at its center. His elbows rested on his knees as they bounced impatiently, awaiting my arrival. Where I counted numbers and said my ABCs to keep my thoughts from straying, Luke used music. I don't know if it was the song choice, or the way his face looked as the pain disintegrated and was replaced with a look of relief. Maybe it was the adrenaline coursing through my body or the realization that everything was over, and we were back together with nothing left to tear us apart. Whatever it was, had me desperate for him as I stood by the door, the water dripping from my drenched clothes and onto the floor. When he stood from the bed, I launched myself at him, my wet body colliding with his, hard as stone, as he embraced me in his arms. He pushed my wet hair, which lay stuck to the sides of my face, and neck out of his way as his mouth claimed mine in a feverish, passionate kiss. His lips moved quickly over my face, hurriedly, but reverently, kissing each exposed area. He lowered me to the bed, his body covering mine as he made quick work of removing the clothes that separated us. When I was naked beneath him, reveling in the feeling of skin on skin as his body heat radiated from him, showering me with his warmth, his frantic pace slowed, and in that moment, he told me everything I needed to know in a single, unhurried kiss that wasn't broken, until the need for us to breathe overpowered our need for that significant connection. When he slid inside me, his pace slow and determined, my eyes rolled to the back of my head as the feeling of him completely filling me and reaching through to my soul replaced everything that wasn't in this particular earth shattering moment. As his hips moved in tune with Counting Crows' song "Colorblind", his eyes penetrated mine. He kept his face close to my own, catching each whimper and moan that escaped my mouth with his mouth. When the passion of our lovemaking couldn't get any stronger, when the feeling of absoluteness had

352

reached its peak, Luke's words took me to a place in the heavens, higher than I ever could have imagined.

"Marry me, Dallas." I looked into his eyes, overflowing with love and compassion for me. His movements never slowed, as he pushed into me, over and over, putting everything he couldn't say in words into measured strokes as he circled his hips, his eyes full of hope and promise never leaving mine. "Marry me. Let me spend forever making you the happiest, most loved woman in the world." His voice was low and breathy, wrapping around my heart and sealing it with his promises. There would never be another day in my life on this planet that could make me feel as cherished as I did in this moment. Before my climax came, before the earth moved and shattered around me, I gave him my answer with a single word, but it was the promise and security he found in the depths of my eyes that told him everything he needed to know.

"Yes."

Saving Dallas Forever

Epilogue

Luke was just as anxious to make me his wife as I was to become it. He had proposed four months ago, and we had agreed that the first Saturday in April would be *the* day. The venue was perfect. We would be getting married at the Abbey, a bed and breakfast I owned in Tupelo. The historical mansion was such a beautiful place that the only decorations required were the fresh flowers that I placed sparingly around the grand room, where the ceremony would be held. A huge staircase centered the room, and the nuptials would take place at the top. Jackie, Gladean, and Pearl, three of the employees at the Abbey, were working feverishly in the kitchen, preparing the food for the reception. Stacy (the man who I considered an uncle, but had also accused of trying to kill me) and I had shared a drink together the night before. Ironic I know, and I was glad to see he held no ill will toward me, not that he should, because there was no way in hell I would ever give him a reason to. Some things were just better left unsaid. He, like Jackie, Gladean, and Pearl, had been working his ass off to ensure everything was ready for this evening.

The ceremony would be dedicated to, and in honor and memory of, War, a fallen brother who had lost his life on the night I was attacked. His service not only to me, but to the club, would forever be remembered and a shadow box filled with a replica of his cut and a single precious item, would be hung in the clubhouse as a reminder of his sacrifices. The body of War had never been recovered and Luke refused to hold a funeral, in the hope that he was still alive. But Jeff (my ex-boyfriend, who dumped me for a one-night stand with a chick who worked at Arby's, compliments of Regg, and was a key factor in the takedown of Charlie) was not the useless piece of shit I remembered, and had informed Luke that Crazy and Dennis had confirmed War's life was taken from him the same night he went missing. Jeff did not partake in the killing nor was he informed of it at the time. Luke still wasn't convinced that he was gone, but Ronnie was going to talk to him, or so he said. Jeff was told to disappear, and he did just that. He was last seen driving a Honda.

I finally got my trip to the beach. Luke and I left the morning after 'operation take down Charlie', after the news confirmed his death. Two eye witnesses claimed to have seen two men who had been staying at the hotel drag Charlie from an SUV and force him into their room. Less than ten minutes later, they heard gunshots and called the police, who ruled it as a fatal shootout between three men, resulting in all of their deaths. Charlie had a whole twenty seconds of fame before a cute kitten dancing for a treat stole his spotlight. Fiji was beautiful. We were there a total of two days before I got stomach flu. It took Luke a whole day to convince me that no one was trying to kill me. He said everyone who had any issues with me, or with anyone I was close to, was dead. This brought up the subject of what had really happened in that hotel room after he left. Our silence seemed to tell one another that we didn't want to talk about it, but he finally asked, so I told him. I never uttered the words "I killed Charlie", because that would make him an accessory; he had taught me that. So, instead of actually telling him, I simply said 'Plan B.' After my forty-eight hour stomach flu, I actually got to enjoy myself. We walked on the beach, snorkeled, rode jet skis, swam, fucked, and ate, and Luke bought me a ridiculous solitaire, princess-cut diamond. All of this happened in one day. After I received my ring, I suddenly felt homesick. I asked Luke if he would be mad if we went home early. Of course he wasn't and we left the next morning. We flew into New Orleans, and when we stepped off the plane, I was miraculously cured of my homesickness, so we spent the remainder of the week in Lake Charles. I thought I'd played it really well, but Luke was on to me. When I burst through the door of the clubhouse, I did not greet my sisters nor did they greet me. The first words spoken were "let me see." Yeah, I probably should have thought that one through. Luke wasn't mad, though; I made it up to him.

    The Red Strip is now a successful strip mall located on highway ninety-eight and it was named after my favorite stripper. I'd meant it as a joke, but the way Red's face lit up when I informed her of the name I planned to use forced me to make it official. The mayor signed a deal regarding the pipeline, and it is now being laid a mile south of Hattiesburg, instead of through the heart of it; the result of an idea from my brilliant assistant, who I plan to let replace me as CEO in the very near future. The mayor was rolling in the money, but the big picture was that many businesses were saved from sacrifice, and now Red could see her name every time she went home, which wouldn't be often considering she still spent the majority of her time at Luke's; which would soon be known as Luke and Dallas'.

I looked around the extravagant room, closing my eyes as I inhaled the scent of the flowers that reminded me spring was here. The only thing I would miss about the cold weather was the sight of Luke in leather chaps. We had a long weekend ahead of us. The ceremony was formal, and the reception, consisting of hors d'oeuvres, champagne, and dancing would take place here, immediately following 'I do.' Tomorrow would be the biker reception, where attire was optional and catering would consist of grilled food, liquor, and beer, as well as strip poles covered with Lindas', or so I hoped. Then after that, it was off to spend a week in the city of love, unless of course I got homesick.

I walked up the stairs, pausing at the top to look down at the empty room that would soon be filled with the faces I loved. I made my way down the hall to join Red, who waited in my room to help me prepare for the first day of the rest of my life.

"Would you hold the fuck still?" Red murmured, the safety pin she held between her teeth impairing her speech.

"Would you put that fucking cigarette out?" I asked, eyeing the cigarette that was wedged between her fingers and dangerously close to the back of my arm. I stood with my arm extended over my head, while Red attempted to pin my dress, which was missing the hook and eye, because her impatience had got the better of her when she had tried to latch it the first time.

"Shut up. I need it to concentrate." Red said, pausing to take a drag, gracious enough to blow the smoke out of the side of her mouth, other than onto my gown. I had decided to wear my mother's wedding dress. I wanted to feel as if a part of her was with me as I walked down the aisle. The dress fit perfectly, but I wanted to add my own touch of splendor, so it had been in the hands of Luke's mother, who I had found was a wonderful seamstress. She removed the long lace sleeves, so that the dress lay perfectly across my chest, using some of the leftover material to make a garter, and the rest she promised to keep-in the event my daughter would like to one day use it on her own wedding gown.

My daughter.

I like how that rolled off my tongue. Luke's mother and father were happy to see me, welcoming me with open arms the moment I stepped into their home. I could imagine my children running across the hardwood floors of their home, and opening Christmas presents as we celebrated the holidays with their grandparents.

As a family.

Soon, I would be Mrs. Carmical, and I couldn't fucking wait.

Maddie joined Red and I, her smile bright as she ignored an annoyed Red, and handed me a small box.

"I have something for you."

"Red?" I asked, anxious to put my arm down and receive Maddie's gift.

"I'm done." I watched as she gave Maddie a reassuring squeeze on her arm and a warm smile, before leaving us alone. I took the box from Maddie's shaking hands, a look of sadness claiming her face, although she tried to shield it with a smile that didn't reach her tear-filled eyes. I opened the box to reveal a pair of simple, pearl earrings.

"They were my mother's. I thought you might like something borrowed." I was speechless, as Maddie pulled them from the box and placed them in my ears. I turned around and immediately became teary eyed, as I found the ghost of my young mother in the mirror. The gown I wore was covered in lace that fit tightly to my curves and covered my feet. The back of the dress swooped in the middle of my back, and curved perfectly over my backside, before spreading out to form a three-foot train. My hair was pinned up, held in place by two beautifully crafted hair combs covered in pearls, a gift from my MC sisters, and now my I wore two perfectly matching pearl earrings; a gift from my blood sister.

"Maddie, they are perfect," I managed to choke out, overwhelmed by her gift.

"And now, so are you." I pulled Maddie to me, hugging her tightly, before we were interrupted by something that sounded much like a herd of cattle barreling down the hall.

"Hey!" My infamous group of sisters greeted, as they herded into the room.

"You look beautiful, baby," Brooklyn said, her eyes shining with unshed tears as she kissed the air around me to avoid staining me with her bright, red lipstick.

"Okay, we gotta see the shoes, sista," Mary said, looking down at my feet, as I lifted my dress to reveal my bright orange Jimmy Choo stilettos.

"They are so hot!" Katina said, fanning herself with her hand.

"And look extremely uncomfortable," Katelan added, with a worried look.

"Girl, hot and comfortable are two of those things you can only have one at a time," Chi Chi added, giving me a wink.

"You gonna bust your ass and we gonna have to call the paramedics," Punkin said, the ashes from her cigarette threatening to fall to the floor just any minute. When Katelan offered her an ashtray, she waved it away, and I laughed.

"Shit! I need something blue!" I said in a panic, causing everyone's eyes to search the room in the hope of finding something. A knock sounded at the door, and Red pulled it wide open, greeting a grinning Regg with a smile.

"You know what would make that dress better?" Regg asked, motioning with his finger up and down my dress.

"What?" I asked, looking over it in a panic. Was something wrong? When I didn't find anything, I looked up to find him smiling wide.

"If you just pulled the top down just a little-"

"You're a fuckin' perv Regg," Red snapped, but I could hear the smile in her tone. "What do you want?"

"I was hopin' to find y'all naked."

"Get out."

"Babe."

The sound of voices was tuned out, as I focused all my attention on the man emerging from the room across the hall. Luke looked stunning in an ivory tux that matched the color of my dress perfectly. My eyes traveled up his body, excitement filling me as they zoned in on the bulge between his thighs, knowing that in only a matter of hours, I would be seeing him, tasting him, and feeling him as he pulsated inside me. I dragged my eyes over the lapels of his tux, which hid what I knew were rock hard muscles, begging to be caressed with my touch and teased with the biting sting of my nails as they dug into him; a result of the pleasure he gave me. The silk necktie he wore was orange in color, matching my shoes, and reminding us to stay true to the double life we both lived. His hair was a dark blonde mess, styled unintentionally by his hands, which he ran through it whenever he was anxious or mad. His lips were parted, and showed the slightest hint of the two perfect rows of white teeth that sat behind them. Those lips would be on me soon, sealing the lifetime promise we would make to each other with a kiss. I found his eyes, filled with fondness and pride as he took me, his soon-to-be bride, in all of my dressed grandeur. He gave me a wink and butterflies fluttered in my stomach, causing my heart to skip a beat, before it continued hammering against my chest. His eyes shone brightly, and reminded me that I already had something blue, and they would be with me at the altar.

The door was slammed shut and Luke's face disappeared. My ears tuned into the chatter in the room as everyone offered up something blue, from an Aleve that Brooklyn pulled from her purse, to the panties Katina was willing to remove and allow me to wear. I declined all their gifts, with a laugh, letting them know that I had forgotten I already had something.

I had a host of sisters from both Hattiesburg and Lake Charles, but it was the eight that surrounded me that I wanted to stand next to me as I said my vows, making Luke roll his eyes at the thought of having to convince eight brothers to wear a tuxedo. After much consideration, we decided that we would not choose who stood with us, but would ask them all to stand behind us, as we began our journey together as husband and wife. It would be only Luke and I who stood at the altar and only our family and closest friends would be present. I thought of how each one of the women in the room held a special place in my heart.

My beautiful sister Maddie; looking at her now, I realized that the days of my past were dull compared to the ones I now shared with her. She was my sister in more ways than one, and I now that I had her in my life, I couldn't imagine living without her.

The foul-mouthed, hard-headed, big-hearted Red, whose tough exterior was only half the reason I loved her. It was the passion she had for life and the ability to love fiercely that filled the void in my heart, which I didn't even know was there until she came along.

Mother to us all and leader of our pack, Brooklyn, who paved the road that we all traveled to be a part of the MC life. My heart had been stolen by Luke. There was never a time when I felt like I couldn't love him, but it was Brooklyn who had shown me how to love LLC. She had taught me how to be an ol' lady, and how to love a biker, and the life that went with it.

I might not have known the other ladies that were in my room for very long, but I loved them all. They were dear to me, because they had played a significant part in molding and preparing me for the life of an ol' lady that I was honored to live. They showed me it wasn't what others portrayed it to be, a group of weak women who stood behind their men in fear of their lives, due to the constant drama and violence that being in an MC entailed. What they showed me was the truth. Being part of a sisterhood was about trust, loyalty, and pride, but above all that, it was about love and friendship. We were not weak women who stood behind our men, we were strong women who stood beside our men with the promise of trust, and behind our men with the promise of respect. When problems arose, we faced them head-on, ready to fight, and even die, for what we believed in; the right to be a part of a life where you no longer lived as one, but you rode as many, on a steel horse that was banded with the pledge of love, loyalty and respect; a promise that would last forever.

Acknowledgements

I would first like to thank my MC family. My sisters, Brooklyn, Punkin, Candice(Maddie), Katelan, Mary, Katina, Chi Chi, Melissa and Angela. Without your reassurance and crazy ass stories, this wouldn't be possible. For my brothers, Ronnie, Possum, Marty, Rick, Chris, Big Al(with yo fine ass), Kyle, Bryce and Shark. You are the reason I am so passionate about this life. To the Whiny Goat Pussies-yeah, I altered that a little-your support and willingness to listen to me bitch will forever be appreciated. Amy-without you, I would still be in bed only dreaming of writing a book. You are what fuels me. Regg-I didn't cook for you did I? Sorry about that. I promise to try not to be a hoarder in the future. I will share with you starting today. My Mom and Dad who have always been so supportive and always believed in me. Monkey and Jay, thanks for loving me even when I am a bitch and don't answer your calls. Joe and Heather-those names look good together huh? Yeah, you're welcome. Paul Kirkley and Lindsey Mooney-the cover says it all. Mandy-you effin rock! Just in case you forgot. Rock Chicks, fans, family, friends, Kathy Pepper, all the Pepper girls, Misty, Lori and everyone else. I'm sure I forgot someone. If so, I apologize and your name goes here_____. I love you all so much! Thank-you!

Look for Red's story coming Summer 2014!

Made in the USA
Columbia, SC
14 July 2019